THE WRONG MAN

AMANDA BROOKFIELD

Boldwood

First published in 1995. This edition first published in Great Britain in 2023 by Boldwood Books Ltd.

Cover Design by Alice Moore Design

Cover photography: Shutterstock

Every effort has been made to obtain the necessary permissions with reference to copyright material, both illustrative and quoted. We apologise for any omissions in this respect and will be pleased to make the appropriate acknowledgements in any future edition.

A CIP catalogue record for this book is available from the British Library.

Paperback ISBN 978-1-83889-644-7

Large Print ISBN 978-1-83889-643-0

Hardback ISBN 978-1-78513-799-0

Ebook ISBN 978-1-83889-645-4

Kindle ISBN 978-1-83889-646-1

Audio CD ISBN 978-1-83889-638-6

MP3 CD ISBN 978-1-83889-639-3

Digital audio download ISBN 978-1-83889-642-3

Boldwood Books Ltd
23 Bowerdean Street
London SW6 3TN
www.boldwoodbooks.com

FOREWORD

'The Wrong Man' is a revised version of a novel called 'Walls of Glass', which I wrote thirty years ago. It tells the story of a mother of two small children who dares to own up to the unhappiness of what everyone around her assumes is a blissful married life. No one greets her revelations well, least of all her husband...

It is a strange business meeting your younger writing self. It catapults you back, not just to the task of writing that particular book, but also to where you were – physically and mentally – at the time. At the time of writing this story I was a happily married thirty-one-year-old with two little boys, settling back into London after a decade of living abroad. Life was good. I found it an enjoyable challenge to create Jane Lytton, a woman at a similar life-stage to me, but in a contrastingly panic-stricken state of realisation that she has taken the most terrible wrong road.

Destinies turn on pin-heads. The paths we choose are so often 'Plan B'. There are things waiting for us round corners. Good things, bad things. This is one of the reasons I am drawn to storytelling. Jane Lytton had lost her way, but I could help her find it again.

Back out in the real world, of course, resolving the 'plot-twists' of our own lives can be somewhat trickier; a fact reinforced for me when my own marriage imploded eighteen years on from having conjured up the experience for Jane. Re-reading the novel three decades later has therefore been unnerving. Jane Lytton's circumstances were entirely different from mine, but all the big emotions rang true. To have got so much right! Without a crystal ball! Yikes. Talk about the mysteries of creativity...

Or maybe there are no mysteries. Maybe the answer is simply that the dilemmas I threw across Jane Lytton's path are ones that we all face in different guises as our lives unfold; dilemmas to do with love, sacrifice, loyalty, loss, to name but a few. Relationships lie at the core of our well-being. Each one of us is feeling his or her way along, on a perpetual quest to find joy and equilibrium. And as with my fictional heroine, we are blind not just to the pitfalls, but also to the happy endings – or beginnings! – that might lie in store.

In many ways Jane Lytton was ahead of her time – finding the courage to speak out in a world which still expected a woman to stay silent and put her own happiness last. I have not changed the original story; but revisiting it has been a wonderful opportunity to craft it into the best version of itself that it could be, including giving it a new, punchier jacket and title. The single life suits many; but the question of whether – how! – to find 'Mr/Ms Right' always hovers in the shadows. Invariably, it as much about luck as good judgement. The only certainty is that there are no easy answers, or crystal balls.

Amanda Brookfield May 2023

In Memory of Lucy

1

As Pippa pushed open the rusting black gate, its lopsided hinge emitted a strangled screech that sent tiny vibrations shooting down into the roots of her teeth. After a few moments of standing at the front door, she remembered that Jane and Michael's bell no longer worked and rapped briskly on the splintery wood. Pippa's own home, an airy four-bedroomed Edwardian house in Dulwich, was lovingly repainted and cleaned in a methodical way throughout each year, so she could not resist a silent tut-tut or two at the sight of the Lyttons' obvious neglect of their own property. But at the same time, she loved – and almost admired – them for it. It took courage to neglect things, she sometimes thought, a courage which she lacked completely.

'Coming,' shouted Jane from somewhere deep inside the house.

Pippa got out her handbag mirror to check her bun; her hair was so fine that it slipped out of the pins and clasps no matter how many she applied. She smiled quite warmly at her reflection, not out of vanity (she was not beautiful – her nose was too pointy and her mouth too thin), but because she was happy. She always enjoyed taking time out of her carefully constructed bustle of domesticity to visit Jane and the children in all their glorious chaos. And on this occasion she had some rather exciting news to impart, when the moment was right.

The door burst open, giving Pippa a snapshot impression of the familial warmth and brightness within.

'Heavens,' exclaimed Jane, pushing her thick, dark fringe from her eyes and hoicking baby Harriet higher on to her hip, 'is it eleven already? Lovely to see you, Pip – come in. Mind the trains – Tom has spent all morning building the longest train in the world, haven't you, love?' She stooped to stroke her son's messy brush of hair, before leading the way through to the kitchen. 'You look well, Pippa – you make me feel a total wreck – which I am – roll on the spring term – coffee or tea?'

'I'd love some tea.' But more than that, she wanted to hold Harriet, who was pudgy and square and smiley.

'Could you take the baby, do you think?' Jane, who knew of the Crofts' fruitless – and now abandoned – quest to have a child of their own, was never sure whether to push her offspring onto Pippa or keep them at bay. 'I almost burnt Harriet with the kettle once, trying to juggle cups and things – it was when the health visitor was here – which was lucky, if you see what I mean.'

Jane moved deftly round her cramped but cosy kitchen, the soles of her black plimsolls squeaking on the cracked linoleum floor. Being so petite, she had a tendency to make Pippa, who was by no means tall, feel clumsy and large. She wore a green hairband that morning, a thin strip of dark velvet that did little to control the glossy jumble of her hair, but which drew attention to the brilliant emerald of her eyes, so deeply set into the pale, elfin face. Pippa had always thought Jane very striking to look at, not in a way that made her envious, but so that she couldn't help wanting to stare. To manage to look scruffy but attractive was an achievement far beyond Pippa's own aspirations, as was Jane Lytton's way of appearing higgledy-piggledy but happy. Pippa knew herself to be incapable of reconciling such opposites. For her, happiness was impossible without orderliness, just as attractiveness was out of the question without a good deal of thought and attention to detail.

The little L-shaped kitchen always reminded Pippa of a fully equipped caravan – everything was reachable and functioning so long as it stayed in its correct place; one thing left out or put away badly threw the whole system into chaos. Tom's paintings, together with innumerable creations made out of tin-foil, cardboard and string, filled every inch of space between the bulging cupboards and shelves, giving the effect of some crazy wallpaper of modern art. Along the window sill which overlooked the back garden, several trailing plants fought for space amongst pots of herbs, cookery books and a large bowl overflowing with safety-pins, paper-clips and rubber-bands.

'Any news of the extension?' she enquired brightly. Ever since the Lyttons had moved to Cobham, a couple of years before, they had been talking of building on at the back.

Jane sighed. 'Oh, I don't know, Pip. It's so much money. Michael says we'd be better off moving again, but it's a bad time to sell because the economy is so rubbish – we just go round in circles when we talk about it. I've rather given up, to be honest.' She sat down at the small pine table opposite Pippa and stirred milk into their mugs of tea. Thinking about the extension only made her cross. The move out of London had been her idea to begin with, but Michael had got very enthusiastic in the end. They both fell in love – as she remembered it – with the cottagey feel of number 23, Meadowbrook Road and had enjoyed making plans to improve and enlarge it. But when their requests for planning permission ran into trouble, Michael started to go sour on the whole project. His recollection of their house-moving episode was now based on the belief that Jane had pressurised him into making a decision before he was ready. Perhaps she had. Perhaps he was right. Jane wasn't sure any more. She wasn't sure about a lot of things.

'Well, Tim said that Michael is keen on going ahead, even though you've still only got permission to add on one room.'

'Really?' Jane wondered if other wives found out quite so much of their husbands' thoughts from other people. She laughed quickly, before issuing an automatic excuse for her ignorance. 'Michael's been working very hard recently – it makes him absent-minded – I keep telling him he'll leave his head at the office one day and not just his briefcase.'

'At least that bank of his has eased up on the travelling side of things. When Tim's gone it's for weeks at a time. His trips are longer than the holidays he's selling.' Pippa sighed. 'I do get lonely, you know,' she added in a bleating baby voice to Harriet, who looked puzzled and put Pippa's amber necklace in her mouth by way of a response.

'She's teething, as you can see,' said Jane, offering her daughter a rusk. She hoped Pippa was not going to start on about the wearing demands of Travelmania – the tourist business that Tim had started after leaving the city, which boasted exotic trips at affordable prices. Pippa was unremittingly sweet, but prattled on a bit sometimes, in the way that some people did if they had no burning commitments in the hours ahead. During the early years of their acquaintance, when Jane had not progressed much beyond filing tasks for Moretons publishers, Pippa had an enviably pres-surised job as PA to the managing director of a prestigious London advertising agency. But after a couple of years of failing to conceive a child, Pippa's doctor had warned that stress at work might be taking its toll on her hormones and recommended that she take a break. Though her resignation from the agency was billed very much as a temporary measure, taken for prudence's sake alone, it somehow became permanent and – like the desire for babies that had prompted it – impossible to discuss. The instant success of Tim's business seemed to erase the last traces of a possibility that Pippa might return to work. She even started hinting, with wry little smiles, that Tim would disallow such a thing – as if it had become one of those male-pride issues that she had decided to indulge rather than resist.

While Pippa talked about Tim's long absences, Jane tried but failed to keep her mind from drifting upstairs to the five or six loads of washing that lay strewn across the landing and bedroom floors, together with the thought of Tom's wet mattress, which needed scrubbing and drying before the smell of pee was completely absorbed into its soft foam interior. As her musings moved on to an alarmingly broad shopping list of food, clothes and shoes, she began to wonder vaguely why Pippa had been so insistent on inviting herself over and how long she was planning on staying. Since their relationship had arisen from the longstanding friendship between their husbands rather than any instinctive liking for each other, what intimacy they managed never felt entirely natural.

Having quietly wished Pippa was gone Jane immediately felt guilty and invited her to stay for lunch.

'Oh, I'd love to, if I won't be in your way.'

Harriet was wriggling impatiently, clearly bored with her allotted lap and looking for new distractions. Soggy rusk stuck in blobs to her face and bib. A few gooey fingerprints were visible on Pippa's fluffy jumper. She tried to wipe them with a tissue when Jane wasn't looking, but Jane had already seen and was ready with a damp cloth and apologies on behalf of her daughter.

'Silly of me to wear it, I know.'

'It was certainly a little optimistic to visit this house in such a lovely thing.' Jane touched the soft grey wool with the back of her hand, suddenly conscious of the grubbiness of her own sweatshirt and faded jeans.

'Tim gave it to me. It's got llama in it or something. He brought it back from Peru – for my birthday,' she added shyly.

Jane clapped her hand over her mouth. 'Oh Pippa, I forgot, you should have told me. Oh no, I feel awful.'

Pippa was blushing, regretting a little that she had dared to mention it.

'It's only a wretched birthday. Thirty-eight is not exactly a reason to celebrate – especially not in my case.'

'But of course it matters. I mind terribly about my birthdays. I love presents and being taken out to dinner and all that sort of thing—' Jane stopped quickly, remembering that her birthday that year had been quite horrible. It was a Saturday. Tom, wanting to mark the occasion, had promised to deliver breakfast in bed to both his parents. Michael had to be forced not to go down and intervene while the smell of burnt toast curled its way up the stairs. The toast was quite black, heaving with butter, but otherwise okay. The boiled eggs had been put into water in a saucepan but never boiled. Jane, who was relieved that Tom had heeded six years of warnings about never touching the knobs on the stove, even given the desire to cook an egg, bravely cut the top off her runny offering and dipped a wedge of the charcoaled bread into the grey-yellow slime. Tom stood in solemn silence, watching from the end of the bed.

'Tom,' said Michael, 'you haven't cooked the eggs. This isn't cooked, see?' He picked up his egg and held it out. 'It's still cold. When you cook something, it goes hot. But these are all liquid inside, so Mummy and I can't eat them.'

But Mummy, charged with a fierce reflex of protective love, was spooning large dollops of the phlegmy offering into her mouth and rolling her eyes with pleasure.

'Jesus, Jane – how could you?' said Michael with a laugh. 'You'll be sick.' He turned back to his son, still smiling. 'Well tried, Tom – just ask for help next time, okay?'

But it was not okay, as Jane had known it would not be. Tom's day was ruined. Her day was ruined. Just one mouthful would have been enough, just one mouthful for love's sake. But he wasn't like that, her husband. Michael liked things one way or another, black or white, like his tables of figures at work. If something wasn't cooked that was meant to be cooked, you didn't eat it – whatever the circumstances. Such an attitude no doubt worked wonders in meeting rooms, when heady negotiations for debt rescheduling and long-term loans hung in the balance, but it did not do so well at home. Michael, who felt it was wrong to be chastised for honesty, said that Jane, as usual, was being over-protective of their first-born, refused to melt and admit he had been wrong. Jane, out of some kind of inverted revenge, refused to go out to dinner. Michael ate bread and cheese watching telly while she pretended to read upstairs.

'There's nothing more depressing than a bad birthday,' Jane told Pippa firmly, shaking off the memory. 'I bet Tim's got something lovely lined up for tonight.'

'He usually gets tickets for a show or something, but he never lets on till the last minute. One of those funny rituals we long-married couples go through... though, actually...' Pippa got up to look out of the window, her fingers fiddling absently with the yellow beads of her necklace, 'Tim *has* been a little moody recently. I know he's a bit of a one for sulks – not like Michael at all – but this time I really feel something is up.' She eyed Jane, who was stacking the dish-washer very busily behind her. 'He hasn't said anything to Michael, I suppose?'

'Not that I know of.' Jane pulled a bottle of white wine out of the fridge door. 'Let's celebrate just a little. It's only supermarket stuff, but quite nice. I've got lots of tail ends of smelly cheeses to go with it. A birthday lunch of sorts.'

'You're very kind, Jane. I don't know where I'd be without you.'

Such comments always threw Jane off balance, since she never felt able to respond in kind. Pippa was a friend, but not one that she relied on totally. Not like Julia, say, whom Jane had known since school and whose presence in her life – usually down the end of a phone line – was intermittent but vital. Like Pippa, Julia had no children, but didn't mind at all. She was not married either, or even close to it. Having recently opened her own antiques shop in North London, she was totally involved with that.

With Pippa, there had always been a subtle imbalance in the relationship, brought on by Pippa's at times embarrassing admiration for Jane's marriage to her husband's best friend. The fact that the Lyttons had managed to have children quite effortlessly only heightened Pippa's perception of their marital bliss, at the same time fostering a tic of awkwardness between the two women which no amount of goodwill could entirely smooth away.

They sat down to French bread and cheese while Harriet slept and Tom watched *Thomas the Tank Engine* on the telly.

'I made a big decision last week,' blurted Pippa, now frantic to broach the subject beating in her head like a pulse.

Jane sipped the wine, which was a little tart, but pleasantly cold.

'Something exciting?'

'Very.' Pippa cut off a wedge of Brie and put her knife down. 'I'm going to go for IVF. I know I always said I wouldn't – that if nature wouldn't take its course, it was wrong for us to interfere – but I've changed my mind.'

'Pippa – that's – that's amazing.' Jane's mind floundered in search of appropriate words, wanting badly to say the right thing. 'How terribly brave. What are the chances? Isn't it very expensive? Will it hurt? What does Tim think?' A couple of years previously, the Crofts had formally resigned from the ranks of would-be parents, confessing to close friends that the strain was too much and they wanted to concentrate on enjoying themselves instead.

Though Jane had nurtured suspicions as to Pippa's true commitment to such a way of thinking (compared to Tim who had shown unqualified relief at their decision), she never imagined her turning round with such a bold reversal of opinion. But on seeing the warm glow of hope in Pippa's round and usually quite solemn face, she was immediately thrilled for her. She wanted to be encouraging, to will her towards the outcome she craved. She reached out instinctively and touched her hand. 'Oh, I do hope it works, Pip. You deserve it, of all people.'

Pippa's smile was brilliant. She pushed some wisps of her fine hair, glinting now with an occasional sliver of silver, out of her eyes. 'If points for trying count, we do deserve one, I suppose. I know this sounds terrible,' she went on carefully, 'but I think I would have liked to have had a miscarriage, I really would. Just one... I mean, at least it's closer to being pregnant. Whereas I'm just barren, like those women in the Bible – unblessed and infertile.'

'Oh Pippa, don't say that. Anyway, some of those Bible women had babies when they were old and supposedly past it.'

'Well, I'm starting to feel I'm nearly past it, which is why I've decided to take drastic action. It's now or never, Jane.'

Jane rummaged in the fridge for a bunch of grapes to add to their spread. 'And Tim is all right about it, is he?'

Pippa took a deep breath. 'Tim doesn't know. Not yet.'

Jane stopped, bunch of grapes in hand. 'That's a little fundamental, isn't it? Are you sure he'll—'

'Yes. Absolutely. He's got to.'

Jane knew they were on dangerous ground. The desire to have a child was totally primeval – unarguable, once it took hold. She knew because Tom hadn't been planned, not for one second, and yet when she found out that she was pregnant, one drizzly morning three years into her marriage, she sensed at once that she was in the grip of a force far stronger than anything she had ever experienced.

It was inconvenient to say the least, and certainly unwise. She was by then working as an editorial assistant. Michael had just started a phase of extensive travelling and she felt very distant from him. He would come back exhausted but hungry for sex, pushing into her in a way he never had before, ungenerously, without tenderness. It was confusing. To be wanted in such a basic way was new to her – she was scared by the lovelessness of it all. Out of bed they ticked along as before, as if nothing had changed. It had made Jane start to wonder if love mattered after all, lying buried as it did, behind the daily negotiating and arguing of married life. But when Tom was conceived as the result of one such unemotional sexual encounter on a humid August night after Michael had been on a business trip to Eastern Europe for ten days, Jane decided at once that she should have the child. It felt like fate – out of her control entirely. And then, after the birth, it felt like love, the real thing, the thing she had always hoped to get from marriage.

'Are you going to have any more?' asked Pippa, as Tom appeared, looking screen-dazed and pale.

'No, I'm full thanks – but you go ahead.'

'I mean children, silly, not cheese.' They both laughed, which made Tom suspicious and needing an explanation. Jane was grateful for the deflection. It seemed mean to admit to Pippa – of all people – her certainty that she did not want any more children. Harriet, loved and treasured as she was, had been produced more for Tom's sake than anything else. Jane was very careful about contraception now, even when Michael was all rough and lustful.

2

Michael sipped his mineral water, enjoying the silent expectancy, the power he wielded in the meeting room.

'It's not a question of *if*, Antonia, but *when*.' He looked round the table of faces, knowing he now commanded their full attention. Antonia, a bristly and ambitious newcomer to the department, began making a few notes, to cover the moment of put-down. She wondered if Michael Lytton disliked her, whether his frequent challenges were personal or professional.

'It's a market we can no longer ignore,' went on Michael, deliberately looking at his watch to show that he felt the meeting should draw to a close. 'I'd like to see detailed data on investment opportunities relevant to our special interests by the end of the week. Antonia, perhaps you would like to head up that research?'

She nodded, not sure whether to be pleased or offended. It would be a lot of work, but then there was the enticing prospect of earning brownie points by doing it. Everyone began packing away their papers and shuffling out of the room.

'You are happy to take on this job, are you?'

She looked round in surprise, having thought the room empty. 'Absolutely. No problem, Michael.'

'Good. If you need any help getting started, don't hesitate to knock on my door.'

'Thank you.'

With a quick smile he left the room, leaving Antonia with a blurred impression of businesslike kindness riding on whiffs of strong aftershave.

Michael sauntered back to his office with his hands in the trouser pockets of his double-breasted suit, whistling quietly through the tiny gap between his two front teeth. It was a noise he made when he was happy, when life played into his hands and he felt in control of its multifarious demands. Adrenalin still pumped through his veins from the meeting, from handling it – and the prickly but promising Antonia Fielding – so well. Although it was Friday night, he felt in no hurry to head home, wanting instead to climb down more gradually from the high generated by a hard but successful week's work. A quick drink in the bar they all used, a half of bitter with some colleagues, before hacking back to Cobham. The idea was tempting.

As Michael made his way along the maze of plush, neon-lit corridors that linked the offices of his firm of city bankers like sections of a honeycomb, he tried not to think about the journey home. He dreaded the swarms of rushing commuters, the crush on the train, the fifteen minute walk the other end. It had been mad to move out of London. Extension or no extension. Their next move, when the market picked up, was going to be right back in again, he would see to that. Never mind Jane's rural idyll. It was totally impractical, unless one could afford a flat in London as well. But Michael did not relish that idea either. He had never liked being on his own and had no desire to revert back to a part-time bachelor existence of cheese on toast and baked beans out of a tin while watching junk on the telly. Home life might be noisy and grating at times, but there were many comforts that made up for it.

In the end he persuaded John Procter to have one for the road. But then a few others joined them and they decided to make it two. As Michael was on the point of leaving, the MD himself strolled in and started asking how far his department had got in looking at the Polish market. Feeling on the ball and superbly able, Michael updated him at length, before rushing back into the office to leave a note on Antonia's desk, asking to have her presentation ready three days earlier than he had originally said.

* * *

'Tom waited up for you.'

'You shouldn't let him. I've told you before—'

'You said you'd be early.'

'Did I?' Michael frowned, having genuinely forgotten the promise that was lightly made by him, but hungrily received by his son. 'I got held up. Things began to happen just as I was leaving.'

Jane, who had heard all the excuses many times before, mechanically set about laying the table and serving food. She wasn't in the least bit hungry. The meat had held up well, but the baked potatoes were hollow and tough, their skins like cracked leather. It was nearly ten o'clock. Michael didn't like it if she ate and went to bed without him.

'It was Tom's concert,' she said, 'he did his solo on the recorder.'

'Oh shit.' Michael, who was ravenous, spoke with his mouth full. He chewed vigorously and swallowed before continuing. 'Jane, love, I'm sorry.' He reached out and put his hand on her arm.

She continued eating very slowly, putting only the smallest amounts in her mouth – a flake of potato skin, half a mushroom, a soggy carrot. She did not want to forgive him. The pattern was all too familiar. The repetitiveness of it all depressed her immensely. Last time it had been a parents' evening. Next time it would probably be the carol concert.

'It doesn't matter.' Jane pulled her hands onto her lap and fiddled with her wedding rings. One of the many tiny gold claws holding a small diamond in place on the engagement one had begun to stick upwards. Sharp as a needle, it sometimes caught on things like scarves and jumpers. She pressed it now, hard, into the top of one of her fingers, feeling at a great distance from the pinpoint of pain.

'I'll apologise to Tom in the morning. Was he very upset?' Michael took another mouthful.

She was honest enough to hesitate before answering. Tom wasn't a child who got very obviously upset. At the tender age of nearly six he had already developed a daunting capacity for suppressing his emotions. Jane knew about his feelings from the way he walked, the set of his face, the funny voices he used.

'He didn't say much about it, but he wouldn't eat his supper.' An urge to scream suddenly pressed at the back of her throat. She wanted to yell, to blast the words out, that of course Tom minded – because a promise had been made and broken, again; because he barely saw his father and when he did, he was often critical and cross. But such outbursts, she knew from experience, got them nowhere. Michael would rant for a while about how much he slaved for his family and how little understanding he got in return, and then follow this up with a hurt silence that could last for days. She always ended up having to make the peace.

'Jane, I've said I'm sorry.' His big brown eyes took on the soulful look he used to tell her it was time to step down and relent. 'Work is crazy at the moment.' He mopped up the last of his gravy with a piece of bread and wiped his hands and mouth on the oven glove that lay on the table beside them.

'Work is always crazy,' she said quietly, leaving the room to lock up the house and go to bed.

Michael, feeling guilty, but cross with his wife for being the instrument of that guilt, stayed in the kitchen for much longer than he really wanted, looking at a catalogue of home furnishings that had been put through their letter box the week before. Jane didn't throw newspapers and magazines away until the house threatened to be overrun by the damn things. Michael hit the glossy pages with the back of his hand in a sudden rush of frustration, causing the magazine to fall to the ground with a slap. He stared down at a chic sitting room of navy blue and sandy yellow, complete with a designer mother and child playing happily on a colour-coordinated hearth rug. Engulfed in the bright squash of his own home, Michael felt a rush of despair. When – if ever – did the gulf between how one wanted life to be and how it really was, begin to narrow? he wondered bitterly.

Upstairs, Jane had left his bedside light on, laid out his pyjamas on the pillow and turned on her side to sleep. But in spite of her closed eyes and the quietness, there was an atmosphere of unease in the room, generated by their conversation over dinner and all the things that the two of them had thought, but failed to say.

'Are you awake?'

'Hm.' She curled herself up more tightly into a ball, wanting very much to be left alone.

But Michael wanted reassurance. He needed to feel that he was master of his own life, master in his own home even, though he would never have put it like that himself.

He turned on his side so that he was facing her curved back. After tracing one finger down the ridges of her spine, he reached across her, his hand seeking her breasts. Jane kept her arms folded into her, protectively. She felt the hand arrive, knew what it sought and curled up more tightly still. Not now, she thought, please not now.

But the hand persisted, firmly pulling her arms out of the way, finding its way up under her nightdress, stroking, caressing, determined.

Jane did not want to make love. She was tired and angry. But she was also resigned. An honest woman – a woman who loved her lover – would say no, she thought. But Jane, as she realised with a terrible self-loathing, had got beyond the point where such honesty felt possible. Michael pushed his knee between her legs and settled his weight upon her with a grunt of satisfaction. She turned her head away and closed her eyes as he started to move in the old familiar rhythm, while his hands stroked and kneaded in a show of giving pleasure which lacked commitment and reflected his own needs rather than hers.

'Did you enjoy that?' he asked sleepily afterwards, to put the seal on his warm sense of reassurance.

'Yes,' she lied, because she was tired and wanting to sleep, and because dishonesty was so much easier than truth.

3

Mattie could not remember when she last felt less like doing anything, let alone Sunday lunch in Cobham with big sister, Jane, and her inscrutable husband. Even to contemplate living in a place like Cobham seemed to Mattie, who had a terrible hangover and who had never lived further than a few tube stops from the West End, to reflect something close to insanity. But then, while being enormously fond of her sibling, she had never really understood Jane's motives for doing anything. She often thought that if their parents hadn't died, their car skidding on a sheet of black ice and into the wall of an old Roman bridge when Mattie was still in her teens, the two of them would have remained indifferent and distant. But the accident changed things for good; ever since then Jane had tried to look after her – or at least been there for her, even when she wasn't wanted. And Mattie, while resisting the sisterly mothering, was wise enough to be grateful, knowing that she would almost certainly have fallen apart without it.

Her headache was particularly intense that morning. Yet, it was entirely usual for her to feel lousy on a Sunday. Indeed, a weekend without a throbbing head smacked of failure. Mattie, although almost thirty, liked to dance, preferably in large nightclubs with strobe lights and the first drink free with your ticket. The anonymity of it appealed to her most of all; there were none of the hideous social rituals associated with the ill-fitting mould of her teenage years – of having to have partners or pauses between songs. To be safely alone, yet part of a symbiotic crowd, soothed Mattie's endless ruffles of insecurity. It was also very good for the figure, she found, to dance all night long, several times a week. Popping tablets (which contributed to the headaches) was the silly and expensive part, but then it was the tablets that gave such an edge to the atmosphere and energy of the thing.

After taking three paracetamol and drinking a Coca-Cola, Mattie began to feel fractionally better. She ran a bath and dozed off in it for a few minutes, her head of crazy corkscrew curls trailing in the water like dank seaweed. The painful notion of mustering energy for organised movement was just beginning to peck at the edges of her consciousness, when the sound of someone tapping on one of the windows by her front door brought her fully awake. Mattie groaned, hastily pulling on a towelling dressing gown and padding through her basement flat, dripping wet and full of yawns, to see Julia peering through the smeary glass of the porthole window into her kitchen.

'You were expecting me, weren't you?' she called, tossing her astonishing curtain of shining fair hair over one shoulder and laughing at the sight of Mattie. 'I'm giving you a lift to Jane and Michael's. Sunday lunch. Remember?'

'Oh, yes – thank you and thank God. Come in, come in,' Mattie croaked, opening her door. 'I'm nearly awake, I promise. Can you make coffee? I must do something about my face and hair – I can't face the world without a face...'

'Run along. I'll see to coffee,' soothed Julia, who was used to Mattie and rather fond of her.

* * *

'I just don't see why you had to invite them, this weekend of all weekends.'

'But I told you about it ages ago. Tom, you're spilling your drink. And what do you mean "this weekend of all weekends"?'

Michael shook the paper hard. 'I could just do with some... time. I don't know, Jane, you book so much in – we could have gone away somewhere, as a family.'

Jane almost laughed. They never went away anywhere, and certainly not over a weekend. Even their summer holidays were usually spent in Kent with Michael's father. Fond as she was of the old man and his comfortable old house, it irked her that they always ended up there, falling back on the easy option – the only one requiring neither money nor organisation. The year before, she had invested a considerable amount of energy in trying to sell Michael the idea of a family camping holiday, leading on the economy of it. But he wasn't a rubbing-sticks-together kind of chap, Michael had protested, and never would be. Jane sometimes looked at other families she knew and wondered enviously at their regular escapes to cottages and hotels in England and the rest of Europe. She knew that it wasn't really money or time that prevented her and Michael from doing similar things, but a fundamental lack of inclination, a sinister shadow within their marriage, like a dark smudge on an X-ray.

'It's only my sister and Julia,' she reminded him more gently, not wanting the day to face ruin so early on. 'We haven't seen either of them for ages...'

'Nonsense. You and Julia are always jumping around doing those exercises together.'

'Very rarely now – with us living down here. It's not jumping around anyway, it's yoga and I haven't been for ages.'

Michael folded the newspaper neatly back together and crossed his arms. 'It's just the thought of enduring all you women that I find a little daunting.'

'I tried to invite Tim and Pippa, but they were busy.'

Michael humphed and disappeared in the direction of the lavatory, taking the paper with him.

As she cleared up the kitchen and set about peeling apples for the crumble, Jane seriously tried to think who else she could have invited to make Michael feel his own needs were being better catered for. She knew none of his work colleagues, since he had never invited any of them back to be entertained, even when they had lived in London. While Jane would have hated sweating over recipe books in the interests of pleasing the expensive palates of Michael's various bosses and their wives, she could not help wondering about it. The fact was, that apart from Tim Croft and an old mate called Des, whom he rarely saw, no name sprang to mind – unless she counted Michael's younger brother, Christopher, who lived in Oxford and to whom he'd never been particularly close.

Jane, on the other hand, was on amicable terms now with several mums in the area, mainly through school and sitting in playgrounds, and would have loved to stretch some of these friendships to include husbands. But Michael was very resistant to such notions. He worked too hard to be bothered with any superficial socialising, he said, claiming to prefer spending what little spare time he had relaxing with his family. But as Jane heard Tom bang on the loo door and Michael's muffled roar of response from within, the notion of a relaxed family life seemed little more than a shimmering mirage, vanishing as quickly as it was glimpsed.

The moment their two guests arrived however, Michael came alive. Having spent the previous two hours pointedly burrowing through sheaves of work papers – much to the consternation of the children, who wanted him to play – he leapt to his feet for Julia and

Mattie, issuing drinks and witty small talk as if it was the most natural thing in the world. And Jane marvelled, not for the first time, at how much more fluently he communicated with people he knew less well, people who offered no threat of intimacy. It was incredible, seeing him now with her sister and her best friend, his bad mood apparently forgotten, his face breaking into smiles that showed his handsome teeth and made them feel welcome. It was like watching a different person. Yet, who was she to criticise the clicking of such switches? Everyone did it, Jane told herself, suppressing a twitch of something like envy. It was a long time since her husband had put on such an act for her.

A blast of unseasonal February warmth made it just possible for them to take their after-lunch coffees outside on the patio, while Hattie napped and Tom let off a bit of steam. The garden was a simple rectangle in shape, not exceptionally large, but perfect for a family. At its far end, a tree-house, a sand-pit and a long swing, graced the outstretched limb of a small oak, filling the lumpy, unkempt bit of lawn which ran alongside a tangle that had once been a vegetable garden.

Mattie sat cross-legged on the grass instead of a patio chair, blowing tremulous smoke rings at the bright blue sky and jigging her legs to some silent tune playing inside her head. Jane, watching the faint grey circles rise and fall apart on the chilly spring breeze, shivered as she shifted her chair nearer. Beside her, Michael and Julia talked in an animated way about the art of French polishing.

'How are you, Mattie?' she asked, the tone of her voice communicating the sincerity behind the question.

'Oh, you know me – up and down.' She fiddled with a dangling bit of skin near the cuticle of her left thumb. All of Mattie's fingertips were stubby and raw where she had gnawed at the soft flesh. Once upon a time, their mother had painted her nails with a thick, repellent varnish called 'stop 'n' grow', guaranteed to cure the habit.

But Mattie, being Mattie, had pronounced the stuff to be delicious, and feasted on her chipped fingernails with more cannibalistic fervour than ever. Jane smiled to herself as she remembered the episode and then immediately felt sad. Where had it gone, all that easy anger of childhood, when the things to fight against were so obvious, so deeply felt? Grown-up enemies and sorrows were so much more of a blur; there were no goodies and baddies any more, just a confusion of feelings.

'Have you been painting?'

Mattie squirmed and looked away. 'Not really. Too bloody knackered half the time. I'll do a bit in the summer, I expect, when the light is better. It's still so dark in the evenings – by the time I get in from work anyway.' She shook her dark curls and shot Jane a mischievous grin, out of nowhere, causing her sister a familiar, but painful, stab of motherly emotion. 'I've become a movie junkie. I curl up on the sofa with my duvet and a few bars of chocolate – it's great.'

Jane, knowing that Mattie was probably seeking a reassuring reprimand or two, deliberately held back, simply shaking her head with a smile. Mattie was a good painter; it was sad that she felt so little compulsion these days to do it. Being someone's personal assistant didn't suit her – she was almost certainly lousy at it – but it paid for her rent and cigarettes. And chocolate. Judging from the blotchy pallor of her sister's face, she had been consuming little else.

'Just you take care,' Jane said softly, leaning forward to brush her fingers across Mattie's marbled cheek.

'And how about you, big sis, are you well?' Mattie stood up and put her sunglasses on as she asked the question.

'Me? Oh, I'm fine,' replied Jane automatically, staring up at the giant reflector lenses, seeing a warped image of herself, a hunched woman in a chair. Then quite suddenly she started to cry, terrible tears that simply spilled down her face of their own accord.

'Jane? What the—' Mattie quickly knelt beside her and took her hands. Then Julia noticed that something was wrong and came leaping to her other side waving a handkerchief. Jane felt spectacularly embarrassed and acutely aware of Michael, sitting helpless in his chair, watching the scene of his weeping wife and the clucking women probably with horror. She knew herself that it was a truly dreadful thing to do – to burst into tears at a Sunday lunch for no reason at all. But it had crept up on her out of nowhere, stealthy and appalling, like a sudden sickness. And once she had started, it took several minutes to stop. She blew her nose hard on Julia's immaculately ironed hanky.

'I am sorry, all of you – I don't know what got into me.'

'Don't tell me, it was my new sunglasses – I can take it. I'll burn them the minute I get home.'

'Dear Mat, I love your glasses.'

'Would a drink help?' It was the first thing Michael had said.

'Thank you, Michael, but I'm fine now.' There was an expectant pause, as if all three of them were waiting for an explanation. But she had none to give.

Julia and Mattie left soon afterwards. At the door, Jane laughed reassuringly with them and blamed it all on hormones.

'I'll call you,' said Julia with a firm look.

'What was all that about?' Michael asked, when they had gone.

'I – I don't know.' Jane concentrated hard on clearing the table, instinct telling her that she had something to hide, though quite what, she wasn't sure.

'Nobody just bursts into tears without there being some kind of reason for it.' Michael stood in the kitchen doorway, arms folded across his broad chest, his strong, square face set in an expression of vigorous determination.

'I suppose... I suddenly felt sad.'

'Crying and sadness are commonly associated, this is true.' The impatience in his tone made her rattle the plates. Upstairs, Harriet began to cry in her cot. 'Perhaps you could be a little more explicit? After all, I don't think your behaviour could exactly be described as normal.'

'Normal?' Jane looked at him for an instant before returning her attention to stacking plates. 'I don't know, Michael, I don't know,' she burst out, feeling close to tears again. 'I'm sorry, but that's the truth of it.'

'Steady on, we don't want to scare the children with all this hysteria, do we?'

Tom was standing beside his father, holding a complicated Lego construction up for approval. For an instant Jane felt that the child understood more than the man, that he was tuned into her in a way so deep that it made Michael a mere stranger by comparison.

'I say, you're not pregnant, are you?' he went on, holding Tom's creation but not looking at it.

'No, Michael, I am not pregnant. There are other reasons that women cry.' She wiped the table mats and stacked them back into the box, the sides of which were badly battered and held together with stiff, ageing Sellotape. They had been a wedding present from some distant relative of Michael's who now lived in New Zealand – brilliantly coloured birds of the world, laminated so securely that their plumage shone with as much brightness as they had on the day they were unpacked.

'Good. A baby is about the last thing we need.'

'It's a space rocket,' said Tom for at least the fourth time, but very loudly now, so that Michael had to respond and Jane could escape. At least it felt like escape, as she sidled past the two of them and got on with the immediate demands of her daughter and a messy kitchen.

But all through the domestic chores of that day and the rest of the week, the unprompted outburst of crying sat in Jane's mind like an unanswered question. She was greatly alarmed by it. To have embarrassed herself was bad enough; but far worse, was the sense of not having been in control. Some fundamental ground in her life was shifting and she was losing her balance.

4

'You need a break,' remarked Julia a couple of weeks later in a tone of voice that was both scolding and kind. 'Too much bloody domesticity – baby dribble and Hoover bags – it drives most women to drink in the end. Lay down the rubber gloves and demand a holiday for yourself.'

'Oh Julia, I can't.' Jane was trimming the fatty edges off some pork chops. The telephone was wedged between her ear and shoulder, causing considerable neck-ache, since the conversation had gone on for some time. 'You know I can't.'

'I know you won't, which is quite a different thing.'

'Michael would have a fit and who would look after the children and where would I go?'

'Rent a nanny from one of those agencies and go to a health farm. Tell Michael it's that or a divorce.' She laughed. 'Be bold, woman, demand your rights.'

Jane sighed, not in the mood for her friend's flippant confidence. 'Rights are complicated things when you're married. And anyway, all your suggestions are outrageously expensive. It's impossible.'

'Nothing is impossible, Jane,' she retorted, 'you're going woolly-headed, that's all. You're not seeing anything beyond the wallpaper.'

Even for Julia this was curt. 'Well, thanks for the advice,'

'Don't go all defensive. Tell me to shut up or bugger off, but don't curl up in that bullet-proof shell of yours – it's very distressing for those of us left outside in the cold.'

Jane put the phone back on its wall slot next to her shelf of kitchen jars, feeling dazed and alone. Once upon a time, it had been easy to love Michael. She looked at the pile of raw pork in front of her, pink and moist, streaked with white fat, and wondered if human flesh looked like that, beneath the skin. These days love did not come to her fresh and inspirational as it once had; now it was a stale remembered feeling that she had to dig from her mind with force. She started to cut the meat for the stew, but her knife was blunt and the pork resisted, its fatty streaks so interwoven with the pink flesh that she could not separate them. The fat with the meat, she thought, the rough with the smooth, for better for worse, and she gave up on her task, tearing the meat into big pieces and throwing them into the pan regardless.

Michael must have missed his train. Outside, a failing sun was casting its last beams across the garden, illuminating the spring-green of the grass and making the young faces of the leaves stand out against the dusky sky like jewels on metal. The blurred screen of a television flickered on in the upstairs room of the house next door; from the other side of the fence, the hollering of an angry child broke the stillness of the evening. Jane, whose own children had been asleep for half an hour at least, took a glass of wine and sat in one of the patio chairs still parked at odd angles from the not entirely successful Sunday lunch a couple of weeks before. The chair's once shiny metal frame was now thick with rust; orange speckled with black and brown. She rubbed and picked at the worst patches with her fingers, knowing it was futile, but wanting the shine to return.

After a while she gave up and checked her watch, before going to the little shed beyond the oak tree at the bottom of the garden, where she had hidden a pack of ten cigarettes and a lighter behind an old paint tin. Having lit one, she inhaled slowly, closing her eyes, enjoying the dry burning at the back of her throat and the faint sensation of giddiness. Perhaps Julia was right; perhaps some time alone was all she needed. Time and uninterrupted sleep. Jane took another drag, aware of the smell of garlic and onions on her hands and the tiny shreds of pork still stuck under her fingernails. The faint sound of a slamming door gave her a jolt. She hastily dropped the cigarette and set off back towards the house, balancing on the balls of her feet to avoid the worst of the late February mud.

'Oh, there you are.'

'My God, Michael. You startled me. I thought you'd be on the later train.'

'So, I can still surprise you, after all these years.' He was in a good mood, smiling, saying nothing about the cigarette – though he only kissed her on the nose. 'They've changed the train times – British Rail strikes again, so to speak.' He sniffed the air, which smelt of mint – sole survivor of an inherited, erstwhile herb bed – mixed with smoke. 'The garden isn't looking too bad.' He tugged a small twist of bindweed from the nearest shrub and put it in his pocket. 'What's for supper?'

'Pork. A sort of stew.'

He blew vigorously on his hands and rubbed them together. 'Great. It's bloody cold out here. Let's get inside.'

'It's not that cold, it's lovely. I was going to sit with my drink for a bit.'

'Really?' He gave a snort and stomped back inside, only to return a couple of minutes later wearing an anorak and bringing the wine bottle and a glass with him. He placed them carefully on the table before sitting down in the chair nearest hers.

'Good day?'

'More or less.'

'Children all right?'

'Tom wailed at the school gates and Harriet lunged at the shelves of the supermarket like a mini sumo wrestler. So pretty normal all round. What about you?'

'Monstrously busy.'

'You always say that.'

'That's because it's always true. Will supper be ready yet?' He patted his stomach which was flattish but soft.

'Shall we talk about our marriage instead of supper?'

'Whatever for?'

'It might be interesting.'

'I highly doubt it.' Michael laughed, pouring himself some wine.

There was a terrible complacency in his aspect which struck Jane with such force that for a moment she could not speak. Had it always been there, she wondered, or had it edged into him, an early, teasing component of what he would become.

'Why are you in such a good mood anyway? Have you been given a pay rise or found a mistress or something?' she countered, with a wicked urge to knock all the smugness out of him.

But Michael looked even more pleased, enjoying her banter. 'No such luck on either account, I'm afraid.' He stretched as he grinned, thinking of the crisp perfection of Antonia's presentation and the neat pleated slit at the back of her pinstripe skirt. 'Perhaps I feel good because I'm almost thirty-five and not yet bald or fat or poor or lonely.'

'Those are all negatives. It's not the same as saying I'm slim and rich and surrounded by people I adore.' She eyed the thick curls of his hair. 'You're certainly not bald.'

'And I do adore you.' He reached out and patted her hand.

Jane sat unmoving, unable to respond, suddenly rigid with cold. It wasn't enough and it wasn't true. Michael adored her according to his moods; if he felt good, he said he adored her. It had nothing to do with love. She withdrew her hand and cupped her wine glass to her chest, staring into the yellowy liquid, watching a bobbing fragment of cork on its surface.

'I'm starving. And Christ, now it *is* cold.' He jumped up from his chair and walked briskly down the garden to where she had dropped her cigarette. Gingerly, he picked it up, holding it as he might a dead worm, before hurling it into the mass of variegated ivy that grew along, through and round their garden fence in a collage of greens.

Jane went inside to boil some water for peas. Why was trying to talk about the real things so hard, she wondered, when, in many ways they knew each other so well. Once it had been simple enough. When her parents were killed and Mattie went off the rails, Michael had empowered her. Just the sound of his voice had been soothing. She had loved his unflurried rationality, the way he weighed up what had to be done, assessed things, sorted them out, tackled them head on without fear.

Though she put on a sweatshirt and sat in the kitchen chair nearest the radiator, the cold had entered her and would not leave. The pork had turned brown and tender at the mercy of the oven, but all Jane saw was pink flesh and squidgy ridges of fat. It was like seeing into the heart of the things and it made her feel sick and sad.

Julia banged the side of the steering wheel with the flat of her gloved hand and then resignedly pushed the gear stick into neutral. She should have gone another way – along the embankment and across one of the city bridges perhaps. After scowling at her reflection in the rear view mirror, she looked again to check her make-up. The colour on her lips was very red. Too red. She pressed them together several times and then dabbed at the edges with a tissue from her pocket. The driver in the car behind pressed his horn. The Hammersmith traffic had shifted forward by five feet at least and she hadn't even noticed.

Her fingers reached for the radio, but stopped short. Her car had been broken into the week before and all its contents swiped, even the floppy box of tissues she kept on top of the dashboard and a shapeless mohair sweater that her mother had knitted years before which she hated but couldn't throw away.

Without the distraction of music or news, Julia found herself mulling over the prospect of the evening before her. She was almost as baffled about being on the guest-list as she was about why Pippa Croft should have taken it upon herself to organise such a party in the first place. Celebrating promotions was surely a wife's job. She had said as much to Jane, who was irritatingly pragmatic about it. Pippa was on an 'up', she explained, looking for reasons to be jolly, and if that included throwing surprise parties for Michael, then that was fine by her. Julia had wondered then – as she did now – whether her friend spoke the truth. She couldn't work Jane out at the moment; she couldn't get her to talk any more, either to complain or to have a laugh. Everything was fine, she kept saying, her lips closing on the word like a portcullis.

It had been hard enough maintaining a friendship like theirs over the years, given all the hoops of marriage and motherhood that Jane had chosen to fling over herself. They had had to work at it, the two of them, like some off-beat married couple who only met when other commitments allowed. As a result, the intense intimacy of their student years had been stretched and moulded into some-thing rather more dilute. Sometimes, Julia even feared that the friendship only survived by virtue of what had gone before. There was so little now to fuel it in the everyday sense of having things in common.

By the time Julia accelerated across the relative freedom of Wandsworth Bridge she was already late for the party. She whistled quietly at her own audacity as she shot through a red light and turned on to the south circular. The evening might be fun after all. Mattie was going to be there, as was Michael's brother, Christopher, whom she hadn't seen for years, and a man called Des, who was a friend of Michael and Tim's from way back and whom she vaguely recollected as being quite amusing. Since it was some time since she had experienced anything approximating to a 'relationship' with a man, Julia could not help allowing herself a heartbeat of speculation at renewing such acquaintances.

As Julia Durnford's looks had emerged from the challenging cocoon of late adolescence, she had discovered the fundamental and most disturbing fact that to be what society regarded as classically attractive was frequently the most terrible burden. There was little she could do about it; no visual aids or clever dressing were required to draw attention to her glassy blue eyes and lustrous blonde hair. And her figure was the racehorse kind – that breed apart – with naturally toned long legs, strong hips, a slim waist and broad shoulders. Men, it seemed, read from an entirely different score when presented with such looks. The most obviously desirable qualities in a partner, or at any rate the ones Julia found herself scanning for, such as sincerity, understanding and an equal capacity for intellectual as well as sexual pastimes, were invariably buried under much less enticing features – possessiveness, vanity and insecurity, being the most striking traits of the men she had attracted so far. In short, practically all her affairs had been a disaster, apart from one with a married man, which she tried not to remember and from which she had eventually extricated herself with more regret than she had ever before experienced or wished to know again.

* * *

The Crofts' sitting room, with all its sweeps, folds and tucks of flowery cottons, reminded Jane of a Laura Ashley furnishings shop. Although several years had passed since Pippa had designed it, the effect was still crisp and new; a picture-perfect garden of silky, pastel shades, unsullied by grubby finger marks and juice dribbles. To complete the picture, Pippa floated amongst the floral scene like some pre-Raphaelite flower girl, one of those wan, gowned women on the arty calendars that Jane and Mattie had bought each other as birthday presents in their early teens. In honour of the occasion, Pippa's long, limp tresses had been loosely – but very carefully – pinned to the top of her head so that long wisps fell down about her ears and neck, trailing decorously amongst the large hoops of her earrings. Her dress, like her curtains, was covered with flowers and swept almost to the ground. Jane, who wore a plain silk shirt and baggy black trousers, felt, with a familiar jolt, the chasm that separated her from the wife of her husband's oldest friend.

'This is wonderful, Pippa, you've gone to so much trouble.'

'I never guessed – I thought we were going to the bloody cinema,' said Michael, not for the first time, slapping his knee and looking happily round the room at the small group of people Pippa had invited to celebrate the latest success in his career.

'He was hell to get out of the house,' put in Jane, touched, in spite of herself, by Michael's obvious delight at Pippa's surprise party and willing herself to join in the spirit of the event.

'I could never have organised it without your help, Jane – you've been a marvel,' said Pippa happily, picking up a plate of enticing miniature vol-au-vents to take round the room.

'I have done nothing,' said Jane, truthfully. Had Pippa hesitated at all before suggesting the party, she wondered suddenly, and why did it bother her – as Michael's wife – so little? Life was so much easier if you just let it sweep you along, that was the truth. It was amazing how many things seemed to happen of their own accord.

'How are everyone's drinks?' asked Pippa, clapping her hands to vent some of her panic about the evening in general and the meal in particular. She had written down exactly when each dish had to go in and out of the oven, but still kept forgetting. The real intention behind the dinner, so simple in conception, had been as a pretext for cheering Tim up, stirring him out of what had become unremitting glumness. But her plan, perhaps wavering under the weight of the secret hopes heaped upon it, was refusing to cooperate. Michael appeared cheerful enough, but Tim's contribution to the festivities had so far amounted to little more than a menacing silence, one of those that made Pippa sure she had done something wrong, something as yet unidentified but wholly unforgivable. Des had added greatly to these anxieties by bringing a very young and noisily confident girlfriend – barely out of university by the look of her. The prawns had shrunk alarmingly from grilling, and were going to have to be spread very thinly indeed; as was the home-made garlic mayonnaise, which had curdled twice and which she wished she'd never started. The book said the salmon only needed forty minutes, but it had looked so huge – so disturbingly chunky and raw – that Pippa was allowing twice that amount of time. It was the salmon that was hardest to keep at the back of her mind as Christopher asked her how she was and exclaimed that they hadn't met since Harriet's christening.

'We're just lovely, thank you, Christopher,' she chimed, smelling fish and resisting the urge to run to the kitchen. 'Do you know Des Frewin and his er—'

'Cassie,' said the girl quickly and confidently, stepping forward to shake Christopher's hand with a great half-moon of a smile that might have been more reassuring without the purple lipstick that outlined it. 'I'm in television. Documentaries mainly. Des and I met working on a programme on inner city violence. I think he's the best producer on the circuit.' The large smile never left her face as she spoke, nor did she seem to breathe between sentences.

'I must check out his work in that case,' said Christopher, with a slight bow to them both.

Des shook the ice cubes in his glass, looking embarrassed but pleased. 'Steady on, darling, from what I recall our friend here isn't exactly a fan of the media.'

A dim memory of a drunken argument about the intrusive power of the press stirred at the back of Christopher's mind. It might even have been at Michael's thirtieth. He was drinking a lot around then.

'Age has softened my views considerably,' he said, laughing

easily and rocking his tall frame back on his heels, 'though I have to confess to the unforgivable crime of not owning a television.'

'Are you serious?' Cassie turned incredulously to Des, giving Christopher the opportunity to cast his eyes round the room and raise his glass of orange juice in silent toast to Michael.

'Don't take it personally, please,' he went on, deftly flicking his attention back, 'if I had a television, I'd never read a book or listen to music. I'm totally undisciplined. If there's a box anywhere near, I switch it on. It's a very alluring machine.'

A gentle nudge on his elbow from behind saved him from having to continue.

'Excuse me a moment,' he said, as politely as he could, before turning away, inwardly cursing himself for having come. He should have known better after all this time.

It was Jane who had touched him. Pippa was hovering at her side.

'We're needed in the kitchen, apparently.' Jane, he could tell, was pretending to look solemn. 'The salmon is misbehaving.'

Pippa wrung her hands. 'I need to get it on to a plate and it's sort of falling apart.'

'Don't panic, Pippa. Jane will take the feet and I'll manage the head. You can direct operations.' He kissed his sister-in-law lightly on the cheek. The room was like a greenhouse, but her skin felt cool and smooth. 'How are you?'

'Fine. How's Oxford and academia?'

They followed Pippa through into the kitchen.

'I'd hardly call teaching little boys an academic challenge—'

'Well, you're writing a book as well, aren't you?'

Pippa, who had two large pink blotches on each cheek, blew a few straggles of hair from her eyes and handed out cloths and cooking slices. 'Can you save your chatting for later, you two, and no more jokes about head and feet. If this bloody fish falls apart, I shall scream.'

'That might be rather fun – to have a screaming hostess.'

'Christopher, behave,' whispered Jane, who could see that Pippa was indeed close to some sort of minor breakdown.

The fish wobbled dangerously on its journey from pan to dish, but held together all but part of the tail, which was easily wedged back into place. The two helpers watched as Pippa lovingly planted sprigs of parsley along its sides and spread lemon slices across its belly, including a sliver to hide the loose bit of tail.

'It looks lovely,' said Jane, avoiding Christopher's eyes, which were twinkling irreverently.

'Thank you so much for your help,' murmured Pippa, absorbed in her task. 'Would you mind asking the others to go and sit down? If we don't start on the prawns soon, this monster will go completely cold.'

It took a while for the party to get going, for the single, stilted conversation between all of them to scatter into happy fragments of more natural dialogue. Jane, listening with strained intensity to Des's views on the role of the welfare state, felt her face aching from being fixed in appropriate expressions. She felt deeply uninteresting and uninvolved. When Des gave up on her and turned to Mattie she experienced a surge of relief, followed quickly by a jerk of panic that her life somehow amounted to nothing more than this room full of people, whom – as it suddenly seemed – she barely knew and who certainly did not know her. Only when her eye caught Julia's did the panic subside. She was wearing a short, black velvet cocktail dress that pencil-lined the smooth curves of her body and made her long, fair hair shine like silk. She was smiling and nodding at Cassie, who had been talking very energetically at her for several minutes. Julia was clearly on her best behaviour, nodding intently and shooting intermittent looks of encouragement at Christopher, who appeared either preoccupied or left out.

But it should have been Michael, thought Jane suddenly, the panic returning; it should have been Michael who made her feel she belonged. He was sitting opposite her, his legs so close under the Crofts' long, narrow dining-table that she could feel the brush of his knees against hers when he shifted position. He was smiling deeply, running his fingers through the dark waves of his thick hair, sipping champagne, nodding with Tim about something, enjoying himself.

She stared so hard at him that he turned to look at her, raising his eyebrows questioningly. Caught off guard, she could think of nothing to say except to ask if he was having a good time, which sounded like a probe for congratulation. At least that was how Michael read it.

'This is marvellous – I didn't guess. Truly, I didn't guess for a second.' He raised his glass and offered a toast to his wife and to the chef.

Pippa blushed and waved her napkin.

The prawns were well received. Especially by Cassie, who listed the vitamins to be found in shellfish and announced that she had recently stopped eating meat. This prompted Pippa, despite the good fortune of her fish-based menu, to confess that the hollandaise sauce was positively loaded with egg yolks (they had helped considerably in the long battle against curdling), and that the rice had been cooked in chicken stock. After making a big to-do of forgiving her hostess these inadvertent oversights, Cassie, clearly a lover of limelight, proceeded to flutter her ten, heavily ringed fingers and talk at length about her visit to an abattoir, the stench of the blood, the screams of the dying animals and the depravity of mankind in general.

'Just as well shellfish don't have feelings then, isn't it?' remarked

Christopher, glancing up with a sharp smile from a project that involved lining prawn heads round the rim of his plate, so that their depleted antennae drooped decoratively over the edge.

Cassie opened her mouth, but Michael, too padded by good wine and good humour to pick up on any subtleties of tone, from his brother or anyone else, got there first.

'Thought you were looking a little thinner, mate,' he said to Des, 'now I know it's too much bloody rabbit food.'

'Oh, I'm still a raw steak man through and through,' Des assured him quickly, sensing that he was defending far more than his eating habits.

'What about you, Mattie?' put in Jane quickly, brought to attention by a sense that the conversation was in danger of collapsing into something a little less cordial, 'Weren't you off meat for a while?'

'Yeah, until I nearly hacked my thumb off chopping through one of those endless concoctions of onions, peppers, swedes and parsnips. I converted to chocolate on the spot and I've never looked back. No chopping, no mess, no washing up.'

'Chocolate?' said Cassie, as if the word disgusted her.

'Except for breakfast when I have cereal or toast. You have to wash the bowl or the plate then, of course, but nothing's perfect, is it?'

Jane sat back through all this, enjoying the way her little sister was never afraid of saying the first thing that came into her head, and then simply following it through to see where it led.

Non-plussed, Cassie grabbed the reins of the conversation again by announcing to the entire table that she was about to start work on a documentary about marriage. 'My personal view – not that it will affect my presentation of the facts – is that marriage is almost always lethal.' Her eyes skewered Des's, lovingly, for the split second it took for everyone else to notice. 'So don't go getting any ideas, darling.' She threw back her head, slowly widening her mouth into its designer smile and unconsciously flinging the largest of her permed tresses across Christopher's cheek. He wiped the spot where her hair had touched him, absently, continuing with the other hand to twirl the stem of his wine glass.

'What a load of bullshit,' remarked Mattie, dabbing at a drop of hollandaise with her finger and sucking it noisily. 'Not that I want to get married,' she added, when in fact she sometimes did and sometimes didn't, depending on fluctuating levels of self-confidence. 'I mean, I can't help thinking monogamy must get to be a little dull.' There was a faint shuffling amongst those members of her audience torn between wanting to defend their capacity for sexual adventure and anxiety not to provoke any twangs of discord with their partners. Mattie however, appeared happily oblivious of such stirrings. 'It must be like the same person painting the same thing over and over again – in the end, surely, there is a limit to its creative potential...' She faltered, as unwelcome thoughts of her own unfinished canvases, their faces turned in disgrace to the wall, and the forty hours a week she spent staring at a screen in an overheated office, interrupted her flow. 'I suppose it's all about imagination... fantasies... I bet loads of marriages would fall apart without *that*, anyway,' she concluded, aware of having rather lost her thread.

'Perhaps you shouldn't make judgements about things you haven't tried,' suggested Michael, a little stiffly, wishing the conversation hadn't been allowed to grow so dull.

'Hear, hear,' echoed Tim, giving his friend a look of unqualified allegiance.

'You forgot to mention love, Mattie,' put in Julia cheerfully, 'not that I could claim to be an expert on the subject.'

At which point Jane slipped away into the kitchen to see if she could help Pippa with the pudding. When she returned, bearing a jug of cream, Michael was pulling his brother into the conversation with a distinct vibration of challenge in his voice.

'Your turn, Christopher,' he said, folding his arms and smiling not altogether pleasantly, 'what's the bachelor view of love and marriage then?'

Christopher's response was slow, almost languid. He looked across the table at his brother, their dark eyes meeting fully for the first time that evening. His hair was much blacker than Michael's, cut very short, giving even more prominence to the high Lytton forehead and the peculiar paleness of his skin; which looked sort of fragile, Jane decided, watching him closely, like it was a thin porcelain mask that might shatter from the slightest tap.

'Oh, I'm a die-hard romantic, I'm afraid – all in favour of lifelong commitments and happy marriages.' He paused gravely. 'Though of course I keep it as well hidden as I can.' He laughed and everyone else followed suit, some element of relief ringing through the air.

The rest of the evening passed very slowly for Jane, who, as the designated driver could not help feeling sober and tired. Christopher left shortly after dinner, politely declining Pippa's offer of decaffeinated coffee or chamomile tea and murmuring about the long drive back to Oxford. He was soon followed by the others, Julia kindly offering to give Mattie a lift. Jane and Pippa spent the best part of the next hour in the kitchen, tidying up and talking in hushed tones about the chances of getting pregnant through clinical intervention, while their husbands discussed asset trading over large glasses of brandy.

'I've sort of broached the subject and then flunked out. I'm terrified Tim's not going to agree. It's so wretchedly expensive – but still, we'll have to go private. There's a three year waiting list on the NHS – by which time it could be too late for me – and even then, they ration how many goes you can have.' Pippa paused, an empty wine bottle in each hand. 'The thing is, Tim is just not himself at the moment. So I keep putting off talking to him about it.' She laid the wine bottles carefully on top of many others in a box in the corner before continuing. 'Did you notice anything tonight? Don't you think he seemed a little... preoccupied?' Pippa gave a nervous peek round the door to check that they were in no danger of being overheard. 'I'm really rather worried about him.'

'I suppose he was quite quiet,' conceded Jane, struggling to think how she could be reassuring. The truth was, she had never found Tim easy to talk to. He had always struck her as being very much a man's man, one who made a point of steering well clear of what he regarded as the dangerously emotional conversational territory of women. 'But then, Michael didn't exactly say very much, did he? Come to think of it, none of the men did. I'm afraid Mattie did rather a lot of talking.'

'And Cassie.'

They both laughed.

'But I like Christopher.'

Jane hesitated, as always uncertain about her brother-in law. 'Yes, I like him too. But he's sort of moody – I never quite know what to make of him. Like tonight. He was really quite jolly at the beginning, but by the end he had gone all broody and silent, as if he'd had enough of us all. I never know what he's thinking but always suspect it's something rather critical.'

'Well, he helped me a lot in the kitchen, which I thought was lovely,' pronounced Pippa, folding the last drying-up cloth into a tidy rectangle and leading the way through into the sitting room.

On the way home Michael put his hand on Jane's knee and, inspired by a sleepy gratitude, squeezed it on and off all the way down the A3.

'It was good to see Des after so much time – good-looking young woman he's found for himself too. Not my type though.' He yawned deeply. 'Christopher's a pompous ass, though. I'm always pleased at seeing him and then wonder the hell why.'

'I'm not sure he's pompous exactly—'

'Yes, he bloody well is. Ivory tower nonsense,' he muttered, adding more strongly, 'and he couldn't even hack that, could he?'

Jane had no desire to listen to Michael's familiar tirade against his younger brother, how he had thrown away all chances of adult success by swapping university life for a small prep school, how he was almost certainly gay and in denial.

'You know I hate to say it...' he went on.

Jane braced herself, containing her irritation with a short intake of breath.

'...but I'm sure he's a pansy.'

Michael's choice of vocabulary fell upon Jane's ears like the scrape of a nail on a blackboard. 'That's a stupid, horrible word and what does it matter anyway. I happen to think you are wrong. I don't think Christopher is gay and never have – not that it is any of our business.' She exited too fast onto the slip-road off the motorway, grinding the gears as she changed down.

'Aha! So you thought he was interested in Julia and Mattie, did you?'

'No, I did not. Though he may be, for all I know. I'm just going on my instincts.'

'Ah, instincts. Good, solid things, instincts.'

She realised then that he was very drunk and that it was pointless trying to talk sensibly about anything.

'And that sister of yours talks a load of twaddle. All that nonsense about fantasy.' He yawned again, more deeply this time. 'No one in their right mind would take *her* on for life. Be more like a bloody life sentence than a marriage.' He chuckled and removed his hand from Jane's knee.

By the time they reached the outskirts of Cobham, Michael was sound asleep, his cheek pressed against the window, his face squashed, mouth open, like a dead man.

A heavy rain was falling. As Jane strained her eyes to see past the frenzied, squeaky swipes of the windscreen wipers, she found herself thinking about things like fantasy, imagination and sexual pleasure with the nostalgic longing of remembering lost friends. In the last few years her capacity for such luxuries had faltered and run cold. Sitting there in the stuffy, car-heated darkness, her husband breathing softly, rhythmically beside her, she could have wept for what was lost. Not just for the sweet explosions of erotic pleasure, but for the faith and intimacy that had inspired them. She practiced deception now; it had begun as the occasional exaggeration of enjoyment – reserved for those odd times when she felt so tired and unresponsive that sex was just something to get over and be done with. But gradually the habit had taken hold. Their lovemaking took less and less time as Michael grew surer of his ability to arouse her and she withdrew ever more expertly into herself, hiding her disappointment behind charades of satisfaction and pleasure. Which would upset Michael more, she wondered, as she switched off the engine and turned to look at him, the duplicity of a full-blown affair, or this silent deceit already coiled deep within their bed, the worm within a rose.

She turned to him and stroked his forehead with the barest surface of her fingertips, exploring his face, tracing the faint frown lines, the baby softness of his eyelids, the sand-paper feel of his cheeks and chin, the dry lines of his lips. He closed his mouth and smiled in his sleep.

'Excuse me.' There was a tap at the window. Jane peered out to see the wide, friendly face of the baby-sitter, Mrs Browne, standing by the car sheltering under one umbrella and offering her another.

'Oh, thank you so much, Mrs B,' she called, prodding Michael in the ribs before clambering out of the car, gratefully accepting the brolly and opening it against the black wetness of the night. 'We're terribly late. I'm so sorry.' She had to shout against the pelting rain. 'Do you want a hand, Michael, darling?'

'You mean, am I so incapacitated that I require assistance for the simple business of walking?' He spoke loudly and not entirely coherently, setting off towards the house, apparently oblivious to getting drenched.

'Did he have a good time?' said Mrs Browne with a wink.

'We both had a lovely time thank you, Mrs Browne,' Jane replied firmly, standing back to let her follow Michael into the house.

6

In the weeks that followed, Jane did her best not to think about anything very much. She threw herself into her daily domestic dramas with an energy specifically designed to leave little pause for thought. Usually, it worked. But every so often she would freeze, sock or loo-brush in hand, and tremble at the terrifying realisation that she wanted to leave her husband. It felt so shocking, after years of mental fidelity, even to formulate such a thought. She took to reading of adultery and divorce amongst public figures, with a kind of wonderment. How did people summon the courage to go through with it? It all sounded so matter-of-fact in print, so unquestionable and obvious. Yet to Jane, crouching in her own goldfish bowl of marital misery, the prospect of the mutual suffering, defeat and logistical difficulties that she knew separating from Michael would entail, was dismal and debilitating.

Michael, meanwhile, showed not the slightest glimmer of an acknowledgement of a problem between them. It was not in his nature to admit to failure of any kind. Where such a mind-set served him well at the office, expressing as it did an apparently unshakable confidence in his own qualities, it left Jane feeling increasingly distressed and unnerved. The more arguments and silences threatened them, the more coolly efficient and briskly communicative he became. With his promotion, he began to work even longer hours. On coming home, he would fire bright questions at her about the children, with a determined interest that dared her to be critical of his absences. He even began, with lazy complacency, to profess jealousy at her easy, homey lifestyle, bemoaning, with a half-smile, the increase in pressure and work-load that accompanied success, ignoring her reminders that returning to the publishing world remained a goal of hers once the children were both in primary school.

Jane began to feel like a dissatisfied employee, with no recourse to or right of complaint. It struck her, in the midst of all this, that for a long time she had been waiting – hoping – for some kind of show-down, a natural climax of discord that would illustrate beyond all reasonable doubt that their relationship had broken down. It was more alarming than anything to realise, as she did on the morning of their eighth wedding anniversary, watching Michael's under-pants and striped pyjamas spin round in the frothy frenzy of the washing machine's last spin, that the situation as it stood could go on forever. There was no sense of build-up in the air – no sense of development towards anything.

They were forced to celebrate their anniversary with the aid of the television.

'I don't believe this,' shouted Michael, when that evening's baby-sitter called in sick at the last minute. 'There must be someone you could phone – how you can just stand there?' When Jane said there wasn't because Mrs Browne was visiting her sister on the Isle of Wight, he banged his hand on the kitchen table so hard that the children's pot of felt-pens tipped over and rolled on to the floor. 'Fuck. A fine bloody evening this is turning out to be.'

Jane rushed to help pick the pens up but he pushed her away. 'I can manage, for Christ's sake.'

She straightened and smoothed out the creases in her dress. It was an old blue silk one of her mother's which, years ago, she had cleverly altered to fit her own smaller frame. The overall effect, with its line of side buttons and high-standing collar, was oriental. The first time she had worn it Michael had called her his 'Exotic Beauty', scooping her up in his arms and swinging her round till she was dizzy. Jane thought of this now as she watched him scrabbling on the floor with the pens, deliberately making heavy weather of the job because he was cross about the evening, cross with her – as she could feel him thinking – for making a mess of the arrangements.

The memory now left her little repelled. It was altogether a weird feeling – to look back at what had been a happy experience and to feel so detached and critical.

'There's some champagne,' she said quietly.

'Well, that's something, I suppose. Though I'll have to go easy. Antonia and I are facing the big guns tomorrow – on the Polish investment project. Make or break kind of thing. If the MD doesn't like this one, we could both be looking for jobs – although my neck is on the line more than Antonia's, which is only natural since it's worth a bit more at the end of each month...'

Jane, who had once grown nervous on Michael's behalf when he mentioned such meetings, drifted into a sort of trance as he talked. He had his back to her and was rooting unsuccessfully in the fridge for the bottle of champagne. It had been a habit of her parents to keep champagne in the house. Her father claimed that it made him look for excuses to celebrate rather than grumble. Thinking of her parents gave her a jolt, as it sometimes did, an electric shock of pain that passed through her without warning, a memento of the loss and shock.

Once the bottle had – with evident irritation – been extracted from the drawer marked 'salad', Michael made a visible attempt to slip into a more appropriately celebratory frame of mind, though the strain showed in the rapidity with which he emptied and refilled his glass and his keenness to escape to the sitting room.

They ate pâté and humus with toast, on their laps, watching television. After the news there was a repeat of a Benny Hill show. Jane reached for the console and pressed the volume switch down a few notches.

'Hey, what did you do that for?'

'I want to talk.'

He rolled his eyes. 'Not now, please, Jane – this is funny.' He seized the console and turned the volume back up. 'Anyway, what about?' He kept his gaze firmly on the screen.

'You're not listening.'

'I am, I am.' He gave her a reassuring look and then laughed loudly at something in the programme. Very deliberately, light-headed with apprehension, Jane got up from the sofa and placed herself in front of the television.

'What the hell are you playing at?' he scowled, reminding her of how Tom looked when one of his favourite cartoons ended.

It wasn't a great moment to have picked, she knew that, but fear at her own courage had blurred her judgement and the careful sense of timing that she usually employed in dealings with her husband. It struck her suddenly that she had shoe-horned both of them through so much that was bad – so much that should have been allowed to *be* bad – by simply pretending that everything was all right. It was a hard habit to break.

'We're not getting on very well, Michael,' she announced firmly, feeling small and melodramatic.

He shook a look of surprised annoyance from his face and extended his hand towards her.

'Come and sit down, for goodness' sake. We're fine.'

'No, we are not.' She ignored the hand and took a step backwards. The hem of her dress prickled slightly as it came into
contact with the static electricity of the TV screen. Benny Hill was
on a horse, singing loudly.

Michael sighed and put his hands to each side of his face before
running his fingers back through his thick hair.

'Why are you doing this, Jane, tonight of all nights?' he asked, in
a tone that expressed frustration rather than the desire for a
genuine answer.

She started to reply, but he quickly turned the volume down
and tugged hard on her arm until she sat down beside him.

'Everything needs working at – marriage and everything else.
We both know that.' He smiled and shrugged as he spoke, as if
making such an enlightened statement absolved him from the
onerous task of putting it into practice. 'So stop looking so bloody
miserable.' He pulled her closer. His shirt felt faintly damp against
her face. It smelt of fabric conditioner mingled with sweat. Jane
went limp, focusing her attention on one of his buttons. It was a
perfect, pearly white, apart from the faintest grey streak between
two of the tiny holes.

'That's better,' he murmured, stroking her head.

When Benny Hill had finished Michael murmured, 'I almost
forgot – I've got something for you,' and produced a crumpled
white envelope from his trouser pocket. Expecting it to be an
anniversary card, Jane was surprised when a small business card
saying *Georgio Beauty Therapists* fell onto her lap. In the top left-
hand corner was scrawled a time and a date. 'It's a present. A facial
something or other. Apparently, Mrs Glassbrook – the MD's wife –
spends half her life at the place. It's supposed to be very exclusive,'
he added, because Jane was so silent.

'Thank you,' she breathed at last, 'how very... special... did you
think of it yourself?'

'I found the card in the street – what do you bloody well think?' In truth, the gift had been Antonia's suggestion when he had let slip that he had to get back early for an anniversary meal. He had asked his secretary to pop round to the salon in person to make the booking during her lunch break.

'I'm afraid I haven't got you anything,' Jane mumbled, disarmed and confused. 'I mean, we don't usually...'

'No, we don't, and I'll forgive you,' he said softly, sliding his hand down to the round of her bottom and squeezing it gently through the slippery silk of her dress. 'There are ways you could make up for it, you know.'

She forced a smile, while inside a lone voice roared its derision and despair. Nothing had changed. She was powerless. The failure felt all her own. Michael pretended not to see – Michael would never see – that their marriage had plummeted to terrible depths, that they were in a silent, secret, dark place where there was no love, no understanding, no hope.

'I'll quickly clear up and shower,' she muttered, sloping off, hoping that if she took long enough Michael would have fallen asleep before she got into bed.

7

'You Lyttons make me sick, honestly, with such romance – champagne and beauty treatments – after so many years, it makes those of us who do nothing but watch telly together feel quite inadequate.' Pippa's tongue curled neatly round her lips in search of stray blobs of cream. 'Tim would never think of giving me a present like that – not in a million years, not even if I spelt it out as a written request. He thinks all this beauty stuff is a big con. If he has to pay more than a fiver for a haircut, he feels he's been robbed. And he hates it if I wear more than a dab of makeup.' Pippa touched the natural flush in her cheeks self-consciously before taking another careful nibble of her éclair which, in spite of her cautionary assault, was still splurging cream out on all sides. 'This is truly delicious,' she sighed happily, 'I can't tell you how pleased I am that you called.'

Jane had given up on her own pastry which was filled with a sickly yellow cream and heavily laced with cinnamon. After the at times painful attentions to her face under the therapist's magnifying glass that morning, she felt badly in need of a cigarette, but didn't want to shock Pippa.

'Actually, Pip, we're about the most unromantic couple you could ever hope to meet. Mostly, we do nothing but watch television. Michael got the idea of a facial from his boss's wife who apparently has her spots squeezed and her face pummelled every week. I'm beginning to suspect,' she went on cheerfully, 'that he wants to turn me into one of those trophy executive wives who nibble expensive spinach leaves for lunch and wear designer jackets to the supermarket.'

Pippa giggled in happy disbelief. 'I bet it was lovely really, though.' She closed her eyes. 'A facial massage, hmm.'

'If you really want the truth, Pip...' Jane leant forward over the table, smiling wickedly, 'it was mostly rather horrible – I felt like an insect being studied and poked at under a microscope. The therapist said I had a "combination" problem and asked me if I exfoliated. When I said not that I knew of, she left the room for a few moments, clearly in a state of shock.'

'Oh Jane, she didn't,' said Pippa, laughing so much she had to put her tea down.

'When she came back to put cucumbers on my eyes and spray me with boiling steam, I thought I was going to suffocate.' Jane, enjoying herself more and more, slurped the dregs of her coffee and looked over her shoulder in a charade of fear at being overheard. 'I will pass delicately over the next ten minutes, the pain and shame of which have to be experienced to be believed. Suffice it to say that I felt far worse than a monkey having its fleas picked.'

'Jane, stop, please. Éclairs and laughing don't go. Anyway, monkeys like having their fleas picked.'

'The only half-way decent bit was a few minutes of massage at the end, but that was when she chose to embark on a detailed description of her grandmother's varicose veins, which sort of ruined the effect.'

'I sincerely hope you won't tell it to Michael like this – it prob-ably cost a fortune.'

'Thirty pounds, to be exact. I'm thinking of taking a course.'

After they had ordered another tea and coffee Pippa asked timidly if she might finish Jane's sticky bun for her. 'I'm trying to relax a bit more – be easier on myself,' she said, by way of an excuse. 'Doctor's orders.' She grinned, dying to get on to the only subject that she ever really wanted to talk about, dream about, worry about.

It was impossible to explain to anyone quite how obsessive the matter had become for her, now that she had let it. Everywhere she looked there were babies, pregnant mothers, prams and push-chairs. Every advert, every press story, every TV programme seemed to be about children or parents or pregnancy. Coming to meet Jane that morning, she had glided past countless black and white images of a teenage pregnant girl, standing under the bold telephone number of a clinic promising counselling before abortion. The very idea – knowing from the pictures in one of her endless books what a foetus looked like after only a few weeks of development – filled Pippa with a nauseous despair. It made her more in need of Jane than ever – the only person apart from her elderly mother in whom she had confided her continuing blight of involuntary childless-ness, so acute that it was beginning to feel like bereavement without a corpse. And like bereavement, it was a subject which people found hard to tackle head-on. Jane was so good at simply listening, without showing judgement or pity. For it was the pity of other women that Pippa dreaded most of all.

But when she revealed quite how far she had delved into the logistics of going down the private IVF route, still without a murmur to Tim, even Jane felt she had to intervene with some advice.

'Pippa...' She spoke gently, aware of the raw sensitivity of the subject, 'if you don't get Tim on board soon you could run the risk of making him feel so left out – and perhaps resentful – that he might set himself against the whole thing.'

'I just want to find out all the details of what's involved, whether I'm suitable, stuff like that. We've had Tim's sperm-count done loads of times in the past – we know the problem lies within me.' She tweaked the string of her tea bag and studied the label for a second. 'There are all these hormone injections you have to have to produce masses of eggs; then they are collected by ultrasound and put in a freezer. It's quite amazing. I've read about loads of couples who've succeeded – sometimes first time round. Though of course the overall statistics are relatively low – a 35 per cent success rate – and each cycle of treatment costs £2,400—'

Jane had to put her hand on Pippa's to interrupt the flow and get her proper attention. 'Tell Tim.'

Pippa sighed and pulled out her purse to pay the bill. 'I know, I know. I just keep waiting for him to snap out of this latest dark mood. It's incredible how he sustains them.' She waved at the waitress and wouldn't hear of Jane contributing. 'It'll all come tumbling out in the end, no doubt – some problem at work, I expect – it usually is,' she added with a forced smile.

Jane deliberately took her time getting home, not minding the bad traffic or the endless series of red lights. Every so often she touched her face, hating its sheeny smoothness and the strong smell of cosmetics. Her skin had never needed much attention – a flannel and some moisturiser were the extent of her daily beauty regime – much to the dismay of the beautician. She had exaggerated the discomfort of the facial to Pippa, partly to make her laugh, but above all to help process her own troubled feelings about it. She should have been grateful, she knew, but couldn't shake the notion that Michael had not been thinking of *her* – and what *she* liked – when he bought it. It made her think of the tea making machine he had given her for Christmas and which he used every morning. Jane only ever drank tea at tea time.

By the time Jane got into the house, she was desperate to do something about the stickiness of her hair – glued to her neck and temples from all the supposedly age-defying creams that had been used – and face. At the sight of her reflection in the bathroom mirror, her hair so flat and greasy, her skin bright pink, she laughed out loud. Fixing her hose attachment to the basin, she proceeded to wash herself back to as much normality as she could, wiping her face with a flannel and shampooing and rinsing her hair until it squeaked.

'Let's have a look then,' said Michael, when he got in late that night, tweaking her chin to make her face him. 'Didn't they do make-up and stuff?' There was disappointment in his voice.

'Nope.' Jane turned her attention back to the stove. 'Sorry, no make-up. Just lots of cleansing and rubbing. It was most invigorating.'

'I thought they'd do make-up.' He poured himself a glass of wine and stood looking at her from the doorway for a few moments. 'You should wear make-up more, you know, Jane, it suits you. I like it when you smarten yourself up a bit. I think it's important for a woman not to let herself go, after having children and so on. Antonia does aerobics three times a week – before work.' And with these encouraging words, he disappeared into the sitting room.

* * *

'Michael thinks I should take up aerobics,' remarked Jane the following week, when Julia had enticed her up to town for a yoga session, with the promise of dinner afterwards.

'Michael is wrong. Aerobics is the closest thing to legal torture known to woman.'

Julia cut a striking figure in the changing room, with her mass of hair coiled into an elegant bun on top of her head, showing off the graceful slimness of her neck. She sat on the bench, a little self-consciously, pulling her long legs into her so that her chin rested on her knees.

'Is Harriet teething or has Michael been keeping you awake with long sessions of torrid sex? You look mildly shattered.'

'Both. And thanks for the compliment. I'm supposed to look great – I went into town for a facial last week. An anniversary present from Michael.'

Julia raised her eyebrows. 'I am impressed.'

'I hated it actually.'

Jane pulled on a baggy T-shirt emblazoned with a cartoon of a frowning elephant under the words *No Pain, No Gain*, and made a silly face at herself in the mirror. All around them the other women were getting ready, trying not to look at their reflections too critically, but doing so none the less, casting hopeful glances at their profiles, patting their stomachs and yanking their costumes down to cover the bulges of their bottoms.

'I ate cream buns with Pippa afterwards, which was much more fun.' Jane put two clips in her hair in a vain attempt to stop it flopping into her eyes and followed Julia through into the carpeted studio.

It was clear at once that the instructor – a celebrated yoga guru, Julia said, called Shiro Yatzuma – took his art extremely seriously and would be quickly irritated by students who did not do likewise. 'Silence, please, ladies,' he murmured, when everyone had found spaces, before closing his eyes and taking up a cross-legged pose to begin.

Although quite broad and muscular, their instructor proved

capable of twisting his body into the most surprising contortions. Beside his mat a small tape-recorder emitted a form of tuneless humming which Jane found strangely soothing. 'We must centre our bodies. Balance, relaxation, breathing, these are the key. These three things will make us feel well tonight.' He moved round the room as he spoke, helping his charges stretch into something approaching the correct positions.

'You are trying too hard,' he said when he got to Jane after a few circuits. 'You have no breathing. Please breathe. Do not strain your body. No discomfort for you, please. Your face and neck are too tight.' He knelt down beside her mat, watching as she lay, face downwards, pulling uselessly at her legs, trying in vain to coax the soles of her feet to touch the backs of her knees. 'Release,' commanded Shiro. 'This is bad. Not good. Everything is too tight.' Ignoring the rest of the class – much to Jane's consternation – he proceeded to place his fingers on pressure points in her neck, shoulder blades and spine, moving his fingers gently but firmly down over each vertebra and into the small of her back.

'I think I'm cracking up,' she confessed to Julia afterwards, as they sat with large glasses of red wine and a frayed basket of stale French bread.

'Aren't we all, dear, aren't we all.'

'I'm being serious.'

'Oh, let's not be serious, please. I've had a filthy week. The weather is weirdly good for early March. People are much keener to browse in antique shops when it rains. Unless things pick up, I'm going to have to sleep with my bank manager.'

'What if I told you that when your yoga guru laid his hands upon me, I was melted to the core?'

Julia let out a small scream. 'And there was I thinking you had fallen asleep.'

'Sleep was the last thing on my mind, I can assure you. If Mr

Yatzuma knew the effect of his expertise he'd probably expel me on the spot.'

'That good, was it?' Julia raised one beautiful crescent of an eyebrow and then tipped her head back to laugh. 'I thought such things weren't supposed to happen to happily married mothers of two.'

'They're not.' At which point two steaming bowls of fettuccine and mushroom sauce arrived, mercifully interrupting Julia's line of questioning.

After a few mouthfuls, Julia gave up on her food. 'I don't know why I carry on coming here – this stuff is too stodgy for words.' She prodded her heap of pasta and grey lumpy sauce with her fork. 'It could be all out of a tin, for all we know.'

'It certainly isn't and I don't care, I'm starving.' Jane, used to her friend's picky eating habits, was not going to be deterred.

'I'll tell you something funny though.' Julia threw a heavy tassel of hair back over one shoulder and sat back. 'That brother-in-law of yours rang me up the other day.'

'You mean Christopher?' Jane stopped eating. 'You never told me.'

'I'm telling you now. It was a couple of weeks after that frightful evening at Pippa's, when Michael and Tim got so drunk and that vegan girl with lacquered hair and a pillar-box mouth kept delivering lectures on how we should all behave.'

'I knew it.' Jane clapped her hands. 'He likes you – I knew he wasn't gay—'

'Gay?' Julia considered the idea for a moment. 'I wouldn't say so, no. But I'm not sure that he likes me either.'

Jane pushed her plate away and reached for her wine. 'Don't play Miss Modesty with me. Of course, he likes you, why else would he ring?'

'I haven't the faintest idea. He said he was coming to London and could we meet and then a few days later he said he was awfully sorry but the whole thing was off and he wasn't coming after all.' She eyed her friend for a moment. 'How well do you know him?'

Jane shrugged. 'Not very well at all. He's either frightfully shy or terribly aloof – I can never decide which. When Michael and I first met he used to be around quite a bit.' She paused, spearing a limp mushroom with her fork, 'but then I guess he went his own way and we went ours. It's Michael who's always had this thing about him not being into women. They've never really got on at all. Christopher has always done the rebellious things – gone round the world, chucked in a promising career, got pissed at funerals – he was all over the place at their mother's – though he's definitely sorted himself out a bit since those days.'

'A bit like you and Mattie then,' teased Julia, 'one on the tracks and one in the habit of going haywire.'

'Not a bit like me and Mattie, no,' rejoined Jane stiffly, hating, as she always had, the age-old assumption that she would follow a straight path, while Mattie would flounder. 'Mattie and I are very fond of one another, in spite of our differences. Whereas Michael seems to get positive pleasure out of knocking Christopher down, picking holes in him – maybe it's sibling rivalry – hell, I don't know.' She crossed her arms and threw Julia a mischievous look. 'But he must have contacted you for a reason.'

'Don't start match-making, please – you've always been lousy at it.' Julia shuffled in her chair. 'I'm beginning to wish I'd never mentioned the man. Anyway, he's not my type.'

'And what exactly is your type, may I ask?' Jane teased, but Julia chose to take the question seriously.

'Oh Christ, I don't know. For years I thought it was so important to have a man in my life, but now only a small part of me feels that way. It's so much easier only having myself to worry about. It makes life so uncrowded, so uncomplicated. Do you know...' she lowered her voice, 'it's almost two years since I had any sex. And I can honestly say that I hardly miss it at all.'

Having noticed the sidelong glances of appreciation cast at Julia by a couple of the waiters and some of their fellow diners, Jane could not help but think how amazed they would have been to hear such things. Beautiful women were always assumed to have the best sex lives. Even so, she felt a twist of jealousy at the simplicity of living alone that Julia had described. But it also felt impossible to regret her life – its fallibility was integral, unavoidable. Given the time again, she would have made the same decisions, good and bad, she was sure. Then the children came to mind and her stomach turned again at the wonderfulness and awfulness of it all.

So wrapped up was she in her own train of thought, that it was several seconds before Jane realised Julia had said something else and was waiting for a response.

'I have applied to join a dating agency and all you do is blink. I expected mild shock at the very least.'

'I am not remotely shocked,' Jane countered, shaking off her own preoccupations, 'I mean, how very liberated – and brave... except, how can you, of all people, need such a thing?'

'You have no idea,' Julia laughed. 'No one I like pays me any attention at all. But now all my details are to be fed into a computer,' she went on merrily, 'height, brain-power, the circumference of my corns – and in a few days it will spew out the name – or if I'm lucky, the names – of my perfect partners. Modern magic. It's got to be worth a try, don't you think? Because I really don't have time to widen my social circle with night classes in basket weaving or lessons in Mandarin; and all my friends are married – apart from lovely Toby, who's great for going to the cinema and unthreatening cuddles, but who is inclined to get depressed and drag me down with him. The singles' bars I've tried have been no fun at all and, in spite of what I said just now, I *do* sometimes miss a bit of healthy coital cavorting on Saturday nights, especially when the rest of you are celebrating Valentines or anniversaries and I've got nothing but a bedside book on restoring chamber pots to keep me company. More wine?'

Jane shook her head, starting to laugh, but then finding herself saying instead, 'I think I might have to leave Michael.'

Julia slowly put the bottle down. 'Jane, I am so sorry. What on earth has brought this on? Have you had a stunning row?'

'It's not like that... I only wish it were, it would be so much easier. Perhaps if we'd rowed a bit more things wouldn't have got so bad.'

'You are not making sense, girl. Have another glug of wine and try again.' She pushed Jane's glass at her and leaned forward over the table on folded arms.

Jane fiddled with the stem of the glass. 'I remember Mum and Dad arguing – loudly – loads of times, but I'm sure they loved each other.'

'Mine argued too – *very* loudly – and I know they loathed the sight of one another,' retorted Julia, whose parents had divorced when she was in her teens. 'Of course, you don't have to explain anything if you don't want to – certainly not to me – but I think Michael is going definitely going to want some answers,' she added, more gently. 'I mean, is there someone...'

'Someone else? No. I've told you, it's not simple like that. Michael and I... it's just not working... as it should... as I always hoped a good marriage *ought* to work.' Jane struggled to find the words, hating her hopelessness, her inability to spell it out, even to her best friend. 'We don't really fit – I'm not sure we ever have – but it's so hard to own up to these things, even to yourself. For ages I've pretended that everything was all right – helping Michael pretend too. And when things feel really wrong, I look at the rest of the world, at all the other trillions of married couples with children and mortgages, living in suburbia, making love on Friday nights after a drink or two, yelling at the children and at each other about money and fairness, and I think perhaps misery is normal. All these other people accept it, so who am I to complain?'

'You could do a lot worse.'

'That's what I've been telling myself for ages,' Jane wailed, 'but it doesn't help. Whatever we had has long since dissolved – though Michael wouldn't admit it for the world.' She squeezed her fists and pressed them hard into her forehead. 'The awful thing is, I can still remember how it used to be, how I used to need him – but now I think it was all tied up with Mum and Dad, what I went through having to cope with Mattie flipping so badly after they died.'

'You're stronger now, that's all,' said Julia. 'You're a little more independent, you—'

Jane shook her head slowly. 'No, it's much more than that. Apart from Harriet and Tom, there is this great nothingness between us. I cook for him, clean for him, sleep with him – but there is no affection. We no longer touch each other in the real sense – not inside where it matters.' She laid both hands flat on the table and studied them hard, noting how dry the skin looked, how blue and thin the veins were. 'We have been going through the motions of marriage – and not even managing that very well.'

'You've got to laugh,' said Julia dryly, 'here are you trying to get rid of your man just as I'm starting an earnest search for one. There's got to be a lesson in there somewhere.'

Having made her confession, Jane immediately felt a combination of relief and regret. An illogical urge to reassure Julia overtook her. 'I'll probably never do anything about it. It's probably just a phase. Christ, is that the time – I'll have to fly.' And in a flurry of dividing up the bill and grabbing coats she bustled herself out into the blissful cool of the streets, feeling more burdened and confused than ever.

Julia tried poetry instead of porcelain chamber pots in bed that night, but her mind would not focus. She thought instead of the steely shutters of marriage and the secrets nurtured within, out of loyalty, fear, habit and, perhaps, love. Though shocking, Jane's admission made sense. All her recent uncharacteristic swings of mood, the brooding silences, the tense cheerfulness, had a context now.

In the midst of her compassion, she felt an irrepressible and complex blend of guilt and betrayal. Jane should have told her earlier. Their friendship should have allowed her to speak up long ago. The fact that it had not – that their own relationship too had failed in this way – led Julia's mind along the labyrinthine paths she hated most, towards the painful conclusion that no amount of lovers or friends or children could prevent each person from being alone. Which led her on to the thought of the dating agency and the ridiculous gamble and possible humiliation to which she had so recklessly committed herself.

But you've got to try, she told herself, as she replaced Wendy Cope's slim volume on the side table and turned out the light – you've got to try to connect with people, to understand them, even if it ends up driving you mad.

8

Michael fiddled with his executive toy. The heavy metal balls clacked rhythmically together, the momentum of each swing starting the next. He felt jaded and fragile from a bad night's sleep. He was never any good without sleep. When Jane was breast-feeding the children, he had been driven to using earplugs. But last night Tom had crept into their bed during the dawn hours, crawling up under the duvet to lie between them, his arms round his mother, his small cold toes seeking warmth along his father's legs. Too tired to do anything about it, not wanting to make the child cry, hoping Jane would do something about it, Michael had tossed on the uncomfortable borders of sleep until the buzz of the alarm on the tea machine sounded in his right ear.

He picked up the picture of Jane and the children that lived on his desk and began fiddling with that instead. The frame was loose. The three of them smiled at him. Or rather, they smiled at the man behind the camera, just as they had allowed their hair to be brushed for him and given him their full attention when he asked for it. Sometimes Michael envied that photographer, whom he had never met, who had been doing a 'special' on family sittings in a corner of British Home Stores when Jane strolled through one afternoon with Harriet in a pram and Tom toddling beside. How much easier it would be to enjoy his family, he mused, if, every so often, they sat still like that for him, contented and unquestioning. As it was, family life was rushed and snatched, full of noise and things that made him cross.

Holding the photo at a distance, he tried to look objectively at his wife, to see if he could perceive something beyond the familiarity of her face. Her smile was fixed and sure, but those cat-green eyes looked away, out of the picture somewhere, to some distant horizon behind his left shoulder. Hetty was propped on her knees, floppy, pink and plump – too plump, he had said to Jane at the time – which had made her furious – though since then his daughter's stocky limbs had begun to elongate with quite alarming rapidity. Tom sat beside them, a little apart, hands self-consciously folded in his lap. A bubble of sentimental pride burst in Michael's throat, quickly followed by a spasm of frustration. It was a devilish business being a father. The children were so demanding; they seemed to reserve all their extremes of behaviour for him – either deliriously happy or deliriously vile. They never hurled themselves like that at Jane, hollering and tugging for attention.

Tracing a finger through the thin film of dust on the glass, Michael indulged in a recollection of his wife as he had first come across her, when she was a history student at Durham. Since he had been studying economics and business studies, their paths – to begin with – had rarely coincided. Later on, when they grew intimate, he marvelled that he had not taken more notice of her sooner, with her lustrous tangle of dark hair, such a dramatic frame for the small round face and startlingly sensual eyes, heavy-lidded, bewitching. He remembered suddenly the first time they made love; how she had stared and stared, holding his gaze, not letting go, even when she came, with three short gasps, her mouth slightly open, lips wet from kissing. Such intensity was new to Michael. It sharpened the focus of his life, brightened the colours of his world, made him want to get out of bed in the mornings and go jogging round dark, empty streets for the sheer thrill of being alive. The fact that such intensity had now gone was not something he liked to think about much, beyond the fact that he was sure it was normal. They still had sex about once a week, which he reckoned was pretty good going, even if they took considerably less time about it and Jane's eyes were invariably closed.

They had had their first proper conversation one sticky June night in a queue outside a cinema. Each was waiting for their partner at the time to show up. He was going out with a Scottish girl, Fiona Yarrow, a mathematician with brilliant-red hair, film-star lips and pale, freckled skin. Jane was with a medical student called Dougie Craven, a strong scrum-half and something of a college hero. She had seemed so small and serene that when Fiona finally appeared, running round the corner, all legs and arms, she had struck him as being somehow gangly and inelegant, a giraffe beside a deer. When the couples separated to find their seats, both Jane and Michael turned for a quick look back, exchanging a glance of mutual interest. It was a line cast between them, the ensnaring moment, the moment that ensured they would take the trouble to meet again. Still dating seven months later, they were with a bunch of student friends in the Austrian alps, when the call came through about Jane's parents. Jane had fallen apart and he had helped her through. Sometimes, Michael missed those days.

'Am I interrupting?'

Michael hastily put down the photograph. 'No, Antonia, no. I was miles away. Come in. Help yourself to coffee.' He gestured at the percolating machine which lived on a shelf by the window and stretched himself out in his chair. 'You couldn't pour me one while you're at it, could you?' He nudged the photo back into place and flipped open his briefcase.

'Not having trained as a waitress, I don't like pandering to such requests, but seeing as you look half asleep, I'll treat you just this once.' Her tone was dry and sure. She had come a long way in the last few months.

Michael wondered, as he had many times before, whether she found him attractive. It was irrelevant of course, a mere indulgence that would have no effect on his assessment of her research into eastern European money markets. But it did add an edge to office life to have even the possibility of such a notion dangling over him. He especially liked her hair, which was long and black and straight, as crisply cut as her suits. She was tall – almost as tall as him in her high heels – and flat-chested, like one of those waif-like models who posed in shrunken vests and baggy socks.

'Terry's asked me to do some work on South America.'

'Don't worry – I'll have a word with him later on today.' Michael began sorting through the papers in his briefcase. Tom had drawn a bright red line across the front of his main notepad, together with a large, tremulous rendition of the letter T. Maddened, Michael hurriedly turned to the page where he had jotted down a list of issues to go through that day. But here too, on what had once been the blank page opposite, Tom had left an even more extravagantly creative mark in the form of a green and orange pirate ship, decked liberally with cannons and pirates with pin legs, posing at unlikely angles among snarls of rigging.

'What an original plan for the day,' laughed Antonia, who had quietly approached his desk and was leaning over with interest.

'Bloody children.' Michael ripped Tom's picture out of the book and screwed it up into a ball which he hurled, with perfect accuracy, into the bin in the corner. 'Sorry about that.'

'Don't apologise, I thought it looked rather good. How old is your boy?'

'Five... no, hang on, six. Nothing but trouble at any rate. I assume you're not in any danger of cluttering up your life with infants?'

'Christ, no.' She straightened up and briskly yanked the jacket of her suit down, pulling out imaginary creases, before seating herself in the wide luxury of one of Michael's brown leather chairs. 'About Terry – I think you've misunderstood.'

'I've told you. I'll sort him out,' Michael muttered, rummaging for a column of relevant figures from his in-tray.

'But I want to do the work, Michael. It's on Argentina and Chile. The whole place is really opening up – the opportunities in emerging markets are fantastic. It should be a great project. Don't worry about the work-load, I'll manage easily.' She clapped her hands together and stood up to go. 'If I didn't have to come in on Saturdays, I'd feel I wasn't doing my job properly anyway.' She chuckled, causing Michael a quite unexpected sting of envy, before other considerations crowded his mind.

'But you were assigned to work for me, Antonia – it's not as simple as you seem to think. It would be ridiculous to work on Eastern Europe and the southern hemisphere at the same time – that's not how we operate here, it—'

She coughed politely to interrupt him. 'I have already taken the liberty of speaking to Mr Glassbrook about it – I guessed that was the most sensible approach, given that straddling departments is not usual policy.' She tucked a glossy wedge of hair behind one ear. 'He seemed to think it would be fine, so long as neither you nor Terry start to feel that I am falling down on my commitments.'

There was nothing more to say. Antonia was well ahead with all her work – one step ahead of him half the time.

'You weren't beginning to think you owned me, were you, Michael?' She shot him a grin, before swishing lightly out of the room, a millimetre of petticoat lace flashing under the short hem of her skirt – a parting shot of teasing contempt, it felt like.

When Tim Croft rang an hour or so later to ask if he was free for lunch, Michael leapt at the chance. The exchange with Antonia had unsettled him. While coping deftly with the straightforward aspects of office politics and competition, Michael was not so adroit when it came to the management of other people. He hated not knowing where he stood; wheeling and dealing in international markets was one thing, but when the matters at stake were blurry issues of feeling and opinion he invariably struggled. Most riling of all, was the loss of face in being forced to share the increasingly acclaimed services of Antonia with one of the other partners. The whole business left him feeling subtly, but profoundly, threatened.

Michael's bad mood lingered on as the taxi edged its way through the sluggish West End traffic. Halfway down the King's Road, frustration so overcame him that he got out, resolving to walk the last mile to the pub that Tim had suggested – a favourite drinking haunt of theirs on the riverside near Wandsworth Bridge. Since he had left so promptly, he had loads of time to spare.

But walking was hard work too. An uncharacteristically mild day had brought shoppers and tourists out in droves. Feeling like a visitor from another world, Michael did his best to walk briskly, but got trapped behind a trio of spindly, leather-clad creatures with cartwheels of red and yellow spikes on their heads where most people settled for hair. There was a tattoo on the back of the shaven neck of the middle person in the trio, a large pair of lips with a tongue sticking out that Michael couldn't help staring at until, as if sensing his gaze, the cartwheeled head suddenly spun round, presenting a girl with flaring nostrils and staring black-lined eyes that made Michael afraid.

He ducked into a bookshop and, with Jane vaguely in mind, wandered into the cookery section. Michael didn't read much himself, apart from the occasional thriller. Having flipped idly through the pages of a weighty manual entitled *Your Wok and You*, he moved further along the shelf, to find himself in the biography section. And there, without warning, was his brother Christopher, his dark eyes watching him from out of a black and white photograph on a book which had been put back face downwards. In the image, he looked spruce and serious, like a parody of a devout intellectual, Michael decided, picking up the book, which was called, *Clough's Life and Works*. Although it had been out a while – he and Jane had their own signed copy at home – and its content held little appeal, Michael flicked through the pages with the faint shimmer of an expectation that he might learn something new. '*Perhaps the first truly "modern" poet...*' he riffled back to the front summary of his brother's life:

Christopher John Lytton was born in 1955 in Newcastle, second son of the Reverend Ernest Lytton. After attending St Peter's College for boys, he was awarded a scholarship to King's College Cambridge, where he gained a First Class Honours degree in Classics. His PhD thesis on Greek mythology and the twentieth-century novel was greeted with considerable acclaim. Research fellowships followed, at Trinity College, Cambridge and Christ Church, Oxford. He then travelled widely, living in France for a period. He returned to Oxford in 1985, where he now lives and works as a teacher of English and Classics at St Stephen's Preparatory School. *Clough's Life and Works* is Christopher Lytton's second published work. His thesis was adapted for publication in 1980.

Michael closed the book and studied the photograph again. All his earliest memories of his brother were tied up with feeling sorry for him. Poor little Christopher, clinging to his mother's sturdy legs; too small to climb a tree, or kick a ball, or stay up late, or fight back. And by the time he was old enough for such things, Michael had given up waiting for him, busying himself instead with school-friends and intricate airfix models that couldn't possibly be done with little brothers hanging around, fingers up their noses, asking silly questions.

Even though Michael had long since been forced to accept that Christopher was a steely-willed, deeply independent character who would doggedly pursue his own mystifying course through life, a shadowy image of the poor, shunned little brother remained. Perhaps it was partly this that had prevented them from ever crossing the tricky threshold of true sibling friendship. But there were other, more serious chasms too, based on yawning differences of character. For Michael, university had been a necessity more than a pleasure, even after he met Jane. During all of his time as a student he had itched to be done with it. To get a job, to make money – he burned to get on with the real business of life.

The fact that Christopher had been content to indulge himself for so long as an academic, only to chuck it all in, seriously affected his elder brother's opinion of him, confirming deep-rooted suspicions of foppish laziness and a weak character. None of his extensive travels seemed to improve him in the least. Trading his scholar's gown and scuffed suede brogues for a rucksack and leather sandals that showed off his long, slim feet, he would simply vanish for months at a time, only to reappear quite unchanged, without warning or explanation. Even after the lengthy spell in France, he was the same Christopher, fluent in French maybe, but still single, still unnervingly quiet. If he regretted hopping off the academic treadmill just as he seemed to be getting the better of it, he never said a word.

Michael slotted the book back into the shelf, beside something with a silver cover that looked a lot more enticing, and hurried out of the shop. All that time in hand and now he was going to be late.

9

Not so very far from where Michael and Tim were ordering ploughman's lunches and pints of real ale, Pippa Croft was trying on a pair of pink Bermuda shorts and frowning. Her stomach had expanded in recent weeks, risen and smooth like a perfect cake, as if in anticipation of being pregnant. Perhaps because of this association, Pippa found that she did not mind the extra weight at all. She even pondered the notion of phantom pregnancy, fascinated by the idea of such a thing – the force of human longing to which such a condition bore testimony.

After fighting with the waistband of the pink shorts for a few minutes, she gave up with a resigned sigh. Of course, phantoms had nothing to do with it in her case. For Pippa, food was all about the art of relaxing. She had been treating herself a lot recently – mostly without any guilt at all – embracing how it helped her to feel more content instead of worrying all the time.

If she had any problem with her figure, it was with regard to her knees. Pippa had often thought that she deserved something better than the dimpled puddings that covered her knee-caps. Many attractive fashions had been wistfully jettisoned on account of them, including hot-pants in her early teens, when her best friend, Matilda Johnson, had acquired a pair of purple velvet hip-huggers that had set Pippa's heart afire with envy.

These latest endeavours to expose her legs in a favourable light stemmed from Tim's astonishing announcement, on returning very late from work the night before, that he wished her to accompany him on the big African trip – Kenya, then Cape Town – he was planning for early May. The invitation had been issued from behind a vast bunch of flowers, an explosion of gladioli, irises, chrysanthemums and carnations, that provided the secondary service of shielding him from the intensely questioning silence maintained by his wife. When his morose, cherubic face did emerge – when he finally thrust the lavish bouquet into her arms – she had noticed that the usually irrepressible curls of his hair lay flat and damp with sweat. He looked full of guilt – sodden with it, in fact. A few weeks before, Pippa had watched a compelling, awful soap-drama in which the long-suffering wife confided to a friend that she knew when her husband was starting a new affair because he always brought her flowers. It was to this fictional wife that Pippa had found her thoughts lurching as she exclaimed her delight and set about unwrapping the bouquet.

'But I don't think Africa would suit me, to be honest, Tim.' She had reached into the cupboard beside the sink for her biggest vase. Ask him if there is someone else… ask him, ask him, sang a voice in her head. But she knew she wouldn't. For all the wrong reasons – despicable ones, probably, to do with being nearly forty and wanting a child. Because Tim was her best – her only – hope of that. Because that mattered more to her than putting up with infidelity and the grim fact of still loving him.

'I want you to come on this one, Pip – I really do.' His face was the picture of anguish and concern, so much so that she had even found an absurd compassion welling in her heart for how rotten he must feel, having a secret lover.

She had taken his face in her hands, touching the deep dimple in his chin with her thumbs. 'Oh Timmy, you fool,' she murmured, brushing his lips with a kiss. 'You don't have to take me – I'm too grown up to mind about your travels these days. I'll spoil myself while you're gone – how about that? I'll watch soppy films and eat chocolates in bed, I promise.'

She had returned to the flowers, arranging them with quick, skilful movements, tweaking off the occasional leaf and droopy petal.

'Pippa – I love you so much—' He had stepped up behind her and put his arms over her shoulders, burying his head in her neck, breathing hard, smelling distinctly of alcohol, even though he had supposedly been in the office. 'Please come with me – for this one – please.'

Pippa had thought again of the wronged wife in the soap, and gripped the edge of the sink. Taking a deep breath, she closed her hands over his. 'Okay. If it means so much to you. I'll come.'

Having wrung the decision out of her, Tim had retreated, as if exhausted by the effort it had taken. He had plucked a bottle of beer out of the fridge and swigged at it, gasping between long, throaty gulps as if his thirst might never be quenched.

'You'll need some new clothes,' he had declared at breakfast, his hair springy from the shower, but his eyes puffy and pink.

Pippa, whose knowledge of Africa – East, South or otherwise – was confined to Hollywood depictions of men in khaki shirts, darkened with circles of sweat, and sultry women languishing under ceiling fans and being waited on hand and foot, feared what she might have to suffer from the heat. Her skin was naturally pale and fine; excessive heat brought her out in red blotches and patchy rashes; it made her thin baby-hair cling to her scalp with all the panache of a used dish cloth.

'I'll need a hat too,' was all she had replied to Tim, offering up her cheek for the ritualistic kiss of farewell.

'Have you anything a little longer?' she asked the sales assistant now, peering out from behind the curtain of her box-cubicle, despising her own timidity.

'Longer than Bermudas, madam?' replied the girl, in a tone that contained a hint of amused disdain.

'I mean – sort of just below the knee.'

'Culottes?'

Pippa nodded, but without hope.

The girl strolled off for a few minutes, only to return with a pair of heavy red corduroy shin-length culottes that were clearly useless. Pippa took them, to be polite, but left them on the hanger. She pulled her own clothes back on, all the while doing a quick mental check-list of her summer wardrobe. There were a couple of things that would do – her cotton cream trouser suit and a blue linen skirt, both with stretchy waistbands. There was also plenty of time. No need to panic.

Standing on the escalator, she could not help glancing at herself in the mirrored wall. Her cheeks were flushed and her hair a mess. One earring dangled askew. She twisted it back into place and tried to raise her spirits by thinking about lunch.

Just as she stepped from the moving stairs on to the third floor of the department store, she caught sight of a man who looked like Tim walking away from her through haberdashery towards the sign for the lifts. A tall blonde woman walked beside him. He had his hand on her arm, held just above the elbow, self-consciously.

Pippa stopped, started, then stopped again. In a few seconds they would be gone. In a few seconds she would never know. She began to run, dodging women with large handbags, children in push-chairs and signs about price-cuts and fashions. She got there as the lift was closing, only just managing to put her hand to the door in time. As it pulled back to allow her access she saw, not Tim, but Julia, standing with a man whose face looked nothing like Tim's, although his hair and build were similar.

'Pippa—' Julia, who was with a person spawned by the computer dating-service, blushed helplessly. 'How nice to see you – this is Alan...'

'Lambert.' The man held out his hand with a formal smile, revealing a gap of at least two millimetres between his front teeth. 'Which floor?' His finger hovered over the panel of buttons. He wore several heavy rings.

'Ground, please.' It seemed an age before the doors slid shut so the lift could begin its lumbering descent.

'Lovely dinner for Michael, Pippa – thanks so much. It seems ages ago now.'

'Yes, it was fun, wasn't it.' Pippa clung to her handbag. 'Tim's taking me to Kenya and South Africa soon. A five-week trip, so I thought I'd better do some shopping. Can't find a thing.'

'How exciting.'

'Julia and I have only just become acquainted,' said Alan Lambert, in a voice just high enough to make you notice. 'We are going to have lunch, just around the corner.'

'How super,' said Pippa, aware of Julia's tightening expression and wondering about it.

The doors finally opened and the three of them stepped out amid an awkward jumble of 'after-yous'.

'We've been having coffee on the third floor,' added Julia in a rush. 'They've just opened it. Lovely place – full of hanging plants and the smell of coffee beans. But I expect you'll get plenty of that in Africa – Kenyan beans and all that.' With a look of embarrassed apology, she turned to follow her escort out of the shop.

'Have a nice lunch,' called Pippa, suddenly flooded with a shaking relief that the man had not been Tim, that – for that day at least – she had been saved from the horror of confrontation and its consequences.

* * *

Michael returned to the table with a packet of crisps between his teeth and a pint of beer in each hand. 'They'll bring our food out to us. We're number twenty-two, but it won't be long, they said.'

They were sitting at a wooden bench in a courtyard at the back of the pub, crammed with people trying to enjoy the early burst of spring warmth. Several flies darted between sticky empty glasses and plates sporting abandoned crusts of bread and half-eaten clumps of chilli con carne.

'Christ, it's warm for the time of year, isn't it?' Michael wiped his forehead with a paper napkin and studied the result. 'Look at that.' He held the napkin under Tim's nose. 'Lovely London grime. We'll all be wearing face-masks soon. Cheers, anyway.' He raised his tankard to his lips and let the first swig of beer trickle slowly and smoothly down the back of his throat. It was against his principles to drink at lunch time, but the Antonia business had left him feeling in need of a pick-me-up. 'So, how are things?'

Tim had plucked a large crisp from the packet and was holding it up for scrutiny.

'Not good, Michael, not good.'

'Join the club, as they say. I'm beginning to think about making a move – switching to another bank – what do you think?'

Tim shrugged as he ate the crisp and then said nothing even after he had swallowed – an usual reaction, since such questions usually prompted a volley of hearty advice. Having escaped the confinements of answering to an employer, he liked to comment sympathetically on the career paths of his less adventurous friends.

'So, what's up with you, then?' Michael enquired, a little grudgingly, because of no take-up on his own cri de coeur.

'Oh, nothing much... at least...' Tim sucked in his breath, 'nothing more than bankruptcy.'

He spoke so quietly and dismissively that Michael failed to register anything was genuinely amiss. 'Bad month for business then?' He nodded thanks to the waitress who set down their plates of bread and cheese, and quickly set about tucking in, dolloping pickle on before taking a bite.

Tim, ignoring the arrival of his own food, was laughing wildly and shaking his head. 'A bad month – yes, you could say that – and coming after many, many bad months.' He took a swig of his beer and carefully set the glass back down, exactly over the wet mark it had already left on the table. 'Indeed, I am shortly to join the esteemed ranks of the totally fucked. The word, as I said, is *bankrupt.*'

'My God, you're serious.' Michael slowly lowered his half-eaten baguette.

Tim looked away, down towards Wandsworth Bridge and the sludgy swirls of the shrinking river. He pulled a packet of small cigars from his breast pocket and lit one, inhaling deeply. 'Don't tell Pip, there's a good man – about the smoking, I mean.' He slapped his thigh. 'That's good isn't it – don't tell her about the really important thing—'

'Doesn't Pippa know? Not about the smoking, but the—'

'No, she does not.' Tim shook his head, preoccupied with swallowing a cough that sounded almost like a sob.

'But are you sure things are really that bad, Tim? I thought it was all going so well—'

'Oh, it was, it was. Back in the blooming bloody eighties. But it's the fucking awful nineties now, Mike. I guess I over-reached myself. At one stage it looked like I couldn't put a foot wrong, I was so sure...' He tailed off and Michael didn't know what to say.

'Pippa doesn't have any idea. I just can't bring myself to tell her yet.' Tim pushed his untouched food away and leant on his elbows, head in his hands. 'She loves that sodding house. And the garden.' He thought of their garden, a kaleidoscope of colour – hundreds of flowers and shrubs, none of whose names he knew, bobbing in trim lines round the rich green of the lawn, like patterned lace. And thinking of this brought to mind the small hands of his wife, working neatly with her trays of bulbs and buds, pressing the earth around them, settling them gently but firmly, for hour upon hour, kneeling there, sprinkling them, cosseting them, nourishing them. 'You see, not having had any luck in the children department...'

'Sure, Tim, okay.' Where a woman would almost certainly have encouraged the spilling of such unmentioned agonies, wanting to draw them out, knowing the relief of release, Michael opted for the safer option of changing the subject. 'I'll get us some more drinks, shall I?'

For the rest of the time, they took shelter in the business aspect of Tim's predicament. Small travel companies were folding all the time; people simply no longer had the money for adventure holidays. Travelmania was so deeply in debt that there was no hope of attracting a buy-out.

'I should have seen the writing on the wall. If I had sold up at the beginning of last year I'd be laughing now.'

'Don't, Tim – there's no point in looking back.'

'How right you are.' He clapped his hands with a bright energy that fooled neither of them. 'I've got a trip coming up – Melindi, Mombasa, then Jo-burg and Cape Town – checking out some resorts – a last hurrah. It was organised and paid for months ago.

I'm taking Pippa. A final treat...' His voice trembled. 'I'll probably break the news while we're out there.'

'Well, that will be good – the trip I mean...' Michael had the grace to feel inadequate. Calamity on such a scale was not something their friendship was used to and he could not think how to tackle any further discussion of the subject without making Tim feel even worse than he did already. 'Look here,' he blurted, 'why don't I have words in a few ears – see what leads I can rustle up in the city—'

Tim cut him off with a dismissive wave. 'It's far too late to go back into that world. Thanks all the same, though.' He stood up, taking a deep breath and briefly pressing his fingertips to his temples, where the veins were standing out. 'I expect things will sort themselves out somehow.' He smiled bleakly. 'The first thing is to tell Pippa.'

'Yes, of course. Exactly.' Michael downed the last mouthful of his pint, and then felt bad, in case it looked like he didn't care. But Tim was already on his way towards the exit, a traipsing, deflated figure he hardly recognised.

10

At first glance, Ernest Lytton's house looked like something out of an American country suburb rather than rural southeast England. This illusion was created by the porch, which Ernest had tacked on himself, during the months immediately following his wife, Edith's, death. He was a good carpenter and could have completed the job within a few weeks; but since it was fulfilling a greater, unspoken need within his lonely self, he dragged it out, seeking perfection within perfection, so that many months passed before he pronounced the project finished to his satisfaction.

The porch, or verandah, as its creator preferred to call it, ended up running round all four of the grey stone walls of the old farmhouse and was generally regarded as something of an oddity, like the old man himself. Neighbours, (albeit quite distant ones, since the house possessed two acres of rough land and was several miles from the nearest village), scoffed at this grandiose, incongruous attachment, murmuring that, with sweet old Edie gone, the old boy really had gone soft in the head. But Ernest Lytton had got safely past the age where he gave a damn what other people thought. With the English summers turning so much hotter, it made sense to have a sheltered place outside from where he could appreciate the bright sun and blue sky without being harmed by them. He now spent many an hour sitting with only his pipe for company in an old wooden rocking chair, staring dreamily into the middle distance, across the tangled copses of his own land to the plump hills that skirted the coastal town of Crestling beyond. The first two summers following the completion of his wooden masterpiece turned out to be among the wettest on record. But he sat outside nonetheless, watching the raindrops form along the bottom of the painted slats of timber, dabbing his eyes, which these days watered of their own accord, as if making up for a lifetime of being set in a face too proud to cry.

He still thought of himself as being married to Edie, despite it being over eight years since she had died. After three decades in the north of England, they had moved south hoping the warmer climes would improve Edie's always weak lungs. But when, eventually, mesothelioma took hold, no amount of sea air or warmth could stop the process of slow suffocation that the illness involved. She bore it all with a wrenching stoicism. Even when the very worst of the coughing would start, when her bird-like frame could barely stay upright under the strain of each thick, rasping hack, she would keep one hand raised in the air, fending him off, shaking her head till he backed away.

Once a religious man, it was Ernest's relationship with God that had taken the biggest battering over the years. His calling had come as a result of the war, or, more specifically, as the result of a deep friendship with the regiment chaplain, one Harry Hughes, who died of hepatitis on the way home, three days after armistice. Ernest's belief had been relatively easy in the beginning, with the fervent memories of the war still pulsing through his system and the bright banner of Hughes' faith to light the way. The questioning started later, after the girls were born, so shrunken and pink, when Edie nearly died of a broken heart and he could think of nothing to say – not one thing – to ease her pain, or his. Until, thank heavens, the boys had come along, Ernest reminded himself, getting up from his porch chair to greet Michael as he strode towards the house.

'Dad, hello there.' Michael, never natural with his father, offered a hand to shake, ruffling Tom's hair with the other, glad to have his son there, between them, deflecting the focus of the reunion.

'Jane with you, I take it?'

'She certainly is.' They both turned to watch Jane, who had organised the weekend visit, emerging round the side of the car and coming towards them. She was bent sideways, to accommodate a precarious Harriet – on one hip – while her free hand gripped the handles of an over-stuffed canvas bag. She started to smile at her father-in-law long before she was close enough to greet him, her affection radiant as always. None of his old man habits, like grinding his teeth when he ate, or farting when he thought no one was within earshot, had ever bothered her in the slightest, while they left Michael cringing with suppressed irritation.

'Let me take her,' said Ernest at once, reaching for Harriet as soon as he had kissed Jane's cheek.

Oh God, thought Michael, Harriet will cry and cling to her mother. But Harriet sat proud and high in her grandfather's arms, allowing him to carry her round the garden, pointing out flowers and birds, between tickly-pokes to the tummy.

The joy that Ernest derived from his two grandchildren had come as a pleasure – and something of a surprise – to them all. Though he adored Christopher and Michael, he had never been a particularly hands-on father. Edie was more than happy to take the parental lead, and he had always been so busy, either holed up in his study or bouncing off round his parishes in his dirty green

Morris Minor, often helping out in matters that had little to do with the Lord.

After the car had been unpacked, Ernest turned to Tom, solemnly requesting his assistance on a trouble-shooting tour of the woods. 'We'll take good care, won't we now?' he said, when Tom gleefully accepted. 'And we'll make sure we're back before your Uncle Christopher gets here, at any rate. That's for fighting the wood monsters,' he added, handing Tom a sturdy stick and chuckling when his grandson raced off with a war cry.

'I didn't realise Chris was coming,' said Michael, as Ernest was about to set off in pursuit.

'Didn't I mention it? He's on his spring break and I thought it would be nice to have a proper family gathering. He should be here by tea time... Tom, wait!' he called, hurrying towards the field gate that Tom was already climbing.

'Silly bugger's getting so forgetful,' remarked Michael, as they stepped back into the kitchen.

'Oh, I wouldn't be too sure about that.' Jane busied herself with unloading bottles of milk and cereal packets.

'What's that supposed to mean?'

'Perhaps he thought that if you knew Christopher was coming this weekend, you would find a reason not to come yourself.'

'I've never heard anything so ridiculous.'

Jane, not wanting to tip Michael's irritation into anything more serious, spent several moments reading the small print on a cereal packet.

'Christ, Jane, you come up with some absurd ideas sometimes—'

'I'm a great fan of absurd ideas,' she murmured.

'Christopher,' they both said at once, as the sight of the very subject of their conversation appeared in the open doorway, making each of them wonder how long he had been there and what he might have heard.

'How are you both?' He gently placed a small hold-all on the kitchen table and pulled out a bottle of red wine, its label smeared and torn. 'An old one from college wine cellars – the best off-licences in the world.'

'Still got your academic contacts then,' joked Michael, a little harshly, Jane thought, as she went to kiss her brother-in-law on the cheek.

'You look well.'

'Thanks, so do you. And where are the children?' Christopher sat down, directing the question at Jane who, having run out of things to unpack, was busying herself with stuffing empty plastic bags into her canvas carrier.

'Tom is finding monsters in the copse – with your father – and Harriet was here a moment ago...' Harriet toddled into the kitchen as Jane spoke. She was clutching her lidded drinking beaker, which she placed carefully on the table, next to Christopher's wine bottle, before patting her uncle's lap and making clip-clop noises with her tongue.

'Hatty, not now—' began Michael.

But Christopher immediately hoicked her up onto his knees and embarked on such gratifyingly energetic a rendition of 'Ride a cock horse,' that his niece whooped as she bounced between moments of gawping at him in sheer wonderment.

'Come here, you,' said Jane, when Christopher finally stopped and then had some trouble prising a reluctant Harriet free.

'She looks so like you,' Christopher laughed, 'it's incredible.'

'Really? Most people say the opposite.' Harriet flopped in Jane's arms, worn out suddenly. 'I think she needs her nap – excuse me.'

When Jane returned to the kitchen, Michael and Christopher

were drinking beer and talking about football. Not wanting to disturb the filial accord and eager for an excuse to be outside, she found an old trowel and headed down to the overgrown patch where Edie had once grown vegetables. Ernest was good with his hands, but only when they wielded a hammer and nails. Gardening held no allure for him at all, though – thanks to a small tractor of a lawn-mower, which Edie had given him the year she died – he liked cutting the grass. In the summer he could be seen twice a week at least, steering his old machine round and round the garden, taking the corners at full pelt, like a child with a small racing car. Though the vegetable patch had long since been reclaimed by briars and weeds, sometimes treasures – a beetroot, clusters of potatoes, the occasional carrot – could still be unearthed for the price of a few scratches and stings.

After a bit rummaging, Jane found two carrots to pull, and several sticks of rhubarb. I will tell him tonight, she thought suddenly, straightening herself, aware of the heat of the spring sun on her back. It has gone on long enough. I must tell him. Her stomach heaved and she closed her eyes to steady herself. When she opened them again, it was to see her brother-in-law approaching, carrying a small tatty trug basket and with a wide-brimmed straw hat of his mother's, perched Huckleberry Finn style, on the back of his head.

Christopher had been watching his sister-in-law for some minutes before making his approach, intrigued by her look of absorption, hesitant of intruding.

'I've come to offer my services.' He waved the basket.

'What's Michael doing?'

'We fell out over Arsenal,' he said with a grin, edging nearer, cursing the persistent clinging of the brambles. 'I left him rummaging impressively in his briefcase, in search of worthier pursuits, no doubt.'

'He's never far from his work,' Jane agreed, in as neutral a voice as she could manage.

'Dad and Tom have returned,' he went on, 'plus one rabbit without a hop.'

'Poor rabbit.'

'Conserve your compassion. They are, as we speak, designing the most elegant of cardboard homes – complete with window shutters, a sprung mattress—'

'Wall-to-wall carpeting and a fitted kitchen – I know.'

They laughed together.

'He is the most perfect grandfather,' she sighed, smiling.

'First rate. Making up for his ineptitude with the last generation. Rich pickings there, by the way – well done,' he said, indicating the vegetables in her hands. 'But move in a bit deeper, can you – you're hogging all the best bits.' The two of them, now tightly ensconced in the prickly thickets, continued their hunting, Jane finding another carrot, and Christopher a doughty stem of purple sprouting broccoli. They continued to talk as they hunted, with an ease that seemed to arise quite naturally from the simple business of being involved in a common task.

'Ernest wasn't really inept as a father, was he?'

Wanting to answer truthfully, Christopher hesitated and frowned before answering. The rims of her eyes were red, he noticed suddenly, under-shadowed by grey smears. She still doesn't look happy, he thought, remembering similar thoughts at Pippa's awful party and wishing he could ask her why.

'I wouldn't say inept, no,' he answered carefully, 'just a bit... distant. A rather formal father, but then they were different times and he's more than made up for it since.' He nudged the tip of his boot under what looked like a half-buried potato, but which turned out to be a stone. 'I think sometimes that maybe Michael and I arrived too soon after the death of the girls, my sisters. People say that if babies die you should have another one quickly, but I'm not sure. Grief can take its time, can't it? I have wondered too,' he went on quickly, suddenly talking in such a low voice, that Jane found herself holding her breath and straining to catch all the words, 'whether... at first, anyway... a part of him might have been too scared of loving us, in case he lost us as well. That perhaps he held back a bit to protect himself in some way. Does that make any sense?'

Jane nodded, a little amazed, both at the depth of such conjectures and the fact of him sharing them with her.

'Love is such a troublesome business, don't you find?' he added, grinning.

'It certainly is,' Jane murmured, her thoughts flying back to Michael and the realisation that she couldn't say what had to be said after all. She had nothing really to complain about and was an idiot. She sucked a trickle of blood off a small scratch on the back of her hand. 'So Ernest has discovered fatherhood in grandfatherhood.'

'That's a neat way of putting it.' Christopher nodded as he considered her words. 'Yes, I like that.'

'Perhaps Michael will do the same,' Jane blurted, having had no intention of saying any such thing, and adding hastily, 'you know, because of how he has to spend so much time working.'

'I understand exactly,' Christopher said kindly, 'and I bet he will.'

Just then Michael's head appeared at a top window of the house.

'Jane – Harriet's bawling her eyes out.' He cupped his hands round his mouth to make sure he was heard. 'Can you come?'

Jane and Christopher exchanged a look and burst out laughing.

'On my way,' she called, embarking somewhat gingerly on the

return journey, through all the long prickly tendrils that had bounced back into place.

'Jane, are you coming or what?' shouted Michael, as Harriet's shrieking began to spiral out of the window.

'Yes, yes, oh hell – I'm caught – ow.'

'Don't pull – I think I can reach. Keep quite still.' Several inches of a thickly barbed briar had hooked itself into her hair. 'Here – hold my basket and stop fidgeting.' As Christopher reached across the thickets, his fingers working firmly but gently to tease the bramble free, she caught a faint smell of him, a sweet, sweaty, manly smell, and shivered involuntarily.

'There,' he announced after a few moments. 'A free woman.'

'How kind – thank you.' Jane went the rest of the way as fast as she could, only looking back to wave when she was almost at the house.

11

Jane and Michael were in the master bedroom. Soon after Edie died, Ernest had moved himself into the smallest of the three spare rooms, as if he were a lodger from the old days, when a steady stream of scrawny schoolteachers and students had wolfed down quantities of Edie's crispy bacon and fried bread, contributing measly but vital sums towards their household running costs. Now, Ernest felt comforted by the lack of space, by the way his narrow bed hugged the wall, cornered into it by the chest of drawers that had belonged to his father and the side table which Edie had chosen on a rainy day at an antiques fair in Durham. The smell of Edie wasn't so strong in that room. He could bear everything else – all her embroidered seats and cushions, her collection of miniature ceramic cottages, the painful sharpness of memories triggered by photographs; but the faint odours of her clean, sugary scent in their bedroom came at him like salt to an open wound.

Jane moved steadily, blindly, through the rituals of preparing for bed. The bedroom was large, with a soft, grey carpet and curtains of faded pink. Being on the corner of the house, it had windows on two of its walls. She had opened both of these to their full extent when they arrived, hoping to shift some of the stale air that settled on the top floor through lack of use. The children lay peacefully in the room across the landing, both on their stomachs, their faces flushed, their arms and legs spread-eagled under the covers.

Michael was in the small bathroom that adjoined their bedroom, cleaning his teeth rigorously. His cheeks were rough and dark with stubble. Having spat into the basin, he looked up at her reflection in the mirror when she appeared beside him. 'You've caught a bit of sun.'

Jane nodded, saying nothing, studying the two of them in the glass as if they were unknown characters in a play, a woman with slightly red cheeks, the man tousled and unshaven. She felt nothing as she looked, nothing except the chill of the cold linoleum on her bare feet. It brought a wave of courage back, the need to try – again – to confront reality.

'Michael,' she turned round to face him, her hands feeling for the familiar chip along the edge of the old basin.

'Christ, I'm tired.' He padded through to the bedroom, leaving her there, on the edge of the precipice. She had to go to the toilet before following him out; fear had liquidised her stomach, drained her head of blood.

Michael lay on the bed in his pyjamas, hands behind his head, eyes on the ceiling.

'There are cobwebs all over the place. In fact, this room is filthy. I'm sure it's making my eyes itch.' He rubbed savagely at his eyes with his knuckles. 'Let's make our excuses and head off early tomorrow. That way we'll miss the worst of the traffic – have time to sort ourselves out the other end—'

Jane leant against the bathroom door, curling her toes into the carpet as if to secure herself more firmly. It was tempting to respond to the small issues – the dirt and the leaving early – but she knew that if she did, she would lose herself, drown in detail and perhaps never claw her way back to the rocky resolve that had been coming and going all afternoon.

'There is no easy way to say this, Michael,' she began, her voice hoarse.

'Let me guess.' In one abrupt movement he swung his legs over the side of the bed and sat up. The left leg of his pyjamas stayed hitched up over his knee. 'You don't want to go back early. You never do. You want to pick manky vegetables and dawdle down here until the point where it will take us four hours instead of two to get home again.'

'No, I want – I mean, I think we should separate.'

'Separate?' He was so unprepared, despite everything. And even for her, after all the months of silent arguing with demons inside her head, the moment, now that it had come, was horrifying.

'I've tried to talk to you about this before, but you never... we've been separated, mentally, for years, Michael... I can't – I won't – live like this any more.'

'What do you mean *like this*?' He swung himself off the bed and stood up. The hitched pyjama dropped to the appropriate ankle.

Jane dropped her gaze to his feet, to the sprouting dark hairs on his toes, as she shifted position so that her back was against the greater solidity of the wall. 'I just meant...'

'You *meant*? What is this, Jane?' Michael's mind, grappling with shock, took refuge in anger. 'Separate?' He gave a laugh that was more of a shout as he shook his head in disbelief. 'I work my balls off twelve hours a day – ship the whole family to bloody Cobham just to please you – and this is the thanks I get. *Separate*? You've got to be bloody joking.'

Michael clenched and unclenched his fists, struggling to think clearly through the maelstrom of emotions engulfing him; outrage, suspicion and then a great sense of injustice overwhelmed him. What about all of Jane's inadequacies and infuriating ways? Did she think it had been an easy ride for *him*? He was about to embark on this tack, when a clear spark of suspicion caught light, bursting through the confusion.

'What's really behind this?' He threw himself back against the pillows and studied her through narrowed eyes, silently congratulating himself on displaying such composure. 'Come on, out with it. What's really going on – or should I say, Who?'

Jane licked her lips, which felt dry and crusty. An urge to laugh almost overtook her. Given that her life was spent largely in the company of domestic appliances and shopping trolleys, the thought of having the opportunity – let alone the time – for any sort of affair was ludicrous.

'There is no "who", as you put it.' She hugged herself, feeling very vulnerable suddenly in her flimsy cotton nightie. 'There is nobody else.'

'Oh yes, I see.' He folded his arms. The anger was almost palpable now; his arms trembled from it. How dare she, how dare she.

'It's just no good – we are no good – we don't talk or care or give – we don't love...' The word trembled. Jane let the sentence hang, and moved across to the largest of the windows – further from Michael, seeking more courage, more air. But outside all was strangely still; a quiet, moonless, starless night, stuffed with cloud, offering no cosmic perspectives of beauty or mystery to ease troubled souls.

Down below, a small square of light fell across the lawn from where Christopher lounged on the sofa with a final glass of wine and a book on the stately homes of England. He stared not at the book, but out of the window, at the same blackness beheld by Jane. A large moth was trying to get into the room, throwing itself at the wrong side of the glass, with all the drunken determination of a flagging boxer. As Christopher watched, the creature's efforts grew weaker and weaker, until it finally dropped out of sight.

Upstairs, Michael was fighting with a dry, gagging lump that had lodged at the back of his throat, like the stopper on a rising swell of panic. Until this moment, he had always been absolutely sure of his power within his family – a subtle, heady power to do with being a successful husband and father, as well as a promising businessman. Thanks in part to years of acquiescence and protection from his wife, Michael's fine, solid image of himself had never before been called into question, remaining fundamental to his own lazy self-regard.

'Please, Jane,' he begged, swallowing the lump, which hurt and which only sprang back again, exploding into sobs that shocked him quite as much as her.

She went to sit next to him on the bed, taking his head in her arms and pressing it to her chest. The urge to comfort was reflexive, arising out of pure pity. She stroked his hair and rocked him, as if he were Tom, woken by a nightmare and needing her comfort in the dark.

And Michael let the tears flow, crying for himself, rather than their marriage. Even as he buried his head in the familiar musky smell of her, feeling her warmth, a cold secret part of him mushroomed with loathing at this desperate show of weakness on his part and at all her emotional claptrap about not giving and not loving. But he let the strange dry sobs go on, surrendering himself to them, sensing that for the moment at least they were his keenest weapon.

* * *

A storm broke that night, exploding into the stillness.

Christopher, who had fallen asleep on the sofa, awoke with a throbbing head and a furry tongue shortly before six. He moved his neck slowly from side to side, massaging the stiffness. He had got out of the habit of drinking so much. A few years back, before France and after, twice that amount of wine would have left him with a clearer mind.

Something more than the drumming rain had disturbed his sleep, of that he was sure. He crept into the hall and peered up the staircase. All was dim and silent. Then the kitchen door banged. He ran through just in time to see Jane standing on the verandah, struggling with the zip of a large black anorak.

'Do you know something the rest of us don't?' He had to shout to make himself heard against the wind, which was flinging the rain at them, slinging it sideways through the open arches of Ernest's porch.

Jane jumped round, her face pink and wet. 'Oh, Christopher, I'm going on a walk.'

'So I see.' He couldn't help smiling. 'And in my coat.'

'Your – oh, I didn't realise – only I didn't bring a wetproof and—'

'I'm not complaining, indeed I am flattered.' He cocked his head at her, wiggling his toes in his socks, which were already soaked through from the puddles of rain on the verandah floor. 'I don't suppose I could ask why and where you are going to walk at six o' clock on this delectable morning?'

'Not really, no.'

'I thought so. Will you be long?'

'Not long, no, I shouldn't think.'

'Not doing a Captain Oates on us or anything then?'

'A what? Oh, I see.' She smiled then and some of the startled look dissolved from her eyes so that the green of them looked softer and less dazed. 'No, not this morning anyway.'

'Fine.' He rubbed his hands together briskly. 'I'll put the kettle on then. Does madam take tea or coffee with her breakfast?'

Jane hesitated, distracted for a moment by the thought of Michael's tea making gift, which seemed to sum up so much. But then, what *did* it sum up, exactly? Deprived of sleep, her mind kept darting off in different directions, not hanging on to any sense.

'If you don't want to discuss that either, then that's fine by me – some things are just too private.' He eyed her carefully, wanting to evoke another smile. She looked so forlorn under the giant hood, her pale, pixie face half-drowned in its blackness.

'Coffee would be lovely,' she said briskly, turning suddenly to make her way down the steps.

'Careful not to slip,' he called, because he wanted to say something and that was all that came to mind.

Jane slithered through the mud towards the phone box half a mile down the lane. She needed to talk to Julia and was fearful that Ernest's big black heap of a telephone, which made a violent tringing sound for every number dialled, would wake the whole household.

* * *

Julia wasn't very good in the mornings. Coherent thought or speech was unthinkable before at least three cups of strong, black coffee and several bouts of news, blasted first from the radio next to her bed and then from the mini TV, which lived in the kitchen, squashed between her toaster and a small potted plant that never flowered but steadfastly refused to die.

When Jane called, she was asleep, not deeply but pleasantly so, lost in a fantasy of speculative pleasure about a man she did not know, a man who was most definitely not Alan Lambert. The dream was full of the promise of erotic sensation, of things felt rather than things seen, a writhing, crimson indulgence from which she withdrew with some reluctance. Her telephone was set into the tiled wall of her kitchen, below a calendar of medieval brass rubbings.

'Jane? Are you in a call box? Has someone died?' Her voice was croaky with sleep.

'I've woken you up – I'm sorry.'

'No, no, I always leap out of bed at six thirty on Sunday mornings – hoping to receive calls from my dearest friends.' She groped in her fridge for some orange juice, drinking straight from the carton.

'I'm sorry—'

'For God's sake stop apologising and tell me what's going on.' With one eye on the sheeting rain unburdening itself on to the rooftops of Marylebone and Paddington, Julia reached over to press down the switch on her kettle and then settled herself on a kitchen chair, pulling her knees up under her nightshirt for warmth.

'I told Michael last night that I thought we should separate,' Jane blurted. 'We're at his Dad's. I'm in a call box. I *told* him, Julia. He cried – it was so unspeakably awful – far worse than I could have imagined.'

'Oh, no – Jane, I'm so sorry.'

'He said he wouldn't agree, then he got cross and then just terribly sad. I didn't know what to do.'

'I don't mean to sound brutal, but you didn't really expect him to leap at the idea, did you? Have things really been so bad?'

Jane leant her head against the grimy panes of the phone box, trying to ignore the unmistakeable stench of tobacco and urine. She felt as if she was running out of love, that one day she would look inside her heart for affection and find that there was nothing there, just the dried kernel of a person who had once had something to give.

'I don't love him,' she said simply. 'And I know he feels very little for me. He won't admit it – he wants us all to conform to some grand image of a "normal" family that functions in all the expected ways. He just doesn't seem to believe that the emotional side of things is necessary or important. He never has.' She paused, but Julia said nothing.

'The awful thing is, that's what probably attracted me in the first place – when I needed someone cool and hard-headed to keep me from falling apart.'

The switch on the kettle popped amidst great billows of steam. 'But love changes,' Julia ventured, 'even I know that. After years of marriage, it must do...'

'Oh, I know, I know.' Jane traced her index finger round the scratched image of a heart – half buried among the layers of much less romantic graffiti covering the grimy walls on either side of the phone. 'But this is far, far more than that. It's not just that I'm losing the plot – though I probably am – it's that... I am not sure we should ever have married...'

'Jane – do not say such things, it isn't remotely helpful.' Julia wanted to mention the children, but felt it would be too mean, too obvious. Instead, thinking fast, she suggested a compromise, in the form of a two-week family holiday. 'I know it sounds corny, but it just might help. You and Michael haven't been away for years. Go somewhere hot and exotic. Change the rhythm. It could work wonders.'

Jane took some persuading. The thought of the pair of them under the spotlight of each other's scrutiny, away from all the safety valves of home routines, the props that helped them communicate or ignore each other without it being so obvious, was positively frightening. It would be so false, so raw. But in the end, she agreed. Because of Tom and Harriet. Because, after so many years, it was the least she could do.

She traipsed back up the muddy lane to the house where Christopher's pot of coffee sat waiting.

'I'm planning a holiday,' she said brightly, towelling her wet hair with a tea cloth.

'A surprise for Michael?' He eyed her quizzically.

'Sort of.' She stirred her coffee hard. 'Thank you so much for this, it's just what I need.'

12

Thanks to the timely cancellation of a divorcing couple, the travel
agent in Guildford informed Jane cheerfully, a gleaming white
family villa in southern Portugal was immediately available at a
knock-down price. One phone call to a simmering but subdued
Michael, and the rescue plan was under way. Situated in the
concrete outskirts of what had once been the fishing village of
Milfontes, the luxurious facilities of the house included a swimming pool and a housekeeper called Maria-Marta, whose beady
black eyes immediately alighted upon the children as a legitimate
pretext for neglecting almost every domestic duty itemised on the
list that had been provided by the agent.

Michael, who minded about this more than Jane, devoted
considerable time to communicating these shortcomings through
an elaborate sign language that had little effect beyond prompting a
series of nodding smiles from the housekeeper. The beds remained
unmade and the bare floors quickly became covered with a film of
invisible grit that worked its way between the toes and into the
bottom of the bath. Dirt of a more obvious nature, together with

quantities of a mysterious fluff, rapidly accumulated in impressive piles under the beds and round the edges of each room.

Jane found it hard to care. She even came to enjoy Michael's gesticulated confrontations with their employee, all the while nurturing a secret admiration for Maria-Marta's carefree obstinacy. What mattered most to Jane was that the children – for whom the trivial question of language presented no insurmountable barriers – were happy. Clearly sensing that here at last was a true grown-up ally, both Tom and Harriet entrusted themselves to their new Portuguese friend from the moment she beckoned to them with a shy smile and two small lollipops. After a couple of days, assorted black-eyed nephews and nieces began to appear from behind gates and bushes, eager to join in with orgies of ice-cream eating and endless games in the shallow end of the pool. While Michael huffed and waved his hands, Jane could only smile, enjoying this unexpected relief from parental responsibility.

Between her and Michael, politeness raged. Never had Jane believed that kindness could feel so cold. Michael enquired how she was more times in a day than he usually managed in a year. He asked if her book was good, whether she was thirsty or hungry, hot or cold, tired or refreshed. Any attempt of Jane's to break this mould, to force him into a discussion of the bigger issues that towered, invisible and hard, between them, were either quickly rebuffed or simply ignored. On the odd occasion that Maria-Marta was not there, Michael would embark on self-consciously jolly rituals to entertain the children, horsing round like a child himself, supposedly having fun, but with one eye nailed to his wife.

Jane would take refuge in the shade of the patio with a novel or a pad of paper, trying not to watch her husband as he was watching her. Each display of civility and merriment seemed to her to be tinged with contempt and a sickening self-righteousness. Look at me, he was saying, look at me being perfect; you have no grounds for complaint, Jane Lytton; the failure is all yours.

The patio was besieged by flowers: scarlet bells, white clusters, purple horns with long furry stamens that dangled like earrings from the velvet cases of their homes. Jane's fingers slid down the pen and her palms stuck to the paper. By the morning of the seventh day, she succumbed to the temptation to write to Julia; but then, having put the date, couldn't think how to start. She looked down at the beads of moisture clinging to the tiny fair hairs between her breasts, like tiny glass insects. Her turquoise bathing costume, accustomed only to the neon lights of the Guildford swimming pool, had faded quickly in the sun to an unbecoming mottled green. Nothing felt real. But maybe writing would help make it so.

Dear Julia,

I hope you are well.

Here is a report from the front line:

Michael and the children are asleep, wrung out by the heat. Apparently, it's unusually hot for late April. No matter how much we drink, it all pours out in buckets. The children are on salt tablets, which they loathe. I bribe them with melting chocolate buttons as rewards, while Michael scowls disapprovingly in the background. But then, he's never understood the moral value of bribery where small children are concerned.

I suppose it's rather lovely here – flowers and birds in Technicolor etc. – but give me a windy seaside in England any day. The air-conditioning works, after a fashion; it groans every five seconds or so, like a beast in pain. I've grown to know it rather well; I even feel sorry for it, sometimes, in the mad small hours.

But I suppose you are wondering about other things. Michael is, I have to say, trying very hard. So hard, indeed, that he has given new meaning to the notion of civility. And I am nice too, violently so. We pass the salt and discuss whether to apply lotion before or after a swim; we read our children bed-time stories and drink wine together until the clock has edged its way round to a respectable hour for going to bed...

Having taken the precaution of hiding the letter in her bag and hurling the stub of her cigarette well into the bushes, Jane walked to the edge of the kidney-shaped pool. She could feel the heat of the stone rising through the thin soles of her espadrilles. Not the faintest ripple defaced the surface of the water – a perfect pearly-green, so shimmeringly bright it made her eyes ache. She plunged straight in, a messy dive, which none the less felt glamorous and daring as the balmy cool engulfed her, sucking her down to the bottom of its mosaic-tiled walls. *Oh, for a life of sensations rather than thoughts*, sang her mind, from some dimly remembered Romantic poet, while she blew irreverent bubbles and then surfaced to float on her back, humming a tuneless tune as she luxuriated in the extended caress of the water.

She opened her eyes to find Michael watching her from behind the flimsy façade of his sunglasses and an open book. It disturbed her, like the thought of an eye through a bathroom keyhole.

'This isn't so bad, is it?' He grinned. An air of self-satisfaction was creeping back over him; his confidence, badly knocked by recent events, visibly reassembling itself. Still smiling, he patted his stomach which had developed a small – almost dainty – pot since their arrival and offered her a swig of beer.

'No thank you. I'll get my lemonade.'

Michael watched her climb the steps out of the pool and walk over to the table to fetch her glass. She seemed to move very deliberately, very tightly, with only the faintest swing of her slim hips. She was so small, almost like a woman in the guise of a girl. Her hair, which she had kept short for so many years, had grown quite long again and reached almost to her shoulder blades. The dense curls were thicker than ever, making her head look very wide from behind. He could feel the distinct stirring of arousal as he studied her. She looked so separate and determined. It was infuriating and provocative. An urge to grab her took hold; an urge to be rough – to shake her, to pull her, to press himself on to her, into her, to make her submit physically, if nothing else.

'Shall we go for a walk?' Jane suggested, having drained the last warm dregs of her drink.

As they strolled down the cobbled street that led into Milfontes, Michael took her hand. They had left the children with Maria-Marta and could have been two lovers, on a second honeymoon, out for a Sunday amble. They headed towards the old part of town that lolled around the crumbling ramparts of a medieval castle that sat on the edge of a sandy estuary, a couple of miles from the open sea. A stray cat scurried past them, angular and wary. The rest was silence, the closed-shutter quietness of siestas, interrupted only by the brief bark of a dog, the cry of a child, the slamming of a door.

After crossing the main square, past the rusted bronze statue of a conquering hero, Jane released Michael's hand and followed him up the long stairwell of chipped and loose steps that led to the most preserved of the castle walls. Once at the top, he made a big show of looking through a tourist telescope while she sat with her legs dangling carelessly over the warm, smooth stones, her toes pointing to the water a hundred feet or so below. A whisper of a breeze, as soft as muslin, blew over her face. Jane closed her eyes, enjoying the feel of it in her hair.

Michael had begun wrestling with the telescope which, in spite of having consumed several coins, still offered no vision beyond a cloudy blur. He shook it and then hit it hard with his fist. Two coins tumbled back out of the slot and landed at his feet. Having pocketed the money, he strode along a portion of the rampart, and squinted at the glinting sea. Whatever poise he had recaptured earlier on in the day was gone. He felt unbalanced and cross. Jane's dreamy silence only riled him more. How dare she, he thought, not for the first time, and without quite pinpointing exactly what it was she had dared to do, beyond shattering his sense of equilibrium.

'Come and sit down, Michael,' Jane murmured, her eyes still closed, her chin lifted slightly, pointing towards the lemony sun.

Michael stomped back and perched on the wall next to her, facing the other way – at the ruined castle wall rather than the view. He took a deep, dramatic breath, wanting her to know that he was prepared for this long-awaited attempt at a proper reconciliation. He would make her eat humble-pie, he vowed, he would not cave in easily.

Instead, Jane said, in a voice of deathly quiet and certainty, 'It's not going to work, Michael. You and me, it's over.'

'Jesus Christ.' Michael slapped his legs and swivelled angrily to face her.

They were side by side, very close but not touching. 'What do you want, Jane? What the fuck do you want?'

'I don't know.'

'Well, that's great – so the rest of the world sits around waiting for you to decide.'

'I only know what I don't want...'

'Oh, that's charming, I must say. But perhaps you could endeavour to throw a little more light on this intriguing state of mind? Please, spare no thought for my feelings, not that you ever do.'

Taking a deep breath, Jane stood up to face him. 'I feel as if I've been living in a daze, as if I've been steadily losing touch with myself.' She spoke fast, fearful that even pausing for breath might cause her to lose courage. 'I just wanted things to be all right day by day. I never faced up to what was really going on. But it has buried me. I have forgotten how to be happy. I literally have no idea what I like, what makes me laugh, what makes me get out of bed in the mornings, beyond the fact that you've got a train to catch and the children are howling for food.'

Michael was not really listening. She was using the tone of voice that meant he always hated the things she said. Still sitting on the wall, he reached out and grabbed both her hands. They felt moist and hot. 'Why are you being so melodramatic about life suddenly? Everybody has things to put up with that they don't like. My job drives me crazy half the time—'

'You love your job. And if you don't, then you should leave.'

He stood up, shaking free of her so roughly that she stumbled on the loose stones and almost fell. A young couple, with identical white-blonde hair and chunky, tanned bodies, had arrived at the telescope and were having a friendly tussle about who should look through first. 'For God's sake,' Michael hissed, 'how can you say such stupid things and pretend to mean them? Life is not perfect, Jane, and it never will be – the sooner you realise that, the better for everybody.'

A tiny thought entered her head then, to do with reaching forward and pushing him so hard that he somersaulted backwards into the drop beyond the wall. She had seen something similar once, a long time ago, as a child, with her parents on a beach; a woman had lost her footing on a sea wall and fallen, arms and legs flailing. But the drop had only been fifteen feet or so, and somehow, the woman had got to her feet straight away, pooh-poohing the buzz of concern. 'But haven't we got to try and make life perfect – as perfect as possible—'

'I give up,' Michael interjected, any semblance of patience or a desire for peace suddenly deserting him. Instead, self-pity coursed through him, a heat. 'I have tried everything. I've done my best. But I see now that there is no point. That nothing will ever satisfy you.' With these words, he strode away, swinging his long arms fiercely, the back of his dark head set firmly against her for good.

The young couple, engrossed now in a serious embrace, felt neither threatened nor interested by this public separation of the Lyttons. That others could not love as they did, was no surprise.

Jane finished her letter to Julia later that night, while Michael pummelled pillows and sighed loudly in the next room:

I'm afraid that things remain as bad as ever. The problems lie too deep for salvaging. Michael will not face up to the blank feeling where once there was a kind of love. He believes we should soldier on regardless. But I have realised that if I do that, I shall simply become more deeply unhappy, more embittered – like all those grim-faced women you see in supermarkets who steer their trolleys like battle tanks and yell at their children because they themselves are full of misery.

It is selfishness, I suppose, to want to leave Michael. But it feels like bravery too.

Before their return to England Michael also wrote a letter – or rather a postcard, which he concealed in an envelope.

Tim, I have to say I feel pretty bad being over here while you're going through such dreadful trouble over there. (I haven't breathed a word to anyone, by the way.) But I may as well tell you that I too am experiencing something of a crisis – though of a rather different nature. The plain truth is, I don't think that Jane and I will be together for much longer. This whole business was started by her. I've pulled out all the stops but nothing I say or do seems to make any difference. Taking her on this holiday to southern Portugal was my last effort and it doesn't seem to have worked. The thing is, I was wondering if you and Pippa could see your way to putting me up for a couple of nights, just while I sort myself out. We get back on Friday. Yours as ever, Michael.

13

So it was, that by the end of April, Michael and two suitcases had gone to Dulwich, leaving Jane in a confused state of relief and guilt that focused, alarmingly, on a fresh longing for her parents. Childish conversations with them would start up in her head, little-girl voices begging for their understanding and some home-spun wisdom to see her through.

In practical terms little had changed. The safe trench of daily life, with all its comforting rituals of feeding and clothing two small children, was still there; but so was the full weight of what had happened, sitting like a road-block in her mind, making it hard to focus on anything else at all. She told Tom and Harriet as much as she dared, explaining that Daddy would see them often, knowing that they had no hope of yet grasping what had happened, but wanting above all else to be honest. In spite of trying not to, she fretted terribly over the two of them, irritating them with unwanted hugs and tiptoeing into their room long after they had abandoned themselves to sleep, so that she could watch the innocence of their moon-shaped faces and suffer, a little self-consciously, on their behalf. It was only in the evenings, when there was no requirement of a 'proper' meal to worry about, no conversation to be negotiated, that her heart would sometimes surge with a kind of happiness – a fragile confidence that she had acted for the best. And she would sit quite still then, watching and listening in the lovely late hush of the night, as if waiting to see what might emerge, what she might do next.

'Of course you'll have to find yourself a lover,' remarked Mattie, stabbing a long chip into a blob of tomato sauce and sucking the end.

'Dearest Mattie, not all of us are so completely tied to hormonal impulses as you. A lover is – to put it bluntly – the last thing I require at the moment.'

'What's a lover?' asked Tom, his mouth bulging with hamburger and soggy bun.

They were in a McDonald's on a rainy Saturday in early May, after a speedy tour round an exhibition of modern art. Having spent some time pretending that the bored caterwauling of her niece and the simulated machine-gun fire of her nephew were not disturbing other patrons, Mattie had finally given in and confessed a longing for large quantities of junk food. The declaration proved popular and was acted upon at once.

'A lover is someone you love,' said Mattie promptly, 'and don't talk with your mouth quite so full. Try half-full like mine – see?' She opened her mouth wide, revealing the congealed remains of her chip and then made a roaring noise, which was greeted with loud applause from the children.

The family excursion had been Mattie's way of trying to help her big sister through her crisis. Given that Jane had initiated the separation herself, Mattie found it hard to understand the extent of the drama, or the look of dazed glumness that overtook Jane's features whenever she was off her guard. Personally, Mattie had never liked Michael very much. And now that Jane was apart from him, she felt at liberty to express herself freely on the subject.

'Michael was so pompous and correct,' she said, talking as if he were dead, rather than merely absent. 'Crippled by propriety – I read that somewhere – but I do think it is apt. It was this guy in a book – brilliant read, though not quite your thing – anyway, this guy was so knotted up about the right way of doing things that he never truly let go, that is, not until he meets this girl—'

'Mattie, sorry to interrupt, but we'd better go. These two look terribly droopy.' Jane spoke loudly, telling herself she had no right to be disappointed at her sister not saying the right things. It had been reckless to imagine that Mattie could begin to appreciate the weird cocktail of emotions that besieged her each day, the bewilderment of being alone and yet so tied up in the lives of other people.

'I do feel pretty sad about it all too, you know,' she ventured, when they were back in the car and giving Mattie a lift home.

'Poor Jane – of course you get lonely. Believe me, I know all about that. Which reminds me. I could have a visitor this evening... and should probably prepare...' She tipped the contents of her bag on to her lap as she spoke, picking out an eye-liner and a hand mirror and starting, expertly, to re-blacken the heavy coatings round her eyes.

Jane was on the point of enquiring further, when she noticed a little polythene bag filled with small green and white capsules.

'Are you ill?'

'No, why?' Mattie was examining her teeth, running her tongue along the edges and clacking them together.

'The pills. They look like antibiotics.'

'They're nothing.' Mattie began stuffing things back into her bag.

'If they're nothing, why are you behaving so weirdly?' Jane retorted, pulling up outside Mattie's basement flat.

'I am not being weird. You're just so bloody nosy sometimes – it drives me crazy.'

Jane set her lips together, determined not to say anything predictable, an exercise of control which was rewarded by Mattie taking pity on her at the last minute and bending down to the car window.

'They're pick-me-ups. An American friend gave them to me. They're clinically-everythinged and they make me feel very good. Okay?'

Mattie's face, now powdered and highlighted, looked sinister to Jane, like make-up on a little girl.

'Fine. Great. Thanks for telling me.' She drove away very fast, hating the unavoidable burden of feeling like a worried parent – as if her own two weren't enough. She glanced at them in the rearview mirror with a tummy-lurch of love. They had fallen asleep – Harriet in her car seat and Tom leaning against her – two floppy puppets with ketchup-stained cheeks and open cherry mouths. The journey home would be quiet, and easing them into their beds too, if she was lucky.

* * *

Where Mattie's attempts at consolation tended to get sidetracked by preoccupations about herself, Julia shied away from them altogether, no doubt having decided – with her usual brand of pragmatism – that moping would do no good at all. Whenever they spoke, Jane found herself bombarded with a volley of practical suggestions that left no room for the admission of sadness. Her marriage needed mourning, she felt; it hurt that not even her closest friend would acknowledge this properly.

'You'll need to get a job. Brush up your cv – put in phrases like "articulate self-starter" and "motivated high-achiever" – that's the kind of stuff that goes down well these days. Pretend you haven't got children and put your wedding rings on the other hand. Perhaps you've done that already?'

'No, I haven't.'

'Don't sound so icy. I'm only attempting to inject a soupçon of realism into that dreamy head of yours. It's all very well jettisoning husbands, but the consequences have to be confronted. I know I sound fierce, but you'll be grateful in the end.'

Jane did not feel grateful. She wanted to say that, cowardly though it may seem, she was not yet ready to think too deeply about bank-balances, since Michael, for now, had made no alterations to the account they shared, and – despite any antipathy towards her – had acknowledged that he would never want to deprive his children. Jane also wished she could explain that Tom and Harriet's innocence and trust in her left her weak with guilt; that, while she did not miss Michael himself, she missed the notion of having a husband very deeply. She wanted to say that being a single mother, while often having felt like one during her marriage, was terrifying and that the woman whom she had consulted at the DSS about potential income support while she hunted for part-time work, had displayed all the warmth of an iceberg.

The exchange left Jane with a feeling of isolation that was not improved by a phone call from Pippa a few days later.

'It's me. How are you?' she rasped.

'On top of the world, thanks,' replied Jane dryly. 'But you sound ill. Have you lost your voice?'

'No. I'm whispering because Michael and Tim are next door.'

'Pippa,' said Jane somewhat wearily, 'I'm sure there's no need for that. You're allowed to ring me, you know. I'm a friend who has separated from her husband, not an escaped convict.'

'Oh Jane,' Pippa, speaking more normally, sounded close to tears, 'this is all so awful.'

'It will all work out,' Jane told her gently, with a confidence she did not feel, inwardly marvelling at the recurring sense that she was the one being called upon to offer reassurance, when it was her own life that was imploding. 'Maybe call me another time, when you're on your own and feeling strong. I'm all right, and so is Michael, from what I can gather. Thank you both very much for taking him in. It means an awful lot.'

But Pippa was too nervy and distraught for another phone call. Instead, she wrote to Jane, posting the letter on the early May morning that she and Tim set off for the airport to catch a plane to Nairobi, for a trip about which she still knew nothing except her husband's decidedly uncharacteristic determination that it should include her.

Only used to receiving Christmas cards, Jane found Pippa's tiny, spider-writing hard to decipher. It was quite faint too, as if the biro was close to running out, although there was nothing weak about the message it contained.

Dearest Jane,

I cannot not tell you how sad I am that you and Michael have run into some trouble. But something has happened to me recently, which I feel bound to share with you, because I just know it will help. Tim, I am now certain, has been seeing someone else. There we are – it looks so simple and easily managed when it is written down like that, as a fact. At first, I was resolved to leave – all the expected feelings of betrayal and rejection overwhelmed me for a time. But then – partly because of the importance to me (to us, I hope!) of having a child – I worked through all that to a realisation of how important our relationship is. I have come to appreciate just what a volatile thing marriage is, that it lives and breathes and cannot therefore be boxed or pinned down to conform to a set of rules. And I realised too, that in spite of everything, I love Tim very deeply. Oh dear, I'm being long-winded and sentimental, which I didn't intend at all.

Although I know no details of your situation, I suspect that Michael, like Tim, has perhaps given you similar cause for grief. They are attractive, our men. We should not be so surprised if temptation beckons and they fall prey to it. Forgive him, Jane, but ask to have him back. He does look so lost without you. If my experiences with Tim are anything to go by, guilt and remorse will make him kind – kinder perhaps than he has ever been before. There is always good to be had from bad.

I feel so much better for writing to you. I could never have said half of this to your face. We set off on our travels tomorrow morning, leaving your dear husband to hold our fort for us. I hope so much that we return to an empty house.

With fondest love, Pippa.

Having stuffed the letter into her bag on the way out of the house, Jane ended up reading it while standing amongst an assortment of parents and push-chairs at the gates to Tom's school. So amazed was she by its contents, that she emitted a small shriek and clapped her hand over her mouth.

'Good news, I hope,' ventured a mum whose son played with Tom sometimes, and who had heard rumours of the separation and wanted to say something kind. Jane was friendly, but not one of those that volunteered much about herself.

'What?' Jane, skimming the letter again for some redeeming feature, glanced up at the kindly face. 'No... just something unexpected from a friend.' She hurriedly slid the envelope into her pocket and set off to join the other parents starting to gather in the playground, cementing her reputation for wanting to be left alone.

* * *

For Michael too, the effects of the separation were confusing in ways that he least expected. He told his secretary at once, in the hope of minimising the rumour-mill round the office, and proceeded to throw himself into his work with a frenzied determination. The disquieting sense of being the focus of sympathetic curiosity – the feeling that one's name had been on everybody's lips just moments before entering a room – lasted only for a week or so. Far more humiliating, was the bungle he made with Antonia during the course of a Friday lunch, when the lion's share of a bottle of wine induced him to mistake the gleam in her eye for something other than raw ambition. Although Michael's ego had, by and large, fought admirably on his behalf, slaying demons of self-doubt on all sides, there still lurked a prickly sense of failure with regard to Jane, which no amount of extra paper-work and office-hours could erase. Unhappily encouraged by alcohol, this tingling insecurity surfaced over their meals that day in the form of a severely ill-timed proposition.

'I suppose you know you're extremely attractive as well as brilliant.'

The razor-look of Antonia's eyes should have warned him. 'Oh yes, I know that all right.'

'I don't see so much of you these days. I'd like to see more.' He let his gaze travel down over what the restaurant table allowed him to see of her body, lingering on the large gold jacket button which he imagined marked the point between her breasts. She sat back and folded her arms across her chest, a movement which gave Michael – for some unfathomable and misguided reason – enough hope to continue.

'We're grown-ups, after all...'

Antonia stood up and reached for her bag.

'Yes, we are, Michael, and you are pissed and seriously out of order.' She slung her bag over one shoulder and bent near his face.

'If you talk to me in such a way again, I shall submit a formal claim of sexual harassment.' The central gold button was now very near his nose. 'As it is, I shall now be asking Mr Glassbrook if I may commit all my time to the South American markets.' She yanked three ten-pound notes out of her bag and threw them onto her side plate, where they stuck firmly to a small pat of butter. 'Don't worry – I won't tell him why. Not this time.'

It may have been this incident that lay behind the slovenliness that now overcame Michael when he was on his own, manifesting itself like the onset of some insidious disease. For he was not, by nature, a slob. Indeed, it was one of the more obvious discordant themes of the past, that while he liked to return to a house free of clutter, Jane could step – happy and unseeing – between heaps of laundry and discarded toys.

Now, every morning, Michael pulled a new bowl out of the cupboard in order to eat his cornflakes. When the regular set had all been dirtied, he spent several minutes looking for the special Noritake crockery he knew the Crofts had, rather than placing his hands into the greasy log-jam in the sink. He applied the same principle to his use of cutlery, progressing from stainless steel to silver – the latter requiring him to break open Pippa's lovingly wrapped felt and cellophane bundles in the heirloom of a canteen that resided in the top drawer of the dresser in the dining room. His supper invariably came out of cartons and boxes, the remains of which were then rammed into one of the bulging, smelly bags which slowly multiplied in the far corner of the kitchen.

He rented films nearly every night, usually from the 'adults only' section at the back of the video shop. But the gratification they provided was so short-lived and filled him with such self-disgust, that he rarely watched any of them all the way through. He became a channel-flicker par excellence on the television instead, juggling images in his head – sandbags against loneliness, which only succeeded in keeping him awake, since his mind, unlike the television, could not be switched off at will.

Whenever Jane rang, he found it hard to concentrate on anything beyond the desire to make her feel bad. She would enquire – using an infuriatingly soft voice, hitherto reserved for when the children were sad or sick – when he wanted to see Tom and Harriet, whether he wanted to collect more things from the house, and then fling out flimsy promises about complying with any route to the quickest, cheapest divorce possible, so long as it was fair. And he would fire back short, stalling answers, hoping to make her feel guilty and wretched – not because he wanted her back, but because his feelings were crystallising into a kind of hatred and he wanted her to suffer.

'This is hopeless,' said Jane one night, after a particularly acerbic, aimless exchange. 'We're getting nowhere.'

'I couldn't agree more. But this is what you wanted.'

'No, it isn't,' she cut in. 'This is just a mess.'

Michael looked about him. There were three socks on the rug in front of the television. Empty beer cans were lined up on top of the television and round the skirting boards, a sign that the wicker waste-basket in the corner had long since toppled over from too great a demand on its modest capacities to accommodate such items. Ancient rice grains were strewn across the coffee table, amongst several vintages of pizza-crumbs, solidified blobs of melted ice-cream and many mugs, the remains of each of their contents layered to varying degrees with a custardy scum.

'Well, it's not my fault,' he retorted, before slamming down the phone.

But he rang her back, much later that night, when his head was spinning and his stomach ached from too much cheese and wine.

'Just tell me,' he croaked, trying to sound more pained than he really was. 'Is there some other man? Someone I know?'

Jane was lying flat on her back in bed, her hair a dark fan against the white of the pillows. Through a chink in the curtains, she could see the moon, the merest thumbnail of a silver. A thread of hope, it felt like, hanging on in the dark.

'There is nobody else, Michael. Truly.'

'I'll ask for nothing in the divorce if you swear never to marry again.'

Jane sat up at once, wide awake, gripping the phone with both hands. What new kind of game was this? 'Don't be absurd.'

'So, you don't rule it out then?' he said, in a tight voice.

'I don't think about it.' Jane snapped. 'But no, I suppose not. I don't rule anything out.'

He was silent for several seconds.

Jane looked at her watch. It was nearly two o'clock. 'Michael, you had no right to say that, even if it was a sick joke. We are no longer together because we did not make each other happy. I want a divorce, amicably if possible—'

'You'd better start looking for a job, then, hadn't you.'

'I already have, but...' Jane faltered, experiencing with fresh intensity the curse of having allowed herself to become so completely dependent, so tied to a person by money and material needs. The whole system was meaningless without love.

'We need to sell the house,' Michael muttered, breaking the silence, 'but it's a bad time now – the market is crap. You can stay there with the kids until it improves. Then I want to agree our own terms, without bloody lawyers.' He sounded sleepy suddenly, as if the fight had gone out of him. 'I miss Tom and Harriet,' he added, after a long pause.

'Yes,' Jane replied softly, her eyes filling with tears, knowing he spoke from the heart.

14

Although it was several miles from Hendon to Paddington, Christopher decided to walk. He wanted to clear his head. The party the night before had been a classic of its kind, burgeoning from something quite mellow into rowdy scenes of unbecoming abandonment that had lasted well into the small hours. For the first time in a very long while, he had lost control. Ruthless images of things he had said and done kept cutting into his mind, adding the pulse of self-reproach to the painful throbs of alcoholic dehydration.

Having taken the opportunity of summer half-term to come up to London for an informal meeting with his publishers, Christopher had invited himself to stay overnight with Greg Chambers, a wild friend from his college days, who endeavoured to prove that wildness grew more frantic with each passing year. Cocooned for weeks in the hubbub of school, with very little contact with the outside world, Christopher had felt much in need of the break.

It had felt good to get away from the teaching routines, the clatter of the boys, the oppressive beauty of Oxford and all its associations with his own muddled past – all those messy decisions and blurred opportunities. For many years Christopher had clung to the assumption that, as life unfurled, the picture would become clearer, that confidence in himself would blossom from the bitter bud of youthful uncertainty – which had so sharply flavoured his adolescence – into something more concrete, more reassuring. Instead, though objective perceptions of the world and of aspects of learning developed steadily enough, his own self-regard, together with any true sense of direction about the life he led, remained murky and full of doubt.

Teaching was his refuge. He felt safe amidst the bantering hierarchy of the staff room, where he was known for a dry wit and an amusingly irreverent view of the world. In the classroom he was securer still, sure of his ability to inspire fear and laughter amongst the bobbing, cropped heads of the prep-schoolers, all the while plugging and planting them with facts – just enough to see them through exams but not so much that they grew listless. He handled them well, remembering only too vividly what it felt like to be twelve: to be bored, yet afraid, desperate to be manly, yet longing for home and the soft, bosomy embrace of a mother. All that vile confusion of growing.

He walked fast, hands tucked into the baggy pockets of his faded-green corduroy jacket, shoulders hunched against the world. For June it was chilly. The red-brick faces of Hendon suburbia crouched behind the sparse protection offered by their front gardens. Overhead the sky was patched with grey clouds that teased the sun with gaps, before closing ranks in panels of steel. As Christopher turned on to the upper stretch of the Finchley Road, already jammed with a medley of impatient vehicles, uncomfortable snap-shots of Jane's sister pushed themselves at him, thrusting through the fog inside his head.

Mattie had been at the party. She appeared in the doorway of the kitchen just as Christopher was banging an ice-box on the rim of the sink. Several cubes had flown into the air and skidded across Greg's terracotta flagstones, stopping inches from Mattie's painted toes. She wore a purple and lilac kaftan, with a wide black belt pulled tightly round her small waist; black leather sandals with intricate cross-straps encased her bare feet. Although unusual, the outfit suited her well. A blue scarf was entwined prettily amongst the bushy ringlets of her hair, drawing attention to the heavy blue of her eyes and the darkened lines of her brows. She was clearly Jane's sister – dark-haired, with that small, neat figure – yet in every detail of line and colour so completely different. Jane's eyes were a rich green, her nose was longer, her lips fuller, her chin more pointed. Whereas Mattie's petiteness was focused on the tidy features of her face, the close-set, penetrating eyes, the sharp triangle of her nose and the fine lines of her lips, tonight carefully defined with a pinky-rose gloss.

Mattie had had a bad week. The pills had all gone, as had the friend who had supplied them. Without any chemicals to ward it off, self-doubt had been seeping through the cracks in her system, dampening her confidence and drowning her hopes. Where once the monotony of her typing job had fired her determination to continue as an artist, it now did little more than dull her senses with its tedium, utterly defusing whatever nerve it was that had once empowered her creative drive. Too much time had passed without change. These days the only artistic encouragement she got came from men who gasped dutifully at the bright, angry splashes of her work, before pushing her through to the bedroom and gasping rather more loudly amongst the bedclothes.

'I'd prefer a drink with my ice,' she said, using the tip of her sandal to kick the nearest ice-cube back across the floor.

'What are you doing here?'

'I believe there's a party. Or do all these people pay rent?' She had to step back to make way for a girl with spiky white hair and a cigarette glued between ruby lips. As the girl bent down to get something from the fridge, the red-frilled edge of her panties peeked out from beneath her skirt, which was shiny-black and tight, and made Christopher think of dustbin liners.

When Mattie saw Christopher staring so intently, a wry half-smile on his face, a shiver of irrational envy passed through her. The girl was very young and tall, with pencil ankles that balanced precariously on the tower-block heels of gold-flecked shoes.

'And what – come to that – are you doing here? I thought you lived the cerebral life of an Oxford schoolmaster.'

'It's rarely cerebral,' he laughed. The skinny girl, now in possession of a large wedge of processed cheese, darted back out into the hallway, nibbling her find like a wary animal.

'Greg's an old friend,' continued Christopher, 'we meet about once a year. Our lives have taken rather different roads, as lives tend to do.'

Christopher's state of mind was not so very far removed from Mattie's, though he had already imbibed enough to float, temporarily, above it.

'So you are in London to see Greg?' She sipped her drink and leant up against the fridge.

Christopher swung one of his long legs astride a chair, resting his head on his arms across the back of it, fighting tiredness as he focused on the conversation. Strains of lively music drifted in from the sitting room, where chairs and tables had been pushed aside to make room for dancing.

'And to see my agent – and my publishers – that sort of thing.'

'Another definitive biographical critique on the way? We'll have to queue for your autograph soon.'

'I highly doubt it.' Christopher put his hands to his temples, which were pounding. If his bed had not been piled almost to the ceiling with coats, he would have retreated to it. The work meeting, which had been about his idea for a novel, had not gone well. Both his agent and editor wanted another critical book first, for marketing reasons. Christopher had lost his temper and ranted unattractively about the urgency of personal creativity.

Mattie asked him if he had a joint. She was jigging from one foot to the other, twitchy and wide-eyed.

He shook his head and shrugged, watching the walls of the room heave with a kind of detached interest.

'You don't want to dance, I suppose?' Mattie put her glass down on top of the fridge, next to a large packet of breakfast cereal, and turned to him with a pouting smile.

Christopher, for whom the prospect of rising to his feet suddenly seemed daunting, felt little inclination to accept the request. But Mattie stepped daintily forward and helped him up from the chair.

People of all ages and sizes lined the walls of the house, slouched in doorways, sprawled on the stairs and along walls. Christopher and Mattie tunnelled their way through to the sitting room. The leggy blonde girl was dancing opposite Greg, swaying slowly with her eyes closed. Greg, his tie fastened round his head and his shirt unbuttoned to expose a line of dark, silky hairs, was gyrating furiously, mouthing the words and striking at imaginary guitars.

The two of them joined in with a more conventional disco-jig. Christopher, who found it hard not to lean at dangerous angles when he moved his upper body, clapped loudly at the closing chords of the song and jerked his head towards the kitchen, with the plan to pour himself a glass of water.

But by now Mattie had other notions inside her head. A new challenge had presented itself and she wanted to see it through. The next song was soulful and slow, impossible to dance to alone with any conviction. Christopher started to walk away, but Mattie moved closer and put her arms around his waist. It was good to be held – he felt much less giddy in the frame of her embrace. As he stared over her head, his nose tickled by a frizz of hair, his eye was caught by a framed photograph of a young version of Greg, sporting boyish hips and skinny arms, his head thrown back in laughter. It was a far cry from the businessman now slumped on the sofa beside them, one arm round the blonde, the other flopped across the swell of his belly. His chin had fallen onto his chest, revealing the sparsity of the thatch on top; the glimpse of circular flesh underneath looked white and afraid. Christopher closed his eyes, wishing he could close his mind as well. Mattie pressed her fingers gently into the small of his back, drawing him nearer still, feeling the familiar stirrings of arousal at the prospect of a new man.

Christopher had by now reached the outskirts of Hampstead. The shops began to take on a glossier look; window displays had lost their washed-out air of neglect; coffee shops released aromas of freshly ground beans and baked croissants, instead of the greasy whiff of fried eggs and sausage. He marched onwards, head down, trying not to tread on the lines of the pavement squares, fixing his mind on any detail that might block out the night before. It was a long time since he had made such an ass of himself.

A few yards short of Swiss Cottage, he succumbed to the sweet, creamy froth of a cappuccino, relishing its warmth in the empty pit of his stomach. It was well past ten o'clock. On seeing a payphone next to the door to the toilets, he debated whether he should call Julia first. He had decided to see her because of something Mattie had said – one of the sharp splinters of memory embedded in his head from the night before.

Jane and Michael had split up, Mattie said, after they had screwed each other, hastily, exploring the blind alley of lust that led to nothing but itself. They had used his bed, after the last coat had gone, to the background of Greg's snores through the wall.

Jane and Michael had split up – for good maybe, she wasn't sure – but Julia would know, because Jane always told Julia everything and Mattie nothing. After their intercourse, she had licked his shoulder with her dry cat's tongue and began to trail her fingers through the mass of wiry curls across his chest. But Christopher had pushed her away. He had needed water and aspirin. He had needed to think.

Sitting on the hard stool of the coffee bar, the full force of Mattie's tipsy tears of rejection came back at him, stoking up the guilt and the regret. If only she had told him before. Before they had shimmied their way down the corridor in the inviting, quiet aftermath of the party. Before he had unbuckled the thick black belt round her waist and moved his hand up under the swirling purple of the kaftan to feel the moist warmth of her skin.

While blaming himself, Christopher was also struck by the gross unfairness of what had happened. It was months since he had kissed a woman, years since he had got so drunk at a party that he had encouraged the attentions of a female whom, in the sober light of day, attracted him not at all.

It seemed the cruellest irony that Mattie should have materialised before him like that, all sad and silky-mouthed, when all along she held within her the breathtaking fact that Jane and Michael had separated.

* * *

Julia's shop was artfully arranged – seeming full, without appearing cluttered. Table-sized cabinets of trinkets dominated the centre of the room, while the larger pieces of furniture, together with displays of china and glass, were set back against the walls. Christopher entered, setting off the jangle of her doorbell, just as she was wrapping a seed-pearl brooch for an old lady who had asked for three duplicate copies of the receipt. The lady smelt strongly of lavender eau de cologne and possessed a face so heavily powdered that the bracket smile-lines beside her mouth were visibly clogged with the stuff, like deep gullies of fine beige sand.

'There we are.' Julia handed over the receipts and flicked her eyes up to locate Christopher. He was standing before a small rose-wood desk in the furthest corner of the room. She walked up behind him, noiseless on the royal blue pile of her imitation Windsor carpet, and lightly tapped his shoulder. He jumped round, his pale face pumped for an instant with the blush of surprise.

'I am honoured indeed. Are you being charitable, sociable or genuinely interested? Or is this to make up for cancelling on me before?' She smiled, wishing he did not look quite so alarmed.

'Ah, no... sorry about that. My plans changed. And now... well, I'm certainly not here to be charitable,' he blustered, recalling the earlier abandoned attempt to see Julia, which had also been about Jane – an urge to try and find out why she had seemed so run down at Pippa's party – until he had thought better of it. 'You've got some exquisite pieces,' he went on hastily, 'especially this.' He touched the desk. 'Is it Victorian?'

'Queen Anne. And I'm afraid it's got rather an exquisite price on it too.'

Christopher examined the small white tag dangling off the top right drawer and whistled. 'Out of my league. I'm afraid.'

'What a shame,' Julia teased. 'When I've made my million. I'll start doing discounts for chums – and their relatives. Though I should be quite sad to lose this, I have to confess. Look.' She proceeded to pull out some of the small pencil drawers, unable to resist showing off the clever jigsaw of tinier drawers and spaces behind. Her long hair fell forward over the desk, satin on shining wood. She handled the parts of the desk very gently, as if wary of causing pain. 'You see, it looks so simple – so straightforward – on the outside, when really it's a maze of complexity on the inside.'

'Like a person.'

'I beg your pardon? Oh, I see.' She eyed him curiously. 'Yes, I suppose so. But some people are pretty complicated on the outside too.'

'Yes, yes, indeed – of course they are.' Christopher cleared his throat and jangled the change in his pockets.

Julia clasped her hands, trying not to appear baffled. 'Did you want anything in particular?'

Behind her, the doorbell chimed as someone else entered the shop.

'There's always lunch,' he said suddenly, looking at his watch.

'Oh, I'm sorry, Christopher – I don't close for lunch on a Saturday, it's just too busy. I scoff Mars bars behind the counter instead, when no one's looking. Was there something that you wanted to—?'

But he was already backing towards the door, worn out by embarrassment and the dawning sense of the impossibility of discussing the subject that drummed in his head. 'I was just passing. I do that sometimes – act on impulse – that sort of thing.'

'How marvellous. I'm a dreadful one for planning things months in advance – can't do a thing unless it's inscribed in the diary.' She pursued him to the door. 'Thanks for coming.'

'Not at all.'

He sped off, cursing his hangover and his ineptitude.

15

'You look funny,' remarked Tom, eyeing his mother's made-up face with suspicion.

'Mummy's trying to look extra nice so that someone will give her a job.' Jane placed two squares of buttered toast in front of Harriet and licked her fingertips daintily, mindful of disturbing her lipstick.

'A job like Daddy's?' continued Tom.

Jane hesitated, unsure where the interrogation might be leading and wanting to have some control over its outcome.

'Yes, like Daddy's, but in a different place. So that we have more money.'

'Don't you have enough then?' For Tom, whose piggy bank was impressively weighted with coins, the concept was puzzling.

'I have heaps at the moment, but we might need some more later on.'

'I wish Daddy was here – and I'm not going to school,' Tom shouted, shaking Jane's hand off as she reached down to touch his head.

The rebuff hurt, pulling at the ever-present noose of guilt and injecting her eyes with tears. Quickly turning away so the children wouldn't see, Jane tore off a square of kitchen paper and dabbed carefully at her mascara. Having nonetheless succeeded in removing most of her eye-liner, she screwed the paper into a ball and hurled it despairingly in the direction of the kitchen bin. It did not matter to the children that Michael had, in many ways, been negligent as a father, that he had always been more readily responsive to the demands of his work than the needs of his family. Though Harriet was still too young to show obvious signs of stress at Michael's absence, Tom's increasing awkwardness sometimes made Jane long for the bad old days, with an intensity that scared her.

Tom was now staring at the cartoon figures on his empty plate, swinging his small legs back and forth underneath the chair, very fast.

'You have to go to school, Tom, and Daddy's taking you to Chessington Zoo next Sunday, remember? Just the two of you men together.'

'I'm not a man, silly – I'm a boy,' he shouted, jumping down from the chair, seizing Harriet's remaining piece of toast, and running into the hall.

As Harriet screamed, Tom began a jeering triumphal-dance in the doorway.

Jane was on the point of brokering peace when the phone rang. It was Mrs Browne from down the road, trumpeting coughs and apologies to say that she couldn't manage Harriet that morning after all and did Jane mind.

'Of course not,' Jane replied dully, the sound of poor Mrs Browne's catarrh-laced cough making an appeal impossible. 'Get better soon,' she added, saying what had to be said, while her heart plummeted at the prospect of a bad day getting worse.

The traffic in Guildford was not sympathetic to the predicament of a panic-stricken woman map-reading her way to her first inter-view in ten years, with a whiny toddler for company in the car-seat behind. Made reckless by desperation, Jane hurled biscuits and juice-boxes at Harriet and tried to keep her eyes off the flickering green figures on the dashboard's digital clock. The minutes advanced with disturbing rapidity, while the car got sucked round the mysterious ducts of a one-way system that seemed to bear little relation either to the map or to her intended destination.

By the time Jane – with Harriet in her pushchair – stepped into the lift of the high-rise rotunda that catered for the multifarious requirements of Grove Employment Agency, they were thirty minutes late. Harriet, on seeing the lift buttons, wanted to try and press each one. Frustration at being forbidden this small indul-gence induced a magnificent howling, followed by an unhappily conspicuous entrance into the hushed concentration of the open-plan offices of the fifth floor.

Cabinets and desks crouched amongst rubber plants and rippling blue walls like props in a surreal holiday commercial. Jane steered her weeping charge between them, ignoring the turning heads and trying – with less success – to block out the sense of the great divide she now faced: the Workers and the Home-Stayers. Those to be admired and those to be pitied. This is not life, she told herself, this is a bad day. She hummed a song about a rabbit into Harriet's ear and imagined recounting the details to Julia later on; how she would make her laugh.

Mr Jenkins, who sat at a desk with expansive views of a multi-storey car park, did little to alleviate Jane's sense that she had entered a war zone. Though Harriet's sobbing had quietened to barely audible sniffles, he peered at the two of them over the top of his metal-framed oval spectacles in a schoolmasterly manner that suggested the requirement of absolute silence.

Harriet found solace in a crumbling breadstick (the last in a pack stowed in the side pocket of Jane's handbag), while Mr Jenkins started asking questions and filling in boxes on forms with ticks and squiggles. But peace, like the breadstick, was predictably short-lived; once Harriet had grown tired of sprinkling crumbs on to the carpet, she turned her attention to the tasty array of items on Mr Jenkins' desk. Between fielding questions about her career ambitions and her decade of experience in publishing, Jane had to dissuade her daughter from eating two biros, a saucer of paper clips, a stapler and the apparently delicious curly flex of her interrogator's push-button desk telephone.

'You have arrangements for child care, I take it, Mrs Lytton?' he asked, without looking up from a particularly intricate squiggle.

'Absolutely,' Jane shot back; though in truth she still hadn't quite asked Mrs Browne about needing her for more hours – only hinted, to prepare the way, terrified that she might refuse. Harriet was very fussy about her friends.

'Recent experience?'

'As I said, Moretons Publishing...'

'Yes – I think we've covered that – but anything a little more recent?'

'No. Just the children. They're quite an experience.'

His smile was deeply polite. 'Yes, I'm sure.'

I'm quite clever, she wanted to say. I got a uni prize for my essay on parliamentary reform. I could have been quite the career woman; but things took me in other directions, as things do.

'There's not much, I'm afraid. The recession is hitting hard.'

'I thought there was a great demand for part-time women in the workplace. Isn't that what the statistics say, at least, I thought they did...?' Jane's courage dissolved at the realisation that he was bored with her.

'I don't know about statistics, Mrs Lytton. What I do know, is that a lot of people are looking for work – especially part-time – and it's very hard to fit you all in.'

He removed his glasses and began polishing the lenses with a tissue from a box on his desk. The skin around his eyes looked white and puffy and an angry red crevice was carved deep into the bridge of his nose. It made his face look so raw and unprotected suddenly, that Jane, on a surge of something like compassion, found herself looking away until he had finished.

'I'm afraid I have nothing for you in any of the areas in which you have expressed an interest – though in London you might be luckier, of course.' The spectacles were safely back in place. 'The only local possibility,' he thumbed expertly through a file, 'ah, here we are.' He blew on his hands and rubbed them together.

Jane watched him intently, full of hope and dread.

'Guildford General Hospital requires a couple of part-time clerical assistants, receptionists, that sort of thing. Not bad money either.'

She swallowed. 'Is that it? Is there nothing else?'

'Not unless you are prepared to consider full-time employment.'

'No. Not full-time. Not yet.' She hugged Harriet, who had curled into a sleepy ball on her lap.

'They're interviewing from tomorrow. Here are the details.' He pushed a sheaf of papers at her.

'Tomorrow?' Her tone was incredulous.

He let out his breath very slowly before speaking. 'The interviews will be conducted over several days. I could perhaps arrange for you to be seen early next week.'

'That would be better. Thanks so much.'

He extended one hand across his desk. 'We'll be in touch then.'

Jane reached round the sleeping Harriet with difficulty to a handshake that was limp and moist.

She rang Julia the moment she got home, only to be greeted

with the unsympathetic beep of her answering machine. 'I'm aiming for a career in filing,' she said into the silence that followed. 'History degrees and publishing experience were a definite no-no, but when I said I could tackle tea bags things really took off. Fingers crossed for the interview. Call me when you can.'

The only consolation came in the form of a card from Michael's father.

'*Come down with the children any time,*' said the loopy scrawl on the back of a picture of a vase of roses, '*open house here as always.*'

16

It was unfortunate for all concerned that Pippa and Tim chose to return from their trip a couple of days early without forewarning their house guest. When Tim, carried away on a swell of bravery induced by three pina coladas, had at long last broken the news of their impending bankruptcy, Pippa had insisted on going home. Instead of breaking down as he expected, a steeliness he had never known before seemed to take hold of her, a cold control that shut him out and was worse than anything. Though she assured him, many times, that she did not blame him, what he had always regarded as the feminine frailty in her, that inner essence that made her need his affection, seemed to vanish overnight, almost as if that too had been a luxury allowed by money.

'At least we don't have any children to worry about,' she said, shortly before they touched down at Heathrow, her face flat and grim, her hair pulled back into a tight, thin pony tail that imprisoned the wisps he loved.

Michael was in the shower when they arrived, which spared him the sight of their faces when first confronted with the grimy chaos that he had created and fed, like some cadaverous monster, during the five weeks they had been away. While he lathered his belly and armpits, humming and rubbing to a spirited rendition of 'My Way', Pippa was spinning through the downstairs rooms, emitting high-pitched gasps of horrified disbelief. Tim followed slowly behind, equally appalled, but his mind working along the more pragmatic lines of assessing damage and the possible effect on the already depressingly low likely sale price of the house.

Slightly moved by the heartfelt gusto of his own singing, Michael had embarked on a throaty repetition of the chorus and was just stepping from the shower onto the peach pile of the bath mat when Pippa appeared in the doorway. He broke off mid-note and dived for a towel; but Pippa, who stood closest to the heated rail and whose instincts were following a somewhat baser trail, immediately pulled all the towels to her, forcing him to stand cowering with his hands cupped over his groin.

'Please, Pippa,' Michael begged, now shivering visibly.

If Tim had not arrived on the scene, Pippa would have withheld the towels indefinitely. She loved her house more simply and more completely than she loved her own husband; years of tender work had gone into its decoration and maintenance. She had been longing to get back, to enjoy a few last, precious months of living there before they had to sell and move somewhere poky and cheap to start their lives again. What Michael had done was, in her eyes, nothing short of desecration. If there had been a knife to hand she might have stabbed him.

'For God's sake give the man a towel.' Tim wrenched one from her and threw it at Michael, who wrapped it hastily round his waist, feeling miserable and foolish.

'Hello, both of you... I'm so sorry – I wasn't expecting...'

Pippa turned on her heel and left without a word.

'Tim – I know it's a bit of a tip,' Michael went on, feeling much better now that it was just the two of them, 'but I'll clear it all up.'

'It's a fucking mess,' said Tim softly, 'and at some stage in the near future we've got to sell this place for every penny we can get. You've seen how Pippa is... she's so... Christ, Michael, what's got into you?'

Michael was struggling with his underpants; in his eagerness to get dressed he hadn't dried properly and the result was making everything hard to pull on.

'I'm truly sorry – I was going to have a grand tidy-up – I'll get cleaners in, hordes of them...'

'Talk about abusing a favour.' And with that Tim also spun out of the room to follow his wife.

When Michael came downstairs carrying his suitcases and a bundle of laundry ten minutes later, he found Pippa sitting motionless on a chair in the hall. She stared straight ahead, her lips pursed shut and her hands laced tightly together in her lap.

Tim was in the sitting room, stuffing debris into a large cardboard box. Michael hastened to help him.

'How many slobs were living here anyway?'

'Just the one.'

Tim stopped and looked hard at his friend.

'I'm guessing then, that it's still no-go between you and Jane?'

Michael nodded, keeping his head bent so that Tim could not see the tears of self-pity suddenly blurring the patterns of the carpet.

'It's only mess, after all,' said Tim more gently. 'I'll finish up here. Why don't you make a start on the kitchen? Then we'll call some cleaners or whatever.'

After the obvious things had been tidied up and Michael had reiterated his promise to foot the cost of professional cleaning, he left to stay in an over-priced London hotel near the office. Of all the nights he had spent in the two months since separating from Jane and leaving Cobham, this was by far the worst. Throughout the black, indulgent misery of it all, the mindless channel flicking and munching through mini-packs of over-salted peanuts, Michael knew – even as he endured it – that he had reached the lowest point, that he would never permit himself to feel so bad again. His feelings for his wife took a fresh turn that night, reaching a fever pitch of frustrated rage. Jane alone was responsible. She had done this to him, reduced him to a sleepless night on a rock hard bed in a stuffy hotel when he should, by rights, be tucked up in their soft king size, the dark outline of her body curved reassuringly beside him, there to touch if he wanted.

Anger did wonders for his resolve. After a late, hearty breakfast of solidified egg and cold toast in the hotel restaurant, he phoned his secretary to say he would be taking the day off. Drawing up the high-backed bedroom chair to the dressing table, as if it were a desk in an office, Michael proceeded to make a list, on a blank page at the back of his pocket diary:

Cheque and letter to Tim
Ask Des for room
Check house-price trends
Hair-cut
Julia

The list helped enormously, like a signpost for the way forward. Several times during the course of that day he patted his breast pocket, where he could feel the comfortable shape of the diary, slotted next to his wallet and fountain pen. There were things to be achieved after all; a way ahead.

Towards the end of the afternoon, with the first two items on his list already seen to, Michael went into his favourite barbers for the full works, including a quite unnecessary blow-dry of his thick, trimmed hair. Having tipped the hairdresser very generously, he walked briskly towards the tube station, whistling softly through the small gap in his teeth.

17

'Thank you for coming – Michael's told me everything,' said Ernest, as he kissed Jane's cheek, before she had time to feel awkward. 'Things will work themselves out. They always do, in the end. I'm making a stew for our supper, which I hope is all right, what with this horrible cold June weather.'

Jane's expressions of gratitude were drowned out by Tom, who, having done a little dance of delight to be out of the car, began pulling at his grandfather's hands and trousers, calling, 'How's my bunny? How's my bunny?'

'Fat as a cat and big as a house,' chuckled Ernest, sucking on the empty pipe he had popped between his lips, and feeling in his pocket for a grey hanky, which he dabbed at the drip on his nose.

'Come on. Grandad, let's see.'

Harriet, certain that she was being left out of something, but not entirely sure that whatever it was warranted the stressful business of abandoning her mother, buried her head in Jane's kneecaps, whimpering with indecision. Prehensile clinging was a new, distressing hobby of her toddling daughter's for which Jane – interpreting it as a sign that the separation had started to take its toll –

blamed herself. If one parent could leave, what was to stop the other following suit – unless she was held very tightly, all the time?

The hallway was chilly and Jane was grateful for the old black aga pulsing heat round the stone tiles of the kitchen. She set about boiling water for hot-water bottles, to air any dampness from the beds, humming quietly as she moved around, enjoying the familiar creaks of the floorboards and all the grunts and whispers of the old house. It felt safe – unthreatening and simple – to be in the country with the old man, the perfect way to spend the last three days of half-term. Guilt, for what she was putting the children through, beat inside her like a pulse. With Ernest, however, it eased. Somehow, the dear man knew how to let her be, keeping any judgements he might have to himself. He pottered along as he always did, absorbed in his routines, letting her and the children fit round him, happy to help if he thought he could, but never to interfere.

Upstairs, looking out of the window onto the back garden, she saw Tom and Ernest staggering under the weight of a hefty plank of wood, skirting round the brown, earthy humps of the molehills, which Ernest lamented but couldn't quite bring himself to destroy. It was typical of him to let Tom carry his full share, to know that stretching his grandson would make him far happier than fobbing him off for not being up to the job.

Jane sighed and smiled, hugging the hot-water bottles to her chest and rocking slightly, like she was a child herself, clutching a favourite toy. The fringe, which had been flopping further into her eyes all year, now tucked smoothly behind her ears, showing off the full, strong triangle of her face and her smooth pale complexion. Without any hair straggles to hide behind, her dark green eyes looked and felt somehow bigger and deeper, as if they were starting to see the world more clearly.

At the entrance to the big bedroom, she paused before stepping gingerly inside, half expecting to hear dim echoes of all the failed conversations of her marriage coming at her in waves from the dark corners of a room that had seen it all. But the creaky hush felt kind. A bunch of leafy stemmed yellow roses had been squashed unceremoniously into a tall glass vase on the dressing table, where they bathed in the balmy light of the afternoon sun. He was right, she thought, looking down fondly through the bedroom window at Ernest, now pushing both children in the swings that he had made for them, the one for Harriet with high sides – things might just work themselves out in the end. Michael, for all the bursts of anger when they spoke, certainly seemed to have entered a new phase of acceptance of the situation. He had been managing to see the children by driving down from time to time, usually at very short notice, to whisk them off to MacDonalds and the park. But there had been no question of having even Tom for a visit over half-term, because of work being mad and still settling into a couple of rooms let out by Des in a large south London house. It was a stop-gap, Michael said, and she was to be in no doubt that everything he was having to shell out for would be factored into their settlement – just as soon as the property market rallied enough for them to sell. And if she got it into her head to consult lawyers in the meantime, then she would be paying for them too.

Which was only fair, Jane told herself, suppressing a shudder of apprehension about the continuing uncertainty, but also thanking her lucky stars that the dire state of the economy was at least granting her a breathing space.

A couple of hours later, with the children asleep and the smell of Ernest's beef stew wafting up the stairs and into her bedroom, Jane slipped out of her clothes and into the soothing luxury of a deep, hot bath. Liberal amounts of red wine, garlic and onions had gone into the preparation of supper, she knew, having watched in admiration, as Ernest carefully peeled, chopped and tasted his creation with the expertise of one used to living alone. Thinking of her own now customary evening snacks of cheese and tinned soup, she had felt something like shame. Cooking was the perfect way to spoil yourself, the old man had remarked, if you had no one else to do it for you.

Sinking low in her bath, her chin resting on a frothy plateau of bubbles, Jane felt rather spoiled herself. She raised one leg, dripping and crested with foam, and eyed it critically, like an object apart. If she held it straight, the small silver stretch marks on her inner thigh barely showed. Raising her other leg out of the water, she pointed both sets of toes at the ceiling and did a few small scissor movements, crossing her ankles back and forth, until her stomach muscles burned with the strain. Letting both legs down with a splash, she held her nose and thrust herself backwards under the water until she was completely submerged, the back of her head resting on the hard bottom of the bath. She stayed like that for as long as she could, enjoying the tickling in her ears as the water filled them, feeling every quick thud of her heart, starving her lungs until they were ready to explode. She surfaced panting and happy, intensely alive.

Once the steam had cleared from the mirror, she attended to herself with much greater care than usual, meticulously combing out her wet hair and massaging moisturiser into her face with none of her usual dabbing aggression. I want to look after myself, she thought, feeling pleased at the idea, knowing that it meant progress of some kind, deep within her.

'Well, well,' said Ernest when she appeared in the kitchen, her cheeks glowing, her hair just dried and full of shine.

They drank beer together – a sweet, thick home-brew that slid, velvety-smooth, down her throat, making her dizzy and warm. While he stirred and sniffed at the casserole dish, Jane drained carrots and peeled the tin-foil off their baked potatoes. A comfortable silence settled between them, punctuated only by the rhythmic ticking of the kitchen clock and an occasional comment about the meal or the children. As they sat down to eat, Jane found herself marvelling at the strangeness of life – at how uncomfortable she had grown to feel in the company of a man she had known, intimately, for a third of her life, while his father, this old man whom she knew half as well, could fill her heart with such a sense of calm and well-being.

They had barely raised their first mouthfuls to their lips when there was a sharp knock at the front door.

'Ah, I think I know who that must be,' said Ernest, pushing back his chair and disappearing into the hall.

'Who?' Jane asked, but getting no reply.

Through the wall, she heard muffled greetings, followed by the front door slamming. Then Christopher came into the kitchen, matching her look of astonishment with his own. 'Sorry to intrude – Dad didn't say that you... it's my half-term...' He faltered, tugging at the hem of his jumper, which was grey and shapeless, and hung low over faded jeans and trainers so old that splits on both sides revealed bulges of purple sock.

'It's ours too. Nice to see you. There's loads of food,' Jane replied, speaking in a rush to cover her own awkwardness, wondering suddenly what he did – and didn't – know.

'Trust you to arrive just as a meal's being served,' growled Ernest happily, already at the aga and dishing up a plate of food, which he placed on the table with a glass and a knife and fork before returning to his seat. He flashed Jane a rare, broad grin as he sat down, showing off the full graveyard of his uneven yellow teeth. 'He said he'd probably come tomorrow. I meant to mention it. Here, get some of that down you, Chris – you look like you could do with it.' He pushed the jug of beer across the table.

'No thanks, Dad, not tonight.'

'Really?' Ernest shook his head, topping up his own glass and Jane's.

If he had heard about her and Michael, he would say, surely, Jane told herself, as she carved chunks of beef into unnecessarily small portions and took dainty sips of her beer. For whatever reason, Christopher certainly continued to appear ill-at-ease, shuffling in his chair and concentrating with equal intensity on his plate of food. The easy calm of the evening was rather shattered, she reflected ruefully, trying to think of something neutral with which to start a conversation. Only Ernest appeared undaunted, eating vigorously and pointing his fork at his younger son as he said, 'On the wagon again, are you?'

'No, Dad, nothing like that.' Christopher got up to fill his glass with water, 'I just over did it a bit recently, and am taking a break. Punishment.' He smiled properly for the first time. Unlike his father's, his teeth were pressed close together and unusually white. His lips were thin and his mouth wide, attractive when spread into a smile, but alarmingly severe when closed.

'Because he did have a bad patch with the stuff, didn't you, Chris – a while back now.'

'I am sorry,' Jane murmured, recalling the somewhat wild behaviour after Edie's funeral which, at one point, had included lavishly anointing the vicar's forehead with wine.

'I drank a lot, rather too often,' Christopher declared, sounding, if anything, more relaxed. 'Dad sorted me out, didn't you Dad?'

The two of them exchanged a look of mutual appreciation and fell silent. Sensing the bond between them – such a far cry from Michael's relationship with Ernest – Jane found herself wondering that she had never noticed the extent of this alliance before. It made her feel, not for the first time that evening, that her sensibilities had entered a new, heightened state – as if a layer of her own guardedness had dissolved.

'I was very mixed-up at one stage,' Christopher went on easily, 'with an awful lot of pointless things to prove to people who weren't even looking.' He paused to cast a glance at Ernest, who was chewing slowly and steering a last piece of meat through what remained of his gravy. 'I was shamefully unpleasant to my mother. And then she died and I did a guilt trip in classic style.'

'By drinking.'

'Among other things.'

Jane raised her eyebrows, but he said no more.

'He was a right pain in the arse, if you want to know, Jane.' Ernest patted Christopher's arm and then carefully placed his knife and fork together in the middle of his empty plate. 'Don't hurry, you two. I'm off for a smoke.'

And they were left, the flagon of dark beer between them and their plates still half full of food. The subject of Michael, his glaring absence, ballooned in the silence that followed.

'Michael and I—'

'I know. I heard. I am so very sorry.'

'I'd rather not talk about it.'

'No, of course. I understand.'

'Thanks.' Jane managed a stiff smile. She longed to push her plate away and escape into the sitting room. If only she had known that Christopher was coming – they could have arrived earlier or not arranged to stay for so long. She was tempted to ask when he planned to leave. Instead, she found herself saying, 'I had no idea you and your father were so close.'

He looked up, an expression of pleased surprise injecting some colour into his pale face.

'We understand each other, I suppose. We've got better at it as we've got older.'

Jane gave up on the last of her stew, which was rich and filling, and poured a little more beer into her glass. She offered the flagon to Christopher, who shook his head absently, too busy watching the way the kitchen light shone down on to her head, illuminating shadows of dark auburn and black amongst the rich brown.

'So...' Jane took a deep breath. 'How did you hear? Did Michael call you?'

Christopher slowly swung his head from side to side, using a mouthful of food as pretext for delay, wondering how much to tell her, wishing he could tell her everything. 'Julia,' he said at last, 'I saw her last weekend.'

'Julia?'

'I was up in London, staying with an old friend not far from her shop. I dropped by on a sort of whim.'

'That was nice... now I come to think of it, she mentioned that you had been in touch, a while back.' Jane spoke brightly, while an odd prickle at the back of her neck – a frisson of some emotion that she could not identify – made her disinclined to pursue the subject.

'How are you really, Jane?' he asked suddenly, before slapping his hand to his mouth. 'Oh god, I'm an oaf,' he groaned, 'Forgive me. Don't answer.'

'It's all right...' Jane hesitated, aware that the candour of the recent admissions about his own difficulties had generated a sort of trust. 'I don't know how I am,' she said carefully. 'I really don't. I feel as if I'm still waiting to find out.' She dropped her eyes to a brown blob of gravy to the right of her plate. It was small and pear shaped, like a perfect, muddy tear drop. 'It was the right thing – to split up – I'm sure of that – just. Michael and I – we didn't *work*, so I am not going to start allocating blame...' She gave a dry half-laugh. 'But there are so many other terrible things, what with the children and everything. Harriet is more or less okay but Tom is being pretty impossible – with me, anyway. And then there is the other guilt, of having failed at the fairy-tale ending – at not having managed to live happily ever after.' She paused to breathe. 'I did it for myself, you see – that's the hardest thing. It felt almost brave at the time but now I wonder if I haven't just been the most unforgivable coward. Michael and I really weren't good for each other, that's all I know.' She picked up the tin-foil from her baked potato and compressed it into a tight pellet, thinking how Julia, who meant well, interrupted all the time, while Christopher said nothing. 'The joke is that I miss him – but for all the wrong reasons.'

'What reasons?' he asked after a pause.

'Because being a single mother is grim. Because I get the spooks locking up the house late at night on my own. Because of worries about money – Michael is being really decent, but when we finally get to splitting everything, there is no doubt that life will be a lot tougher...' Jane bit her lip. 'Because Harriet once grabbed the legs of a man in the park saying Daddy. Because Tom is unremittingly horrible. Because I feel so guilty at what I've done to them all that I don't think I can ever be happy with the result. Which makes me wonder if I have been mad as well as cowardly.'

'It's hard to be sure of anything where feelings are concerned.' He had locked his fingers together and was squeezing the knuckles hard. 'What we want from other people is so complicated, so tied up with what we want from ourselves, what we want for ourselves.'

For a few moments neither of them spoke.

'Michael and I were skiing – in Innsbruck – when my parents died – but then you knew that.'

Christopher nodded.

'We flew back at once, only to find that Mattie had disappeared.'

Christopher did not flinch, though his heart lurched at the sound of Mattie's name. A week, and the shame and regret had, if anything, deepened. Keeping his face composed, his eyes burning, he willed Jane to go on. Inside, he could not help relishing this unexpected gift of finding her here, let alone this fragile intimacy of being cast in the role of confessor.

'Michael was incredible. He took over. Locating Mattie, the funeral – everything. It transformed him for me – from being a student boyfriend with grand ideas and too much impatience, he suddenly became a wonderful man who could save the situation and then keep me safe. In the midst of it all, I thought I had grown up too. By the time we found Mattie – squatting in some armpit of a place calling itself an artists' commune – I believed myself to be awash with common sense and authority. I, the big sister, would see her through. Getting married to Michael was so obvious after that. It was like the next step in coping – in showing that I had grown up and survived. Does that make any sense?'

He nodded again, smiling now. 'Most of us couldn't begin to be half so coherent about what we have done in our lives and why.'

'The worst thing,' Jane rushed on bleakly, 'when I think back to those times, is realising that losing Mum and Dad was what brought Michael and me so close. It's as if grief can somehow magnify everything, make all other emotions seem bigger, disproportionately so. Did you find that, with your Mum, I mean?'

'I was too busy running away to notice such niceties.' Christopher shot her another, broader smile, wanting – somehow – to cheer her up.

'Have you ever been in love, Christopher?' she asked suddenly.

'Oh, my word, yes,' he laughed, enjoying the unexpectedness of the question. 'I was mad about an actress once, during my artist-in-a-garret phase in Paris.' He put his hands behind his head, tipping his chair back onto its two rear legs. 'I was rather stubborn about it, as one is about these things. It took a visiting professor from Milan to bring me to my senses.'

'Oh? Because you fell for her instead?'

'Ha – no.' He hooted with laughter, letting the chair drop back into place. 'That would perhaps have been preferable. No, the prof was a *he* who so lost track of time making love to my actress one afternoon, that they were still at it when I got back.'

Jane put her hand to her mouth, trying to feel horrified, but laughing because Christopher was.

'Well, it certainly brought me to my senses…' he chuckled, 'the sight of all that heaving flesh in my bed.'

'Oh dear. I'm so sorry.'

'Really, there is no need to be,' Christopher assured her quickly, his spirits plummeting as images of a much more recent bed – of Mattie – started whirling round his head.

'What is all this?' boomed Ernest, startling them both as he appeared in the doorway. He scowled, waggling his wild eyebrows in mock admonition. 'Haven't you even put the coffee on yet, you pair of useless so-and-sos?'

18

It was with the best intentions that Julia accepted Michael's invitation for a drink. He wanted to talk about Jane, he said, sounding unremittingly forlorn, and conjuring up poignant images of a man in mourning, needing to recapture some essence of the person he had lost. Curiosity, too, played a part in Julia's compliance, as did a tenuous, mushy hope that she might even act as an agent of reconciliation and bring everybody to their senses. Jane had been sounding so hopelessly forlorn herself that Julia sometimes found herself thinking that the separation had been ill-advised in every aspect. Being such a resolutely independent soul, she found it hard to dish out heavy doses of sympathy for anyone who had made such a drastic bid for freedom – even Jane – only to show so many signs of not coping with it.

Michael's own motives were more blurred. It felt daring to contact Julia, and he liked that. But he was also troubled by pestering clouds of non-comprehension; discovering a logical reason for the breakdown of his marriage would make it more tolerable. He was clinging therefore, to the pragmatic belief that it was just a question of seeking answers in the right places. His wife's closest friend was an obvious, and most attractive, starting-point.

As their date approached, Julia had found herself irritatingly preoccupied by it. It felt odd to be meeting Michael – odd enough for her not to mention it to Jane and for her to spend some considerable time determining what to wear. Without being sure of her exact role in the proceedings, it was hard to settle on the appropriate clothes. Everything looked either too dressy or too sombre. With half the contents of her wardrobe strewn across her bed and floor, she angrily pulled on her dressing-gown and padded through to her kitchen with the intention of fixing herself a drink and calling Jane. If she told her, she would feel better, she was sure. But though the drink was poured – a dissatisfying weak gin without lemon and barely a bubble to the tonic – the phone-call was never made. She lay on her bed instead, flattening a heap of rejected outfits and mulling over the irony that her first 'date' in weeks was to be with the almost ex-husband of her best friend. Her commitment to the dating agency had faded fast after her rendezvous with the yawningly dull Alan Lambert and a couple more like him, who – with an almost endearing lack of awareness as to their own boringness – had undertaken the business of starting a relationship with all the delicacy of heat-seeking missiles. Romantic dinners, phone calls, theatre outings, holidays, sex – they had wanted it all from the get-go, long before any mutual knowledge or affection had been established to warrant such things. Feeling disappointed, but resigned, Julia had fallen back on the rigorous demands of book-keeping and French polishing, interspersed by the occasional outing to avant-garde films with her old friend, Toby, who was often in the throes of existential angst or heartache himself, and always terribly kind.

'It was good of you to come,' said Michael, swinging open the door of the two-room bed-sit he was renting from Des, and kissing her swiftly on the cheek. It always took him a moment to register quite how tall Julia was – her head level with his even in her velvet pumps. Jane, he couldn't help thinking, would have barely reached his chest in such flat shoes.

'Not at all,' Julia replied, surreptitiously scanning his face for signs of strain and noting that, though a little thinner, he appeared impressively composed.

The bed-sit was spacious, and well-situated in one of the residential streets off Clapham High Road, but lacking in furniture and warmth. As Michael led her into the mustard-walled living room she effused about its potential to hide her dismay, thinking what a far cry it was from the bright, cosy squash of Cobham, with all its heaving bookshelves and rampant pot plants.

'Jane's keeping the furniture and everything else for now,' he said, as if reading her thoughts. 'I'm not bothered, quite honestly. I've got an eye out for a nicer short let, if I can find one at a reasonable price. All of it is a holding operation, until we sell. And frankly, there's a sort of freedom to the whole business – a beginning again feeling which isn't too bad.'

'You're being brave,' Julia scolded, feeling suddenly very sorry for him.

'Oh, I'm not saying it's been easy – far from it. Staying at the Crofts' place was pretty hellish... not that I wasn't extremely grateful,' Michael added hastily, detecting her pity and wanting to scotch it. Though part of his motive for the evening had been the appeal of evoking Julia's sympathy – of winning her as an ally – other instincts were now also kicking in, including the desire to show strength and resilience to impress her. 'They're in the midst of their own troubles, the Crofts, as you may have heard.'

'No, I haven't. What troubles?'

'Tim has gone out of business. They're having to sell everything.

He's talking of moving to Cornwall – some place near Helston – and running a camp-site, of all things.'

'Oh dear, though that might be fun, I suppose – leaving the rat-race – and maybe if you like the great outdoors...' Julia faltered, as the limitations in her own life, which had been looking pretty dispiriting in recent weeks, seemed to gleam with potential, given all the disarray around her. 'But how very difficult for them – I am so sorry.'

'We should all appreciate what we have while we have it, I suppose,' said Michael brightly, 'so please do take a pew while I fetch us a glass of wine.' He gestured at two shiny brown velour armchairs, whose single redeeming feature seemed to be that they blended well with the muddy decor. Julia, who had an almost physical need to surround herself with beautiful objects, perched on the very edge of the seat of the nearest one, feeling out of place and increasingly out of her depth.

'Red or white?' Michael asked, elaborating the question with a theatrical flourish of two bottles.

'White would be nice... though I am not entirely sure what you hoped to achieve by asking me here, Michael,' she added quickly.

'Neither am I.' He threw her an anxious grin. 'Perhaps to get a woman's perspective? Cheers anyway.' He poured white for himself too, and chinked his glass against hers. 'I thought we could go round the corner for a bite.'

Though Julia had never entertained the idea that the evening might continue long enough to involve food, the prospect of escaping the oppressive tawdriness of the flat was instantly appealing. 'Okay, why not.' She took an unseemly swig of wine. 'Jane is really cut up too, so you know,' she began, wanting to launch into the only subject that mattered, 'and also pretty close to getting herself a job—'

'Is she now? Good for Jane.'

On hearing the snarl in his voice and seeing the sudden flush of anger across his face, Julia felt her flutter of an idea about brokering a reconciliation recede. 'Just say whatever you want, Michael,' she blurted, gripping her wine-glass hard, 'get it off your chest, ask questions, moan. Do whatever you want.'

He studied the texture of his trousers for a few seconds, flicking at an imaginary speck of fluff. 'What I want, principally, is to *understand*.'

'Oh, is that all?' Julia smiled, vaguely flattered that he should believe she could help with such a thing, but also grappling with the sudden, strong certainty that it would not be wise to let the conversation get too heavy. 'Well, I wouldn't mind a morsel or two of understanding myself. It's pea soup for me, I can assure you, uninitiated as I am into the mysteries of co-habitation, let alone marriage.'

'But you two talked,' Michael said helplessly, having only a dim notion of apparently effortless female intimacy, a notion which had always left him feeling profoundly threatened.

'Oh yes, we're great talkers, Jane and I – usually about nonsense on the telly, or things that make us laugh. I'm afraid we've never been ones for rip-roaring discussions on the inside leg measurements or earth-shattering secrets of the men in our lives.'

Michael said nothing, not quite believing her, sensing only the loyalty that had always made him feel shut out.

'I think Jane has changed a lot in the last ten years,' Julia blustered, feeling compelled by his downcast silence to attempt an explanation – albeit for something she barely understood herself. 'Perhaps more than you have. Those changes added distance between the two of you – a distance that Jane could no longer manage.' She stood up, looking at her watch, wanting to nudge the evening onward. 'Though I can also see that in some ways she has been what some might regard as a little reckless...'

'Reckless?' Michael leapt on the word, sounding hopeful.

'Oh,' Julia continued quickly, eager to quash the hopeful tone and to get them out of the flat, 'only in the sense that she did have many things that people long for – kids, a relationship, a home – and so from the outside, to give that up... but then that shows how much she felt she *needed* to do it,' she stumbled on, cursing her useless big mouth. 'Jane has never lacked courage,' she concluded firmly, and with a fondness that was wasted on Michael, still busy absorbing her earlier comments with a degree of relief and self-justification that, had Julia perceived the extent of it, would have alarmed her greatly.

Indeed, so successfully had Julia unwittingly defused his sense of failure and awkwardness, that later on, in the restaurant, he felt bold enough to lob out a very personal enquiry about why she wasn't married herself. Since Michael had always assumed that such decisions were made on the basis of opportunity, not personal choice, it had long puzzled him. Julia was so good-looking. Just making their way to the table everybody had turned to stare, even the women.

'Sometimes it is a great burden to me,' Julia replied in her candid way, unfazed, 'as I think it is for many women in their mid-thirties – which is grossly unfair. We should all be able to live the lives we choose, in the way that we choose...'

Michael studied her as she talked, deciding that she possessed something like indifference to the impression she made on other people, which only succeeded in spicing up her attractions.

'Actually, I wouldn't mind a partner,' Julia went on blithely, 'but seem to be marvellously efficient at attracting the most unsuitable characters. After a while, both parties – including myself – feel misunderstood and hurt, and withdrawal takes place under a hail of self-inflicted fire. It's all very tiring.'

'My goodness,' Michael muttered, unused to Julia's hyperbolic style of self-mockery, 'that sounds sort of... tragic.'

'Oh lord, then it's time I went home. I am the opposite of tragic, but I do talk too much. I need to be told to shut up occasionally.' Julia pushed the plate of salad niçoise she had chosen to one side, aware that she had been in danger of enjoying herself and feeling guilty. 'I thought we were here to talk about the situation between you and Jane. I wish I could be more helpful.'

'But you haven't finished your food,' Michael pointed out, 'and it has been so good to spend time with someone on the other side of the fence, so to speak. Work has been fairly hellish,' he said in a dejected tone aimed at eliciting sympathy and getting them back on the track he had been enjoying.

'I've had enough to eat,' said Julia firmly. 'But tell me this, would you want to get back with Jane?'

Michael thought of Tom and shrugged. 'Maybe.'

Julia, imagining it was Jane who had crossed his mind, reached across the table and gave a quick pat to the top of his hand, before catching the eye of their waiter to signal for the bill.

Michael looked at his hand – the spot where she had touched him – with a welling-up of surprised gratitude. In truth, any remaining tenderness towards Jane herself now constituted only the finest thread in the tangled web of his mind, charged as it mostly still was with anger and hurt pride. Indeed, as the evening had progressed, any desire to understand the failure of his marriage had grown less and less urgent. Instead, conversing with Julia had left him feeling more alert and engaged than he had in months – almost like his old self.

'I'd like very much to do this again,' he ventured, after having won a fight to pay the bill. 'I can't tell you what a help it's been.'

'Really?' Julia countered coldly, 'I'm not sure how or why.' While the evening had been rather more pleasant than she had expected, she felt all the inappropriateness of repeating it. They should have spent more time talking about Jane, or the logistics of divorce. Aware that he was trying to catch her eye, she made sure to avoid it, leading the way out into the street. 'Perhaps you just need to start going out a bit more,' she suggested briskly, preparing to turn in the opposite direction to his flat, no matter that it was the wrong one; 'get used to being a single man again.'

'You could help me feel that way,' Michael quipped. 'I mean, perhaps we could help each other...' He took a step towards her, enjoying the quickening of excitement in the pit of his stomach.

Julia held up her palm, like a policewoman stopping traffic, and glared at him. 'I have helped all I can,' she said tightly. 'I apologise if agreeing to this encounter has misled you in any way. I really did believe that you wanted help – over Jane, and coming to terms with—'

'But I did – I do – that's exactly what I mean.'

Julia eyed him steadily, her blue eyes fearless and distrustful. 'It had better be, Michael.' There was a trace of regret as well as a warning in her voice. What a fool she had been to come. What an even greater fool to speak so freely about herself, to be borne along by the misplaced confidentiality that their meeting had enabled.

As he watched her stride off down the street, Michael felt a surge of something like triumph. She had enjoyed herself, he was sure of that; never mind what she had said at the end, when he pushed things a little too hard. He would leave it for a while, he decided, then call her again.

19

Nosing deeper into the soft down of the pillow, Jane stretched her legs luxuriously, seeking the cooler, untrammelled regions of the wide bed. Her mind drifted back towards the outposts of sleep, dimly alert for waking-up noises from the children across the landing. But all was quiet.

After a few minutes of trying, unsuccessfully, to return to a dream that had left her mysteriously content, she threw back the sheets and padded over to the window seat. Her head throbbed slightly in protest at being brought upright, reminding her of Ernest's beer and the rather astonishing frankness she had shown in conversation with Christopher the night before. An uncomfortable shyness now stole over her at the prospect of seeing him again. He had said something about going off for the day. She half hoped he had made an early start.

Lifting one weighted corner of the old pink bedroom curtains, she caught sight of Ernest in the garden below, putting the finishing touches to a new extension on the climbing frame. He wore a checked tweed cap, which he kept tweaking at his handiwork, as if doing little salutes to the bits he liked. His lips were pursed together, a whistling position to do with concentrating that reminded her of Michael.

The sun was high in the sky, coyly dodging behind cotton-fluff clouds of the kind that Tom now liked to draw, wedged between squadrons of battle-planes and clusters of stars. Thinking of her eldest, and realising that all was far too quiet, she dropped the curtain and hurried out onto the landing. The door to the children's bedroom was wide open, displaying an empty cot and Tom's train pyjamas lying in a heap beside the potty. Harriet's rag doll, wedged between the wooden slats of the cot, surveyed the scene with unblinking button eyes.

They were in the sitting room, wearing a startling cocktail of clothes, but well covered and certainly happy. Christopher had a mauve tea cosy on his head and was brandishing a wooden spoon. Tom wore a dented Panama, pulled well over his eyes, while Harriet was curled, tortoise-like, under an old wide-brimmed straw hat of Edie's.

'We're playing a hat game,' remarked Tom by way of an explanation.

Christopher touched the tea cosy with a self-conscious grin and shrugged helplessly. 'I'm just following orders.'

'I'd no idea it was so late.' Jane pushed her hair back from her face, still trying to focus her thoughts. 'I've left my watch somewhere.'

'We thought we'd give you the morning off. I hope you don't mind.' She looked so sleepy and surprised, standing there in an old dressing-gown of his mother's, the stitching loose at the collar and one pocket ripped at the seam, that Christopher quickly turned his head to hide his enjoyment of the sight.

'Mind?' Jane cried. 'How could I mind being given my first lie-in in six years? I just hope they haven't been a bother.'

Harriet, recognising her mother's voice, wriggled out from under the hat to wave, before burrowing back again.

'Harriet wants to be a whale,' complained Tom.

'Can't whales wear hats?'

He rolled his eyes in despair.

'I took up a cup of tea,' Christopher said, 'but then didn't have the heart to wake you.' He gave a playful tweak to Tom's hat.

'Oh.' Jane was momentarily nonplussed. 'Have they eaten any breakfast?'

'Bowlfuls.'

'Gosh. Thank you.'

'We've had a good time, haven't we, Thomas Lytton?'

'Uncle Chris is cool,' conceded his nephew.

'High praise indeed.' Jane smiled, aware suddenly of her state of undress, and pulling the old dressing gown more tightly about her. 'But now it is time to come upstairs. Your poor uncle needs some peace. He's got other things to do today besides entertain you two.'

Christopher removed the tea cosy, momentarily looking as crestfallen as the children. 'Actually, I was going to visit a church. Perhaps you would all like to come too? It's for some research I'm—'

'That's very kind, but I don't think so – thanks all the same.' He was taking pity on her, Jane realised, and it was hateful.

'But the Normans built it,' Tom shouted, jumping to his feet. 'They threw the bell in the river and it's got real skeletons inside.'

'Skeltings,' echoed his sister, having crawled clear of the hat and begun trying to pull out some of the looser threads of straw poking out of its brim.

Christopher looked sheepish.

'Oh.' Jane, feeling ambushed, tried to slip her hands into the dressing gown pockets, only to find air, like feet missing a step. 'Well in that case... I mean, given the skeletons... I suppose we'd better see it,' she murmured, shooting Christopher a reluctant smile, 'but only if you two are upstairs on the count of five...'

Half an hour later, after Jane had managed some breakfast for herself, they set off in Christopher's car. Ernest had resisted several invitations to accompany them on the grounds that a lot still needed doing in the garden, including painting his handiwork. The car was a big old tank of thing, with wide leather seats and no belts in the back. The children, rolling from side to side like pillion riders, thought it heavenly. Jane, sitting in the front, sank low inside her coat, steeling herself to remain cool and strong, still inwardly lamenting the unguardedness of having invited this man – of all men – to trample round the mess of her life with doses of unwanted compassion.

Christopher spoke little during the drive, instead devoting a dangerous proportion of his attention and energy to a slim cassette player, which was slotted into the side pocket of his door. Watching him eject a tape and then hunt for another – mostly in the area round his feet – Jane was on the brink of a snide remark about valuing the lives of her children, when a glorious, mellow trumpeting sound began filling the car, floating out of two small black speakers she hadn't noticed under each of their seats. Christopher relaxed visibly at once, his shoulders dropping and his head moving slightly – as if the music was moving through him in waves, Jane observed, a little fascinated.

'It's Handel,' he sighed, keeping his gaze on the road, 'simple, but heart-grabbing. I love it. But do say if you don't, and I'll find something else.'

'No, it's fine... very nice,' Jane murmured, soothed by the music in spite of herself, as well as grateful for how it removed any pressure to converse.

Aided by the fact that the children were in an advanced state of uncle-adulation, the outing proceeded with astonishing smoothness, taking Jane's reservations with it. It was a history lesson of sorts, after all, she told herself, and from someone who knew a lot about holding the attention of children.

It was a wonder for her too, however, to step inside the big-stoned, square-towered church some twenty minutes later, where even the air felt old and not one of them – not even the children, felt able to talk above a whisper. On being shown the promised box of bones – relics of a saint that were kept in a cabinet by the pulpit – Tom emitted an awestruck gasp, beckoning to his little sister, who until then had been practicing her toddling walk up and down the central aisle, to come and share the thrill.

'What did you say your research was for?' Jane asked, once they were back outside and following the path through the graveyard, which Christopher promised was the exact the route along which the bell had been carried on its doomed journey from tower to river.

'A book.'

'Yes...' Jane rolled her eyes. 'My limited intelligence had staggered that far all by itself.'

'Sorry. It's just that – well, it's a different kind of book.' He stooped to pick up Harriet, who was dawdling, and placed her on his shoulders. She clung tightly to clumps of his hair and to his ears, but he didn't seem to mind. 'I'm trying to write a novel – much to the disgust of my agent – and I've discovered that I can't do it without fixing real places in my mind. Even if I barely describe them, I find that I have to be able to see the background properly in my head in order for any coherent thoughts to emerge. It's a tiresome business really – I expect I shall give up long before the end.'

Jane wanted to ask more, but they had reached the riverside and Tom was performing some alarming acrobatics near the edge, as if bent on diving in to retrieve the legendary chimer himself. To divert him, Christopher told them all the full story of the bell – how its watery end had been brought about by villagers believing it brought bad luck – before suggesting they drive on to the beach and have fish and chips for lunch before returning home.

The tide was quite high and they sat a few yards from the waves to eat their picnic, the pebbles bruising their bottoms and an unseasonably brisk wind cutting up under their legs and coats. The children ate only chips, not liking the fish, after which Harriet began to nestle against Jane, blinking sleepily, while Tom's wiry six-year-old frame remained in perpetual motion, venturing nearer and nearer the water. Christopher laughed aloud when Jane finally gave in and suggested a mother-son paddle in the sea. He remained sitting, with Harriet on his lap under the lee of his wide black coat, continuing to laugh as Jane hopped and tugged – with obvious reluctance – to help Tom off with his socks and shoes and to remove hers.

'You're frowning and the wind might change,' he called, 'then where will we be.'

'Shut up,' she retorted, throwing a shoe at him, which he caught and promptly lobbed back again. 'You are getting off very lightly, so I should keep quiet if I were you.'

'But I'm looking after Harriet,' he cried, feigning affront, 'someone's got to.'

Jane set off towards the water, stepping gingerly and with difficulty between the sharpest looking stones, cringing at the cold squidge of sand between her toes. Tom was already ahead, prancing in the froth of the breaking waves, looking tiny beside the heaving grey sea.

'We shall have to come back on a much warmer summer day, Tom, with our swimming things,' she shouted, beginning to enjoy herself, as the stones became sand and her feet numbed.

They returned some fifteen minutes later, fairly soaked but triumphant, cheeks burning, their hair wild. As soon as they were in the car and back on the road however, Jane found herself breathing deeply from nausea rather than exhilaration. After an unseemly panic to wind down the window, Christopher pulled over in a layby so that she could finish vomiting into a bush rather than down the inside door of his car.

The children sat, curious and subdued, watching the ever-unfolding mystery of adult behaviour through the car windows. Christopher, after a moment's hesitation, got out of the car too.

Feeling a steadying arm across her shoulders, Jane was too wretched to shake it off or to bother with embarrassment. The retching turned into a kind of sobbing, as it often did with her. She found a clean large blue hanky being put into her hands, with which she wiped her face, and then finished her crying into his shoulder.

'Was it the fish or the company?' he murmured.

'Definitely the company – or perhaps just the company's car,' Jane muttered, shuddering as another urge to retch ebbed and died. 'Where did you get such a tank anyway?'

'An auction. I'm very fond of it. In fact, I'd much prefer you to blame me than my vehicle.'

She pulled herself free, still dabbing at her face with the blue hanky. 'I am so sorry, Christopher. I'll wash all offended items, of course – including your beloved car.'

'No need – I can easily do that. There's no harm done. Are you sure you're all right?' Christopher asked urgently. Her composure felt like a door shutting him out; hard to take when the impression of her was still tingling in his arms, the warmth and shape, so long imagined.

'Oh yes, fine now. Better out than in, as they say. And sorry again – sisters-in-law shouldn't be so much trouble.'

'Or ex-sisters in law,' he ventured, as they got back into the car, but she didn't smile.

Despite claiming to be fully recovered after taking a shower and some paracetamol, Jane declined supper and took herself upstairs shortly after the children. Christopher knocked quietly a couple of hours later, expecting her to be asleep, but she opened the door herself – attired once more in his mother's tatty dressing gown – and nodded meekly at the idea of soup.

'I hate being ill,' she admitted gloomily, when he returned a little later and placed a tray of tomato soup, bread and a glass of water across her knees.

'Yes, that much is clear.' There was a pout to her upper lip, he noticed, a very small one, that moved as she spoke and disappeared every time she smiled.

'Are you happy, Christopher?' she asked suddenly, when he was at the door.

He turned slowly. 'What a question. I think I prefer you languishing in humble gratitude at my accomplished nursing skills.'

'But, being a teacher – do you like it?' she persisted.

He put his hands in his jean pockets and leant against the wardrobe at the end of the bed. 'Ah, that's easier. Yes, I like being a teacher very much. Though, when I started it was a part of that running-away I mentioned – failed academic flees in terror.' He shook his head ruefully. 'I couldn't take the pressure of trying to get into print all the time – having to scrape out an unexplored area to claim as one's own – it dried me up completely. For years I barely wrote a thing. But the moment I moved into the school the writing came easily.'

'I am afraid I've never read your book on Clough.'

'I'm relieved to hear it. Unreadable stuff – specially designed for verbose undergraduates and mediocre tutors. It would probably put you off poetry for life.'

'I don't believe you for a minute. I will read it one day. Though I should probably read some Clough first.'

'That might help,' he conceded with a chuckle.

She sipped at a spoonful of the soup and scowled, wrinkling up her nose.

'That bad, is it?'

'Just hot,' she rasped, fanning her mouth.

He suspected that she wanted him to go, but couldn't quite bring himself to move. 'What about you then – seeing as we're on impossible questions – what makes you happy, Jane?'

She studied her spoon. 'Once upon a time I thought I knew, but now...'

'And what did you once think it was?'

'Love,' she said simply.

'Oh, dear me, is that wrong then?' He feigned panic, but she didn't smile.

'It's just too complicated for happiness. Even loving the children is fraught with danger. Like Tom terrifying me by that river today – loving brings this terrible fear of losing. It's a kind of suffering.'

'But isn't that just the point?' He pushed off from the wardrobe and thrust his hands deeper into his pockets. 'There has to be a price. Without the suffering there's no value.'

She sighed and took another sip of soup. 'I suppose so. But it's full of trickery too.'

'That's half the fun—'

'Realising I didn't love Michael wasn't fun,' she countered quietly.

'No, no, of course not. Sorry, I never meant to make light of that. Forgive me.'

After leaving the room, closing the door softly behind him, Christopher remained outside for several long seconds, gripped by an almost palpable urge to rush back in and tell her what had happened in London. Not saying anything felt as bad as lying. But in the end, rational argument got the better of him. Mattie would probably never mention the incident anyway. She knew, as well as he, that it had all been a mistake – two drunken adults, copulating because they were sad. The only lasting relevance of what had occurred was that, had he known of Jane and Michael's separation, it would never have happened. And how was he ever going to explain that, Christopher mused bitterly, without saying a lot of other things that would – he had no doubt – make his sister-in-law either laugh in his face or run for the hills? At least the way things were, he could occupy the same space as her, sometimes, when serendipity allowed.

20

The following day, Christopher was lying on his belly inspecting the entrance to a rabbit burrow with Tom when the house phone rang. The tone was only faint, but he looked up nonetheless, a pin-prick of foreboding in his heart. Harriet was close by, being pushed by Ernest in the box-swing. She had kicked off her pink wellingtons into a patch of stinging nettles by the garden fence and was flapping her little legs in celebration of the achievement.

Jane, feeling much better, was sitting at the kitchen table dissecting a cauliflower and therefore nearest the phone. One tiny green caterpillar had already wriggled indignantly on to the chopping board and she was undertaking a thorough search for its mate. The cauliflower, which had clearly been resident in the house for quite some time, had been presented to her by Ernest on finding her rummaging in the freezer for something she could turn into a hot lunch for the children.

'Cauliflower cheese?' he humphed, 'there's plenty of cheddar in the butter-dish.'

Cheese in the butter dish. Of course. Where else would cheese be? Remembering the conversation, Jane smiled to herself as she reached for the receiver – at full stretch since the phone, for some unidentifiable reason, lived on top of the fridge, behind a stack of Edie's cookery books.

Mattie's voice, nasal and whiny with a heavy cold, came on line. She sounded very poorly and appeared, in some measure, to hold her elder sister responsible.

'It's taken bloody days to run you to ground,' she sniffed, omitting to mention that, in fact, one call to Julia had easily solved the mystery. 'I thought you were supposed to be job hunting.'

'What's up, Mattie?' Jane leant up against the side of the fridge and stared out into the garden as she talked. Christopher glanced in the direction of the house, but was quickly tugged back down to the ground by Tom. She wondered what they were doing, beyond the understandable pleasure of rolling amongst Ernest's beloved mole hills.

'Oh, nothing's up – nothing at all.' There was a loud, snorting sound, as Mattie made a big show of blowing her nose, followed by an uninviting silence. 'How are you then?' she asked at length, so grudgingly that Jane couldn't resist saying that she had thrown up the day before, but was now feeling fine – surprisingly happy in fact.

'Oh, well, I don't want to drag you down or anything—'

'Come on, now, Mattie.' Jane turned to face the gleaming blankness of the fridge in an effort to wrest her mind from the dreamy, unfocused state induced by watching the intriguing activities going on outside. Tom and Christopher had started beating at a thatch of towering stinging nettles with long sticks, like knights charging at the lists. 'Talk to me properly. I can tell something is wrong, so please, let it out.' She rested her forehead against the cool metal. Her voice, so soothing and kind, worked on her younger sister as it always did, in the end.

'I'm a mess,' sobbed Mattie at last, 'I hate myself.'

'I'll be back in Cobham soon – come and see me next weekend. Stay the night and we'll have a proper talk. Michael's probably taking the children out for the day on Sunday and Julia's coming over – but not until lunch time.'

'No – I mean, I can't wait – I need to talk now.'

This was dramatic, even for Mattie. Jane felt the palms of her hands go clammy. Maybe something had happened. And a terrible fear, based on the ineradicable insecurity of having once before had the worst news imaginable down a phone line, an international one, to a ski resort in Austria, seized her somewhere about the neck and throat.

'Whatever is it, Mattie? What has happened?'

'Don't sound so panicky, for God's sake. I just need to talk to you about something – I can't tell you on the phone – I just can't... could I come down there?'

'I'd have to ask Ernest...' Jane faltered, her alarm being replaced by a flicker of resistance at the notion of Mattie disturbing the peace of her weekend in Kent.

'Ask away,' boomed Ernest, coming in from the hall with Harriet in his arms, her socks caked in mud and her boots jammed on to her hands like fluorescent boxing-gloves.

'Hang on a minute,' Jane covered the receiver with her palm. 'It's my sister – Mattie – something has upset her – she wondered if she might come here—'

'Arrange anything you want, love,' said Ernest easily, more intent on rubbing some warmth into Harriet's toes. He pulled off her socks and blew noisy raspberries into the soles of her feet, before rubbing them briskly between his bear-like hands.

'Ernest says that's fine – if it really can't wait until I get back.'

But Mattie was already enthusing, uncharacteristically, about fresh country air and the delights of rural life. 'It'll take me a couple of hours to get sorted up here... has Ernest got a washing machine?

I'm right out of everything but laddered tights – I might bring a load or two – thanks so much, Jane – I'll call from the station.'

When Jane told Christopher of the imminent arrival of her sister, he nodded quickly, as if he had been expecting it, and then went noticeably quiet. With the strong sense that she was somehow responsible for ruining something, yet unsure exactly what, Jane found herself apologising. 'I'm sorry – but she did sound a little desperate – I really felt I couldn't say no.'

Christopher smiled, nodding. 'Of course, you couldn't. You're close, you two, as siblings are supposed to be.' He spread an old newspaper on one end of the table and began easing small clods of mud out of the ridged soles of his boots with a long, pointed knife.

So, he doesn't like Mattie, thought Jane, aware of a small reflex of protection on her sister's behalf.

'Did she say what the matter was?'

'No, but I think I know.'

'Really?' He stopped, knife in hand.

'Oh, it will be man trouble, I expect,' Jane said breezily, unaware of Christopher's racing heart. 'And her painting. And her hateful job, playing errand girl for a stingy, ungrateful group of architects – every so often all of it blows up in her mind, bringing misery because of not yet being where she wants to be in life, and I have to remind her that most of us are miles off being where we want to be, and that feeling muddled and overwhelmed is pretty normal.'

'Does she always tell you everything then?'

'Everything,' Jane replied, with some pride, brushing aside the thought of the little pills in Mattie's handbag. 'I might just hand this back to you,' she teased, picking out a mud pellet which he had inadvertently pinged with his knife into one of the yellowy heads of cauliflower on her chopping board. 'Mind you, with all the invertebrates to chomp on, the children probably won't notice the odd crunch of dirt.' She gave the cauliflower head a vigorous shake.

'Ernest is determined we should eat this thing, but it's proving something of a caterpillar metropolis. They're green but quite sweet-looking – no hairs or goggly eyes. I've spotted three so far, but they're good at wiggling out of reach...'

'I suppose sisters are always going to be good at confiding in each other,' Christopher said, putting the boots down.

'But we're not,' Jane protested, laughing. 'Mattie has always loved to talk about herself – to splurge out all the gory details – but I'm not like that – not usually anyway.' She shot him a quick smile, thinking of all the things she had told him without quite meaning to.

'Me too,' he murmured, busy now folding up the newspaper that had received the boot mud and squashing it deep into the bottom of the bin.

Jane turned her attentions to grating cheese for the white sauce, aware that something in him had closed down and deciding to ignore it. He hovered in the doorway for a few moments while she got on with her task, trying to brush the hair back behind her ears with her wrists, only for it to fall forward over her face again.

'I think I'd better be getting back.'

'Right now?'

'I'm afraid so.' He ran one hand back across the top of his head and looked away. 'I've loads to be getting on with, what with the book and so on.'

'Of course.' She smiled, to hide her surprise.

'I shouldn't really have come at all,' he muttered, leaving the kitchen at great speed and reappearing some ten minutes later with his hold-all packed and the shapeless grey sweater back on. Jane was at the sink, her hands in the washing up bowl. He approached quickly, kissing the top of her head, taking an invisible nanosecond to inhale the faint soapy smell of her hair. 'I'll see you around. I've said farewell to the children, and Dad.'

'Hang on.' Jane was struggling to peel off her rubber gloves.

'I really do have to go, Jane, sorry.' He gestured towards the hall and the front door.

'Okay. Bye then.' Jane had to blow into the second glove to get it off. 'Maybe we'll coincide down here again one weekend. Let me know if you're planning a visit.'

'Sure. Cheerio. Back to the tank.' He jangled his car keys and strode away, as if he couldn't wait to be gone by the look of it.

Jane followed slowly to watch his departure from the front door. Ernest appeared, carrying Harriet, to say a final farewell. Tom, busy with something in the grass, shouted a goodbye and got one back. Ernest managed to give Christopher a half hug, because of Harriet being in his arms and then watched, like Jane, until the big dusty car had disappeared round the bend in the lane.

It didn't take Mattie long – just two roll-ups and a cup of tea – to get to the point. They were sitting toe to toe on the window seat in the spare bedroom where she was to spend the night, a box of tissues between them, like huddling teenagers. Bruised by self-blame and her usual insecurities, total honesty was not Mattie's highest priority in telling her tale to her sister. Truth was there, but padded out with wishful thoughts and muddled regrets that had taken place only in the morning-after recriminative ferment of her mind. Without such fictional trimmings, her story would have sounded too much like a path of her own choosing to evoke the sympathy she craved.

'Christopher? Christopher Lytton? Michael's brother? Are you sure?'

Mattie, hunched over her mug of tea, her second cigarette wedged between two bitten nails, was too absorbed with curating her own version of events to register the scale of reluctant disbelief in her sister's voice.

'Yes, it was your dear brother-in-law – I am hardly likely to *not* know that, am I? I couldn't believe it – seeing him there, at Greg's. It was like – I don't know – fate or something. He didn't waste time, I can tell you.' Mattie shook her dark curls, which looked dull and slightly greasy. 'Talk about being taken advantage of...' She gulped, assailed by a fresh wave of self-pity.

'Poor Mattie.' Jane touched her arm.

'He *used* me... Christ, I know I didn't actually tell him to stop, but it would have been nice to even qualify for a post-coital cuddle.' She rolled a fresh cigarette, offering it to Jane, who vigorously shook her head. The desire to smoke had, curiously, departed with Michael. She had been watching her sister's smoking, the ash being tapped into her empty tea mug, with revulsion more than anything, most of her energies directed at trying to process the awfulness of what she was being told. Mattie certainly did look quite terrible, the worst Jane had seen her since her teens when she had done her vanishing act and then tried to starve herself to death.

'I mean, that's the usual joke isn't it,' Mattie went on, exhaling plumes, having lit the new cigarette herself, 'I bet even you've experienced that.'

'What?' The smoke was starting to make Jane feel sick. She swung her legs to the floor and took refuge on the bed.

'Oh, come on, you know – the man falling instantly asleep after bouts of supposedly meaningful, torrid sex, leaving you to confess heartfelt emotions to a wall of snores.'

'I don't think I'm best qualified to talk about torrid sex,' Jane said quietly, wanting suddenly to be left alone.

'Well, Christopher,' persisted Mattie, 'didn't even have the decency to fall asleep. He just lay there, blinking and not talking. When morning came, he said he had to make an early start and he was sure Greg wouldn't mind if I wanted to stay and help myself to breakfast. Which I did, but honestly...' She threw up her hands, scattering a fine spray of ash over Ernest's faded blue window seat cover. 'No lover of mine,' she spoke gravely, 'has ever treated me with *that* much disrespect.'

'It sounds awful, Mattie, I'm so sorry,' Jane murmured, thinking what perfect, sickening, sense Christopher's hasty departure that day now made – the man who ran away from things. People never changed.

'These bloody Lyttons, now they've ruined both our lives,' Mattie declared, in a tone so full of melodrama and relish that Jane couldn't bring herself to agree, excusing herself instead to go downstairs and see to the children.

After the bedroom door had closed, Mattie pulled a small leather pouch out of her jacket pocket and examined the contents. Four pills left and one squashed joint. Having carefully restored the little reefer's shape, rolling it gently between her fingers and patting the makeshift filter in more securely, she placed it carefully back in the bottom of her pocket. She would save it till later – smoke it out of the window when everyone was asleep. The tablets, which were the kind she had once reserved for all-night partying, were less easy to resist. Her energy levels were so low these days. After some consideration, she broke one in half and nibbled it slowly, loving the buzzy feeling it brought and the way her head began to clear.

21

Back in Cobham, the house felt cold and unwelcoming. With her interview for the hospital job looming, and still preoccupied by the unsettling conversation with Mattie, Jane busied herself with some unseasonal spring-cleaning, telling herself that juggling work and motherhood would mean less time for such niceties.

She was standing in her dressing-gown on the Sunday morning, absently ladling sugar into a bowl of bran flakes, when Michael turned up early to collect the children for their Sunday outing – to Wisley Gardens, he said, because there was lots of space as well as a lovely café. He seemed full of bounce, greeting her with a disarming smile, while Tom and Harriet screamed their welcomes and pulled on his arms. Something's happened, Jane thought at once, he looks different.

She was still puzzling over it when Julia arrived.

'Michael looked odd today.'

'Oh?' Julia, browsing through the colour supplement that had arrived with the morning papers, glanced up briefly. 'What sort of odd?'

'I don't know – pleased with himself.'

'Perhaps he's finding his feet,' Julia murmured – in a very un-Julia like way, Jane decided, watching her friend return her attention to the magazine, as if profoundly bored by the whole subject. A little put out by the indifference, but knowing better than to show it, Jane set about preparing their lunch. 'I'm stir-frying chicken, with all sorts of bits, including sprouts. I love sprouts and they were on special offer. I hope that's okay.'

'Sprouts in June, that sounds grand,' said Julia, at last throwing the magazine to one side and helping herself to a raw carrot from the pile Jane had just peeled. 'Did I tell you I saw Christopher recently?'

'No, you didn't, but I know anyway.'

'How come?' She gnawed neatly round the entire carrot, leaving the long sweet core till last.

'He was at Ernest's for a bit, when I went there with the kids. He mentioned it.'

'How did he seem?'

'Fine.' Jane was at the draining board now, hacking great chunks off the bottoms of the sprouts, causing clusters of tiny green leaves to flutter everywhere but on the board.

'I only ask,' Julia went on, 'because he seemed rather out of sorts when he came by the shop – positively distracted – quite the mad professor. I half wondered if he was ill.'

'He was probably rather tired,' Jane said dryly, scooping the sprouts into a colander and running vicious jets of water over them, making them jostle like penned animals. Julia, meanwhile, started banging cupboards and drawers open and closed in a haphazard search for useful things to lay on the table.

'Actually,' Julia continued, between her cupboard-banging, 'he did look *very* tired – all black-eyed and dishevelled – rather handsome, really, in a gaunt kind of way. Where does the pepper mill reside in this worthy establishment?'

Jane pointed with her knife towards the table, where the salt and pepper cellars could just be seen peeking out from under Julia's discarded magazine.

'Ah, good.' Having given up on her half-hearted attempts at assistance, Julia perched with her bottom on the edge of the table, facing Jane's back. 'It was sort of astonishing, him popping in like that, out of nowhere and with absolutely nothing to say. But there was that other time too – do you remember? – when he rang, and said he would come by, and then didn't.' Julia giggled. 'Do you think I should start getting ideas?'

'I think that is rather up to you,' Jane said tersely, hurling the sprouts into a saucepan of water, and having several goes at getting the gas to ignite.

'Jane, whatever is the matter? Is it because he's Michael's brother – not that I am *remotely* interested anyway—'

'Sorry to snap. Sorry, sorry, sorry,' Jane groaned, running her hands over her face, and then taking a deep breath to compose herself. 'Look, I wasn't going to mention this, but the reason Christopher was in London a couple of weeks ago was for a party, where...' She crossed her arms, doing her best to sound matter-of-fact rather than angry; '...where he met Mattie. Apparently, the two of them ended up in bed together – which is, I suppose, neither here nor there, except that he led her on, Mattie said, and then left without so much as a goodbye, and visited you, by the sound of it, before returning to his lair. Oh, and then he dropped by for a couple of quiet days with his father a week later, when I happened to be there. The ubiquitous Christopher Lytton. It's just all a bit weird.' Jane bit her lip, fighting again the dim sense of having been taken in by her soon-to-be ex-brother-in-law's charm. 'Needless to say, he made no mention of Mattie to me – she came rushing down to Kent to pour it all out and was pretty cut up, as you might imagine.'

'Goodness.' Julia was intrigued. 'That does sound a bit much... but... he didn't do anything awful, did he... like force her...?'

'Oh, no. He was just very full on, Mattie said, and then took off early the next morning, leaving her feeling rotten.'

'Golly. Christopher and Mattie...' Julia rolled her eyes. 'Who would have thought?'

'There's no need to get all gleeful about it.'

Julia blinked in surprise at the reprimand, inwardly abandoning the resolve to get her dinner with Michael off her chest. How Christopher had behaved was undeniably reprehensible, but she found the vehemence of Jane's response puzzling. Mattie, from what Julia had gleaned over the years, was more than capable of handling her own lovers, without requiring her big sister to take up arms on her behalf.

'Let's leave the subject of your erstwhile brother-in-law, shall we?' she suggested with icy sweetness, 'it seems to be making you rather cross.'

After such uncharacteristically tense exchanges, the two of them found it hard to regroup into anything like their usual easy way of being. Though Julia stayed for coffee after their meal, she left much earlier than she had intended, slightly worn down with frustration at Jane's unreachable state of mind. It caused her to think how, when Jane had been harnessed to Michael, there had at least been a fixed stand-point from which she could rejoice or complain, and for Julia to respond to accordingly. Now, with this new prickliness, Julia sometimes found herself wondering, not for the first time, whether Jane staying in an imperfect marriage wouldn't have been the wiser choice after all.

As she pulled away from the kerb, offering a cheery, departing toot at Jane's closing front door, she resolved to leave her old friend alone for a while, to give them both time for some readjustment.

22

With the interview proving to be little more than a formality prior to starting the job, Jane's energies were soon diverted into the challenge of learning how to navigate the vast filing systems of Guildford General Hospital. Her life hit what felt like a timeless new rhythm that comprised of juggling the children round school, Mrs Browne and her new working hours. The sporadic visits from Michael continued, sleepovers being impossible he said, thanks to a new, hectic work phase and ongoing plans to move out of Des's into a more suitable flat. Apart from occasional weekends with Ernest, making sure always that there would be no other visitors, and Julia checking in with the odd phone call, Jane therefore found herself alone a lot, and enjoying what felt like a much-needed breathing space. The big, final upheaval of divorce, with all the inevitable wrangling over asset splitting, would come soon enough. In the meantime, it felt good to be earning some money of her own again, and to have the chance to grow into the feeling of being truly separate, rather than part of a broken couple.

For Christopher, the second half of the year rolled slowly by. It seemed obvious, inevitable – only right – that Mattie should have told Jane everything, scotching any hopes he might have had of running into her again. The old demon of self-loathing, which he thought he had slain for good, began to creep back over him, like an enemy intent upon revenge.

As summer edged into autumn, and then winter, the possibility of a family Christmas fuelled his hopes for a while. But in the event, he and Ernest dined alone at the close of the year, while Jane and Michael tried their hands at some stiffly executed festive charades in Cobham for the sake of Harriet and Tom. There was limited pleasure to be had in either camp; though, like Jane and Michael, Ernest and Christopher applied themselves to the festive rituals as well as they could. Ernest asked no questions, but his son's downcast spirit was plain to see, infused as it was into every angle of his bony body, and the way his dark eyes were hooded with all the old wariness of the world.

Back at school, Christopher took on every extra-curricular activity available, much to the surprise – and some puzzlement of his colleagues. The more sensitive among them guessed that he sought such distractions for unenviable reasons, while others began to whisper, less generously, about the new, juggernaut thrust of Lytton's ambitions. Outings, plays, poetry groups – nothing, it seemed, was safe from the voluntary involvement of the once somewhat endearingly disengaged English master.

If ever Christopher found himself alone, without one single essay to mark, not one lesson to plan, he worked on his novel – not out of love or any heated desire to create, but with gritted teeth and a burning mind, fearful of being sucked into the downward spiral that whirled within. It was escapism of sorts, bringing little satisfaction, but at least dulling the edges of his brain with tiredness so that sleep without whisky was possible. He never drank alone now, for fear of where it might lead. When all else failed, he clung to the feather of a hope that Mattie had been too proud to say anything after all, and that it was mere coincidence that Jane Lytton never seemed to cross his path.

23

One of the few people in the world Jane had ever trusted to drill holes in her teeth was a Mr Philip Newel, who practised near Dulwich, in a quiet residential road off Denmark Hill. Pippa had recommended him when Jane was pregnant with Tom and all the nerve-endings in her mouth had felt as though they were trying to crawl out of her gums. So it was that, when a piece of tooth landed on her breakfast plate one early March morning, dislodged by a challenging crust of toast – to the delighted astonishment of the children – Jane arranged for a day off and drove to south east London.

Reclining with her mouth open to the glare of Mr Newel's angle-poise light, enduring an examination with a silver hook that she tried not to think about, it was Pippa who kept coming to mind.

'We can save the tooth,' announced Mr Newel happily, 'no need for a crown at all.' He started pulling on thin rubber gloves; condoms for the fingers, thought Jane, her brain pinging with fear, fixing her gaze on the ceiling while the inevitable, unimaginable needle was prepared.

The subject of Pippa continued to provide a welcome counterpoint to the speckled paintwork overhead, distracting from the certainty that searing pain was merely biding its time, coiled deep within each vibration of what Philip Newel was doing with his unspeakable gadgets.

Pippa's ill-judged letter, begging Jane to give Michael another chance in the immediate aftermath of their separation, felt a world away. In subsequent months, intermittent efforts by Jane to communicate, via phone messages and one heartfelt letter, had met with no response whatsoever. It was only through snippets – reluctantly divulged by Michael – that she knew of their continuing dire financial straits and the still unfulfilled plan of moving to the West Country. Julia had grown impatient with the whole subject of the Crofts, as she seemed to with so much else lately, advising Jane to let it go, saying she should regard Pippa and Tim as one inevitable casualty of her break-up with Michael; but Jane could not help feeling uneasy about the rift. She knew Pippa had many problems and very few friends. It seemed too awful to give up on such an essentially good, sweet person without the tiniest fight.

By the time Mr Newel had reached the final stages of the treatment, when the hinges of her jaw were aching and her dry lips were crying out for a tongue lick, it had occurred to Jane that Pippa might be acting under pressure from Tim; that perhaps he had taken it upon himself simply to forbid her to get in touch. The thought blossomed wildly. Perhaps Pippa was no better than a prisoner, a slave to Tim's philandering and to his unfortunate mishandling of their business affairs.

'Rinse thoroughly, please.'

Jane did her best, most of the pink liquid dribbling unmanageably from the numbed side of her mouth.

A little while later, when she tried to smile into the bite-sized mirror in the surgery's toilet, her lips merely quivered, looking lopsided and unconvincing. The point of her nose was frozen too, and there was a numbing sensation in her right eye socket, as if cold water had been injected up under the cheek bone. She drove down Denmark Hill with one eye closed, massaging the right side of her face with her fingertips.

At the end of the Crofts' smart little front path, bordered that morning with rows of dazzling daffodils, there was an estate agent's sign emblazoned with the word *SOLD*. I am too late, Jane thought, pulling into a space behind a van across the road and keeping half an eye on a very plump woman half way up a tall, sturdy ladder at the front of the house cleaning a first-floor window. Despite the spring flowers, the weather was still bitter; and yet the woman wore no coat – only a long wide tartan skirt, thin flat shoes, and a voluminous olive-green jumper with both sleeves pushed up to the elbows, revealing forearms as big as shelves. She was polishing the glass in sweeping circular movements, her wide skirt swinging with each motion.

It was only when Tim emerged through the open front door with a mug in each hand that Jane realised the woman cleaning the windows was Pippa. She sank lower in her car seat, watching in some disbelief as Pippa descended the ladder to take her tea. Her face, Jane could see quite clearly, remained almost unchanged, as fine boned and sharp as ever, apart from being set in a wider framework and looking incongruously small atop the new rounded shape of her body. Her hair, which was swept tightly off her face into a thin pony-tail, had also grown considerably, its longest strand pointing well down between her shoulder blades.

Jane found the physical transformation of her old friend deeply disconcerting, almost as if it was a reminder of how profoundly the world had changed for all of them. For a few moments she clung to the steering wheel, tempted just to pull out and accelerate away. The Crofts, now standing talking with their mugs of tea, wouldn't notice. But that would be cowardly, Jane scolded herself, gently pulling the keys from the ignition and flexing her thawing mouth into what felt like a normal position. She was in the area anyway. It was the perfect opportunity to offer support – to show she cared. Just to slink away without saying a word would have felt like failure of the most unforgivable kind.

'Hi there,' she called, even before she had crossed the road, wanting to give them fair warning. Tim looked first, angry incredulity darkening his face, while Pippa turned more slowly, as if she already knew what was coming, her expression inscrutable.

'This not a good idea, Jane,' Tim said loudly, marching towards her and then planting himself in her path, arms folded, as if Pippa needed protection, it felt like.

'I've come to see Pippa,' said Jane firmly, feeling shaky at the very physical sensation of being so unwanted by people who once had welcomed her company. 'I'm so sorry about your business trouble, Tim. I've tried several times to call but...' Through the open door behind him she glimpsed bare floorboards, pictures propped against walls, a stack of cardboard boxes.

'This is not a good time. I must ask you to leave.'

Jane stood her ground, deliberately not engaging with the almost comically hostile look on Tim's chubby face. Behind him, Pippa was behaving with a nonchalance that encouraged Jane to hope. Having tipped her head back to swallow the last warm drops of her tea, she carefully placed the mug on the window sill and started climbing back up the ladder, cloth in hand.

'Pippa,' Jane called up to her, 'can we talk?'

'Don't you think you've done enough?' Tim took a step forward, coming so close that the possibility he was considering physical restraint even crossed Jane's mind.

'I've done nothing – not to you.'

'Like hell you haven't.'

Jane looked to the top of the ladder where Pippa was back rubbing at her window pane – despite it looking very clean.

Tim was still talking, sounding more confident, getting into his stride. 'It's not just Michael – though what you've done to him is bad enough.' He shook the remains of his tea onto the gravel between them, splashing a few brown drops onto her shoe. 'But the way you led Pippa on too, filling her head with ideas about which you have no authority to speak – special fertility treatments, expensive clinics, getting her hopes up – she told me *everything*,' he hissed. 'As if *you* have any right to offer advice on being a parent...' He stopped abruptly, shaking his head. 'Please leave us.'

Jane wanted to defend herself, to explain how it really was – not just about Pippa and babies, but also about the intolerable loneliness of being married to Michael. But Tim's expression, his whole stance, the way his stocky legs were planted so firmly against her, his hips thrust out, his arms protecting his chest, did not invite explanations of any kind. Instead, she made a sort of run at the ladder, charging in a way that felt at once melodramatic and necessary. Grasping a metal rung with both hands to steady herself, she called up to Pippa again.

Tim strode past her towards the open front door, an odd halfsmile on his face. 'She won't talk to you. Loyalty means something to us.' And with that he disappeared inside. Jane was still staring after him when Pippa began to descend, taking each step very slowly, her wide skirt swaying. Jane waited, relieved that the two of them would at last have the chance to talk alone. But having reached the ground, Pippa simply collected her mug from the window sill and followed Tim inside, like a sleepwalker. The rebuff was so surprising that Jane did not move for at least a minute after the door had closed behind them.

To be ostracised in such a way was almost laughable, she told herself, scampering back across the street on a wave of incredulity and high dudgeon. But by the time she had settled back behind the wheel, any consoling puff of self-righteous triumph had been superseded by a much more wobbly feeling. Her tooth was throbbing badly and her fingers trembled as she groped for the ignition. The white blur of Pippa's face appeared at a window as she pulled out. Jane slowed and stared back hard, hoping – in spite of everything – for some sort of salutation, a flutter of fingers perhaps – some signal that what had taken place was not for real; but there was no movement, not even a twitch.

On arriving home, she resisted calling Julia. The urge to discuss the depressing and bizarre events of her day was strong, but for a while now they had not been talking as often or in the same way. Quite who was holding out on who, Jane wasn't sure; knowing only from her own side that Julia's readiness to make judgements, the quick surfacing of her impatient, witty scorn had grown a little harder to take in recent months. Sometimes, she half sensed some disapproval about her decision to end things with Michael, though she knew Julia would never own up to it.

Or maybe, like everyone, Julia was just busy leading her own life in north London, Jane chided herself, tossing in bed later that night despite her tooth having settled down. Still awake in the small hours, she went downstairs to make herself a hot milk, taking a couple of aspirin too, despite knowing the small white capsules contained none of the answers or help she really needed.

24

Returning to the neon-lit warmth of Guildford Hospital the next day was quite a relief. Right from the start, Jane had derived an unexpected pleasure from being in an environment where nobody knew anything of her background, where there were no expectations of her beyond the manageable demands of her work. She was quite happy to spend large segments of her time on her own, putting away and pulling out trolley loads of fat beige files from the cadaverous basement on the lower ground floor. It was warm and dim in the bowels of the building. She liked the hush of it, the neat click of her heels on the concrete floor and the gentle gurgles of the pipes that pulsed warm air to the upper levels, like the arteries of some great metal heart.

In spite of having been warned, early on, by the dapper, double-breasted head of administration, about the importance of keeping busy at all times, Jane often found herself dawdling dreamily between the long rows of shelves, riffling through X-rays of blurred images and illegible notes on symptoms and treatments. With her own life in such disarray, she found it perversely reassuring to peek into the thankfully mysterious world of human sickness and diagnosis being endured by other, less fortunate souls.

The rest of her duties ranged from answering phones to helping out with the paperwork in busy clinics. With staff shortages being a problem common to every department, Jane quickly got to know her way round the disinfected labyrinth of corridors and stairs, with their slippery, brown linoleum floors and endless stretches of peppermint-coloured walls.

Initially, by far the most daunting challenge had been the vast hospital canteen, where the feeling of being new, part-time and friend-less was unavoidable. But after a while, Jane took to tucking something to read under her arm before joining the queue for food, losing herself in a book or a magazine instead of feeling conspicuous. An awareness that she was starting to like her own company had begun to settle inside. She had felt so abandoned being married to Michael – living with the recurrently thwarted expectation and hope of his company, understanding and support – that it could only feel less stressful to exist as she did now, without no such expectations or disappointments other than those she brought upon herself.

One early, wet April evening, however, someone did at last emerge from the mass of her fellow employees to lure her out of this self-imposed exile. Dr Anthony Marshall, an expert in respiratory diseases who ran a clinic on the third floor, had just turned out of the hospital car park when he caught sight of Jane Lytton grappling with an inside-out umbrella, its nylon material flapping in the wind like the broken wings of a large black bird. The rain had plastered thick strands of hair across her mouth and cheeks; the wide panels of her long blue skirt billowed up round her knees, revealing the slim legs which he had long suspected of existing, but which were always hidden by trousers or long hem lines.

Anthony Marshall liked women; it was one of his most pleasur-

able hobbies to observe them in detail, to second-guess their preoccupations and hopes, and sometimes, to play a key part in
influencing such things. Jane Lytton had caught his eye not only
because of her petite, fine-featured looks, but because she seemed
to exist in a bubble-world of her own, enchantingly oblivious to the
people and goings-on around her. Though he had seen her often
enough in the canteen, absorbed in a book or newspaper, it was
only recently that they had been introduced. He was using patient
data for an asthma research programme which had entered its final
year and which – thanks to incompetence that took a while to come
to his attention – had been in danger of being drowned by unsorted
paperwork. Jane Lytton and two of the other switched-on adminis-
trative part-timers had been drafted in for a few hours each week to
help sort things out, clearing the way for a final analytical assault
on the findings.

By the time Anthony pulled up alongside the bus stop, Jane had
given up on the umbrella and was holding her handbag over her
head – in a desultory way that suggested defeat – while she endeavoured to make sense of the bus timetable. Anthony pressed one of
four buttons on a panel in the dashboard, bringing the front
passenger window down with a slick humming noise.

'Let me give you a lift,' he shouted into the beating rain. 'Just
jump in and I'll drop you somewhere.'

Jane bent down, peering in at a safe distance from the open
window, as if wary of being guillotined, when in fact her main
concern was not to drip into the car. Her hair, heavy and darkened
from the rain, was spreading huge damp patches across her shoulders and chest.

'Dr Marshall... I'm fine really...'

'Nonsense. Get in at once before I'm arrested for illegal parking. No time for politeness in weather like this.' Divine intervention, in the form of a gratifying crack of thunder overhead,

prompted Jane to yank open the car door and slither into the seat beside him.

He pulled away from the kerb at once, with a tummy-turning burst of acceleration that confirmed Jane's suspicion that the car was something impressive.

'Where to?' he asked with a grin, weaving so expertly through the rush-hour traffic that the prospect of asking him to stop did not feel possible.

'This is terribly kind.' She found a soggy tissue in her jacket pocket and blew her nose. 'I'm afraid I'm going to make your smart car horribly wet.'

'Bit of rain won't harm it. Are you warm enough, that's the main thing.' He pressed a switch and a jet of warm air began circulating pleasantly round her feet and calves.

'My car wouldn't start,' she explained, 'it's been sounding funny all week – sort of clunky deep inside – and then this morning it gave one throaty gurgle and died on the spot.'

'I can recommend a good garage, if you like.' He sped through an amber light and pulled out to overtake a bus. 'But what you need, my dear, is a drink.'

'Oh no, I couldn't possibly. If you would drop me anywhere near the main station. I'll be fine – it's only two stops to Cobham...'

'Cobham is practically on my doorstep. I wouldn't dream of dropping you anywhere but your front door. But first we're going to have that drink.'

Jane laughed uncertainly at so much insistence. 'You are very kind, Dr Marshall, but—'

'Anthony, please. And I'm not kind, I'm bloody thirsty. There's a good pub in just a couple of miles – on the Cobham road. We'll stop there for a quick one and you can use the pay-phone to call your baby-sitters – or whatever – and explain.'

Jane, somewhat discombobulated, decided to accept defeat and enjoy the ride. She leant back into the snug curve of her semi-reclined seat, from where she could observe her rescuer without it being too obvious. With her habit of scurrying, head down, through her chores at the hospital, there were few opportunities for scrutinising colleagues. It was only now, therefore, reclining gratefully in the warmth of his purring car, that Jane allowed herself to take what felt like the very large step of noting that Anthony Marshall was probably rather attractive. Though his nose, when considered in isolation, was a trifle beak-shaped and small, it was more than made up for by his wide blue eyes and an impressive shock of silky fair hair that fell forward, a little roguishly, over one side of his face. The smile lines round his mouth and eyes suggested he was over forty, but the overall impression was of a man far younger.

Leg room in the front of the car proved limited. After trying and failing to cross her legs, Jane noticed how Anthony's long body was bent almost double, his knees barely an inch from the steering wheel. It caused a flash of a memory of Christopher to pop into her head – driving to the coast the previous summer, his feet working the pedals of his old green motor like an organist.

'So, you're among the noble ranks of the multi-tasking, working mothers,' said Anthony easily, after he had placed two gin and tonics on the table and she had returned from telephoning Mrs Browne to explain her delay. 'I know all about them, believe me.'

'Does your wife work then?' Jane enquired, happy to get the subject of spouses out in the open, as if doing so lent some justification to the dubious business of swigging gin with an attractive employer and husband.

'My wife, Barbara, runs a boutique in Godalming – Octavia's – perhaps you've come across it?'

Jane shook her head. The gin tasted fantastic.

Anthony watched intently, noting the evident pleasure in the way her throat moved and her eyes closed as she swallowed. 'I told you that you were in need of a drink. Though I must confess, I'm not in the habit of picking women up at bus stops,' he added, with just a tic of a thought about an erstwhile lover called Sally, whom he had rescued from a taxi-rank. 'But you looked like a woman requiring a pick-me-up, if ever I saw one. Tell your husband you're to have a hot bath and a massage when you get home – doctor's orders,' he went on, flirting imperceptibly, enjoying the thought of her neat figure being warmed and rubbed by a man's hands.

'Actually,' Jane cleared her throat, uncertain whether she was now speaking out of a healthy impulse to own up to her new single status, or for less honourable reasons to do with the penetrating blue of Dr Marshall's eyes, 'I'm no longer married. I separated from my husband in the middle of last year. We've yet to sort out terms, but...' She fiddled with the rings, still on her fourth finger. 'I wear these because it makes life simpler.'

'Ah. Well, please forgive me blundering on in that case. I had no idea.' Anthony touched her hand for the briefest moment and then shook his head. 'This really is bizarre. You see, I know exactly what you're going through.' He paused, running one hand through the sleek wave of his hair, his eyes illuminated with the subtlest flicker of suffering. 'Barbara and I are close to going down such a road ourselves.'

'Oh dear.' For one mad moment, Jane debated whether to touch his hand in a mutual show of support, until good sense got the better of her. 'So, you have children?' she asked gently.

'Three girls. We're staggering on. Not much of a joy-ride for either of us – but then you know all about that.'

Jane looked at her glass which seemed to have emptied very quickly. 'I really ought to be getting back,' she said. 'Thank you so much for the drink.'

'The pleasure was all mine, I assure you.' It wasn't until they were in Cobham itself, when he was half-way through a fascinating account of some of the theories behind the rise in the presentation of asthma symptoms, that he suddenly broke off to ask her out to dinner. As Jane opened her mouth to protest, he chipped in quickly, expressing sentiments carefully designed to make acceptance easier. 'I spend a lot of time on my own too, these days, with things the way they are at home. It would really be such a treat to go out for the simple fun of a nice meal and pleasant company. We could do it after work, say, next Thursday. You open negotiations with your squadron of child-minders and I'll book a restaurant.'

By the time he turned into her street, Jane – after several flurries of reluctance – had agreed to the idea, telling herself she could always pull out. Quite flustered by it all, she did her best to make a smooth, dignified exit from the car, only to be thwarted by an inability to locate the door handle.

'Allow me,' he said, reaching across her, so that his head came close to hers and she could smell the unfamiliar scent of his hair and feel the faintest pressure of his arm across her chest.

* * *

'But everything's still completely under control,' she assured Julia, one Sunday several weeks later, as they strolled round the edge of the boating lake in Regent's Park. Tom and Harriet each had a bag of stale crusts, which they were trailing behind them to a posse of waddling ducks. The unexpected boon of an early heat-wave had bestowed something of a holiday atmosphere upon the park; the grass and paths were packed with picnickers and strollers in a care-free mood, prepared for once to smile at each other, as strangers do when acknowledging the simple pleasure of a cloudless day.

'Oh, yes? You've gone all pink just talking about him. Doctors always do that to women – there's something sexy about the idea of them. Maybe it's because looking at naked bodies is often a part of their job; so we have a secret little notion that, because they know the female body so intimately, they should also know their way blindfold round all our erogenous zones.' Julia gave a mock shudder and waved her fingers. 'Ooh, the thought of unleashing all those pent-up desires...'

Jane couldn't help laughing, even though she was exasperated. 'I've told you – nothing has happened. Why can't anyone believe in platonic friendships any more?'

'Because in my experience, when it comes to genders with the potential for mutual physical attraction, they are extremely rare,' replied Julia dryly.

Jane tried to concentrate her thoughts on the burning blue of the day, rather than allow her irritation to show. She was so glad Julia had suggested the get-together, but there was still something steely in how she was responding to everything and Jane was at a loss as to how to deal with it.

By the time they had crossed a bridge and started up the other side of the lake, Tom and Harriet, having long since used up their supply of stale bread, were flagging badly, complaining of tiredness and heat. Carrying a child each, their conversation was temporarily interrupted by a piggy-back race to the ice-cream kiosk, followed by the palaver of commandeering a paddle-boat. With the children squashed on the little front seat, their heads only just peeping out from under enormous life jackets – guaranteed, joked Julia, to suffocate any infant under ten – the two women took charge of the twin sets of pedals, giggling naturally together for the first time that day as they set off in a gentle zigzag across the water.

'This doctor is divorced, did you say?' said Julia, hitching her skirt higher, more intent on getting some sun on her long legs, than in pedalling very hard.

Jane, feeling resignedly unglamorous in her knee-length khaki shorts, slowed her own pedalling so that the little boat could advance in something more progressive than a circle.

'Not quite, but heading that way...' Jane pushed her sunglasses further up her nose and turned to face Julia, who remained staring fixedly ahead. 'Look, we meet for the occasional drink and have had one dinner, during which we talked about our children, asthma and the weather. Honestly, Julia,' – she nudged her with her elbow – 'I was hoping you might even be pleased that I have got some sort of social life at last.'

Julia, now leaning back in her little seat, working the pedals even more slowly, was unmoved. 'Dearest Jane, call me a cynic, but the man is married, you are only quite recently un-married – with nothing sorted in terms of divorce – and so the whole thing sounds just a little bit... unwise.'

Jane gave up, suggesting they let Tom have a go at pedalling instead, which meant Harriet needed consoling at being left out.

It wasn't until they got back to Julia's ground-floor flat and were sitting on the grass with cups of tea in her small, walled garden, that Julia dared to bring up one of the reasons behind her invitation to have Jane and the children over for the day.

'I have something to tell you,' she ventured, ignoring Jane's look of surprise as she produced a small tin of slim black cigarettes from her bag and lit one. She drew on it deeply, eyeing her friend through a swirling screen of bluish smoke as she exhaled.

'That sounds serious,' Jane quipped, giving Tom a wave through the window, where he and Harriet were watching cartoons on the telly. 'And why are you smoking? You don't smoke, at least you haven't for years.'

'The occasional Black Sobranie doesn't count,' Julia replied smoothly, picking a crumb of tobacco off the tip of her tongue and flicking it to the ground. 'I don't know if what I have to say is serious or not.' She plucked at some grass with her free hand. 'It rather depends on how you choose to react.'

'You're getting married.'

'No, idiot.' Julia laughed, throwing the tin of Sobranies at Jane, who caught them deftly in one hand.

'Have one if you want.'

'No thanks. I don't any more, remember?' She dropped the tin into Julia's open bag. 'So, what is it then?'

'Michael is seeing someone else,' Julia declared flatly, 'someone from work, called Lisa.'

'Really? Goodness... but how on earth do you know?' Jane spoke in a rush, aware at some level of being relieved to feel nothing more intense than a jolt of curiosity.

Julia hesitated, stubbing out her slim cigarette, inwardly fighting the rare and uncomfortable sensation of being at a loss for words. 'Because... occasionally... Michael has been phoning me – over the last few months – to talk.'

'Phoning *you?* To *talk?* What about?'

'He hasn't for ages. It was just to try and understand what had happened, he said... a sort of emotional crutch type thing.'

Jane had got to her feet. 'And did it not occur to you to tell me of this blossoming *friendship* a little sooner?' She rammed her hands into the deep pockets of her shorts, thinking bitterly that it was little wonder both that Julia had been so weird for so long, and that Michael had at times been so chipper, like he knew something she didn't; because he did. 'And so, tell me, please,' she went on icily, as a new, even more unpleasant thought occurred to her, 'how does what you have just told me fit in with your recently expressed view that *platonic* relationships between heterosexual men and women are impossible?'

For a moment Julia gawped. In all her many mental prepara-

tions for the conversation, she never anticipated being so spectacularly tripped up by her own glib tongue. 'I said *rarely* possible... and
come on, Jane, that would never... I would never... look, Jane, I'm
sorry. It was a phase. I shouldn't have let it happen and I should
have told you. He hasn't rung in ages. He was just off-loading... I
have been feeling more and more awful about it. I just didn't know
how to tell you, and the longer I left it, the worse it got.' Julia had got
to her feet too, appalled at what a mess she had made of everything;
but Jane was already gathering up her things and heading inside.

'You've both been through so much... and it *would* be
completely understandable if you were a bit put out by the Lisa
woman,' Julia cried, desperately trying get back onto her original
tack as she hurried after her.

'Well, you've got that wrong too,' Jane snapped, having scooped
Harriet onto her hip, using her free hand, first to turn the telly off,
and then to herd Tom towards the door. 'Michael and I did not
make each other happy,' she hissed, lowering her voice, acutely
aware of Tom trying to make sense of their conversation and this
sudden need to leave. 'I am truly glad if he has found someone else.
All that puzzles me is why my oldest friend seems to have turned
against me...'

'Jane, I have *not* – I got it wrong – I am sorry—' Julia did her best
to block the doorway but Jane pushed past. 'I've made a hash of
everything,' Julia wailed, following them to the car, 'I am a clumsy
idiot and an oaf, please stay to talk it through.' But Jane had with-
drawn into herself, offering only the stiffest of goodbyes before
strapping the children into their seats and driving away.

25

Christopher lay on the sofa staring up at the patch of damp staining the ceiling. He had been reading a novel, but could not keep his mind upon it. His own novel lay, complete but for the final paragraph, on the desk to the left of the fireplace. He could not write the closing sentences because he did not yet know whether there should be a stab of hope amidst its dark conclusion. He rather thought there shouldn't.

From his vantage point in the bay window of his sitting room, he could enjoy a picture-postcard view of the school grounds, laid out to his left like patched green carpets, bordered with the feverish colours of the hydrangea bushes, reluctant homes to a medley of lost balls. As the end of term approached, he found himself longing for the boys to be gone, for afternoons such as this when he could enjoy his idyllic surroundings in peace. The energy of the children made him feel stale. Yet the moment they were gone, when the thwacks and shrieks of ball games no longer interrupted his train of thought, he found it harder to concentrate than ever. His ears strained for signs of life outside, as if he needed to feel the existence of others to be sure of his own.

But it was to the mottled shape on the ceiling that his eye kept returning: a shape of infinite possibilities, growing imperceptibly, like a slowly evolving cloud, inviting the imagination to play games. A donkey. A boat. A house. A dinosaur. It was always a dinosaur of one sort or another – long neck, small head, a clump of a tail. The school bursar, a man with beady eyes and a nose for economies, had been promising to replaster the place ever since Christopher had moved in, years before, when the damp patch had been no bigger than a hand print. But now it did not matter. The cottage was to be uprooted, making way for a computer centre. Work was scheduled to begin that autumn.

Christopher had, in a detached fashion, been looking into the possibility of renting nearby. He had also been pursuing, with rather more vigour, an advertisement for a Lecturer in English Literature at the University of Georgetown in Washington DC. An application form, filled out but unsigned, lay beside his typewriter, together with a photocopy of his cv and the passport photograph he had taken in the grimy booth at Oxford station a couple of months before. The picture was not flattering. Christopher, his black hair cropped short, his eyes staring and vacant, had the look of a suspect in an identity parade: motionless, but shifty, hoping to slip by unnoticed.

He got up from the sofa, wrenching himself up with enormous effort, forgetting the book on his chest, which slid to the floor with a thump. It landed awkwardly, a wad of pages folded backwards, tearing the jacket. He crouched down and rearranged the pages tenderly before placing the book in the bottom of an open packing case. As if fearful that any further delay might weaken his resolve, he then moved swiftly across to sit at his desk, picked up his pen and signed his name at the bottom of the application form, before slipping the documents into a large brown envelope. The deed done, he put both hands behind his head and tipped his chair as far backwards as he dared, until only an inch or two held the balance. He maintained the position for several seconds, poised and tense, before letting the chair crash back into place.

Christopher's progress with the packing cases was severely hampered by the need to create order amongst his unruly belongings. Piles of unsorted letters, photographs and papers covered every available surface; a large green sack was propped open by the door, empty and gaping, as if hungry for scraps. After sifting through one such pile and extracting only one used envelope to hurl at the sack, he turned his attentions to the less demanding task of emptying bookshelves. Picking up five or six books at a time, he rubbed the dust off their covers with the sleeve of his jersey, before stacking them into boxes. Having quickly filled all available receptacles, he wandered back over to his desk, pressing his favourite recording of Mozart's Requiem into his tape-deck on the way. The haunting beauty of the music swelled inside him, as it always did, bursting the bubble of efficiency, stirring his emotions into a mood of irresistible indulgence. Only half-concentrating, he reached down and tugged out the lowest of the desk drawers, the one he used the least because its runners stuck so infuriatingly. Sitting with his back against the wall, he tipped the entire contents on to his lap: bank statements, an ink-stained ruler, school photographs – curling and faded – several folders, a pad of paper that looked old but unused. Flicking through the pages, checking to see how many were blank, his eye was caught by some writing at the very back – a spider-script in smudgy biro, which he recognised at once as his own, dating back to a time before the loops and dashes of adult haste had taken over completely. Thinking he had found the draft of an old essay, Christopher started to read, curious to see whether any of his youthful ideas could impress him now, as a washed-up English master:

Another gem of a family row to add to our collection. The usual order of play – the usual trivia to start us all off, like the bell-ring in a family quiz show. Michael took Mum's side against me – what a surprise – while Dad stomped off and left us to it. I mean – HAIR – for fuck's sake. I'm not a kid. Who cares when I decide to fork out to get a shearing?

I sometimes imagine what it would be like to have a sibling whom I could respect. But how can I give a toss for a man who preens himself like a fucking peacock, who reads zero books a year, who thinks poetry is 'gibberish' and who believes Success =Money.

But he surprised me yesterday, turning up with that girl. Jane something. I don't think it's been going on that long. He's brought her home to show her off, before they go skiing to wherever the hell it is. A designer holiday no doubt, perfect haircuts beneath bobble hats and Ray-Bans.

I thought I knew what to expect from Michael's women, but this one is different. There is a lightness to her, a quickness, that makes you look twice, to be sure she spoke, to be sure she's really there. She's very small, with loads of hair and such strange eyes – green with black and brown – that make you want to stare.

Dad looked pretty smitten too, when she kissed him at the gate, her cheeks all pink, her ski jacket zipped up to her chin, with hair tumbling everywhere. All I got was a handshake; her fingers were icy cold and small in my palm.

When Mum and Dad had gone to bed, the three of us played cards. After a couple of rounds Michael gave me one of his looks, which of course made me more determined to stay, sod that I am. But she seemed keen enough to carry on as we were. I fetched some drinks, while Michael sulked, trying to get her attention. He put his arm round her once, but she shook it off, a glimmer of beautiful impatience crossing her face.

Michael, being Michael, played to win. She and I lost outrageously. As Michael steadily amassed his fortune, we laughed at our diminishing piles of matchsticks and formed hopeless alliances against him. I suppose I flirted, but so did she, I think. We were on whisky and Coke, but Michael stuck it out with black coffee and water, a look of self-righteous superiority pinned to the flat mask of his face. Every so often he would try to stop the game, but we were determined to lose everything. He didn't dare get really cross, because of her.

It was juvenile of course, the whole thing. But thrilling too, to feel so in league with someone like her, co-conspirators against my brother. When I finally went to bed my head was spinning from whisky and a weird kind of elation. I kept thinking I could love someone like that; that this thing between her and Michael could not last – that she was too lovely, too true.

But this morning everything was different, like nothing had happened. She hardly even looked at me. Perhaps he braved the creaky landing to enter her bed. Something must have happened to make her butter his toast and pour his coffee like a waitress. After a while I couldn't take any more and left them to it. But I keep thinking of her and of those exotic flowers that only open at night—

Christopher stopped, mildly embarrassed for himself, then and now. Without reading another word, he tore the pages from the pad and threw them into the fireplace, where he tossed a lighted match at them. The paper arched and curled, a second of resistance, before submitting to the flames, sinking down into grey feathers of no substance at all.

Their engagement had come as something of a shock. Christopher, though he was aware of her family tragedy, did not see Jane again until the day of the wedding, which he approached with philosophical coolness, immaculate in his hired top hat and tails, determined to throw confetti with the rest of them. But when she first entered the church, leaning slightly on the arm of an uncle, because of the awful business with her parents, for a moment all he could see was a tiny bird, drowning in a sea of white. Her luxuriant hair, bound on top of her head in intricate sweeps and braids, laced up with ribbons and flowers, looked to him like a strangulation of beauty. His ushering duties complete, he stood with his eyes fixed on the crazed pink plumage of a hat in the next row, unwilling to turn his eyes to the aisle as she walked by.

But, with only a little effort, the moment passed. That she was radiantly happy there could be no doubt. Michael too seemed quite transformed by the occasion, hugging Christopher goodbye as if their brotherly love had never once been darkened by shadows of mutual incomprehension.

Over the next few months, he caught himself manufacturing excuses to visit them, partly out of fascination for the way Michael – his physical presence, his every utterance – seemed to absorb her. It was like watching a person bewitched. She deferred to Michael in everything, presenting her own opinions shakily, with one eye searching the room for his nod of concurrence, as if some spirit in her had lain down in the cause of love. After a time, Christopher could only find such subservience deeply depressing. The spark of intimacy, or whatever it had been on the night of the card game, showed not the slightest sign of reignition. Realising the impropriety of waiting for a glimpse of such a thing anyway, he withdrew from the tramlines of their marriage completely, to get on with pursuing the puzzle of his own life.

In spite of his capacity for such things, Christopher took care not to pass through the next decade like some Heathcliffean figure, punished into an exile of frustration and silent torment. If anything, he went to the opposite extreme. Sometimes, in the heat of other relationships, he forgot about Jane entirely. Only when he saw her again, at a family gathering, or heard her quiet voice down the end of a telephone line, were his emotional recollections set jangling with the faint sense of missed opportunity.

It wasn't until he began to detect some element of real unhappiness in her bearing, during the ordeal of a dinner at the Crofts, that more vehement feelings rushed back upon him, like creatures released from banishment. He was shocked by the pastiness of her face, the heavy look of her brilliant eyes. There she had sat, the husband-pleasing wife, looking so left out, so anxious to be somewhere else, that he had longed to abandon the cheery banter over Pippa's collapsing fish for the cold shock of real conversation. Only fear of embarrassing her prevented him. Meanwhile, Michael continued to bask in the glow of self-importance that Pippa's surprise gathering had allowed, toasting his own success, uncaring and oblivious – so absolutely neglectful of his wife that Christopher had trudged back to his car afterwards feeling quite bruised and powerless. The next day he had got as far as phoning Julia with the aim of finding out if Jane really was all right, but then chickened out of following through. It wasn't his business. It wouldn't have been right, despite how much he wished otherwise.

The dinosaur had turned into a map of North America; a few bits were missing but the essence was there. Christopher frowned at his enigmatic companion. The prospect of Washington was attractive as an escape, but not as a future. America was nothing but a bolt-hole for the monster, a way to survive. Mustering the last reserves of a detached pragmatism for which he had once been famous, Christopher strove to look forward to the prospect. After all, he had been given his chance with Jane and thrown it away with quite astonishing aplomb. Or perhaps, as he now began to wonder, there had never been a chance. Perhaps, during those few days in Kent, the bright scenario of romantic possibilities had clung to life purely by virtue of his own imagination. The tangled history of his feelings for Jane had formed a pattern inside his head alone; there was no proof that she had ever, consciously, played a part in it. And now, there was nothing but the thought of her disdain to contend with, echoing at him in her resounding silence.

After stretching his long body so high that he almost touched the damp shape overhead, Christopher returned once more to his desk, resolved, though by no means refreshed. With the three fingers he used for typing he began to compose the closing lines of his book. There could be a blink of hope, he decided, because there always was. Not that he felt it now, but he knew it was there, lying low, waiting to pop its silly head up just when his eyes had grown accustomed to the dark.

The moment, when it came, one evening in late June, was
something of an anticlimax. The committedly passionate way in
which Anthony's tongue flicked in and out of her mouth felt more
strange than arousing. I do not know this man, Jane thought, as her
lips struggled with an appropriate response, while her hands nonetheless made no attempt to stop him from unbuttoning her shirt
and starting to caress the silky channel of skin between her breasts.
This was what the evening had been leading to – she had known
that, and had played her part in it.

They had been to the cinema, to see a Hollywood remake of an
old classic, in which every nuance of charm from the original had
been sacrificed to the cause of pressures at the box-office. To Anthony's credit, he kept his hands resolutely to himself throughout the
film, even when promising shivers of electricity seemed be charging
haphazardly round their forearms and elbows. Jane was grateful for
this show of self-control, even though she knew such reticence had
nothing to do with what would happen later. It would have been
unseemly to neck in a cinema, that was all. They would do it at his
place instead, at the little flat he had mentioned, where some

supper awaited them, and where she had agreed to go, like some kamikaze fly zooming into a glittering web.

The flat was disappointingly bare, furnished only with the essentials. Jane, knowing full well that she was entering his man's den, having finally conceded – if only to herself – that Julia's stark views on platonic friendships between people who found each other attractive were mostly right, had expected more of a velvet lining to the place. Romance did not exactly dance upon the brown formica table and its four matching chairs. Nor did the sight of the big bed with its padded pink satin headboard make her feel any more lost to the moment. The evening had come into being because Anthony had explained that he and Barbara were trying an 'open-marriage' approach instead of actual separation, Jane reminded herself, as the ardour of his renewed embraces steadily compelled her to fall back into a conveniently horizontal position on the mattress; which meant they were all free consenting adults, able to take whatever actions they chose.

Anthony proved a tender and attentive lover, and looked the part too, his hair flopping becomingly into his eyes as he drew her closer, whispering that he was falling in love with her. While Jane's body submitted welcomingly enough to the intimacies that ensued, her mind obstinately refused to climb into bed alongside. Instead, a curious, almost comical detachment overtook her, focusing unhelpfully on the improbability of her circumstances and the uncharacteristic recklessness of her compliance. It dawned on her that – for all her attempts to cling to moral high-ground – and even before Anthony's revelation about his open marriage – this coupling had somehow become inevitable; an outcome towards which she had moved with a curious, almost existential sense of necessity. Even when the snake-tongue had started its disconcerting darting-ritual, making her long for the slow, sensuous kissing of which she and Michael had once been capable, way back before the hurried mouth-pressing of latter years, even then, she had felt unable and unwilling to call a halt. Deep down, this encounter was what she had expected, dreamed about, flirted for and come for. There was almost a duty about seeing it through to the end.

'I'm not sure you were quite with me,' said Anthony afterwards.

'Oh, but I was,' Jane replied quickly, knowing only too well the paradoxical game of reassuring a man for any shortfalls in her own enjoyment during love-making. 'It was lovely.'

Clearly heartened, Anthony then leapt out of bed, with admirable immodesty, and proposed they adjourn for food. Jane, who felt far less inclined to offer up the flawed attractions of her own body for closer scrutiny, wrapped a bath towel around her chest before following him through into the little kitchen. She was not hungry in the least, but remained fearful of making him feel that their evening had failed in some respect. She sat at the table while he produced smoked salmon sandwiches, pots of exotic, ready-mixed salads and a bottle of white wine from the fridge. Seated at the table, Anthony ate with enthusiasm, his handsome face attractively flushed and full of smiles.

'What lovely food – thank you.' Jane sipped some wine and bit a small corner off a sandwich. She wondered, watching him eat with such apparent abandon, whether thoughts of his wife had invaded his mind quite as much as Michael had entered hers.

'So, Barbara knows about this place of yours?' she remarked, echoing her understanding of the new 'anything-goes' marital conditions to which he had referred in their last few meetings.

'Yes – sort of – I mean, it's more like one of those I-know-you-know situations. Nothing needing to be spelt out.'

'Oh, I see.' So, she doesn't know anything, Jane realised with a jolt. As this truth dawned, she could muster little surprise. Anthony had wanted to get her into bed, and she had gone along with it, enjoying the pleasurable and almost forgotten process of being wooed and won. All the chats about marital break-up and leading separate lives had simply helped her self-justification, as Anthony had almost certainly intended them to.

By the time he had eaten his fill, Jane was still nibbling through her first sandwich. The fish tasted dry and salty.

'Can we do this again?' Anthony asked, reaching across the table to stroke her cheek. He stared hard at his companion, pondering how, in spite of everything, he was left with the damnable impression that she remained aloof from him, that there was some deeper, inner sanctum which he had yet to discover. Jane glanced up, her dark green eyes momentarily startled, before they quickly softened with her smile.

'My baby-sitters will mutiny if I go out much more.'

'They can start a world war for all I care.' Anthony picked up her hand and pressed it gallantly to his lips. 'I need to see you again,' he whispered, thinking at the same time how curiously more alluring it was to pursue a woman than to ensnare her. Though he had found considerable satisfaction during the last couple of hours – Jane's petite figure had proved pleasingly supple and soft – her silence had been the source of some disappointment. Anthony liked a bit more of a show from a woman, more of a sense that he had them in his thrall. 'Same time next week?' he ventured, kissing her hand again, but this time more fervently, sucking her finger-tips. I'll get a moan out of you yet, he thought, his blood starting to quicken again at the thought.

But all he got was a 'maybe,' before Jane firmly pulled back her hand and started to gather her discarded clothes from the floor.

27

An urgent invitation to dinner from Mattie the following month could not have come at a worse time. Not only was Jane still off-balance from her encounter with Anthony, busy trying to avoid him at work and making excuses not to see him again, but Tom was on the point of spending three weeks of his summer holidays with his father – a perfectly reasonable and long overdue visit, that nonetheless made her miserable every time she thought about it. It was the new woman, Lisa, who troubled Jane the most; a visceral revulsion taking hold at the thought of a stranger having the chance to play mother to her precious child. She had broken her silence with Julia on the back of it, phoning for support that was readily, sheepishly, gratefully given; though when Julia suggested coming to visit, Jane had found herself saying soon, but not yet – that she would prefer to handle the situation on her own. 'Whenever you are ready, dearest Jane,' Julia had said quietly, 'I am always here.'

Tom, ignorant of his mother's muddled anxieties, was frantic with excitement. For days he had been boasting to the bewildered Harriet of how many MacDonalds he would eat, how many late nights he would have watching telly with his Dad. 'Not your Dad,' he sniped, when he thought Jane wasn't listening, 'mine, mine, mine,' and then wailing with denials when Jane told him off.

Michael had made a big deal of taking such a long stretch off work for the visit. There had been no question of Harriet going too, because his new flat was too small, he claimed, for which Jane was secretly grateful, while guessing that it was simply because he felt daunted by the thought of coping with the two of them at once. Harriet, at two, was certainly still a lot more time-demanding than Tom, requiring cajoling through the key, challenging areas of food and sleep; but there was also a part of her that was annoyed at Michael ducking the chance to be in full charge. Just as he always had when they were together, accusing her of 'mollycoddling' a lot of the time, while he watched from the sidelines.

A hot July day had turned into a sticky evening by the time Jane descended the steps down to her sister's basement flat. As always with Mattie, there burgeoned the little mushroom of anxiety that something was seriously wrong, that her sister needed bailing out of some pot-hole or imminent disaster.

Jane placed her sandalled feet carefully on each of the narrow black metal steps, dispirited at the sight of the extremely sparse and chipped remains of red toe-varnish they displayed. Applied during the Anthony phase, it seemed to epitomise how inept she still was at managing her own personal life, let alone being qualified to offer the sisterly counsel that would no doubt be demanded of her by Mattie.

Receiving no response from the doorbell, she climbed half-way back up the iron stairway and leant over a congestion of cracked flower-pots and smeary empty milk-bottles to tap on the kitchen window.

'Coming,' called Mattie, in a tra-la-la kind of way that reminded Jane of their mother. Her face appeared round the door a moment later, grinning. Her thick, frizzy hair had been tied into a ponytail on the very top of her head, from where it cascaded over her eyes and ears like a silky mop-head. She was wearing skin-tight black shorts and a lime-green T-shirt that stopped somewhere around her rib-cage. Her stomach looked very white and flat.

'I'm on an up,' she announced brightly, her eyes glinting with a mauve eye-liner that matched the similar, and rather alarming shade on her lips. Having offered her cheek for a kiss, she promptly disappeared into her bedroom, ordering Jane to pour the wine she had just put out and to make herself at home.

Jane did as she was told, sighing at the sight of the dirty dishes and clutter, before picking her way through into Mattie's living room, which was in an even worse state: overturned drawers, card-board boxes, shrivelled pot-plants, untidy piles of clothes and stacks of canvases competed for floor space – it was as if all the inner muddle of her sister's life had finally hurled itself into the open, demanding attention.

'A bit late for spring-cleaning, isn't it?' she called, perching on the arm of a chair and fanning herself with an old magazine.

Receiving no reply, she got up to negotiate her way to the bath-room. This required sidling through a cupboard of a spare room which Mattie had once called her studio, but which now more closely resembled a dumping ground for things that had outgrown their usefulness, but which had not yet been abandoned long enough for assignment to a dump. A dented lampshade and a badly stained blanket toppled off a heap of paintings as she pushed open the door. In bending down to pick them up, her eye was caught by the words *Triangles of Love* written in italic script on the corner of a page. Easing it out, she found herself confronted by a dense mass of black and red triangles, overlapping in dizzy mirror images of themselves. Right in the centre, sat the smallest triangle of all, drip-ping colour at its corners – globules of red paint, like fat tears.

'Oh Christ, not that,' exclaimed Mattie from the doorway, but with a grin that indicated pleasure at the scrutiny. 'My geometric phase,' she snorted. 'You can keep it if you want.'

Jane, who thought the painting horrid, said she couldn't possibly.

'By the way. I'm giving up – that's one of the things I wanted to tell you.' Mattie took the painting from Jane and held it at arm's length, scowling. 'Mediocre Mattie. A little bit good at lots of things. Not very good at anything.'

'Which means you're a damned sight more able than most of the human race,' Jane declared, feeling guilty about not liking the picture.

'That's what you always say.'

'Then I'm always right, aren't I? Anyway, you can't mean it – about giving up. Some of your stuff is excellent.'

'Oh, I do mean it.' Mattie smiled. 'Period. Final. I should have done it years ago. You can't imagine the relief.' She stretched out her arms and arched her back, as if physically embracing her new freedom. 'You simply have no idea how awful it was to live with the *burden* of not painting when I thought I should.'

She laid the triangles canvas gently on top of a battered briefcase which Jane recognised, with a pang, as having once belonged to their father. She felt a surge of love for her sister. They only had each other; looking out for Mattie was not a choice.

'Let's eat,' cried Mattie. 'We can take our plates into the garden. Her upstairs,' She paused to pull a face and gesture at the ceiling, 'luckiest of landladies, is slobbing in Corsica – the third time this year – so we can have it to ourselves.'

It was only as Mattie was spooning mounds of sticky white rice and dollops of livid curry onto two plates, that she got round to explaining the mess in the flat.

'Moving?' Jane exclaimed. 'Where on earth to?'

'I'll tell you when we're settled,' Mattie retorted smugly – maddeningly – leading the way out of the flat, up the steps, past the front door of the main house, and then down along the dingy side alley that housed the dustbins and an entrance into the back garden. An ornate set of heavy white furniture, high-backed and curly-legged, awaited them.

'Come on – this is exciting – don't keep me in suspense,' Jane begged, as soon as they were seated and she had taken a mouthful of food which, despite its lurid appearance, tasted good.

'Things are falling into place at last, Jane, they really are,' Mattie burst out. 'Do you remember my amazing trip to Boston – that cheap flight deal when I slept in the airport to be first in line – when I met that incredible man, who'd been involved in that famous bridge project and the university rehousing scheme?'

Jane, who remembered only that there had been a man, but nothing about bridges or rehousing schemes, nodded, her relief at Mattie's up-beat mood starting to recede.

'Well, the incredible thing is, he called the other day – just like that – and it was like we had never been apart – I mean, it was like we knew exactly what the other was going to say, what we were thinking – it was unreal. And then he suggested...' Mattie swallowed, as if to contain some of her excitement, 'that I go out there – to live with him.'

Jane hoped her face gave only the slightest indication of her feelings.

Mattie was now vigorously spooning curry into her mouth. 'Don't you think that's wild?' Her mouth was bulging, her eyes all poppy and staring.

'It certainly is—'

Mattie put down her plate and pointed a finger at Jane. 'I know what you're going to say, so don't say it. I am going for broke this time. I'm packing up the flat. I've handed in my notice at work. I've been buried in shit, Jane, and it's taken a chance like this to make me realise just how deep.'

Jane did her best to be gentle. 'How well do you really know this man, Mattie?'

'We had those amazing weeks together – it was, like, really intense. Phil was married then, which kind of made things complicated – but that's all over now. He's had a really hard time,' she added solemnly.

'So... do you mind my asking... if you love him?'

'Love?' She picked up a grain of rice from the edge of her plate and placed it on the tip of her tongue. 'Oh, I gave up on all the sloppy stuff years ago. Love doesn't guarantee survival – of itself or anything else. It's a pain in the arse, if you ask me.' She kicked off her flipflops and leant back in her chair, parking her feet on the table next to her plate, showing off a delicate ankle bracelet of twisted coloured threads. 'Phil is okay – really, he is. And what's more important he's unattached and quite wealthy and – for some amazing, incredible, reason – he wants *me*.' She nudged her plate further away, using the side of her foot. 'I tell you, I've had it with one-night stands and getting pissed at lousy parties.'

'But what if it doesn't work out?' Jane ventured, cringing at the image of Mattie hurling herself across the Atlantic like a dice across a board.

'Then I'll stay and make a go of it on my own.' Mattie crossed her arms and stuck her chin out defiantly.

'I'm just anxious for you, Mattie. I'm the big sister, remember? Worrying is my thing.' Unhelpful memories of her own recent imprudence fluttered, but Jane pressed on with the necessary business of being sensible; a process she knew she was better at when undertaking it on someone else's behalf. 'But you need green cards and things over there, don't you?'

'I've got a tourist visa that's valid for sixty days. But once you're in, you're in – everybody says so. Loads of people work over there without proper permits.'

Jane shook her head, unconvinced of the depth of her sister's knowledge on the subject, or indeed of any other aspect of her plans. Mattie's views of the world always tended to be based on the most attractive ideas around her at any given time, a hotch-potch of hope and half-baked truths.

'Why not just keep it as a holiday?' Jane suggested, aiming for a tone that was friendly rather than judgemental.

Mattie rolled her eyes.

'Going away won't change *you*, Mattie,' Jane persisted, more urgently now. 'And that's what I can't help thinking that part of this madcap plan is all about – trying to run away from yourself, from what you are, who you are—'

'Put a plug in it, can't you? Christ, I should have known you'd be like this. *You*, who have made such a perfect success of your own life, right?' She got up and stacked their empty plates noisily on top of one another, so that the cutlery stuck out awkwardly at the sides. 'Get real, can't you, Jane? It's hard work on my own.'

There wasn't much to say after that. Mattie led the way as they traipsed back down into the stuffy flat in silence. Coming in from the shimmering green of the garden, the misty dusk of the summer night, Jane felt more sympathetic about Mattie's compulsion to leave. It must be like living in an airing cupboard, she thought, seeing again the cramped spaces of the basement flat, thinking of the hated job, the discarded paintings, the history of men who never called back.

She was about to go when Mattie, a little mollified by Jane's air of repentance, suggested that she have a rifle through some of the heaps on the floor.

'It's all going. A nice man from the Salvation Army is coming by tomorrow with a van. You might as well see if there's anything you want.'

Since their taste in clothes had never shown the slightest hint of overlapping, it was purely in the interests of their fragilely reconstructed peace, that Jane knelt down to examine some of the rejected items from Mattie's copious wardrobe. She was fighting sadness too, at the realisation that it might be quite some time before they saw each other again.

With some relief, she extracted a silky blue scarf from a pile of crumpled clothes. 'This is very pretty,' she said, spreading it across her knees and stroking out the creases. 'I would love to have it.'

'You're more than welcome.' Mattie made a face. 'A witness to my seduction of your hapless brother-in-law – I don't want the thing anywhere near me on my journey to a new life, thank you very much. By the way, are you and Michael actually divorced yet, and if not, why not?'

Jane had stood up so quickly that something clicked in her spine, not painfully, but with a deep, jarring feeling of elements realigning. 'Not yet, no... but soon... Michael is... we are waiting for... it won't be long now,' she muttered, long used to Mattie's lack of real interest in the ups and downs of her own life. 'But, about Christopher – what did you mean, seduction?'

Mattie smiled, in the manner of one acknowledging her own wickedness. 'Wicked woman – I know – but it hardly matters now.'

'But that's not what you told me before.' Jane was wrapping the scarf tightly round and round her fingers.

'I guess I was just in one of those moods at that party,' Mattie went on ruefully, not really listening, 'you know – looking for an ego boost, sort of thing. I think I'd have slept with a terrorist.' She began to laugh, but stopped the moment she saw Jane's expression. 'Oh Christ, don't play the prude with me.'

'Sorry... I mean, I'm not... but... at the time you said it was the other way round, that he was the one to take advantage. You were upset, Mattie. Very upset... you came to see me at Ernest's, remember?'

'Oh, you should know better than to listen to me when I'm upset,' Mattie countered quickly, thinking suddenly how wonderful it would be to get away from big-sister monitoring. 'I was bloody hungover and down about everything afterwards, which I guess affected what I said. And anyway, he *was* unforgivably cold afterwards, scooting off with barely a friendly word, saying he regretted it and blaming the booze. How was *that* supposed to make me feel? Though I did get my own back,' she added slyly.

'You did?' Jane murmured.

'He wrote a letter – a grovelling apology – which – again – isn't exactly flattering, if you think about it. And then he tried to ring a couple of times, leaving messages with yet more regrets, which I just deleted. It may sound mean, but it was all too heavy, you know? It was just one of those things that happened. Best to let it go, right?'

'Right,' Jane echoed feebly, marvelling at her little sister's capacity to run rings round her – and reality – and saying that it was probably time for her to go.

She was half-way up the steps, their hugging farewells done, when Mattie emerged with the picture of triangles.

'A goodbye present,' she said, laying a breathy kiss near Jane's ear as she handed it over, before scuttling back into her burrow of a home.

28

There was no need to go out that Saturday afternoon. The mini heatwave had come and gone, and the forecast was rain. Outside, a grey drizzle was already speckling the air, flecking the windows with a damp mist. The only communication all day had been a morning phone message from Anthony – left while Jane had been at the playground with Harriet – saying it had been weeks and why was she avoiding him and could they meet. Jane shivered. The house felt unnaturally quiet without Tom. She even missed his war games and the way he slid head-first down the banister in order to beat Harriet to the bottom.

Harriet missed him too, placing far greater demands on her mother to provide entertainment. After a long whingey period after her nap, she had finally settled down to a whispering game involving Tom's trains – hallowed, untouchable objects when her brother was around – and several chair legs. Jane sat nearby, doing her best to cobble together a shopping list on the back of one of the old Christmas cards she kept for the purpose. There was nothing to buy, no reason to go out again at all. Tom was the only one who ever ate anything in any quantity. Both freezer and fridge were stuffed to bursting point. After a few minutes she wrote the word 'broccoli', very slowly and neatly on the back of the old card, and then sucked the end of her pencil, pondering whether she could really be bothered to buy and cook herself something so sensible as a vegetable. Harriet hated broccoli; she had been known to submerge even the tiniest floret in her milk rather than suffer the revulsion of placing it in her mouth. Chucking the pencil down with some impatience, Jane sat back and watched as it rolled to the edge of the table and onto the floor. Harriet grabbed it with a squeal of triumph and began beating a blue engine across the back, scolding it in squeaky whispers for some unforgivable deed.

'Come on, you, we're going on a drive,' Jane said firmly, reaching for their raincoats and ignoring Harriet's yowls of dismay.

It was only as they approached the outskirts of Godalming, when the rain started to pound the windscreen with tropical fervour, as if trying to force her to turn back, that Jane acknowledged to herself that she had come in search of Barbara Marshall's boutique.

With the grey afternoon stretching ahead and Harriet obligingly asleep in her car seat, two trains clutched fiercely to the frilly yoke of her pinafore dress, there was no need to hurry. But a panicky feeling overtook Jane nonetheless, like the sensation in a bad dream when unknowable deadlines and ungraspable challenges press upon the mind, or when some awful truth is about to dawn. She drove jerkily but systematically through the grid of narrow streets round the town centre, craning her neck to see through the sheeting rain. The windscreen wipers worked furiously, squeaking in spite of the profusion of water.

It had been easy not to think about the wife. Throughout their acquaintance, she could see more clearly than ever, Anthony had been very helpful in this regard, never overtly complaining about his marriage, but just referring to it occasionally, along with becoming hints of sadness and weary resignation and affectionate references to his three daughters. By the time the talk of 'open marriage arrangements' and having his own flat arrived, Jane had only the haziest of impressions of what Barbara might be like, picturing a bored, attractive, wealthy wife who dabbled in prissy shop-keeping to fill her day.

The door jingled as Jane and Harriet entered. A ten or eleven-year-old bespectacled girl sat behind the counter, reading a comic and sucking the ends of her pigtails. On catching sight of them, she immediately clambered down from her stool and came round to say hello, cooing at the one train that had been allowed to accompany them this far before unwisely surrendering her glasses to Harriet's determined, grasping fingers.

A woman appeared from a door behind the counter. 'Can I help at all?' she asked amiably, 'Or would you prefer to be left alone?' Her hair was fair and very fine, cut short round her ears and up the back of her neck. She wore a matching set of earrings and necklace – large bobbles of black, to which her fingers kept returning in a fidgety way, as if they were a string of worry-beads.

'I'm just looking, thank you.' Jane shuffled through a couple of racks of clothes, her heart pounding, wishing she had never come.

Everything was on sale – 50 per cent off the marked price. The styles were attractive, sensible without being dowdy. Thinking of her pathetically limited supply of skirts for work, she began to look with more genuine application.

'It seems only yesterday that mine were that age,' said the woman dreamily, refolding some sweaters near Jane and nodding at Harriet, who was going through her lengthy repertoire of animal noises for her new audience.

'How old is your daughter?'

'Trudy is twelve. I've got two more – fourteen and sixteen – all girls.'

So, this was indeed Barbara Marshall. Curiosity, the ostensible reason for her coming, suddenly felt like no reason at all. A chilling sense of something much more unsettling tiptoed up the back of Jane's neck; here she was, no better than a voyeur, dabbling covertly in other people's lives, playing stealthy games with their emotions. Instinct told her to flee at once from this pleasant, skinny woman, with her bony cheeks and big smile, but Harriet was chortling with Trudy and Barbara was still talking about babies.

'I certainly had my hands full when they were small. Oh, but they're worth it, aren't they?' She hugged a sweater to her chest, adoringly. 'My husband would love another – even now. He wants a boy of course, like all men. But I just don't feel I've got the energy to go through it all again. It's been so long – I don't think I could face it. Is that terribly selfish of me?'

Jane took a breath. 'Oh no, I don't think so – not at all.'

Barbara disappeared behind a grey curtain beside the changing cubicle. She was much taller than Jane had imagined, and so painfully slim, it made her want to stare.

'Harriet likes you a lot,' she told Trudy.

'I love babies,' the little girl said dreamily, pushing her spectacles back up her nose.

Jane was on the verge of leaving when Barbara re-emerged from behind the grey curtain, brandishing a dress of emerald green with a cream belt and cream trim round the sleeves.

'I don't often do this,' she said, sounding a little breathless, 'but I really do think this would look rather splendid on you. It was in the stock room. With the closing sale, it's at a very reasonable price. It's wild silk. The colour is just so perfect – for your eyes.'

'Thank you, but I really don't...' Jane faltered. Barbara was swinging the dress from side to side, making it shimmer under the shop's warm ceiling lights. 'Well, I suppose there's no harm in just trying it on, is there?'

'No harm at all,' laughed Barbara, all confidence now, the worry-beads forgotten.

'Did you say this is a closing sale?' Anthony had never mentioned anything about that.

'Unfortunately. Trade has been poor for quite a while now.' She absently twirled her wedding ring round her finger as she cast a regretful look round the cosy interior of the shop, which was decorated more like a living room than a place of business. 'It was so easy when we started out. On a Saturday you couldn't move for customers.'

'This rain can't help,' put in Jane, wanting to be kind.

'No, no of course it doesn't.' She sighed. 'It's a shame to sell. But my business partner and I – we take it in turns to do weekends – think it's best to get out now, before things get too desperate. They say lots of small businesses are being hit at the moment, what with the recession and everything. It's all supposed to be getting better soon, but we haven't seen any signs of it.'

'I'm so sorry.'

'Believe me, so am I.' She gave a short laugh. 'It's really kept me out of mischief, this place – and the girls love helping. I'm a sports widow, you see – used to be rugby, but now it's golf. Does your husband play golf?'

Jane shook her head.

'Well, don't let him,' she warned affectionately. 'Once they start you've lost them for good. My husband – he's a doctor – is always finding excuses to run off and play with his mates. Though it keeps them out of mischief too, I suppose,' she added with a faint smile.

Jane, her heart in her boots, wanting only to run out of the shop, hurried behind the curtains to try the dress on. In her haste, the zip caught in the lining and she had to come out for help. Barbara sorted out the hitch with an expert yank and then stood back admiringly.

'I knew it,' she cried, clapping her hands, 'I just knew it.'

The dress felt smooth and cool. When Jane turned to look at herself in the full-length mirror, its skirt swung out effortlessly with the quiet whisper of fine silk. The main bodice was snug and flattering, following the line of her bust and waist as if it had been specially tailored for her alone. For all the awful confusion of the situation, shame being prime among them, it was impossible not to be thrilled. 'You shouldn't be leaving this business,' she said quietly, 'you're far too good at it.'

'Here, try these.' In an instant Barbara had slipped off her shoes and was offering them to Jane. 'To get the full effect.' They were made of soft black leather with a small pointed heel. Since their feet were clearly of a similar size, and there was no question of achieving the same effect with her own scuffed plimsolls, Jane reluctantly felt compelled to accept. She slid her feet uneasily into the faintly repellent warmth of Barbara Marshall's shoes, her toes curling on contact with the unfamiliar grooves inside. After only one hasty twirl she stepped quickly out of them and handed them back.

'I'd love the dress, but I think I'd better let you hang on to these.'

Barbara carefully folded the dress amongst quantities of crisp tissue paper, before Sellotaping it into a large white cardboard box that had OCTAVIA printed across one corner in large blue letters.

'If your husband throws a fit, you can always bring it back – though I hope you won't,' she went on, sliding the box into a bag. 'You need a wedding or something. It would be perfect for that – with your hair up, perhaps a cream ribbon of some kind...' Having put her hands to her own head to demonstrate, she dropped them with a quick laugh. 'Goodness, you're lucky to have hair like that. All mine fell out after Trudy – it's never been quite the same since.' She tugged ruefully at a few short strands.

'I think it looks very nice,' replied Jane firmly, beckoning to

Harriet who was again showing off her precious train to Trudy. 'Thank you, goodbye – and good luck,' she said, carrying her purchase and handbag in one hand and tugging Harriet with the other, trying to hide her haste to be gone.

Outside, the rain had stopped and the pavements were pitted with puddles. The air smelt fresh and moist. Jane walked as fast as Harriet would allow. She kept her head down, feeling like a spy, expecting every second that Barbara would come racing up behind her, shouting accusations about who she was, what she had done. Harriet toddled happily alongside, trying to jump in every patch of water, gleeful at her increasingly sodden socks and shoes.

The wife was no longer the wife. She was too-thin, and kind, and full of hope. What Jane had chosen to regard as an unwise no-harm-done deviation from the challenge of sorting her newly single life out, now gleamed in the lurid spotlight of base deceit. If love had played a part, Jane might have felt fractionally better. But where its absence had once helped her feel less guilty, now it only made things seem worse. Anthony had been a charming, attractive tonic for everyday pain, nothing nobler than that, nothing addictive or remotely justifiable.

That evening, when a glass of wine had begun to iron out the significant creases of the day, Jane filled her old fountain pen and settled down in the deepest of her armchairs, with a block of writing paper on her knees. The nib, thick and worn smooth, moved with gratifying ease across the chunky whiteness of the page, as if wanting to help her in her task. Contemplative, but sure, she started at once, barely pausing until she had signed her name at the bottom:

Dear Anthony
    I want to tell you that I have valued your friendship very much.
    The reason for my recent silence however, is because I have

been feeling worse and worse about the new territory that friend-ship entered a few weeks ago. In fact, if I could undo it, I would. Since there is no going back with these things however, I must ask you to stop trying to communicate with me – as a friend or anything else.

With my own marriage having failed so recently, I am still trying to find a way of moving forwards and have been making some mistakes along the way. What I am now sure of, is that emotional honesty has to be a part of whatever road I choose.

I have realised also, that I have very little idea of your own marriage. I have done my best not to think about it, to be honest. But I can't resist saying that, perhaps the support you want is there waiting for you, if only you would turn and look. After all, one of the things we each love most in life is to feel needed – it brings out the best in us. Whereas the hardest thing – sometimes – is to show that need.

Goodbye and with best wishes,
Jane

The letter helped ease the guilt. And there was relief too, since, in hindsight, Jane could see that the entire Anthony escapade, including her own willingness to succumb, had brought her close to giving up on all the things in which she still wanted to believe. It felt good to realise that she wasn't quite ready for such a surrender, and made her think more tenderly of Mattie – trying so hard to find her own way through the muddle of life, with the new crazy American plan.

After reading her letter through just once, Jane sealed it in an envelope ready to take to work and slip into the hospital post on Monday. It would not be easy of course, having to continue to avoid encounters, ducking down corridors and behind doors when necessary, but it felt unquestionably right.

Settling herself for bed a little later on, Jane was aware of a new peace of mind – a fresh trust in her own instincts – that brought with it thoughts of Julia. The heinous disloyalty over how she had let Michael – no matter how briefly and one-sidedly – into her life could not be undone; a failure of judgement on an epic scale. But Julia did have a tendency to rush in like a fool; and there was no denying that she had been right about the Anthony situation from the get-go. *Unwise.* Yes, Julia had been spot on, Jane reflected sleepily, turning out her bedside light and falling deeply asleep within moments.

29

Michael shifted the car down into second gear, ensuring that the movement caused the knuckles of his left hand to brush against the exposed inches of Lisa's stockinged thigh. As Julia had correctly reported, Lisa Reubens worked at the bank. Though she had begun as a temp for the whole department, her finger-clicking command of keyboards and filing cabinets had quickly made her indispensable to several of her employers. Her indispensability to Michael, which was of a rather different nature, had been set in motion back in the autumn, thanks to an encounter by the office drinks machine which was choosing a timely moment to swallow Lisa's coins without delivering anything in return.

'This usually works,' said Michael, noticing her exasperation as he was walking by, and stopping to give the machine a good thump. 'Not the most appealing cup of coffee, is it?' he remarked dryly, as a sludgy dark brown liquid spurted into the awaiting plastic cup.

'That might be because it's actually hot chocolate.' She smiled at him, revealing a tiny fleck of her red lipstick on a front tooth. 'I don't like coffee much.'

'Ah. Sorry for jumping to conclusions, in that case,' Michael laughed, feeling a frisson of something from how she was looking at him.

Lisa took a dainty sip. 'I love hot chocolate. Perhaps it's the continental in me. My grandmother was Spanish.' It was one of Lisa's endearing – and yet to some, irritating – habits to talk exactly as her mind worked. Once she started, thoughts could trip off her tongue in quite random sequences, leading down avenues that sometimes surprised even her.

As a single woman in her late twenties, still recovering from the shock of losing a long-standing boyfriend to a flat-mate, Lisa was alert to the possibility of a fresh relationship – preferably with the prospect of some permanence. Michael Lytton, with his swarthy looks, had already been an object of interest, even before Rosie in HR had mentioned the separation from the wife.

She stood to one side, feigning interest in the machine, while Michael fed some coins into the slot to secure a cup of coffee for himself.

'It's not very good,' he remarked, scowling after he had taken a swig, 'perhaps I should switch to that stuff.'

'Oh, you should, Mr Lytton, you definitely should.' And with an instinct perhaps inherited from the Spanish grandmother, who had once graced the Milan stage for a living, Lisa twirled on her high heels to saunter back down the corridor, her impressive chest pushed outwards, the full curve of her bottom rolling with each stride. She paused to cast him a quick smile before disappearing round the corner, a smile that said she knew he had been watching and it made her glad. No harm in being friendly, she told herself – and Rosie when they discussed the incident over lunch the next day.

Although Michael had the wit to recognise a crude bid for attention when he saw it, he was flattered – and lonely – enough to feel inclined to pursue it. Since the run-in with Antonia, now thankfully transferred to their New York office, his only diversion had been trying to crack open the un-crackable Julia. She had given him more than a wisp of encouragement during their dinner together, he was sure of it, and yet all that had followed was a steadfast refusal to do anything but – occasionally – take a phone call, letting him talk, while giving nothing in return. Out of loyalty to Jane, Michael had no doubt, which had felt more and more like pouring salt into his own wound. With his self-confidence teetering,

With Des abroad and Tim wrapped up in his own woes, Michael had been in danger of falling back into something like the bleakness of the immediate aftermath of his split from Jane.

Until Lisa. Having settled the car back into cruising mode for the last section of motorway before their exit, Michael reached for the hand of his girlfriend, and gave it a squeeze. With the prospect of an evening in a country hotel before them, he felt more expansively happy than he had in months. Lisa squeezed his fingers right back, just as he had known she would, and then raised them to her mouth. Her perfect, red heart of a mouth. Michael sighed with pleasure.

Lisa, too, savoured the moment, enjoying the now familiar, slightly salty taste of Michael's skin, and the faint scent of the soap he used. Such closeness – she had not known the like of it. Her ex-boyfriend, now married to the ex-friend-of-a-flat-mate, used to shun all physical demonstrations of affection unless they were a prelude to sex. Whereas Michael's craving for hand-holding and hugs was like an unquenchable thirst. Still holding his fingers, she reached out to stroke his ear with her free hand, enjoying the swell of nurturing love inside her – a swell that had begun the moment she saw him stare with such lonely gloom into the frothy depths of his Styrofoam cup some eight months before, racking his brains for something to say to her, it had looked like – anything to keep her from walking away. It taken a couple of months before things got going – on Rosie's advice she had played a little hard to get – but boy, had it been worth it. Indeed, all her life, it seemed to Lisa, she had been searching for just such a man as Michael Lytton; a man who wanted to be looked after; a man who buried his head in her ample chest as much out of hunger for a mothering love, as lust.

At the touch of her fingers on his ear, Michael kept his eyes fixed on the road, but bent his head slightly towards her, emitting a small groan of appreciation. Every moment with Lisa reminded him of the wonderful, almost forgotten, sensation of being cared for in an overt, generous way, when everything was still to play for, when nothing had turned sour. When they finally went to bed together, many long weeks after their prosaic exchanges about the varying qualities of manufactured hot drinks, he had been almost shocked – not to say thrilled – by Lisa's unashamed desire, by all the writhing and moaning that went with the unhooking of her indescribably splendid underwear. Having stopped believing that women in real life could behave like that, he immediately blamed Jane for his loss of faith.

His wife had never shown him such passionate love, he promptly confided to Lisa, who accepted such confidences greedily, clearly happy to be reassured of her own growing status in Michael's heart. Soon, he was re-writing his entire marriage in their conversations, forgetting the good bits and exaggerating the bad. Jane withheld affection. She was selfish and self-centred. Ungrateful. Demanding. She never had a welcoming smile for him at the end of a long day or listened properly when he spoke.

But Michael did miss Tom, especially since having him to stay. The three-week visit earlier in the summer had gone brilliantly. Without Jane around, and Lisa coming by to help, they got on so much better. Michael could lay down his own rules and indulge or castigate his son as he thought right without fear of provoking any parental cross-fire. Lisa went along with anything he said, while

Tom seemed to enjoy it too, rising well to the challenge of being treated more like an adult. Jane had always babied him so, and Michael told Tom so, man-to-man.

It was partly because he wanted to talk to Lisa about Tom that Michael had booked them into such a splendid hotel for the night. The other, even more practical reason for the indulgence, was that the hotel was on the outskirts of Westerham, only half an hour's drive from his father. Springing a visit on the old man was a key part of Michael's plan – paving the way for the future of which he now dreamed. Ernest was fond of Jane, he knew that much – from what he could gather, she always seemed to popping down to visit him, which was maddening. But the sweetness of Lisa would also win the old man round in seconds – Michael was sure of it, giving them both a much-needed fresh start.

When he told Lisa of the plan however, she wasn't quite as confident. 'But what if he doesn't like me?' she asked, for the third time, as they pulled into the driveway of the Country Inn, the wheels of the car crunching through the deep gravel.

'My love, he will adore you,' Michael assured her patiently, finding all her worry rather touching.

Unconvinced but encouraged, Lisa smiled in response, pulling her skirt a fraction lower, so that it met the top of her knees.

The hotel was as luxurious as the brochure promised. After cocktails, and a delicious dinner that left them replete, they retired to their room to enjoy some inspired love-making that was brought to a rather abrupt conclusion when Michael's condom burst as he climaxed. In the kerfuffle that followed, Michael was aware of being fast-forwarded – ill-prepared – into all the territory which he had hoped to introduce with the utmost tact and care.

'Are you likely to get pregnant at the moment?' he ventured, lying back down on the bed after having disposed of the condom in the bathroom. 'I mean – are you in the fertile bit or the safe bit?'

'You make me sound like a plant or something.' Lisa sat up, tugging down the yellow silk camisole she was wearing and raking some order into her long dark hair. 'Like you wouldn't want a kid of mine anyway.'

'I'm sorry, darling Lisa. Don't be upset, please. It was just a shock. For you, too, surely... I mean... of course, I would want your child...' Michael stroked her shoulder. 'It's just that... well, it would be something of a disaster if it happened now.'

'Our child, a disaster, I like that.' Thick tears spilled down Lisa's cheeks.

Michael, amazed and horrified by his apparent cruelty, hastily put his arms round her. 'Oh, I didn't mean it like that, darling – that was a stupid word to use – forgive me, please – I only meant that... timing-wise... it would not be ideal, because...' he pulled her closer, murmuring into her ear, 'you know by now that I want to spend the rest of my life with you, don't you?'

Lisa went very still, clinging to his encircling arms like a child. 'You mean...?'

'Yes,' Michael said softly. 'I want you forever, Lisa, and to have children with you, if that's what you want...'

'Oh, Michael.' Lisa sat up on her knees to hug him properly, covering his face with kisses. 'I love you so much.'

'I love you too, darling, and all I have been thinking about recently is how and *when* we can be together properly, because obviously there is still...' Michael hesitated, not wanting even to use Jane's name at such a special, crucial moment, '...still a lot to sort out. But,' he rushed on, 'I have been getting my head properly around fair terms for the divorce – the property market is doing better and we aren't far off the two-year mark, when it can all be done easily and quickly – with no one having to be officially blamed and minimal intervention from blood-sucking lawyers...'

'Michael Lytton.' Lisa knelt up, stopping his flow and cupping his face between her palms. 'Are you asking me to marry you?'

'Yes,' Michael said huskily, marvelling again at the power of her. 'Lisa Reubens, I am asking you to marry me. Just as soon as I am properly free. Until that time, I would like you to come and live with me...' He broke off, detecting a flicker of doubt in her face.

'And what if I am expecting a baby now?' She laid her hand on her stomach, keeping her big brown eyes fixed on his.

'It would be wonderful,' Michael murmured, kissing her, inwardly steeling himself for what he wanted to say next.

She nestled against him. 'And I want to live with you and marry you too, Michael Lytton.' She slid her arms round his waist with a happy sigh. 'Whenever God might decide to grant us a child.'

'Darling, there is something else I need to ask you,' Michael began, after they had been silent for a few moments. 'It's about Tom.' He stroked her hair, feeling her shiver of pleasure at his touch. 'An idea I've had. No need to answer now.'

'What idea, darling?'

'That, once you and I are settled, Tom should come and live with us. Properly. Permanently. He likes you so much – anybody could see that – and we did have fun when he came to stay, the three of us, didn't we?'

She drew away a little, looking at him with solemn eyes. 'Yes, we did have fun. He's a lovely boy, Michael. I would always love him anyway, because he is yours. So, what can I say, my darling, but yes, of course your Tom can live with us. Though I might need to give up work...' she gasped, laughing because Michael was hugging her so hard.

'Give it up then – tomorrow!' Michael cried, unable to suppress his relief and jubilation. 'I can look after both of us.'

'Tomorrow is Saturday, *mi amor*,' Lisa reminded him, giggling as she nudged him onto his back and rolled on top of his long body, thinking how, with his hair all tousled, he looked not unlike Antonio Banderas, even though his eyes were grey instead of brown. 'I am going to kiss the life out of you now,' she murmured, pressing her hips more firmly into his, 'my dearest future husband.'

* * *

The prospect of visiting Michael's father the next morning introduced an unwanted thread of unease to their newfound joy – an unease which they both found hard to hide. During the half hour journey they hardly spoke a word, except for each to enquire of the other, every two miles or so, whether everything was okay. To which they took it in turns to answer yes, wishing it were so.

August had brought another wave of heat, and Lisa could feel her hair sticking unpleasantly to the back of her neck, destroying all the hard work with the hair-dryer that had made her late for breakfast. She was a great believer in appearances, as well as in the importance of a first impression. For Ernest she was wearing her best summer frock, which was tight-fitting and bright yellow – her favourite colour – with white broderie anglaise skirting the neck and sleeves. Her legs, freshly waxed for the weekend, were smooth and bare, and her small feet were tucked into yellow leather shoes with spiky heels that sank so deeply into the soft ground of Ernest's drive that she had to walk on the balls of her feet, balancing uncomfortably, all the way up to the porch.

The front door was propped open with a cast-iron hand-bell that Edith had once used to summon Ernest – from the bottom of the garden or one of his foraging walks – back to the house for meals or telephone calls. Entering the cool dimness of the hallway now, with its faint smell of linseed and boot polish, Michael had the sudden, unnerving sense of stepping back in time. He moved closer to Lisa to catch the sweet scent of her perfume instead. The past could be such a lead weight, he had always found, pulling at him for recollection and reconsideration, when, now more than ever, all he wanted was to move onwards.

His father was nowhere in sight. They looked upstairs and down, calling his name and banging doors.

'He must have gone on a walk or something,' said Lisa, worried by the deepening furrows in Michael's brow.

'Damn. We could be here all day waiting for him. He's quite capable of losing track of time. Midday, we agreed, and midday it is.' Suspense, disappointment and a fear of being wrong-footed in front of Lisa, sharpened Michael's tone. 'He's probably absorbed down in that jungle of his that he calls a copse.'

'Absorbed in what?'

Michael shrugged. 'Oh, I don't know. He clears ditches and ties bits of string round broken fences – all that sort of Heath Robinson stuff. Pointless in the extreme, but I suppose it helps him pass the time. There's not much else for him to do these days.'

'Poor old man.'

Michael laughed at that. 'Don't waste your lovely pity on my father. He's fine. Very selfish and very happy. Always has been.' He thrust his hands into his trouser pockets and wandered back out on to the verandah, whistling quietly. 'I suppose we could go down there and look for him.'

'Down there?' Lisa squinted at the ragged horizon presented by the tangle of trees at the bottom of Ernest's broad garden. 'Into those woods?'

'It's hardly a wood, sweetheart.'

'I couldn't possibly – not in these shoes. Surely, he'll be back soon. I mean, he'll want lunch, won't he? Even if he has forgotten us?'

'I don't think he bothers much with lunch,' Michael muttered, 'he's incredibly thin.'

Lisa sucked in her stomach – a purely reflexive action prompted by the notion of a slimness to which she constantly aspired but never quite attained – before marching, with great vigour, back into the house. After a few minutes, she called out to Michael, who was still hovering, very much at a loss, on the verandah steps.

'Come and look at this. What do you mean he doesn't eat? I've found loads of things – fresh bread, cheese and half a chicken. Why don't we lay the table, get everything ready, as a sort of surprise for when he comes out of the woods?' Having made up her own mind on the subject, she started bustling round the kitchen, unearthing plates, glasses, knives, forks – even three napkins— and arranging them all neatly on the table.

Michael felt his frustration dissolve at the sight of her, the way she made herself so at home, arranging things with busy precision, her cheeks flushed, her hair bouncing against her back as she moved. He went up behind her as she was carving a few slices of bread, shifting her hair so that he could kiss the nape of her neck, just above a small mole that gleamed with minute, silky hairs.

'Have I ever told you I love you,' he murmured.

'Not enough, not enough.' She leant back against him, turning her head so they could kiss.

They poured themselves glasses of water which they drank in the kitchen, keeping guard over wilting lettuce leaves and taking it in turns to bat flies off the chicken. Every so often they kissed, only to part at the slightest rustle of a sound from outside. As the minutes chugged by, the tension of waiting began to mingle with the gradual arousal caused by their intermittent embraces. The day was getting hotter. Michael took off his tie and rolled up his shirt sleeves; Lisa kicked off her shoes and put her feet in his lap, wiggling her toes provocatively.

'I can't take much more of this,' he grunted, not making it clear whether he was referring to her teasing feet or the prolonged absence of his father.

'We could always start eating,' She tore off a shred of lettuce. 'He can't be much longer, can he?'

'Silly old fool. What can he be up to?'

They made love on the kitchen floor. The delicious coolness of the tiles helped Lisa forget the discomfort, but their hardness left a small patch of bruising at the base of her spine, a blue stamp of a memento that stayed with her for weeks afterwards. The excitement for her was bound up with a realisation of her power – that she could induce Michael to take such a risk, with no mention of even using a condom this time. For Michael, terror at the thought of Ernest's wrinkled face appearing at the door sharpened the edge of his sexual appetite, intensifying the pleasure of gratifying it. And there was a part of him too, the young boy part, who felt the child triumph over the adult, once and for all.

The exertion and pump of adrenalin left them so thirsty and celebratory that Michael proposed they look in the cellar where he knew Ernest kept a few decent bottles of wine. As he groped his way down the dark steps, Lisa, following closely behind, put her arms round his neck and nuzzled his hair. The light switch was half way down on the left, in the middle of the wall somewhere. The instant he made contact with it, Michael lost his balance and pitched forward. There was time, a split second, for him to anticipate pain, before something broke his fall at the bottom of the steps. He heard Lisa scream before he saw that he had landed on the body of his father.

The sex made it so much worse. The thought that the crumpled body, with its blood-caked head, had been lying just a few feet beneath them as they hip-thrusted into each other on the cold kitchen floor, was too macabre for words. It made Michael feel barbaric and unsafe; unaccustomed to the rawness of such emotions, he threw himself into all the business that followed with a frenzied energy, as if activity alone could shield him from the confusing assault of guilt and sorrow. While Lisa wept, Michael had got on with the task of phone-calls: to 999 and to Christopher, who it took time to reach because he was leaning against a tree in the Parks in Oxford when it happened, watching what turned into a long cricket match.

When he did get to hear the news, Christopher was at first enraged. Those stairs had been a death trap for as long as anyone could remember. Only a few months before, Ernest had said, not for the first time, that he really ought to have the light-switch moved up the wall so that it could be reached with greater ease. Such a stupid minor detail, a design fault, had no right, he felt, to be responsible for the taking of a human life. Something more momentous, more significant in every way should have done the deed.

The two brothers met back in Lisa and Michael's hotel the following morning, after Christopher had visited the hospital mortuary, where Ernest's body had been taken to await a post mortem. Lisa, still full of tears and shock, stayed upstairs.

Suffering, the grey gauntness of their faces, made the two men look more alike than at any other time in their lives. They sat in the mock-Tudor dining room sipping their coffees and struggling to talk, groping for a way of sharing the experience more fully. But a sudden unveiling of brotherly love was not to be, though each had half hoped it might be so. Michael was too absorbed by images he would never reveal – Lisa with her yellow dress up around the white mound of her stomach, her eyes blinking and brown; the eyes of his father, staring, gooey with blood.

'It must have been rough on you two – finding him like that. I am so sorry.'

'You've no idea how rough...' Michael felt again the weight of Lisa, her arms round his neck at the top of the stairs, bearing down on him as he fumbled for the switch. He remembered too the triumph of the secret sex, the sweet taste of it, before satisfaction had turned so sour. And he envied Christopher, as he always had, for being close to Ernest, and now for being able to mourn him simply, with none of the complicated, uneasy feelings that surged in his own heart.

'Have you told Jane?'

'Not yet, no.'

'Would you like me to?'

'You? Christ, no. Why should you? Of course, I must tell her.'

'Will you say Lisa was with you?'

'I don't know – I expect so.'

'Are you quite sure you don't want me to tell her—'

'Stop going on about it, for God's sake, Chris.'

Their fellow breakfasters looked round, momentarily diverted from their buttery eggs and flaky croissants, their expressions radiating vibrations of disapproval at raised voices in such a place, so early in the morning.

Michael lowered his voice to an impatient whisper. 'I will deal with Jane. I have some sense of duty in that respect, you know. There are plenty of other things for you to be worrying about.'

A discussion of likely arrangements for the funeral did not proceed any more smoothly. Ernest Lytton had, to put it in his own words, resigned his commission from God – or at least from the God whose demands were laid out in the books of the Bible he had once preached so evocatively. In the light of this, Christopher suggested that he might appreciate being buried on his own land, in a clearing in the copse, perhaps.

Michael was appalled. 'Bloody hell, now I've heard it all,' he whispered furiously. 'The very idea of getting the coffin and the priest and the rest of the bloody lot of us down there...' He threw up his hands in a gesture of contemptuous despair, flinging himself back in his chair.

'Forget it.' That they were capable of arguing over such a matter was enough to make Christopher withdraw. 'We'll stick to the safety of the churchyard, shall we? Just in case there is a God and he has a strict sense of protocol about such things.'

Lisa chose this moment to make her entry into the hushed elegance of the dining room. She had suffered a great deal, she felt, and walked accordingly. Christopher had met her only once before, when the two of them – much to his astonishment – had come to Oxford to treat him to lunch at the Randolph. It was because they were very 'serious' about each other, Michael had confided, during one of his girlfriend's frequent trips to the Ladies during the course of the meal. Christopher, burying his scepticism, had said all the

right things, noting how much more overbearing Lisa was than Jane
– bossier, but also more cosseting. And maybe that was what
Michael relished, he mused, for the security it brought, the sense of
being so overtly cared about. It would have driven him mad.

On seeing Lisa now, a black mohair cardigan draped over her
shoulders, her face a becoming composition of pallor and sorrow,
he could not help thinking that the part was overplayed somewhat,
given that she was in mourning for a man whom she had never
known. In his own shocked state, he found it hard to think of
anything to say beyond obvious pleasantries and the unfortunate
circumstances of this, their first meeting.

'It was *devastating* – for both of us – to find him like that – oh,
your poor Dad.' She gripped Michael's arm, shaking her head.
'How are you doing, Christopher, love? Michael was so sorry he
couldn't get hold of you straight away, before the...' Tears overcame
her ability to continue.

'If you don't mind – I'll be on my way. I want to go to the house.'
Christopher stood up as he spoke, the need to get away rising inside
him like nausea. 'We'll talk. Whatever you want for the funeral is
fine by me. He's not around to mind, is he?' He managed a ridiculous half-bob of a bow to Lisa, before plunging through the chairs
and tables for the door.

* * *

Before going into the house, Christopher sat in the old rocking
chair in the corner of the verandah, running his palms over the
worn grey wood of its arms until they were warm. The chair smelt
of pipe smoke. Floating on the wisp of a breeze were voices and
laughter, whether from recent times with Jane and the children, or
from more distant days, he did not know. Nor did it seem to matter.
A scruffy sparrow, its feathers tufted and fluffed, landed a few feet

from him, its eye darting to and from a crumb of something near Christopher's left foot. After cocking its head a few times, sizing up the risks, it hopped closer. But at the last minute its courage failed and it soared off into the sanctuary of the silver birch, the one that had died, but which Ernest could never bring himself to chop down. The departure of the bird, its essential timidity, depressed Christopher beyond words, heightening his sense of abandonment.

Inside, the house was stuffy and still. There had been more life outside, Christopher decided, where some substance of the old man seemed to linger in the warm air. He forced himself to open the door to the cellar, to feel his way down the top three steps and grope for the elusive switch, the trigger of death. He had a sudden thought then, poised in the dark, that perhaps it was Michael who had killed their father, squashing the life out of him when he fell. Falling in darkness, like life, he thought.

A pungent smell wafted up from the bottom of the steps; blood and disinfectant. Someone had made a bad attempt at clearing up. A botched job. Something about this, the fact that no one had been caring or strong-stomached enough to clean the blood away properly, broke the last small twig of his defence. Sitting on the bottom step, his feet where his father's head had been, Christopher wept. It was not only from a sense of loss that he cried, but also for himself, for his own derisory attempts at being happy, for all his failures and cowardice, for the fact that he was already halfway through his life – now without even the buffer of his beloved parent between him and the prospect of his own death – and yet still he felt weak and worthless.

With a cloth and a bucket from under the sink he set about clearing the blood away properly. He had only just finished when the phone rang. Though recoiling at the noise, hating the sense of intrusion, he felt bound to answer it.

It was Jane, as yet ignorant of what had happened, calling to invite herself and the children down for a weekend. The shock of hearing Christopher's voice, sounding so hostile and low, made her sparky and false.

'Oh, so you're there this weekend, are you?'

'I, yes, I—'

'How lovely. I'm hoping for an invitation myself – but not for this week or anything terribly soon. Is he there?'

'He – he – he—'

'He's in the garden, don't tell me. Well, don't summon him in or anything – I can easily ring back. Just say I called, would you? Thanks so much.'

It all happened in the weird double-time which accompanies calamity – the slow-motion of the unavoidable that happens in a flash. The moment her voice had gone, Christopher knew he had done wrong. He should have been able to swallow the lump in his throat far down enough to say something. No matter that Michael had staked his claim for breaking the news to her. He, Christopher, should have said *something*.

Without thinking, fumbling with the receiver, he began to dial her number. But when he got to the eighth digit, he made the mistake of pausing – to think the last part through – and promptly forgot it entirely. The numbers simply evaporated from his mind, floated away, like figures in a dream. After redialling, incorrectly, several times, he undertook a frantic search for an address book, a note-pad, anything of Ernest's that might have contained Michael and Jane's number. He had rifled through kitchen drawers, old phone books, even the desk in the sitting room, before the sweet recollection of the existence of directory enquiries eased its way back into his panic-stricken head.

The number, when they released it, was so obvious, so blindingly familiar, that he wondered if he was going insane. With trembling fingers, he dialled for the last time, then settled himself to wait, leaning his forehead against the cold metal side of the fridge, as Jane had done so many months before, when Mattie phoned all weepy and full of crisis. One, two, three, four, five, six, seven rings. There was no reply.

Christopher banged his head hard against his metal support, welcoming the distraction of physical pain. Moving slowly, half-stunned, he then replaced the phone, put the cloth and bucket back under the sink and returned to his car, locking the front door behind him.

* * *

So, Michael got to tell Jane after all. She expressed so little emotion that he almost felt cheated. He hated her control over herself, the way it shut him out. Before calling, he had half imagined her breaking down on the telephone – a fantasy of need in which she sought his comfort, as she once had a long time ago, when they had confused such emotions with love.

Perhaps because of her restraint over Ernest, which Michael's state of muddled shock caused him to receive as some kind of an affront, he was cruelly blunt when it came to his other news.

'Lisa and I – despite the far from ideal circumstances between you and me – have decided that we would like to get engaged. I like to think it might have made the old man happy to know that I— '

'But he didn't know her, did he?' Jane had slid to the kitchen floor with the phone gripped between her ear and shoulder. That Ernest had gone made it hard to concentrate. Her chest felt as if someone had punched a hole into it.

'Lisa? No, but if he had, he would have been pleased for me – for us – is what I mean. And when we… found him, we were going to tell him.' No single aspect of their conversation was proceeding as Michael had intended.

'Oh, I see,' Jane said faintly, not seeing anything at all, except Ernest's broad smile. 'Just so long as you're happy—'

He felt sure she was mocking him. 'Of course, I'm not happy about Dad, if that's what you're implying.'

'No, no, Michael, I didn't mean that,' Jane murmured, wondering when it would be okay to put the phone down.

Michael had jumped to the safer subject of their divorce. 'In six months it will have been two years, which means everything can happen quickly and easily. Markets are beginning to pick up, on all fronts, so before long we should be able to get a decent price for the house – at bloody last. I'll organise the next valuation in due course. In terms of money, I am prepared to continue with what I see as the extremely generous monthly allowance I have been dishing out for the children, until they are eighteen. With regard to you, I propose a lump sum settlement, based on a fifty-fifty split of all assets, but factoring in your earnings, as well as the significant amounts I have since been shelling out for rent. Lisa is moving in with me, but we obviously want to buy our own place, and are considering Wandsworth, so I suggest you start getting your ducks in a row too...'

'Ducks?' Jane murmured, huddling tighter against the wall, as Michael moved on to pension rights. Perhaps this was how he was managing his grief, she told herself, listening to his arguments as to why she had no right to any of his hard-earned pension pot, despite what the law might say on the matter. By the time he finally released her, after a stunned silence when Jane had said she hadn't wanted any of his pension anyway, her entire body was trembling. In trying to put on a tape of cartoons for the children, her fingers jerked so uselessly over the buttons on the remote control, that Tom, rolling his eyes, snatched it from her to perform the simple task himself. Removing the lid from the biscuit tin and leaving it invitingly on the table beside both children, she then

bolted up the stairs, two at a time, to seek sanctuary behind the
bathroom door.

Jane lowered the toilet seat and sat down, reaching for a towel
in which to bury her face as she wept. Like Christopher, she found
it hard to think beyond her own loss. No more of that quiet reassurance, that unvoiced affection of which she had felt so sure; no more
building and fixing jobs with Tom; no more rocking on the
verandah for Harriet, wrapped in his liver-freckled arms, the
rhythmic creaks of the chair soothing her to sleep. And as images of
Ernest continued to form, his thick shock of white hair, the bony
features of his face, the crinkled, stretched-leather look of the skin
under his eyes and around his mouth, the images blurred and fused
into the face of her own father, and how he might have looked, had
he lived so long.

A bathroom had been her refuge then too, in the cramped
skiing chalet full of friends who had taken it in turns to knock on
the door and beg her to come out, fearful – as they later admitted
– that she might 'do something stupid'. Peering over the towel
now, at the pink disposable razor reserved for her armpits, Jane
reflected wryly that her options for death in this bathroom at
least, were slim. Nor had such a dark possibility crossed her mind
that evening in the Innsbruck mountains. She had sat on the loo
seat then too, staring, not at the assortment of shaving appliances
marshalled round the basin, but counting the cracked tiles on the
floor and walls, waiting for something, for some clearing of vision,
some emergent sense of what to do next, before she got on the
plane home. It had presented itself in the form of Michael,
hurling himself through the door, breaking the flimsy lock, like
some superman of the slopes. 'It will be all right,' he had said,
grabbing her hands in his, soggy pieces of the toilet paper that
had served as Kleenex falling to the floor at their feet. 'You will
come through this, I promise you.' It was his strongest moment,

Jane saw now, the climax of all the time they spent together, before or since.

No more weekends in the country, Jane mused sadly, as she soaked a flannel with cold water and pressed it to her eyes. Maybe Lisa and Michael would try to take the house over as a cosy rural retreat for themselves. Or perhaps – more likely – Michael would persuade Christopher to sell the place, so that he and Lisa could afford somewhere really fancy for their future London marital home.

Later that evening, when she had settled Harriet to sleep, she brought Tom downstairs after his bath for a story, pulling him next to her on the sofa and kissing his soft, ruffled hair. He hadn't fought with his sister or sulked with her quite so much in recent weeks, perhaps because she had taken some time off work for the summer holidays. Whatever the reason, he seemed marginally happier and more relaxed – more like the Tom of before, when nothing more serious than an irritating sibling had threatened to cloud his day.

'Darling, I'm afraid I have something sad to tell you.'

He sat up at once and studied her with such a sombre expression that all her bravery threatened to collapse in an instant. 'Grandpa Lytton has died,' she managed, biting her lip.

Tom blinked, frowning. 'Is that because he was very old?'

'Partly... yes, he was very old, so he was going to die quite soon. But he... he died because he fell down and banged his head very hard.'

'Did it hurt him, when he died?'

'No, I'm sure it didn't. It happened far too quickly for it to hurt.'

'So does that mean he's gone to heaven?'

'Yes.'

'Will you die too?' Tom asked after a pause.

'Yes, but not for ages and ages – probably when you are an old man.'

'Does everybody go to heaven?'

'Everybody.' Jane tried to hug him but he remained upright, unyielding.

'So, I'll see Grandpa Lytton again then, won't I? And you, when you die. And Daddy and Harriet, when they die.'

'Yes, we'll all see each other in heaven.' Jane pulled him onto her lap, turning him to face the book they were reading rather than her face. The tears slid noiselessly down her cheeks, salty-warm on her lips and tongue, while he turned the pages and she softly read out the words.

31

Julia arrived on the doorstep the day before the funeral like Mary Poppins, complete with umbrella, carpet bag and hat, the latter being of black velvet with a wide, floppy brim, pulled, twenties style, down over her eyes and ears.

'By the way, thank you for forgiving me – I mean for *properly* forgiving me – so we don't even need to discuss it,' she had declared when Jane phoned to ask for help. 'And I am so very sorry for your loss of that lovely old man. I know you adored him. And he you. Please use me mercilessly for whatever assistance you require. I will never let you down again.'

They hugged hard on the doorstep, needing no words, Jane fighting tears because of being sad, and because of the relief of truly having Julia back in her life. She looked marvellous, though Jane worried for the hat. Harriet had recently developed a liking for hats, not just to wear, but to chew and jump on, or to fling, Frisbee-like across a room. Julia had another bag in the boot – of a smart new silver car, Jane noticed – that turned out to be full of presents, perfectly wrapped parcels with dainty tags, invisible Sellotape and mesmeric patterns of teddy bears and trains. They were to be rewards for when they were good, she explained, little milestones to get them through the next two days with the minimum amount of pain.

It had been Julia's suggestion during the course of the phone call that she come to babysit not for the day, but for two nights – so that Jane could approach Ernest's funeral in peace, she said, with time off either side to prepare and recover. 'I shall arrive on the Tuesday and leave on the Thursday,' she had said in her commanding way, 'whenever you choose to get back. Book yourself into somewhere spoiling – *not* just a cheap B&B – and I shall foot the bill. Don't argue, because I won't budge. Take a swig of brandy whenever you need to. I did it when Dad died and it helped enormously – especially after breakfast, when things have a tendency to look their worst.'

The handover proved longer than Julia had anticipated. After a conducted tour of the fuse box, the immersion switch for the hot water, the surgery leaflet on first aid, the medicines in the bathroom cabinet and the contents of the children's chest of drawers, she ordered Jane to leave.

'But there's the dishwasher. I haven't explained—'

Julia picked up Jane's small suitcase and handbag and held them out to her. 'Kiss your infants and go. Now.'

'Humming's okay – that's normal – but if it gurgles for anything more than five minutes you must switch the knob back to the green bit and then forward to the blue bit again – very fast or it doesn't work. When the humming comes back you can breathe again.'

'I shall breathe regardless. Go away.' Julia, carrying Harriet who was happily fascinated by the purple baubles in her necklace, kept the front door open with her foot, pretending to frown.

'I gave you the number of the guest-house?'

'At least three times. Though I wish it was a five star hotel—'

'And if they're monsters – Tom especially can be horrid – then get as cross as you like – or call me – thank you again so much.'

'If you thank me one more time, I shall run screaming from this house and never return.'

'Don't forget to hide your hat,' Jane yelled through the car window before driving off, her heart lurching with love at the sight of Julia bouncing Harriet, with Tom at her side now too, all of them waving madly from the doorstep.

Though Julia might have groaned at the sight of the Sea View Motel, whose bedroom windows offered little view of the coast except for those patrons inspired enough to have come equipped with a telescope, Jane did not care in the slightest. She felt utterly remote from her surroundings. Disconnected. Luxury of any kind would have been wasted on her. Even when the bath taps began by hiccoughing air and brown water, and the bulb in one of the bedside lights didn't work, she could not muster the strength to mind. She lay on her lumpy, narrow bed for twenty minutes, trying to relax and appreciate her solitude, before giving up and going for a walk.

'Do some shopping at the very least,' Julia had commanded, 'for *yourself*.' Since Jane was too unfocused to do any such thing, she bought T-shirts for the children, white splashed with paint-boxes of colour, and a cheap straw hat for Julia, which she ended up wearing herself because the early September sun was dazzling and she had forgotten her sunglasses.

It was strange to feel so solitary amidst the hordes enjoying the last couple of weeks of summer, strolling in their beach clothes, making their way towards the next ice-cream, the next fizzy drink, or simply back to the patch of stony sand which they had claimed as their own. Having yearned many times since becoming a mother for exactly this sense of being alone – time to herself – Jane wondered now what she was supposed to do with it. Without Tom and Harriet, she felt like a balloon lost to the sky, a pin-point on a blank canvas.

She walked aimlessly, her head buzzing with disjointed images: the children waving on the doorstep, Barbara Marshall's warm smile, Julia's hair, tumbling out of her black velvet hat like a shower of gold; Mattie's horrid triangle picture, dripping red... and poor Ernest... Ernest, of course... that was why she was here... the dear man, broken and bleeding at the bottom of the steep cellar steps...

Jane stopped, holding on to a lamppost as the dizziness surged and passed. But sadness did not mean losing the plot, she scolded herself, as soon as the horizon had righted itself. Spotting a café further on down the street, she took several deep breaths and set off again. She would avoid brandy but food and sleep would help. And grieving. She would manage.

* * *

The stone face of the angel peered down from her safe niche on the pillar, an expression of haughty pity on her grey, pockmarked face. Apart from the two brothers, Jane knew no one. It was a small gathering, made up of locals from the village and distant relatives whose faces were only hazily familiar from family albums and the Lytton turn-out for her marriage to Michael. Ernest had been an only child and Edith's family came originally from the north of Scotland, so contact between the various factions was rare.

Jane had taken the precaution of arriving early, so that she could slide into a discreet position in a back row. Christopher and Michael arrived last, filing in behind the coffin before taking up their seats in the front right pew, several feet apart. A woman, who had to be Lisa – his fiancée now, Jane reminded herself – was already there, waiting for him, buttoned into an elegant black chiffon dress and sporting a pillar-box hat swathed in black lace.

She kept fiddling with the black netting between casting nervous glances at Michael.

The coffin looked far too small to house Ernest's long, wiry frame comfortably. Did the body shrink after death, Jane wondered, without the soul to pad it out? Instead of singing, she was capable only of opening and closing her mouth, while her fingers gripped the order of service so tightly that the edges of the paper were soon damp and torn. She would have liked to have sung, to have wished the lovely old man farewell with her voice; but the notes in her throat wavered so much that she did not trust herself to release them, fearing that uncontrollable tears might follow half a beat behind.

Outside afterwards, a burning wheel of sun in a blue sky mocked their long faces and dark clothes. The handles of the coffin glinted, flashing a last valediction, as the box was lowered into its deep hole. Jane, having continued to keep well back till then, away from the small crowd, stepped forward at the last minute to throw in a tiny bouquet of marigolds as her parting gift. Moments after the 'dust to dust' passage, she tiptoed away, taking the long route down through the graveyard to the back gate, anxious to avoid any post-service small talk or the ordeal of vol-au-vents and sausages-on-sticks that was scheduled to take place at Ernest's house afterwards.

She almost got away. Her fingers were on the rusted latch when a hand touched her shoulder, causing her to spin round at such speed that she cricked her neck.

'Michael, you made me jump.'

Michael stood very close to her, as if unsure how to proceed, a visible sheen of sweat covering his white face. In the background, she could see Lisa eyeing them anxiously from behind the black cage of her hat, her head half bowed. Christopher had his back to them, his dark head unmoving, either ignorant of – or studiously oblivious to – the side show going on behind him.

'Thank you for coming.' Michael pulled a yellow handkerchief from his breast-pocket and dabbed at his temples. 'You don't have to go running off, you know,' he added, wondering how she could look so cool in her long-sleeved black dress and dark tights.

'If that's an invitation to come for the wake, then thank you.' Jane's fingers found the gate latch and lifted it. 'But I've decided it wouldn't feel... appropriate,' she stammered, not up to explaining that she didn't feel she had the emotional stamina required to get through it.

'But there's something I want to give you, something he would have liked you to keep.'

'Really?'

'It's that carriage clock, the one you said you liked, on the book-shelf in the sitting room.'

Jane blew her breath out, moved in spite of herself, and was somewhat at a loss. Michael being kind was the last thing she had expected. 'That's an extremely generous thought. Thank you, Michael.'

'And Lisa would like the chance to meet you properly,' he blurted, flicking his eyes away and fiddling with his hanky.

Jane almost laughed. 'Whatever for?'

'She doesn't want any animosity.'

'Animosity?' Jane turned back from the gate to face him. 'There is no animosity, Michael. There is nothing. What Lisa thinks of me, or I of her, is an irrelevance. It does not enter into the situation at all. I am very happy that the two of you have found each other – truly, I am. I wish you both every success in your future life together. There. Is that enough? Can I go now?'

'Would you say that to her?' He was pleading now, laying bare in the process the astonishing fact that he – obstinate Michael – was acting under the strongest of directives.

'But why should I?' Jane cried, her patience and limited amount of stamina fast running dry. 'Today is about your wonderful father. To grieve and mourn and honour *him*. Nothing else.'

Michael too, appeared to be sagging under the burden of his errand, coupled with the constraints of his heavy black suit.

'But it would mean a lot to Lisa,' he replied miserably, throwing a wary look back towards the church where the mourners were starting to move off, apart from Lisa, rigid as a tree and now glaring in their direction.

Jane took a deep breath, aware of her mostly sleepless night on the lumpy bed catching up with her. What did it matter? What did anything matter? 'Look, I will get into my car and have a think about it, okay? I just need a moment to myself. But if I do come, I do not wish to take the clock – or anything else – thank you,' she muttered, wanting him to know she had seen through his tactics.

'Okay. Thanks.' Michael, dabbing again at his face, turned and walked back up the path.

Jane closed the little back gate behind her and stepped into the cool of the canopy of trees arching over the narrow road like the vaulted ceiling of a cathedral. Only pin-pricks of light broke through the dense, leafy roof, dappling the bumpy surface of the old lane. Jane hurried towards her car, which she had parked up on a verge well beyond any other vehicles. It wasn't until she was half inside that she noticed a small white envelope with her name on pinned under a windscreen wiper. She reached for it quickly and with dread, fearing yet more demands from Lisa, since the hand-writing certainly wasn't Michael's. She settled herself behind the steering wheel before opening it, her mind and body braced.

Dear Jane,

I am sorry I must resort to the drama of a letter. It comes from having lost faith in my own voice. I certainly lost it when we spoke on the phone two weeks ago and Dad was dead and I couldn't tell you. I tried to ring back, but you had gone out.

My silence stemmed, I think, from shock, and, I suppose, cowardice. And Michael had said he wanted to be the one to tell you. All these things made me dumb.

Forgive my timorousness

Yours, Christopher.

Jane was not to know that it had taken several drafts to wring out the yearning that had seeped through Christopher's first attempts like air through a cracked door. In the end, formal brevity had been the only way to block it out. He had planted his letter soon after he saw her arrive, when they were still waiting for the coffin, slipping through the side door of the church and jogging along the lane to her isolated parking spot. The chances of her coming to the house after the service seemed slim, and he baulked in any case at the prospect of handing it over in person.

Having read the letter just once, Jane carefully returned it to the envelope and zipped it into the side pocket of her bag. It was a good letter, honest and to the point. She was very glad that he had written it. Before starting the car, she found herself trying to imagine how he must have felt, returning to the white house on that day, how difficult it must have been, just to pick up the phone, let alone deal with all her chatter.

She drove towards London for a good fifteen minutes or so, before turning round in a lay-by and heading back towards Ernest's house. The world had to be faced sooner or later, she told herself, pulling into the drive a little later. There was no option but to get on with it.

32

Approaching the house, it was Pippa who Jane saw first, carefully descending Ernest's narrow verandah steps, one hand gripping the slender balustrade to her right, the other patting the pin-cushion of a bun on top of her head. Jane froze, half expecting Pippa to float on past her, just as she had all those months ago in Dulwich, refusing even to acknowledge Jane's presence, let alone hear what she had to say.

'Hello, Jane,' exclaimed Pippa, suppressing her own discomfort and surprise, since Michael had just informed her of Jane's decision not to attend the wake, despite apparently heartfelt efforts on his part to persuade her otherwise. 'What a sad reason to meet. Tim and I managed to miss the service because of the A404, but are glad to be here, showing what support we can.' Having made it safely off the bottom step, Pippa offered an air-kiss of a greeting – which Jane returned in kind – as she continued to talk, about being happily settled in Cornwall, and how awful it was for Ernest to have died in such a way, and even more awful for poor Michael to have had to find him.

'How very good of you and Tim to come,' Jane said, when she ran out of steam at last.

'Friends are friends,' Pippa replied stoutly, wishing Jane's small, neat, figure, so tastefully attired in the simplest of black dresses, didn't make her feel like quite such a wheezy heffalump. It made Pippa long to be back in Helston, where their new friends only knew her and Tim as they were *now*, without any of the baggage of the past, whether in terms of body shape or anything else.

Jane, meanwhile, was thinking not of Pippa's size, but of the guardedness in her old friend's eyes, pondering both its true source and the hopelessness of being in no position to enquire. 'I should probably head inside,' she said instead, in as friendly a way as she could. 'Are you just taking a breather? Will you come back in?'

'Yes... no... I mean, I shall come back in, but I have to do something first...' Pippa smiled for the first time, replacing all the guardedness with light. She had told Tim that she would never forgive Jane, for what she had done to Michael – not to mention what she had thrown away by ending the marriage. But now that she was actually alone and with Jane in front of her, it was harder to stick to; because Jane was *nice*, and because it was impossible not to feel bad at how she had callously made use of her as a scapegoat for all the now abandoned pregnancy plotting that had made Tim so cross and despairing. 'Follow me, if you want to see why,' she said, gleefully, setting off towards a car, where two small black dogs had started barking and hurling themselves at the boot window.

'I'm intrigued,' murmured Jane, hurrying behind.

'Meet Lottie and Lionel,' declared Pippa happily, opening the boot and expertly seizing an animal under each arm, while managing less deftly to stop them licking her mouth and ears. 'Scottish terriers, both aged seven months, from different pedigree litters, and somewhat demanding...' She laughed, dropping them to the ground and managing to grab their trailing leads in time to stop them jumping on Jane. 'They're dying for a walk. Poor loves, it's been such a boring day for you, hasn't it? Mummy knows.'

'They are very sweet.' Jane knelt down to pet the dogs, who were too busy leaping on each other to take much notice.

'Don't tell me – child-substitutes – I know.' Pippa grinned. 'I don't care a bit. Tim isn't quite so keen, but he'll come round, I know he will. I keep telling him, we might make some serious money out of it one day.'

'What a wonderful idea. They're gorgeous.'

'We really are very happy in Cornwall,' she declared, after having slammed the boot shut and swapped her party shoes for walking boots. 'Funny how life works out, I suppose.'

'Yes, isn't it just... gosh, I am *so* glad for you, Pippa.'

'Thanks.' Pippa spoke briskly, busy taking charge of the leads which needed untangling from all the playing. 'Maybe we'll see you when we get back from our walkies. Tim's in there somewhere,' she waved at the house, 'though I can tell you now, he won't want to say hello.'

'I'm happy for Michael,' Jane called after her.

'Good,' she shouted, without turning round, 'so are we.'

Jane had to dig inside herself for courage all over again to enter the house. The door was open and she could see at once that caterers in black dresses and frilly white aprons had taken over the kitchen. She was hovering at the bottom of the stairs in the hall, steeling herself to enter the hubbub of the sitting room, when two female voices – one soft and one very loud – came floating down from the landing. As they drew nearer, the more strident one said, 'Michael has decided the son, Tom, should come and live with us. He feels that—'

At the sight of Jane, Lisa's mouth snapped shut while her companion scuttled off into the sitting room.

'I'm Jane. Michael said you wanted to meet me.' Jane spoke in a flat voice, extending her hand. 'What he did not mention was that you are planning to seek custody of *my* son.'

Lisa managed a limp handshake, glancing round her for support. A waiter, a tray of full glasses balanced on the palm of one hand, walked quickly between them with a murmur of apology. 'Drink?' she asked feebly, taking a glass herself.

Jane shook her head slowly.

'I think I'd better find Michael,' Lisa murmured, distressed by the expression on Jane's face.

'I think you had.'

By happy coincidence, Michael chose that moment to emerge from the sitting room. 'Ah, glad to see...' he began, before it dawned that all was not quite as he would have wished.

'She.' Jane raised a finger to point at Lisa. '*She* says that... you... want... Tom.' Jane could feel her fragile composure starting to crumble. She took a step closer to Michael, who now had one arm protectively clasped around Lisa, who was clinging to her wine glass and looking at the floor.

'Tom?' Michael asked, the exact nature of the crisis still only beginning to come into focus.

'Yes, she says you want Tom.' This time, the words somehow came out as a shouty screech, which had the effect of alerting some of the other guests to the unfolding drama.

'It was just... I was going to tell you... to talk to you...' Michael faltered, loosening the knot of his tie with his free hand, while his other arm remained round Lisa, who was sobbing volubly into his shoulder and in need of propping up.

A part of Jane wondered whether she might strike Michael. A slap. Something. She moved closer still, but then someone stepped between them.

'Michael, please take Lisa upstairs until she is feeling better.' Christopher spoke firmly and quietly. 'Jane, perhaps you would come with me.' He had gently taken hold of her elbow, making it easy for Jane to allow herself to be propelled away – back out through the front door, round the side of the house and down to the bottom of the garden where the swing and climbing frame were, looking all the more abandoned somehow for their recent improvements. From the copse beyond came the faint intermittent sound of Pippa calling to her dogs.

'They are planning to take Tom,' Jane cried. 'Did you know?'

'No. I would have told you if I did.'

She slumped down on the swing, while Christopher leant up against one of the supports. Up at the house, the other guests, having gathered snippets of the story, peered out through various windows. Michael too, stared grimly from a top room, arms folded tightly across his chest, his jaw grinding furiously, consoling himself at how lucky he was to be rid of Jane and to have such a loyal and beautiful woman at his side instead. Neurotic and aggressive outbursts would not help her cause with Tom, he brooded vengefully.

Christopher had no idea how to offer comfort. His brother could be determined and ruthless. With the back-up of a new wife and a deft lawyer, it wasn't impossible that he would win full custody of his son. He could not think of a single reassurance for Jane at such a prospect.

She was swaying in the swing, her head leaning against one of the ropes. Her black, rather scuffed shoes were in her lap, and she was using her stockinged toes to trace lines in the mix of dry mud and grass under her seat. 'Perhaps I should give him up.' She sounded dazed. 'Perhaps I should spare Tom the battle. What do you think?'

'That would be hard.' Christopher crossed his arms, to stop them dangling, out of wanting so obviously to reach out to her.

'I'm so sorry about Ernest.' She spoke to the ground. 'I loved him very much. Losing a parent is always such a shock, however – whenever – it happens.'

'You would know,' Christopher murmured, watching her intently, wishing she would look up, but knowing that if she did, he would have to look away.

'It's like the ceiling above you – the protection – has gone,' Jane went on. 'The fun and games are over, and your *real* life begins – the one that is full of all the difficulties you have so far dodged...' She straightened herself, sniffing as she wiped her face with her dress sleeves. 'Sorry. Don't listen to me. Self-pity incorporated inc.' She pulled roughly at her tights, hoicking them up from the ankle, oblivious to the tenderness with which Christopher observed the slimness of her legs, the bony, girlish knees. 'Thank you for your note,' she said suddenly, 'on the car.'

'I just felt so dreadful,' Christopher blurted, 'you ringing that day and—'

'I know. It doesn't matter now. It was very thoughtful of you to write.' She got off the swing and smoothed her hair, tucking the long front pieces behind her ears, before carelessly slipping her dusty feet back into the shoes. 'I'd better go before I assault somebody – a menace to society, that's me. You wouldn't escort me back to my car, would you? I am not sure I could face bumping into anyone. They probably already think I'm mad.'

'Don't be so hard on yourself. Mad people have a lot to offer. Personally, I prefer them to the sane ones... and of course I shall see off any unwelcome approaches,' he quipped, wishing he could do something to cheer her up.

They strolled back the way they had come, following the dusty path that snaked past the old silver birch towards the drive. A dry breeze hit their faces as they rounded the house, more like a blanket than a fan. 'When does life stop being such a bloody mess, that's what I want to know,' Jane said bitterly, kicking at a hard clod of mud, which broke into several pieces, making her shoes even dirtier.

'I'm hardly in a position to comment on that now, am I?' Christopher smiled ruefully. 'I've made the most terrible mess of things.'

'No, you haven't – not really – not compared to me. In fact, the sum total of my achievements is really quite hard to match.' She held up her fingers to count. 'My marriage has failed. I may lose custody of my own son...' She had to stop to swallow down a choke of a sob. 'I have a high-flying career as a part-time filing clerk... and recently have allowed someone to fall in love with me when I had no business doing any such thing...'

Christopher thought for one crazed moment that she meant him, until she muttered that it was someone at work and she wished she hadn't even mentioned it.

'I bet you can't do better than that,' she continued grimly, now rummaging in her bag for her keys, since they had arrived at her car, 'mess-wise, I mean.'

'I am alone, discontented and emotionally dishonest,' Christopher countered, wishing he could think of some way of defying her to ask more about the work person who might be in love with her.

'Oh, but I'm all those things too,' Jane replied airily, her eyes glittering with self-deprecation. 'What a fine pair of no-hopers.' She brushed his cheek with a kiss before getting into the car, winding down the window to say, 'thank you for rescuing me from making a total idiot of myself.'

'About Mattie,' Christopher began, bending nearer so as to be heard over the rev of the engine.

'It's all done with, Christopher. Mattie told me everything. It doesn't matter. None of it matters. Forget it.'

He stepped back to give her space to manoeuvre, and then stood, watching the clouds of dusty air left by her wheels long after the vehicle itself had disappeared round the bend in the drive.

Jane drove much too fast, wanting distance between herself and what had happened. The inside of her cheeks throbbed from all the chewing that had been helping to keep the tears at bay. Free to weep at last, she found that she couldn't. She was too hollowed out. Too shocked. Without Christopher, she wasn't sure how she would have regained any self-control. And thank God for that. Thank God for Christopher. To have lost it in front of all those people, on such an occasion, would have been unspeakable. Christopher's calmness – his kindness – had saved her from that at least. Though if Michael had his way, nothing could save her from the pain that lay ahead.

33

It wasn't much fun at all. In fact, it was really rather awful. Tom's seven-year-old wilfulness, of which Julia had only ever had glimpses, was quite frightening. He seemed to relish the challenge of trying to make her cross – almost as if he knew it was the last resort that she was determined to avoid. Whatever she suggested, he refused, whether it was food or entertainment and when it came to going to bed, Julia found herself resorting to bribery – with chocolate buttons – not even making him clean his teeth again.

'I'm going to eat this rubber,' he announced the next morning, after three bowlfuls of Coco Pops and half the contents of the sugar bowl.

'You'll get tummy-ache.'

'Won't.' Tom raised the rubber to his lips.

'Don't be silly, Tom. Give the rubber to me.'

'Won't.'

'Silly, silly Tom-Tom,' chanted Harriet, in an attempt to show solidarity with Julia which only succeeded in encouraging the opposition.

Tom bit the rubber, his impish green eyes – so like Jane's – fixed on Julia's face.

'I'm not going to watch. I've never seen anything so stupid. Come on, Harriet, let's go and read a story.' Julia swept out of the kitchen, sneakily grabbing the first aid leaflet on her way. Weed-killer, plastic bags and boiling water featured in several sections; but rubbers didn't get a mention. She even tried to ring the surgery but the number was constantly engaged. When Tom reappeared, patting his rib cage and making disgusting burp-like emissions from the back of his throat, she abandoned her search for medical assistance, deciding that death might be the best option after all.

As the hours wore on, with the relentless, repetitive, exhausting business of childcare, Julia found herself clock-watching in a way that she hadn't done since her early days as a sales assistant at Nelson's Antiques, where lolling of any kind had been forbidden and the small of her back had ached to know the pleasure of being allowed to sit down. The second night she got them both into bed even earlier, managing without chocolate buttons – on the grounds there were none left. She poured herself a glass of wine and was just settling down with a plate of the fish pie Jane had so thought-fully made for her, when Tom reappeared, claiming he was starving and that Harriet had peed into his policeman's helmet instead of her potty. This turned into the first of several interruptions, lasting well beyond the ten o'clock news and a documentary on breast cancer that Julia had been keen to watch. When Tom finally surrendered, a small heap of crumpled peace on top of his duvet, clutching a weather-beaten, clearly much treasured spotty giraffe which Julia rather wished had been a part of Jane's briefing, she was too tired to do anything but go to bed herself.

On the morning of Jane's return, they had all been keeping watch at the window for at least half an hour when her grey Rover finally pulled up outside the house. Harriet cantered, yelping, to the

door, while Tom promptly – and with an obstinacy Julia was beginning to recognise – pretended to be absorbed by the dinosaur book
that had been among her many gifts.

Jane looked pinched and tense, though her face broke into a
grand smile at the sight of Julia and the children. 'Oh, I missed you
all,' she cried, trying to hug everyone at once, Tom having been
unable to keep up his pretence of indifference for more than a few
moments.

'Was it ghastly?' asked Julia. 'Have you been miserable? There's
gallons of coffee.'

'This place looks suspiciously tidied-up and spotless,' Jane
accused teasingly as they entered the kitchen, scooping Harriet
onto her lap as she flopped into a chair. 'I expected jam smeared on
the walls at the very least.' She reached out and squeezed Julia's
hand. 'I can't thank you enough. Have they been more or less okay?'

'We've had our moments.' Julia pulled a funny face at Harriet,
unwilling to reveal the full extent of the battles that had been
waged and her own desperation in dealing with them. 'Persuading
them of the joys of sleep proved something of a challenge.'

'Oh dear, they've been awful, I can tell.'

'Not exactly awful, no.' Julia smiled. 'I think they just knew they
had an amateur in charge – and took full advantage. We'd opened
all my presents within about two minutes of your leaving – it was
my fault, I caved in completely. Then it rained for the rest of the day.
Yesterday was better – we spent so long at the park that we got
locked in, but a kind man on a horse found someone to undo the
padlock. Food hasn't been a problem. Tom ate half a rubber
yesterday – but seems to have digested it okay.' She poured out two
coffees and dolloped milk into the mugs. 'Tell me about the
funeral.'

Jane shrugged. 'Grim, but bearable. Until the reception. I wasn't
going to go, but then thought I'd better.' She took a sip of her coffee.

'I saw Pippa there, which was okay, actually.' She pulled a wry smile, Julia having long since been apprised of all the difficulties in that quarter. 'She says they love Cornwall, and introduced me to two gorgeous dogs – Scottish terriers – she wants to breed them, she says.'

Julia raised an eyebrow. 'Dogs instead of babies?'

'Absolutely. Pippa said so herself. She really seemed happy, which was wonderful.' Jane lifted Harriet off her lap and reached for her coffee mug, hugging it to her chest. 'But it was after that when things nearly got out of hand.'

'Go on.' Julia spoke carefully, having noted the tears filling Jane's eyes.

'It turns out Michael wants Tom... I almost punched him,' Jane whispered, reaching for a banana from the fruit bowl and peeling it for Harriet, who had begun tugging on her clothes for attention. 'He wants to have him live with him and Lisa.'

'Jane, I am so sorry.' Julia got up to put her arms round her as best she could. 'But they haven't a hope, surely?'

'I don't know, Julia, I can hardly bear to think about it, to be honest. I mean, maybe having an eager young partner – one who doesn't want to punch ex-husbands in the face – would help Michael's cause. And as for Tom,' Jane lowered her voice again, checking around Julia for any sign of being overheard. 'He is already pretty thrown by what's happened – the thought of any sort of custody battle is unthinkable. The damage it might do...'

'Yes, Tom has a sort of rage about him sometimes,' Julia admitted ruefully, returning to her seat. 'I'm not sure I was terribly good at handling it.'

'I bet you were. I can't thank you enough.'

'No need for *more* thanks,' she scolded. 'It was an honour and I shall do it again, like a shot, whenever you need. Also...' Julia drained her coffee, setting the mug down with a little bang, 'if it comes to needing lawyers to fight your cause, please know that I shall assist with that too. Not to be discussed now,' she protested sternly, as Jane tried to pitch in with refusals and more gratitude. 'I have to be on my way now anyway – to see whether my shop-sitter managed to sell anything in my absence – but you are to call me at *any time*. Is that understood?' Only when Jane had nodded meekly did she disappear upstairs to fetch her things.

'By the way,' Julia said, when they were standing in the hall on the point of farewell, 'your erstwhile friend, Anthony, called. I said I wasn't sure when you were getting back and that you were extremely busy.'

Jane made a face. Julia knew all about the Anthony hoo-ha.

'Did I do wrong?'

'No, you did absolutely right. Thank you. He knows where he stands – and has done for ages. Far more importantly, thank goodness this beautiful headgear survived Harriet,' she joked, tweaking the brim of Julia's black velvet hat as she pulled it on.

'Me too. Though, I fear the small canvas of triangles propped behind my bedroom door wasn't quite so lucky. Sorry, but it somehow got embroiled in a game of hide-and-seek... salvageable, I think. I've rolled it up and am taking it with me to see.' She patted her carpet bag. 'I could put a frame on it too, if you wanted. Strange piece – wherever did you get it?'

'It was a parting gift from Mattie. It gives me the creeps, actually, but I couldn't refuse. Don't worry if you can't fix it.'

'Any word from the migrant sibling?'

'Just a postcard – you probably saw it on the board by the fridge, a New England forest in its autumnal glory – bearing one line of scrawl about having a *great* time. Which is typical, and good, of course, but also worrying, because with Mattie you never really know.' Jane sighed. 'I give it six months at most.'

She summoned the children to come and say a proper goodbye.

Harriet obligingly allowed herself to be enveloped and kissed, but Tom, having slouched as far as the bottom of the stairs, refused to speak.

'It doesn't matter, Jane, really,' whispered Julia, feeling miserable at the sight of his clenched little face.

'But it does matter,' Jane insisted, glaring at her son. 'Julia has been kind enough to look after you for two days, Tom. She has given you presents and taken you to the park. Now, say a proper thank you to her.'

Tom remained silent, looking hard at his socks, his hands plucking at his trousers.

'Please, Tom. Say thank you and goodbye to Julia.'

'I hate you,' he shouted, turning to run up the stairs. 'I hate everybody.'

'Don't worry.' Julia put her bag down to hug Jane. 'He will be all right. He's just in such a muddle right now.'

Jane shook her head, 'I thought it was getting better. Going away probably hasn't helped. I just couldn't face taking them. Which was probably terrible of me...'

'Shush, Jane,' Julia murmured, hugging her while she pondered the delicate balance between offering help and downright interference. 'It was fine to go alone. You needed the space and the time... but further down the line, because of all that has happened, Tom might benefit from some counselling. It's something to bear in mind, anyway,' she added kindly. 'The main thing is to take care of yourself.'

Jane nodded meekly. 'Okay. Thanks, yes. I'll have a good think about everything.'

As they were finishing their goodbyes on the kerb-side, Jane was dimly aware of the house phone ringing. Stepping back into the hall a little later, after Julia had driven off, Tom came bowling towards her, his face transformed by grinning.

'Daddy just rang. He wants me to go to Cornwall with him and Auntie Lisa before school starts again and I said yes. We're going to camp at Uncle Tim's and make a real bonfire.'

* * *

The moment Julia was clear of Jane's road, she lit a Sobranie, wound down the window and put a Whitney Houston tape on at full volume. Her new car, a Japanese make with all mod-cons, including air-conditioning and a phone, felt wildly luxurious. As did the thought of her small, carpeted shop, and her tidy, clean flat, where the single mug, bowl and spoon that she had used for breakfast two days ago would still be sitting in the drainer; where every single one of her solo routines for taking care of herself and her business could continue without interruption by anyone or anything – let alone small children, no matter how dear. Having tossed the cigarette out of the window after just a few puffs, she used the car phone to dial her shop.

'Good morning, Lisson Antiques, how can I help you?' came a male voice with a hint of an accent, which Julia had originally had trouble in identifying, but which she now knew to come from Sweden.

'Olaf, hello, it's me. Just checking in to see if the place has burnt down or been robbed.'

'No. We are in excellent condition. How was your goddaughter and her brother?'

'A lot more demanding than my business, I can tell you. I should be with you in an hour or so. Can you hang on that long? The traffic is unspeakable.' She was sitting in a jam that appeared to stretch right up through and beyond the Kingston bypass.

'Of course. I am getting paid, remember?'

She laughed. Olaf dealt in antiques himself, but only by way of a serious hobby. Having run a successful computer company for most of his life, he had recently sold out and was adjusting to the pleasures of retirement. They had met when he came browsing round the shop a few weeks previously and argued over all her prices. His payment for two days of shop-sitting was, by his own suggestion, a Victorian porcelain figurine of a deer and hunter. He had one very like it already, he said, and relished the idea of an almost-matching pair.

34

Although Jane had read about fathers deciding to fight to take their hitherto mostly ignored children with them en route to a new relationship, she was still profoundly shocked that such a course of action should appeal to Michael. Apart from perhaps the event of birth itself, he had always been such a reluctant parent, so short-tempered and unwilling to be involved, that it was hard not to assume his motives were of the basest kind, to do with getting back at her rather than actually wanting to bring up their son. And she had her suspicions about the awesome Lisa too, as a driving force behind it all.

But how could a mother refuse a child a camping holiday with his father? It would have been impossible to explain her reservations to Tom without alarming him, only adding to the turmoil of his new one-regular-parent world, a world in which grandfathers died and mothers and fathers came and went from the family home, apparently at random.

The night after Julia had gone, weighed down by such preoccupations and aware that it was a while since she had eaten anything hot or nutritious, Jane decided to cook herself a proper meal. Tom, no doubt exhausted by the antics to which he had subjected poor Julia, as well as excited by Michael's camping plan, complied with welcome docility to the process of being washed and shoe-horned into bed, and was fast asleep soon after Harriet.

Jane tip-toed downstairs and opened a bottle of wine from the couple she kept under the sink, before switching on the radio, and starting to prepare rice and vegetables to go with a chicken breast which had been among her purchases for Julia. The radio programme was about black holes in outer space, invisible vortexes of nothingness, from what Jane could make out. She kept trying to concentrate on the scientific explanations, only to find her mind wandering down wilder avenues to do with the possibility of an after-life and God. To believe fully in *something* would be so deeply reassuring, she reflected wistfully – that certainty that there was a grand plan rather a void of pure chaos – but then, even dear Ernest had found it hard. The thought of her erstwhile father-in-law made her weep a little over her grilling chicken, before the realisation that she was getting chilled as well as hungry sent her upstairs in search of a jumper.

In her bedroom, she paused in front of her wardrobe mirror, curious to see whether she looked as bad as she felt, what with all her recent tears and the new, hateful and churning worry about Tom. In recent weeks the weight had been falling off, and it didn't suit her, Jane saw suddenly, having until then been half pleased at her loosening clothes. Her breasts were in danger of disappearing altogether, and her bottom, when viewed side-on, looked almost flat. Her face too, had been altering, she saw now – her chin jutted more and her eyes were too deep in their sockets, all hollow and staring, as if shrinking back from the outside world.

It wouldn't do, Jane scolded herself, picking out a bright red jumper, baggy enough to hide her too-straight lines, and giving her hair the vigorous brushing that still made it shine. Spotting a grey hair gleaming amidst the mass of dark brown, she yanked it out, before hurrying back downstairs, resolved to eat and enjoy every last morsel of her hearty meal.

She was rounding off her feast with a bowlful of bright yellow, easy-scoop vanilla ice-cream, when there was an impatient rap on her front door. Slowly, Jane put the bowl down and ventured out into the hall, fighting unhelpful images of axe murderers and intruders with knives up their sleeves. 'Yes? Who is it?' she called, hopping back in fright when the letter flap opened in response.

'It's me,' a voice boomed through the flap, a voice that she recognised at once. 'I've been ringing the doorbell.'

'The doorbell doesn't work, Anthony,' Jane called back, 'and it's late.'

'Please, Jane, can I come in for a bit? Just to talk?'

With some reluctance, Jane released the upper and lower bolts and opened the door.

'God, it's good to see you.' He thrust a bouquet of red roses at her. 'Say it with flowers, right?'

'Anthony, this is not a good idea...' Jane began, only to find herself suddenly fighting off not only a bunch of thorny flowers, but also Anthony's hands, clasping her back, and his mouth, full of alcohol fumes, travelling over her face. It took several moments to prise herself free. Long enough for Tom, parked on the top stair, to have an unrestricted view of the proceedings.

'Mum.'

'Oh, my darling.' Dropping the flowers onto the hall table, Jane rushed – two stairs at a time – to gather Tom into her arms, where he flopped sleepily. 'I had no idea you were awake, sweetheart. Let's get you back to bed.' She carried him across the landing and into his room, her heart thudding, cursing herself for the stupidity of having opened the front door.

'Hello there,' Anthony called up after them, in a jaunty, slurred voice that made Tom cling to Jane more tightly. 'What a lucky chap to have such a lovely Mummy.'

'Who's that man?' he murmured, as she pulled the bed clothes up.

'Someone from Mummy's work who is going home right now. Now go to sleep.'

'You were kissing.'

'He was trying to kiss Mummy, but Mummy didn't want him to.'

'It looked like love-kissing.' He rubbed his eyes with his fists, screwing his face up.

'Well, it wasn't,' Jane said firmly, desperation mounting. 'I don't love him at all and he's not even a friend and Mummy is going to tell him off for coming to the house when he wasn't invited. You try and get some sleep now, and try to forget all about it. I'll come up again very soon, okay?'

Back downstairs, she found Anthony in the kitchen, drinking wine from the glass she had left on the table. His hair, which she had once perceived as flopping with roguish attraction over one eye, now looked lank and unkempt.

'Anthony, I would like you to leave.'

His elbow slipped off the table as he tried to lean on it. 'But we've got some unfinished business, you and I. Don't tell me you don't remember?' He smiled in a way designed to be alluring, and then frowned when Jane didn't smile back.

'As I explained months ago, in my letter—'

'Oh yes, now there was a waste of paper, if ever I saw one.'

Jane tensed, hearing a nasty edge in his tone. I don't know this man at all, she thought, I never have.

'Anthony, I would like you to leave, please.'

'I'd be a lot happier staying here with you.' He patted his knee. 'Come here a minute, there's a good girl.'

'No.' Jane walked over to the telephone, trying not to hurry. 'I am calling you a taxi.' She picked up the receiver and dialled the number of the local cab company, which lived on a business card pinned to a cork wall board, between Mattie's postcard of New England foliage and Harriet's first picture ever of a human with limbs as well as eyes. Behind her, Anthony thumped the table, making her supper things rattle.

'Put that bloody phone down and come here.'

A woman answered the call just as Anthony, having arrived behind Jane, was pressing his face into her neck and trying to slide his hands up under her jumper. Jane managed to keep hold of the receiver with one hand – fighting off what she could of the unwanted attentions with the other – giving the details of her address in a clipped, loud voice. 'And please hurry,' she gasped, 'there is a man here who—'

'Hurry? There's no hurry, is there?' Anthony had snatched the phone from her and rammed it back into its slot. Jane seized the opportunity to break free and charged into the hall. He followed slowly, shaking his head in drunken bemusement. 'I think you've been playing games with me, Ms Lytton. Come on now, own up.' He wagged a scolding finger. 'Leading me on, eh?'

Jane pressed her back up against the front door, one hand behind her on the handle. 'I wasn't leading you anywhere. It was a hideous mistake and ages ago, and I'm sorry.'

'Sorry? But why? It was fun, wasn't it?' He had arrived in front of her, his face so close she could smell again the sourness of his breath. 'Harmless fun...'

'It was not harmless. There is Barbara. Your wife, with whom you want to have another child.' Jane spoke in short bursts, tightening her grip on the door handle, ready to turn and escape into the street, screaming if necessary. The taxi would hoot. They always hooted. 'I met her. At her shop. And your daughter. Barbara and Trudy. I met them and they are lovely. Barbara and I talked a lot.

She told me about trying for another baby. She was so *nice* – far too nice for you. If you don't leave me alone, I shall tell her everything. I have nothing to lose, you see, Anthony. Whereas I have a feeling that you do, despite all that bunkum about having an open—'

Jane was interrupted by the hoot of a car horn. Anthony had stepped back anyway, his head and arms hanging, the fight gone out of him. Jane opened the door and ran outside to wave at the driver. 'Now go, and never bother me again. If you do,' she hissed, as Anthony shuffled past her, 'I will report you for harassment and get you struck off. Oh, and be nice to that lovely wife of yours,' she snarled, before striding into the house and slamming the door, emerging a few moments later – moving with even greater speed – to ram the bouquet of roses into the dustbin.

* * *

'So, what is she like, this friend of yours with all the troubles and the terrible children?' Olaf placed a kiss between Julia's breasts and then sat back against the pillows.

'Oh, very normal. And the children weren't terrible – I was.' She yawned, reaching back above her head to grasp the bedstead, so that the compact mounds of her breasts rose too, causing her lover to smile in appreciation.

He started to kiss her again, this time with rather more vehemence. She nuzzled the top of his head and then pushed him away.

'I thought you were supposed to be tired.'

'I was. But maybe you should make the most of such times as this – I am an old man, remember?'

'I hate your old man jokes. I won't listen to them.' She threw back the sheets and swung her legs over the edge of the bed. 'It's late. My shop opens in forty minutes. Get some sleep, old man.'

Olaf sat up, sliding his arms loosely around her waist, before brushing his lips over the small mole by her left shoulder blade. 'Let us just talk some more. To lie in bed with you is my greatest pleasure. Don't leave for your workshop yet.'

She loved the way he talked. The grammatical, textbook English, learnt to perfection but still pitted with phrases that sounded somehow incorrect – subtly inappropriate or too formal.

'We shall discuss your friend, Jane Linton.'

'Lytton.' Julia flopped back amongst the pillows. 'Five minutes. Then I'm in the shower. You can brew us some of that wonderful coffee of yours. Why are you so interested in Jane anyhow?'

'Because she is your great friend. And because I am interested in you. Would you like me to meet her?'

Julia had to think about this for an instant or two.

'Do you have an embarrassment about me? Because of my age?'

'Oh no, silly Olaf. It's not that, not that at all. It's just that I haven't told her about you yet – she has so many complications in her own life at the moment – I'd feel almost guilty admitting to being happy myself.' Julia paused. 'And we don't talk like we used to – not nearly as often anyway. We're both so busy with such hope-lessly different lives.'

'That is not an excuse between friends.'

She stroked the thin smattering of grey hairs on his chest. His skin was smooth, but slightly loose-fitting, as though designed for a man one size larger. He had spent most of the summer at his house in the Swedish archipelago and was still tanned a light olive-brown. The hair on his head was steely blond and very thick, and his eyes, though beset by lines – crow's-feet gone wild – were so richly blue that she had at first teased him about suspecting they contained tinted contact lenses. But the reluctant unveiling of some gold-rimmed, half-moon spectacles in the semi-darkness of a cinema had soon put paid to that theory.

'You're right, I know.' Julia paused, torn for the first time in a while between loyalty to Jane and the desire to unburden herself to someone whose intimacy and opinions she already cherished very deeply. 'There was a time – a while back – when I unwisely allowed myself to become embroiled in the break-up of her marriage.'

'You made love with the husband?' The blue eyes were fearless, softened only by concern for her.

'Oh no, nothing like that, thank goodness. But we met once – a big mistake – and then he used to call me a lot. Looking back, I'm sure he saw me as the way to avenge himself on Jane. I don't think he's a very nice man. Anyway, it was a complete loss of judgement on my part, and when I finally mentioned it to Jane – though I didn't tell her everything, only that he had called – it made things very difficult between us for a while. In fact, the whole business of her marriage going wrong really made us lose our balance – I can't really explain it.'

'Call her now. Tell her we shall take her out for a dinner. Tell her it shall be the gift of your good friend, Olaf Lindquist.'

Julia kissed him very tenderly. 'Jane and I are fine now and you are a lovely man. Thank goodness you stepped across my path. We shall take her out to dinner soon – but I certainly won't let you pay. Can I have a shower now?'

'No, you cannot.' He pulled her down beside him. 'Before drinking my coffee, you have first to work up a thirst,' he whispered, brushing the hair from her eyes and kissing her nose.

35

Tom went with Michael to Cornwall for the very last week of his summer holidays. For Jane, time slowed to a crawl. On the days she was at home, she diverted herself with major cleaning and sorting sessions round the house, as if spotless surfaces and stacks of belongings could somehow make up for the continuing dishevelment of her emotional life. She would be glad when the time for selling finally came, she told herself, Michael having said again that they would get more money if they waited a few months more. Harriet, growing ever more mobile and independent, thought all the activity very exciting and did little dances amongst the dusty heaps, flicking Jane's feather duster at dead spiders and pretend-spraying aerosols at the walls. She liked housework to a worrying degree, Jane mused wryly, vowing to indoctrinate her daughter with the importance of sharing such duties fifty-fifty, and never taking any of the nonsense she had.

Early September, the husk of summer, imprinted its own stamp of melancholy on those days. The nights were noticeably darker, the sun, when it shone, less brilliant. The unmistakable heartbeat of winter pulsed quietly in the background, filling Jane with a kind of suspense, a dull, unpleasant sense of waiting that cast a shadow over even the good moments.

Some part of this tension proved justified when, on the final day of the week, she was summoned to the head of administration's cubby-hole of an office to be informed that, due to budget constraints beyond his control, all of the part-time clerical staff were to be 'released' with immediate effect.

'You mean we're being made redundant,' said Jane, which caused some embarrassed squirming, before the discussion was shunted quickly on to the less painful question of the modest financial settlement that would make up part of this mandatory package. An absurd sense of rejection accompanied Jane home – an inescapable feeling of not being wanted, of not having been good enough for even the lowest rung of a ladder.

'How would you feel if you'd failed in the dizzy career heights of clerical assistant?' she wailed, phoning Julia about it later that day.

Julia could not help laughing. 'Try not to take it personally. You are *so* employable, Jane, and when you choose to job hunt again, you will find something much more suitable, I am certain, especially as the country appears – at last – to be rising out of its doldrums. In the meantime, perhaps try and look on the bright side. I mean, there's the pay-out to keep you going, plus no more need to play Dodge the Dreadful Doctor – God, that man is bloody lucky you haven't reported him. Also, what with all Michael's Tom shenanigans, a bit of time-at-home could be just what you need. By the way, has he said anything else on the subject since the funeral?'

'No, thank goodness, but only because he's too busy showing Tom a happy camping time in Cornwall with the Crofts...' Jane took a breath, pulling herself together. 'But I'm fed up of talking about me. Tell me how you are for once. Actually, you sound rather jolly. Have you won the pools or something?'

'Alas, no,' Julia laughed and then hesitated, assailed – for all her reassurances to Olaf – by sudden qualms about admitting to Jane that she had fallen in love with a man thirty years older than herself, a man who wore half-moon spectacles. 'Come up to London and have dinner,' she suggested, longing suddenly to tell Jane everything face to face. 'We'll go out. My treat. We haven't seen each other properly for months.'

'Oh Julia, I'd love to, but could we wait until Tom is home and settled back in school? I don't mean to seem ungrateful. I'd be lousy company anyway. All I'm good for at the moment is chasing dust-balls and filling sacks for the dump. It's very cathartic, actually, not to mention useful. I just need a bit more time before committing to anything.'

On the morning that Tom was due back, Jane's excitement was momentarily diverted by the arrival of a starchy white envelope, addressed to her in the sort of embossed italics she might have expected on an invitation to take tea with the Queen. It turned out to be a request for her to attend the reading of the last will and testament of Ernest John Lytton, at the offices of Masterton and Daniels on 18 September at 10 a.m. She was just marking the date in her diary when the telephone rang. Her hand reached for it absently, her mind still on the letter.

'Jane, it's Michael.'

'Is Tom okay?' she asked at once, engulfed by a reflex panic-surge, which quickly subsided at Michael's easy response.

'Yes, he's absolutely fine.'

'Thank goodness. How was Cornwall?'

'Great, though it rained a bit. Pippa and Tim seem well. They've got these dogs now...'

'Yes, I was introduced – at the funeral. So, when will you get here? Three o clock, like you said?'

'Jane...'

'Why are you phoning, Michael?' She spoke sharply, the panic suddenly back.

'Because... because Tom has asked – begged – to stay here with us.'

'I don't believe you.' Her ear throbbed from the force with which she was pressing it against the phone.

'Believe me, Tom is pretty clear on the matter.'

'You've egged him on. You and Lisa.'

'No, we have not.'

The complacency of Michael's tone made Jane feel sick. She held the receiver away from her and breathed in and out once, very slowly. She needed her wits. She needed to be calm. 'Tom, hardly surprisingly, is confused about everything that has been going on,' she said levelly. 'He doesn't mean everything he says.'

'Yes, a lot *has* been going on, hasn't it,' Michael retorted, in a tone that was snide as well as smug.

'And what do you mean by that?'

'How you're always cross with him. How you favour Harriet. How he hates his school. How he doesn't like some man who comes to stay over – I must say, Jane, I would have expected a little more tact from you. Tom keeps going on about seeing the two of you kiss. It's clearly upset him deeply.'

This was too much all at once – so many missiles against an unsuspecting target. It made Jane bluster and stutter her defence, like the guiltiest of parties.

'The man was nothing – a one-off horrible episode – someone who arrived drunk and uninvited. I kicked him out. Tom hardly saw anything – I mean, there was nothing to see.'

'That's not what he says.'

'For God's sake, Michael.' The notion that she was having to justify herself was enraging. 'Far worse is you and Lisa – don't you think all that might be confusing Tom a bit too?'

'We're very discreet. And anyway, we've made it clear that we are best friends as much as anything, and hope to be so for life. No scary stuff about getting married – yet. Tom gets it all and it's obvious he really likes Lisa.' Michael's tone was placid and slow, exuding the confidence of the player with the unbeatable hand. 'If he was as happy with you, he wouldn't be telling us the things he has, would he now? And as for his school – *you* picked that place, I seem to recall – he clearly hates it. I've never seen Tom more reluctant about anything—'

'He always says he doesn't like school just before term starts.' The fear was getting worse, making it hard not to shout. 'After the first day back he's always fine. But then, you wouldn't know such things, because you were never interested. Which reminds me – I've been meaning to ask...' Jane steadied herself, knowing the importance of not losing her cool, '...how come our son is suddenly of such mighty interest to you, when you spent the first six years of his life barely wanting to be around him, let alone trying to understand his needs?'

'That is a bloody lie.'

'Could I talk to Tom now, please?'

'I've a good mind to say no,' Michael snarled, before, a few muffled rustles later, Tom's shrill voice came on the line.

'Hello, Mummy.'

'Hello, darling. Have you had a lovely time in Cornwall?'

'Super.'

'Tell me some of the things you did.'

'We built a castle with ten towers on the beach, but it was too cold to swim. We stayed in a caravan with a big telly in it at Uncle Tim's and I helped build the fire. And Daddy says I can stay with him much longer if I want to and go to a different school.'

A desperate ache was swelling in the pit of Jane's stomach, pushing up through her chest so that she had to fight to breathe.

'And what do you want, my love?'

'I want to stay with Daddy and go to a different school.' There wasn't even a hesitation. An adult might have paused, to be polite.

'Do you like Lisa?'

'She's nice. She's good at drawing airplanes.' He did stop then, but only for an instant. 'Daddy says I can see you and Harriet whenever I want. He says the new school will be much nicer than my old one.'

'I see. Could I talk to Daddy again now, darling? Remember Mummy loves you very much. I'll see you soon—' But he had already gone.

'See what I mean?' drawled Michael.

'He's barely seven. He believes what you tell him. He doesn't realise the implications of it – how the hell can he?'

'Oh, I think he realises well enough.'

A kind of hatred, a new, raw feeling had taken hold, making Jane's voice deep and hard. 'You can't just keep him, Michael, on a whim. Like he is a parcel that can be posted or held back when it suits you.'

'That's how you treated me,' Michael replied softly.

'So, this is revenge, after all. Christ, that's low – even for you...' Jane was trying not to cry now.

'It is nothing of the sort. Tom is my son too.' Michael cleared his throat, his own emotions in danger of getting the better of him too. Lisa had come to stand beside him, laying her hand supportively on one shoulder. Behind her, Tom was watching a Batman film, using the console to re-run scenes he found particularly exciting. 'Look, Jane, I recognise this is upsetting for you. Would you like me to call back when you're a bit more under control?'

'I will not get more *under control* about this, ever.' Jane raised her voice, mostly to conquer the tears. 'I trusted you to have Tom for this week, Michael. If I had thought for one moment that you would pull a stunt like—'

'It wasn't a stunt. It's what Tom wants – you heard for yourself. Neither Lisa nor I are forcing him into anything.' Michael squeezed Lisa's fingers with his free hand. 'Though I will admit to being pleased. How could I not be? Any father in my position—'

Jane had stopped listening. Having said to Julia that she could not stomach the thought of distressing Tom with an open fight against Michael, she now knew this to be untrue. She would fight for ever, when the time was right. For now, the only sensible course open to her was acquiescence. She stroked Harriet's head; her daughter, guessing from Jane's loud voice that calamity of some sort had seeped into their lives, had crawled on to her lap during the course of the conversation.

'So, when can I see him then? You're not going to change your mind about that, are you?'

'No. But he needs to be allowed to settle a bit first. There's a lot to sort out. No need for any toing and froing with his stuff either – he's got the main things with him, and Lisa and I are happy to buy whatever else he needs. He's growing an inch a day at the moment anyway.' Michael spoke in a leisurely way, relishing the sense of Jane's despair. All he had told her was true. It was as the end of the week approached that Tom had – much to Michael's delight and astonishment – begged to be able to stay with him and Lisa forever. Michael's confidence had never known such a boost. It wasn't how he had envisaged gaining custody, but that made it all the more wonderful. One quick conversation with Lisa and it had all been agreed. 'Lisa has found a brilliant school in Wandsworth, so let's see if we can get that all underway before arranging visitations. I tell you what, I'll call you back when you can—'

'No. Do not call me back. Tell me now. I need a definite date *now*.'

'Steady on there.' Michael winked at Lisa. 'Let's look in the diary, shall we?'

Jane clung to Harriet and the phone, listening to him turning pages. 'How about the last weekend in September? That will give Tom a bit of a chance to find his feet and then we can all see where we are.' The continuing casual tone of his voice made her want to throw up. He could have been a holiday tour operator talking to a needy client.

Jane agreed, because there seemed no immediate, alternative course of action – not without Tom, physically, being torn apart. She then sat in a stunned silence, clinging to Harriet. Her darling boy had asked to live with his father. Tom had not been kidnapped or drugged. He had asked to live with his father and the soon-to-be new wife who drew airplanes. Until she could get some advice on her legal position, there was no good choice but to submit. Yet, Jane was also wary of bringing the fight out into the open too soon, possibly turning Tom against her for good, or making him wretched, which was her worst fear of all.

The rest of the day passed in a blur. She phoned Tom twice and both times Michael passed the phone over immediately. Which was something, Jane consoled herself, as was the late September visit now in her diary. Step by step, she told herself. Step by step, and Tom would come back. That night she brought a confused, sleepy Harriet into bed with her, needing the comfort of her daughter's soft, steady breathing to see her through the darkness.

36

Several strands of thin silver hair stretched across the shiny-pink scalp of the man talking to several people by a bookcase, from the tip of one protuberant ear to the other. Jane couldn't remember the man's name, but she knew he was going to tell them about Ernest's last wishes. There were many things she now had trouble remembering, her mind during the course of the last two weeks having taken to swimming off in directions of its own, dragging the immediate present with it and leaving her stranded in a limbo of dazed nothingness. Her eyes roamed round the room, noting the plush furnishings, heavy burgundy velvet and dark wood.

After sitting quietly gnawing on a bunch of plastic teether keys for ten minutes, Harriet had embarked on a more detailed investigation of her surroundings, plucking at trouser legs and lunging for teaspoons. Jane, who was the only one already sitting down, watched vacantly. The room was hot. If she stood up, she felt she might collapse and drown in the deep wine-red of the carpet.

There were about ten people gathered in all, sipping from thin porcelain cups, waiting for some signal to move into the three rows of high-backed chairs that had been arranged beside them.

Michael, having come over with a few stiff greetings and a hug for Harriet, had gone back to position himself at Lisa's side, with his back to Jane. She found that she could hardly bear to look at him. Tom was fine, he had said, then, and many times over the phone, eating well, sleeping well, managing in the new Wandsworth school.

Twelve more days, Jane reminded herself, and she would see for herself. She could read Tom. She would know what to do. She let her gaze travel again round the room, this time half recognising a couple of faces from the funeral, though they soon all merged into a blur of dark suits and ties. Only Lisa stood out: in an electric-blue dress and matching shoes that lit up the room like a beacon. As Jane stared, she saw that Harriet, perhaps equally mesmerised by the colour, had toddled over to Lisa and started yanking on the crisp hem of the dress, leaving a smudge of fingerprints clear enough to see across the room. Soon Lisa was swiping at her frock with a tissue and Michael, grim-faced, was transporting their daughter, whining and wriggling, back to Jane.

'Really, Jane, this is hardly the place to bring a child.'

'Mrs Browne had a migraine.'

'How unfortunate.'

'How is Tom?' she asked, needing to know again.

'I told you – he's fine.'

'And school?'

'Good, as I have *said*. No problems to speak of...'

'You mean, there are problems?'

'I mean nothing of the sort. Tom is perfectly well – Jesus, Jane, you've spoken to him enough times on the phone. Now if you'll excuse me—'

'The phone is no substitute for...' Jane broke off as a wave of giddiness overtook her. She fanned her face with her hand.

'Michael,' she called feebly, 'it's so hot in here. You couldn't open a window or something, could you?'

'It is a little stuffy. I'll see what I can do. I wish to God Christopher would hurry up and get here.'

'Oh, so that's why we're all waiting.'

'What did you think we were doing? These people have got better things to do with their time – as indeed have I – but then my dear brother has never been exactly renowned for his punctuality.'

At that moment Christopher walked in, wind-swept and out of breath, looking strikingly casual in tatty beige cords and a crumpled green shirt. His hair, which had grown considerably over the summer, was wavy and tousled, contrasting sharply with his brother's new, closely trimmed hair-cut. Someone clapped their hands and everybody immediately began to sit down in the chairs, there being no time, apparently, for the luxury of familial greetings. Jane sat at the back, doing her best to settle Harriet on her lap; but quiet co-operation was not high on her daughter's list of priorities that morning. After resisting fiercely, she tried to stand up, her feet digging uncomfortably into Jane's knees, while her chubby fingers lunged mercilessly at her hair and earrings.

'May I take her for a bit?'

Christopher had crept over from his place in the next row and was crouching beside them. Too relieved to protest, Jane let the eager Harriet fling herself into her uncle's outstretched arms and turned her attention back to the front of the room. The man with the sparse roof of hair was addressing them from behind a small desk with a leather inlay, an angle-poise lamp bent towards his face like a microphone. He had a nasal drone of a voice that made Jane want to close her eyes.

'Thank you all for coming – dear friend, Ernest Lytton – time it's taken – letter of wishes – a few surprises – honour his decisions...'

The words came at her in a broken, meaningless snatches. She leant forwards to check on Harriet, who was pulling on Christopher's nose and having her own tweaked in return.

'...come to the main point. According to Mr Lytton's wishes, his eldest son, Michael Lytton, is to receive liquid assets and stock holdings, amounting to a total value of fifteen thousand pounds. While his house...' here the lawyer cleared his throat and stroked his dimpled chin, 'according to the said Mr Lytton's last will and testament, he bequeaths the house and its contents to his second son, Christopher Lytton and...' he paused again, 'and Mrs Jane Lytton, to be possessed jointly by these two persons.'

Without turning her head, Jane became aware of several things at once: of Lisa grasping Michael's arm, of heads swivelling, of Christopher gently releasing Harriet who tottered to her pushchair to begin a favourite game of fiddling with the seat straps. Jane meanwhile, stared resolutely ahead, into the deep, glossy wooden frame of the chair in front of her. This cannot be, she thought, feeling dreamy and detached, this cannot be.

The rest of the proceedings comprised formalities and details that floated over the heads of the listeners like dust after an explosion. The real blow had already been struck: the younger brother and the ex-wife of the elder brother had been favoured, together. While the elder brother had been slighted, given a mere sop in comparison. An unmistakable whiff of scandal hung in the air, lingering in the silence of unexpressed outrage, surprise and plain curiosity.

When they were dismissed, like a class of new schoolchildren, no one knew quite where to go or how to leave the room. Michael looked as if he wanted to come across to Jane, but Lisa, who had a tight grip on his elbow, led him towards the door, the arrow of her nose aimed firmly at the ceiling. The other attendees followed, murmuring amongst themselves as they shuffled out into the carpeted corridor that circled the wrought-iron railings of the stairwell.

Only the guilty parties remained, the main beneficiaries. There were a few moments of silence before Christopher burst out laughing.

'The old devil. What a trick to play. Poor Michael.'

Jane found herself laughing too, a little hysterical from shock, and the relief of everyone else having gone. 'I can't believe it. Why on earth would your father do such a thing?'

'I suppose... all I can think... is that it was because he saw who needed – who would enjoy – the old place the most. You've got to admire his cheek, though I'm not sure Michael will see it in such terms.' Christopher had edged his way through the chairs towards her, his heart racing with something like euphoria, an exultation that was as full of fear as pleasure. 'Congratulations, anyway. If that's the appropriate thing to say.'

'Of course, it's impossible,' Jane said flatly, struck fully by the impracticability of Ernest's scheming. 'You must buy me out or whatever one does in such situations.'

'Buy you out? I wouldn't dream of it. And couldn't afford to, anyway.' The solicitor put his head round the door and promptly disappeared again. 'As it happens,' Christopher went on, moving to the window from where the roofs of cars and the striped tops of shop canopies were visible in the street several storeys below, 'you can consider the place your own for the next year at least.'

'Whatever do you mean?'

'I'm going abroad.'

'But you can't—'

'Can't?' He spoke quite sharply, spinning round from the open window to face her.

'I just meant...' But Jane couldn't think what she had meant at all.

'What were you going to say?'

The stuffiness of the office came at her again like the blast of a fan heater. 'Nothing – I was just going to ask where you were going.' The straps of her handbag were twisted round her fingers, leather sliding on sweat.

'Washington DC. I've been accepted as a visiting English lecturer at Georgetown University. I applied months ago. I felt I needed a change.' He returned his gaze to the view of the traffic. 'At the school, I felt as if... as if I was starting to merge with the damp on my walls.'

'Yes, I see,' she replied, sounding as distant and dazed as she felt. Harriet had left the pushchair and come to lie on the carpet by Jane's feet, where she was sucking her thumb of one hand and winding the fingers of the other round a little coil of her hair. 'I ought to take her home. She's exhausted. So am I.' Jane tried to stretch a little, but her joints felt bruised and stiff. 'Thank you so much for looking after her all that time. I'm feeling sort of weak today. I think I might be going down with something.'

'You ought to live there,' he said suddenly.

'Where?'

'At the white house – while I'm gone. I don't know how far you and Michael have got with sorting stuff, but if you haven't sold the house yet, you could always rent it out and spend a year in Kent. There's a good primary school in Crestling, I believe. You could grow vegetables and keep chickens and things.'

Jane had to laugh. 'You can't be serious.'

'But I am – deadly serious – at least about you using the house. I'll put it in writing that it's all right by me, the co-owner.' He grinned. 'Then at least you've got the option. What about that?'

'My goodness, I don't know what to say...' Jane faltered, struggling to hide the appeal of the idea. 'But then I would obviously have to pay you some sort of rent or something—'

'If you live in the house, you'll be doing both of us a favour. Rot and wood-worm will take one look at you lot and run like hell. Good.' Christopher rubbed his hands together, as if there was nothing more to discuss. 'Now then, how about a farewell drink? A coffee – anything. We ought to toast our new-found wealth, don't you think?' he urged, seeing her face assume an expression that was almost certainly a prelude to a refusal.

'I really – I think – I had better not.' Jane looked at her watch without registering what it said.

'Are you thirsty, little one?' Christopher had dropped to his knees to talk to Harriet, well aware that it was devious to try and bring his niece into the matter, but keen enough, in that moment, to try anything. For all he knew, it could be years before he saw either of them again.

'Okay, you win,' Jane groaned. 'A quick tea or something then, before I get clamped or towed away.'

They found a sandwich bar nearby, where Christopher bought coffee and a sausage roll for himself and an apple juice and doughnut for Harriet. Jane, overcome by another bout of the dizzy nausea, asked only for water. 'How's your book,' she managed, once it had passed, 'that novel you were planning?'

'Finished.'

'Congratulations.'

'I suppose so.' He frowned. 'At least it will be marginally less painful to receive rejection letters from across the Atlantic.'

'Oh, I think rejection hurts at any distance.'

'Yes, of course it does,' Christopher murmured, feeling a little foolish, but pleased that she had not pandered to a bid for reassurance that she was in no position to give. It reminded him of her honesty, a quality which he believed, increasingly, to be of the rarest kind. He bit into his sausage roll but then panicked at the silence between them and spoke with his mouth full, flaky bits of greasy pastry sticking to the corners of his lips.

'Were you all right after the funeral?'

She nodded and took a sip of the water, which tasted warm and metallic. 'Except... perhaps you've heard... Tom is living with Michael at the moment. He asked if he could.'

The monotone with which she delivered the news did not deceive Christopher as to the emotion behind it. He put the sausage roll down and pushed his plate away. 'No, Jane,' he said quietly, 'I had not heard that.' He pressed his palms together, matching each long slim finger to its counterpart. 'You get to see him, presumably?'

'Not yet, but soon. We have little chats on the phone. He's started at a new school... I hope it is temporary. Tom isn't exactly... communicative, apart from saying that he likes being with his father.' Jane closed her eyes and raised her glass of water to her mouth, draining it in one go, though it did nothing to quench the thirst now burning at the back of her throat.

Christopher watched how her neck moved rhythmically as she swallowed, noticing that she was even thinner than at the funeral, all hair and eyes. 'I wish there was something I could do to help you.'

'But you already have done so much – saying I can use the house – I shall certainly go there for a while. It might do me good to have a change...' She let the sentence hang, leaving him feeling helpless and bereft, unable to think what to offer to fill the new quietness from her. Beside them, Harriet had fallen asleep in her pushchair, half a doughnut still gripped in one hand, specks of sugar on her cheeks and chin.

Jane started talking again, absently. 'So much seems to have gone wrong lately. I can't help believing it must be some failure in me, some terrible capacity for error—'

'No – we already agreed that if anyone has a monopoly on

mistake making in this world, it is me, remember?' He hoped she might smile, but she was busy tearing her paper napkin into thin strips, as if barely aware he had spoken.

Jane arranged the strips into a line. Steady as she goes, she reminded herself. Step by step today, and every day. 'So, when are you off?'

'Tomorrow.'

'So soon?'

'I hung on for the will – they wanted me a week ago.'

'Mattie's over there, you know.'

'Yes, I know, she's in Boston, teaching art to old ladies.' He chuckled, before registering that he had surprised her into paying proper attention. 'She sent me a postcard. I suppose we might meet up at some stage. Boston's only a hiccough away from Washington – by American standards, that is.'

'Yes, of course.'

They left the café, Christopher having insisted on paying, and stepped into the hubbub of the pavement. People streamed by, some of them dodging the pushchair with evident impatience. Saying hello to her is never this difficult, he thought, bracing himself as he tried to conjure some appropriate words of farewell.

Jane got in first, asking him to give her love to Mattie if he saw her. 'You're clearly very honoured, by the way – my postcard only had trees on it and no news at all – not a squeak about teaching old ladies.' The pushchair was between them. Jane wished she could manage something better to say, something about his kindness instead of about Mattie, but it was hard to think straight with her sore throat worsening by the second and drilling sensations going on behind her eyes.

'Let me know about the house. The spare keys are under the big stone round the back.'

'Yes, I know. Thanks.'

'And I might drop you the odd line to you, if you don't mind, that is.'

'No, I don't mind.'

They kissed cheeks quickly across the rain-hood of Harriet's pushchair, before setting off in opposite directions. Jane walked for several yards before it dawned on her that she was going in the wrong direction for her car. She wheeled round quickly, hoping to catch Christopher up, but his tall, striding figure was already lost amongst the lunch time crowds.

37

Pneumonia wasn't diagnosed until several days after their arrival in Kent. When an elderly local doctor gruffly informed Jane that her nausea, fatigue, fever and the coughing now compounding her raw throat, were the symptoms of something rather more serious than a bad cold, she found herself accepting the news with a sense of inevitability. Life was too dense a minefield – things blew up, no matter how carefully you trod. But there hummed an element of relief too, in being able to acknowledge that all this time she had been feeling like hell from an actual *illness*, rather than from not coping and being run down.

When a chest x-ray mercifully proved that she was not ill enough for hospital, the obvious and most sensible course of action would have been a speedy return to Cobham, where there was Mrs Browne to assist during a period which the doctor said could be lengthy, as well as requiring strong doses of analgesics and antibiotics. But such a move held little appeal to Jane, partly because of the simple fact that she felt far too weak to organise it, but mostly because she found herself wanting – very badly – to stay where she was. The original motive for the visit had been something of an experiment, a way to help fill the time before getting to see Tom. Arriving with Harriet, woodlice scattering as she lifted the heavy stone that guarded the key, she even half dreaded the prospect of sharing the house with Ernest's ghostly presence. Instead, she had found the place haunted only by a sense of peace and warmth. Outside, autumn was deepening in glory, the copse a shimmering fire of red and burnished gold. There was a bite and tingle in the air, an alertness, which, despite Jane's imminent state of collapse, affected her deeply, inducing irrational surges of hope and self-belief.

After receiving the diagnosis, and having managed a call to Tom to explain why she might not able to phone so often for little while, Jane – not knowing where else to turn – rang Julia.

'Let me understand correctly. Though you have an extremely serious illness, you wish to take to your sick bed in a draughty old house in the wilds of Kent where neither you nor your daughter have any friends or support. You wish to do this because some sixth sense has instructed you that this is the best place to be.'

'That's about it, I suppose, and because Christopher so kindly insisted that I could use the place,' Jane agreed feebly, waiting for some gentle explosion on the wide-ranging, unintelligible subject of her life choices and personality.

'Well then, at least we all know where we stand.' There followed a pause, in which Jane heard Julia take a deep breath. 'Since I can boast of no private nurses in my small circle of acquaintances, I would consider it an honour to step into the breech myself. I shall drive down at once.'

'Thank you,' Jane whispered, before a bout of hacking overtook her.

After Julia's arrival, Jane's immune system, as if realising that it no longer had to cope alone, surrendered completely. For several days things went very fuzzy. She lay in the wide bed in the smaller double spare room, aware of nothing but heat, body-ache and a cough that intensified the burning in her chest. Her only movements were trips to the bathroom; exhausting, painstaking journeys, sometimes having to lean on Julia like an old lady with a walking frame.

On the morning when she at last felt able to sit upright to a tray of tea and toast, Julia plonked Harriet next to her and perched on the end of the bed. 'I'll have to Hoover the sheets, I can see,' she scolded happily, as Harriet joined in to nibble all the crusts, which Jane hadn't been able to manage.

'Don't worry, this bed's quite big enough to be shared with a few crumbs.' Jane smiled, aware of the comforting sensation of the hot tea and food, settling in the near-empty bowl of her stomach. 'Thank you, Julia.'

'No need. It's given me quite a kick – to feel really useful for once.' She tugged out a crease in the counterpane.

'What do you mean *for once*? You've helped so much it's embarrassing.'

'Bollocks.' Julia reached out and patted Jane's hand. 'Letting people into your life, I mean *really* letting them in, so they can make a difference, is not something that comes very naturally to you, Jane Lytton. Or hadn't you noticed?'

Jane grimaced, licking a fleck of butter off a fingertip. 'It's only ineptitude – nothing deliberate. It's probably just because I blunder along, letting things happen to me instead of taking control.' A wave of fatigue came at her suddenly and she had to flop her head back against the pillows. 'By the way,' she murmured, fighting the desire to close her eyes, 'you know I am having Tom at the weekend...'

'Jane, sweetheart,' Julia spoke as gently as she could, and very softly because of Harriet, now lying asleep in the crook of her mother's arm, 'I think that it would be better to wait until you are properly better. Tom knows you are unwell, so he will understand. Wouldn't it be far better – especially given the current, far from ideal circumstances – to be full of energy for when he does come? Then you and he can have the *best* of times?' Julia added carefully, not wanting to stir up any more of Jane's anxiety about the situation than necessary. 'So, what about pushing the visit back two weeks – to mid October, say? And then insisting to Michael that you have him again, for half-term? I am not being negative, dearest,' she rushed on, seeing Jane's tense, crestfallen expression, 'I am totally on your side, and – as I keep saying – will help pay for any legal help in due course. But you will certainly need your full strength back for those battles too, which is why – in my humble opinion – getting totally better should be your number one priority.'

'Okay,' Jane whispered, using a corner of her pillow case to dab at a couple of rogue tears. She levered herself more upright, pulling a tissue out of the box on her bedside table and blowing her nose in a bid to compose herself. 'I'll call Michael later. When I am feeling up to it.'

'Good. And very brave. And I will be at your side – if you want me to be – ready to snatch the receiver and take over if he plays silly buggers—'

'Silly buggers,' said Harriet, sitting up.

'Come on, you,' Julia laughed, raising an apologetic eyebrow at Jane, 'we're going to make some toast for ourselves now, seeing as Mummy's gobbled the lot.' She lifted her goddaughter off the bed, holding her close for a moment, before setting her carefully down on the floor. 'Let's put jam on ours – heaps of it,' she went on confidingly, bending down to kiss the top of Harriet's tousled little head. 'Strawberry or blackcurrant – or honey, perhaps – or all three –

what do you think?' Harriet whooped and made an eager charge for the door, and then turned to look at Julia because she couldn't reach the handle.

'Sorry, Julia, but one more thing,' Jane called croakily, raising herself onto one elbow in order to speak. 'Would you mind awfully taking those triangles of Mattie's somewhere else?' She pointed at the picture Julia had kindly repaired and had framed, which was propped up beside the dressing table. 'Maybe hang it in the downstairs loo or somewhere. It was so sweet of you, but to be honest, the thing gives me eye-ache. All those sharp points and the red...' She shuddered.

'Consider it done.' Julia slipped Mattie's picture under one arm and picked up Jane's tray, still managing to open the door with her other hand. 'Sleep now. That is an order. Come with me, little one.' Julia smiled to herself as she herded Harriet onto the landing, thinking how Jane's recent traumas had at least allowed the two of them to develop a lovely bond – how bits of good could still could come out of bad.

The next morning, after managing to cajole Michael into agreeing to both proposals – despite bitter threats to sell the Cobham house and contents from under her feet if she was never going to be there – Jane felt a little bit better.

'You've got to get back to your own life,' she told Julia, as sternly as her feeble state would allow, when she brought up a tray of soup and bread for her lunch. 'I am on the mend. Harriet and I will manage.'

'Don't be absurd. You're a sack of bones. A small gust of wind would send you flying into the nearest tree.'

But your shop—'

'I've warned you before not to fret about my shop. I've got help. A friend – a minor patron of the arts – a brilliant haggler over prices. He's taking care of things for me.'

'He?'

'He's a good friend who understands the business... Swedish and terribly capable. We look out for each other,' she added airily, sweeping out of the room.

A couple of days later however, when Jane had improved enough to camp on the sofa downstairs during the day, Julia, who really did have to get back to her shop, produced – like a smug conjuror with a deep hat – a young girl called Karen who was sixteen and lived in Crestling.

'Karen has a bicycle and loves children,' she announced, pushing her guest into the sitting room, while she rushed off to the kitchen to make tea and open a fresh packet of biscuits.

Karen smiled shyly at Jane, before bobbing down on all fours to invite Harriet to press the curled tip of her freckled nose, emitting a squeak the moment it was touched. 'We've got lots at home,' she remarked casually, getting to her feet and lifting Harriet on to her skinny hip in one effortless movement, 'Mum fosters.'

Though the purple shadows under her new employee's eyes suggested a social life somewhat at odds with the homely demands of her working day, Karen's energy and cheerfulness were limitless. Apart from a few cigarettes, chain-smoked at great speed down by the swings whenever her charge was asleep, she devoted herself wholeheartedly to Jane and Harriet's needs, cycling off for groceries, hanging out washing and wrestling with Ernest's dinosaur of a Hoover with only the mildest cursing.

After Jane had invested in a second-hand child's bike seat, Karen would pedal off down the lane with Harriet kicking in delight behind; if they weren't having picnics or running errands, they would ride over to spend the afternoon with Karen's family, where a spoiling choice of playmates was always available. The last vestiges of her daughter's clingy shyness disappeared within days. She no longer picked at her food or whined at Jane to be held. Her elfin face filled out with health and colour. Best of all, night time sleep, which had often been patchy – yet another challenge uncomplainingly handled by the saintly Julia – suddenly settled, sometimes into nine-hour stretches, allowing Jane to catch up on what felt like a lifetime of broken nights.

38

Hanging out laundry after lunch on the Friday that Tom was due to arrive, debating whether the shaggy scraps of black cloud were likely to assemble themselves into something thick enough to make her regret it, Jane kept pausing to relish her excitement. Julia had been right. It had been worth waiting. She felt up to anything. She and Tom would have the best of times. She would apply no pressure. She would simply show him her love, her understanding, the absolute rock-solidity of her being, as the mother who had birthed and nurtured him, and who needed him fully in her life in order to feel complete. The rest would follow. Somehow. She had phoned him every night that week – not caring how much it clearly annoyed Michael and Lisa – though sometimes Tom had picked up first. He had sounded increasingly and genuinely excited too, full of un-Tom-like eagerness to chat, sometimes even asking after his little sister. A weekend together, after so long, was measly, but it was a start. And there was the treat of half-term to look forward to afterwards. One hour would have felt like luxury. One minute.

Jane pegged a last grey bra into place and used Ernest's old forked stick to push the line of clothes higher. It would probably rain now, she reflected wryly, sitting on a tree stump to enjoy a burst of sun through a break in the cloud, pulling her long thick cardigan more tightly about her. Had leaving Michael been wrong after all, she wondered with a sudden shiver, watching Harriet's little tops and dungarees flutter in the wind beside her jeans, shirts and underwear. Was it wrong – pure selfishness – to end a marriage that had lost its heart? Was the old cliché of sticking together for the sake of the children the best wisdom in the end? Would Tom have suffered as much if they had? Would any of them?

The light crunch of car wheels on gravel broke her reverie, followed by the sound of Julia's voice. 'I spotted you from the drive,' she cooed, her tall figure, elegantly clad in a long green coat and black suede boots, appearing round the side of the house a few moments later. 'I've had a rather disappointing scout round some dealers in Tonbridge, and then thought I'd pay you a surprise visit – for the weekend, if you'll have me. I can help with Harriet while you enjoy Tom.'

'Julia, you are a wonder, and I would love you to stay anyway,' Jane cried, running over to fling her arms round her.

'And how is my favourite convalescent?' Julia spoke gently, holding Jane at arms length after they had embraced and studying her face with undisguised concern.

'You are not allowed to call me that any more – I am better, mostly thanks to *you*.'

'Well, you won't be if you stay out in this chill much longer,' Julia quipped, shaking her head in affectionate despair as Jane sat back down on her tree stump. 'Or were you hoping for a double dose next time around – perhaps with hypothermia thrown in for good measure?' She deftly flipped over the empty laundry basket with the toe of a boot as she talked, and then sat down on it next to Jane. 'You never were one to do things by halves.'

'These bits of sun are so lovely. I was just having a think.'

'A highly dangerous occupation at the best of times. Come on then, penny for them.'

'Tom, mostly.'

'Ah.'

'A few hours and he'll be here... and I can't tell you how... oh my word, just to *see* him... I offered to collect, but Michael said he'd drive him down after school. Is that controlling or nice? I can't decide. I can't think straight.'

Julia reached across the space between them and squeezed her hand.

'Because I'm anxious too, obviously,' Jane rushed on, 'I so want it to go well, but also for Tom not to feel worried, or *fought* over... unless – and until – that becomes unavoidable. I suppose it is just a bit hard to feel *safe*, given what's at stake. But then, so much of it is my fault. I should have insisted we put the house on the market regardless of everything and made a clean break of it right from the start. I've let things drift, allowing Michael to call all the shots, and am paying the price.' Jane swiped at a couple of rogue tears.

'I warned you,' Julia said in her kind brisk way, keeping Jane's hand on her lap, 'thinking too much is *never* a good idea, especially for someone who – despite their protestations – is still not back up to full-throttle. Be gentler on yourself, Jane. First and foremost, you are not going to "lose" Tom, who loves you. On top of which, one of the many things in here,' she patted the sizeable handbag parked at her feet, 'is the number of an excellent family law firm – I know one of the partners quite well – for when you are ready. Michael is tricky. He always has been tricky. He's also now got a fiancée he's trying to impress. Yes, it has been a while, but letting a full two years pass means you'll be able to get a quick no-fault divorce, which has to be a good thing, for both of you. So, enough of the self-blame, okay?' She patted Jane's hand and released it. 'I mean, all any of us can do in this world is what genuinely feels right at the time. Even if others might think it unwise. Right?'

'Right.' Jane sensed immediately that there was something else behind her words. Something that – for once – had nothing to do with her own dilemmas. 'Is everything okay?'

'More than okay, actually.' Julia picked something invisible off her immaculate green coat, letting out a very un-Julia-like nervous laugh. 'I think I may have met someone.'

'Not the someone who is terribly capable and Swedish, by any chance?'

Julia tried to hide her smile, not catching Jane's eye. 'Early days etcetera. He is called Olaf and I am bonkers about him. He likes me a lot right back. Not remotely what I thought I was looking for, but then, don't you think so many problems in life seem to arise from not knowing what the hell one *is* looking for? We waste so much time chasing after the wrong thing, not seizing the right one until it whacks us over the head.' She stopped abruptly, standing up and swinging the long straps of her bag over her shoulder. 'I'm going to shut up about it now, in case I jinx things. Can we go inside? My nose is in danger of producing icicles.'

'We can. And... congratulations... or something,' Jane laughed, leaping to her feet to give Julia a hug that was mostly resisted. She looped an arm through hers for the walk back to the house, throwing sideways glances of delight and bemusement which were studiously ignored. 'No one deserves happiness more than you,' she murmured, engulfed by happiness herself at the good fortune of having such a friend. Christopher's generosity floated to mind too. Such kindness, such support, such friendship – from two quarters – really, what more did a person need?

* * *

When Harriet awoke from her nap, Julia whisked her off to visit a nearby donkey sanctuary she had heard about. To give Jane a little bit of time and space, she said, though Jane spent most of it gliding from room to room, picking things up and putting them down, willing the minutes on towards the designated four o'clock arrival time. For tea, she had planned shepherd's pie – Tom's favourite – with peas and baked beans. Having gained sufficient grip on herself to peel some potatoes, she began a haphazard search for some of his favourite toys she had packed when they left London, finding several trains, the beloved dinosaur book Julia had given him and a Lego kit of a space module, complete with little men in moon boots with oxygen masks fixed to their backs.

While the potatoes boiled, she decided to assemble the Lego, taking so long that the potatoes were burnt underneath and soggy on top by the time she checked on them, requiring some vigorous whisking and generous dashes of milk and butter to make them edible. By three, the table was laid, the pie made, the baked beans and the peas in their separate pans, ready for cooking. Another hour. Unless the traffic was terrible, which was more than likely on a Friday. Or Michael changed his mind. For a moment the kitchen floor heaved. Get a grip, woman, Jane hissed, slowly lowering herself into a chair. Placing her palms flat on the table, she closed her eyes and took several deep breaths. She was on the third, when there was a loud rap on the front door. Wondering why Julia, who knew that the door was never locked, didn't just let herself in, she got to her feet and hurried along the hall.

'Hello, Jane.'

'Lisa...' Jane threw the briefest glance at the composed, heavily made-up, unsmiling face of Michael's fiancée, before dropping to her knees to hug Tom – and the football he was clasping – an unnaturally clean football, Jane observed, processing a thousand thoughts and feelings as Tom let the ball drop in order to hurl himself against her. 'Darling heart. I've missed you so.' Jane wept a little as she held him, joy and relief swamping her, not just to have him in her arms, but at Tom's evident delight to be there, hanging on to her jumper, burying his face in her shoulder. 'Thank you, Lisa, thank you...'

A car horn in the drive, signalling the return of Julia and Harriet, made all three of them turn. 'Harry!' Tom cried, charging over the moment Julia lifted his sister out of the car and set her on the ground, enduring Harriet's exuberant squeals and then making her howl by trying to swing her round.

'Could we have a word?' asked Lisa, not bothering to acknowledge any of the mayhem, or Julia, trying to sort it out, but simply pushing past Jane into the house.

'I'll take them for a run-around in the garden,' Julia called, shooting Jane a look as she herded both children towards the path that led round the back.

'Coffee?' Jane said icily, forcing politeness because of how it might matter one day, when the chips were down and she needed to prove to others that she was a decent human being.

'No thanks.' Having crossed the threshold, Lisa found herself hovering in the hall. Apart from the funeral, when everything was safely bustling and different, she hadn't been back to the house since the unforgettable day of Michael's attempt to introduce her to his father. Her eyes flicked over Jane's shoulder towards the kitchen, remembering the flagstones, so hard under her back, and the bruise that had stayed so long, compounding the weird guilt of all the awfulness that followed. 'A glass of water would be nice. Perhaps in the sitting room? If that's not too much trouble. I picked Tom up early to beat the traffic.' She peeled off smart tanned leather driving gloves as she talked, pulling at each finger like a twenties film star, before dropping them into her large shoulder bag. 'First, could I use the bathroom, please?'

Jane, suppressing a mounting fury at the woman's bold imperiousness, said of course, and went into the kitchen to pour her some water. A few minutes later, they were settled in armchairs, Lisa's eyes travelling – unashamedly, it seemed to Jane – round the room, no doubt assessing the worth of everything and wanting to communicate her disapproval. In fact, there was not much in terms of worth, just plain old furniture, faded furnishings and knick-knacks, all still in the exact places Ernest had arranged them. Only odd details hinted at Jane and Harriet's recent occupancy: a small green sock on the arm of a chair, a Postman Pat video cassette on the carpet by the television, a toppling pile of ironing on the stool behind the door.

'A nice house, I suppose, though not my cup of tea.' Lisa took a sip of her water, turning her gaze on Jane over the rim of the glass. 'Michael was very upset, you know, by the will and everything.'

'Yes, I know,' Jane murmured, 'it was very unexpected for me too.'

'He thinks you must have been having an affair with his brother. Have you?'

'No, I have not,' Jane gasped. Through the window, she caught a glimpse of Julia, pushing Harriet on the swing between kicking Tom's ball back to him, agile and athletic, despite the three-inch heels on her boots. Julia, who never took any nonsense, who would know what to say in order to put this terrible woman – and her snide comments – down. 'And I resent the accusation,' Jane went on, rising from her chair. 'I was as flabbergasted as everyone else by Ernest's will, as I have already made clear to Michael, and willingly agreed that its value should be factored into our divorce. Not that it is any of your... why didn't he come today, anyway? He told me *he* would come, so why hasn't he?'

'Keep your hair on.' Lisa leaned forward to set her glass on the little coffee table in front of the hearth, and then turned to face Jane more directly, crossing her legs, which were elegantly stockinged under a tight knee-length skirt. 'The thing is, I am returning Tom to you.'

Jane stared back at her, saying nothing, while her brain whirred. It had to be some sick new game. Maybe between Lisa and Michael. To get at her, she had no doubt. 'What do you mean by that?' She spoke slowly, keeping her eyes fixed on Lisa's.

Lisa fluttered a hand in the direction of the little troupe playing at the bottom of the garden. 'I can guess how you must miss him. Just like Michael did. It really cut me up that, you know, seeing his pain.' Her face, hard to read behind the heavy make-up, had tightened.

Whatever was going on, she was milking it, Jane warned herself, keeping her own expression inscrutable while inside her heart banged against her ribcage.

'I mean, Jane,' Lisa went on, in a steady, colourless voice, 'that I want a *new* life for us – for me and Michael. Tom is a part of what he had before. It's been different between us having him around – not how I want – not how I *need* – Michael and I to be.' She had left her chair suddenly, crossing the room and making a show of studying the pair of photographs of Ernest and Edie that sat on the mantelpiece. 'Michael looks so much more like his mum, don't you think?'

Jane had not moved. The hammering in her chest had got worse. There was no particle of the woman pretending to scan the photos that she trusted. 'Lisa, does Michael even know you are here?'

'Of course, he does,' she cried, with an incredulous laugh. 'We are like *that*, Michael and I.' She held up crossed fingers to indicate closeness, shaking them defiantly at Jane. 'We think the same. Whatever I think, Michael thinks. He couldn't face you today, he said, and I don't blame him... he was *upset*.' She spat the word and then waited, evidently hoping for some sort of reaction.

Jane, incredulous and distrusting, folded her arms. 'You expect me just to believe all this?'

'I said you'd say that,' Lisa cried with something like triumph, reaching into her handbag and pulling out a brown envelope which she placed on her lap to spread out the creases. 'He's written it all down. Fixed visits – one weekend in five – we've talked it through. He's put some figures in there too, for maintenance going forward, and a percentage settlement for you.'

'I'll get a lawyer to take a look,' Jane said, letting Lisa hold the envelope out for several seconds before accepting it. Deep inside, a small flame of jubilation was trying to ignite. But it all seemed too simple, too flimsy. She ripped off the end of the envelope, seeing from a glance that the contents seemed to accord with what Lisa had been saying. 'Okay... well... thank you...' she faltered. 'And Tom...?'

'He hadn't settled too well at school.' Lisa spoke matter-of-factly, concentrating on pushing back a cuticle on one of her long nails. 'I kept expecting him to tell you, but kids are funny like that, aren't they, holding stuff in...' She worked harder at the cuticle, making Jane wonder, just for a second, how she knew such things. 'He was always saying he felt sick and not wanting to go in. I did my best – Michael knows that – but at nights too, he ended up in our bed half the time, none of us getting a wink. Also—'

'Also, what?' An angry, protective love was surging on Tom's behalf – being seen as a problem, being made to go through so much with a woman he barely knew, not even feeling able to tell *her* about it; his little heart trying to resolve all the baffling inner conflicts of trying to love two parents who no longer loved each other. Jane was fighting down the urge to fling some of this at Lisa when she noticed a sheepish smile lighting up her face. 'Also what?' she repeated.

'I'm expecting my own kid now.' Her hands had moved to her stomach, which looked flat and un-pregnant. 'It's very early days yet – but I've been quite sick in the mornings. That's another thing that has made it hard, coping with Tom. I wanted you to take him back sooner, but Michael said no because of you being sick.'

Jane was aware of her mouth opening and closing again, not in shock at Lisa's news, but because of the joy now erupting inside her. This was not a game. Tom was not going to leave after the weekend. Tom was going to stay with her. 'Thank you, Lisa.' She swallowed. 'Congratulations. And thank you for coming. Though, Michael should have done it...'

'He's not been too well either, as it happens.' Lisa dropped her hands from her stomach, snapping into a different way of being. 'He had to take yesterday off sick. It's been hard for him, you know, all this,' she added bitterly. 'And before that, *you* made his life hard – never satisfied, never happy, never grateful. But now, thank God, he's got me.' She had begun tugging her gloves back on as she talked, flexing her fingers in the soft leather. 'We're planning a nice break over Christmas – at my sister's in southern Spain. So, Tom and Harriet can come to ours *next* year. It's all in there.' She nodded at the envelope, still sitting on the arm of Jane's chair.

'Tell Michael I shall check it all over, and thank you again.' Jane picked up the envelope and put it on the table, fighting the sudden terror that if she wasn't thoroughly civil, Lisa might change her mind. She found herself watching the fingers sheathed in the tight gloves, wondering at the determination of the woman in front of her and whether Michael loved it or merely submitted to it. 'Please tell Michael that I will talk to him soon and that I am happy for you both about the baby.'

'Ta. It was what I wanted.' Lisa's brown eyes gleamed, and Jane marvelled again at the power of her, and whether Michael had a clue what he had let himself in for.

'Tom hasn't said much about it all, to be honest,' she remarked breezily, once Jane had led the way out of the house and they were at her car, unloading Tom's small pile of things from the boot. 'We've both explained it as best we can. He is a bit of a one for moods, I must say.'

'I'll make sure we have a good talk and he understands,' Jane assured her hastily, inwardly flinching again on Tom's behalf. 'Goodbye and thank you again.' She stepped back, willing Lisa to hurry up and leave.

Instead, Lisa opened the car door and then paused, giving Jane one of her beady looks. 'Convenient for you though, this job of Christopher's, giving you the chance to play lady of the manor at this place.' She gestured with her nose at the house.

'I hardly think—'

'And your sister's over there too, I gather, in Boston. We know all about it from Christopher's letters. He's been writing to Michael – out of guilt, Michael says, sucking up to him, feeling guilty and quite right too. Christopher says Boston is even nicer than Washington. Maybe, if you play your cards right, Jane, he might never come back. Lady of the Manor for good, eh?'

'Did you want to say goodbye to Tom?' Jane suggested icily.

'Oh no, don't bother him. We did all that this morning. I don't believe in making unnecessary dramas out of things. We'll see him before long, anyway. Cheerio.' She slid into the car at last, and was sweeping out of the drive a few blissful seconds later, gravel flying up from under the wheels.

Jane stood very still, relishing the waves of relief, of happiness. Strains of laughter and chatter were still coming from the garden. She would join them, but Tom's bags needed taking inside first. As she gathered everything up, Christopher came to mind. True to his request, he had written to her too. Just once. A letter full of dry observations about his Washington colleagues and the difficulties of communication in a world where irony was no more than a word in a dictionary. Some of the things he said had made her laugh out loud. But there had been no mention of visiting Mattie in Boston.

'Mum' Tom shrieked, belting towards her the moment she stepped into the garden. 'I just did ten kick-ups, non-stop.'

'He did,' Julia shouted. 'Harriet and I bore witness. He is a genius.'

'I am a genius,' echoed Tom, pronouncing it *geeenus*, and doing one of his war dances to celebrate.

'I have *missed* you,' Jane yelled back, running at his football and booting it so hard it sailed over the fence towards the copse, producing a frozen tableau as they all paused to watch, even Harriet, until Tom yelled, 'good kick, Mum,' and belted after it.

39

For the first time in what felt like a long while, the pieces of Jane's life started to fit together instead of pulling in opposite directions. After securing a place for Tom at the local primary school in Crestling, she wrote to Christopher to say she was taking him at his word and would be staying in the house for a few more months. Much to Michael's slight astonishment and satisfaction, she then organised a short-term let for Cobham, saying he could receive all of the rental income until they had jointly agreed a sale-price and found a buyer. There were still things to haggle over in the brown envelope, but Jane decided to leave those until the need to settle final terms was upon them.

Most of all, Jane concentrated on her children. Harriet, with Tom back, and Karen as a playmate, continued to blossom. While Tom too, despite having to start at yet another new school, seemed much happier in smaller classes and an atmosphere that was clearly more about having fun than achieving targets. His teachers, knowing some of the background, were full of praise for how he was coping with the challenge – a little too quiet sometimes, they reported, but always cooperative. It left Jane daring to believe that therapy might not be necessary; that the bad old days of raging mood swings could be fully replaced by the natural stomping that went with being seven years old and full of plans that were either forbidden or impossible. It helped enormously to have Ernest's vast garden for the venting of such energies, not to mention a mother who felt she had been given a second chance at being happy.

As Jane's strength continued to return, she took to going on long walks, often with Harriet bouncing in a robust carrier on her back, exploring the pathways and thickets surrounding the property that she still had to pinch herself to believe was half hers. She drove herself on until her pulse raced and her lungs heaved for air, loving the slight ache in her body from serious use and the way the muscles in her legs began to reappear. A return to the workplace in some form would come, she knew, but in the meantime it was bliss to enjoy every second of her mothering freedom.

'I'm in danger of feeling content,' she confessed to Julia when she rang up a couple of weeks before Christmas. 'I keep forgetting to check over my shoulder for demons sneaking up behind.'

'You always were a raging pessimist,' replied Julia merrily, 'it was high time you changed your ways.' Julia liked not having to worry about Jane any more. It was much more fun to have the old balance back between them, a balance that allowed her to speak her mind and exercise her quirky sense of humour without fear of the consequences. 'Now then, could we discuss that most joyous of festive seasons, the one that rips through our bank accounts with as much fervour as it does our digestive systems?'

'I take it you mean my invitation to you and Olaf to come and stay over Christmas,' Jane laughed, pulling out a kitchen chair to sit on and letting Harriet clamber onto her lap, where she set about her favourite pastime of trying to chew the telephone flex, dangling enticingly from its socket on the wall. 'I'm hoping you can make it in time for the children's Christmas Eve nativity in the local church. And another thing...' She lowered her voice on account of Harriet, 'I could do with a volunteer for Santa Claus. There would be the reward of lavish refreshments, obviously. Michael used to like beer and cake but the catering department can adapt. Actually, Michael always rather enjoyed all that,' Jane couldn't resist adding fondly, relishing the ability to feel affectionate about the past instead of rocky and hopeless.

Julia whooped. 'A sticky beard and a baggy red trouser suit? I'm sure Olaf would be delighted. But that's partly why I'm ringing. Olaf has some Swedish traditional stuff planned for Christmas Eve, so we won't be with you until Christmas Day itself. Say midday? Staying over sounds good though.'

'Perfect. The nativity gig will have a packed audience in any case. Tom has volunteered – if you can believe it – to sing a solo of 'Twinkle, Twinkle Little Star', and one of Harriet's more respectable dolls is headlining as the baby Jesus, so there's great excitement all round.'

'Glorious. Wish Tom lots of luck and tell Harriet that, as her godmother, I am very proud.'

So it was that fourteen days later, with Michael and Lisa in Fuengirola, Jane had to cope alone with the trauma of watching their son perform publicly for the first time in his life. She sat, rigid with pride, elation and terror, hanging onto an unusually silent and awestruck Harriet for comfort, until Tom, after delivering a shouty, enthusiastic performance, landed on the final note. The round of spontaneous applause was so loud that Harriet burst into tears, saying she wanted her doll back. On stage, Tom, busy waving at them and enjoying his moment, had to be elbowed out of the way by Mary and Joseph trying to join the front line for a bow. A perfect nativity in other words, Jane agreed, laughing with the other parents over mince pies and mulled wine afterwards, while Harriet toddled about, happily reunited with Baby Jesus, and Tom played tag round the grown-ups with his classmates.

40

On the morning of Christmas Day Jane put on the dress that Barbara Marshall had picked out for her. It fell out of its box of tissue in a shimmer of green, as if eager to be released. Though it was uncreased and as alluring as ever, flattering her slim frame, Jane found herself regarding her reflection in the bedroom mirror with something like unease. To look quite so elegant felt almost unnatural, on top of which the dress was a link to past errors that she wanted only to forget. She was fighting with the zip, having decided to take it off, when Tom ran into the room firing the rubber-tipped arrows that he had found sticking out of his stocking that morning, along with a feathered red bow which Jane had already had to mend with heavy-duty sticking tape.

'You look different,' he said, stopping at once and cocking his head. 'Like a pretty lady.' When Harriet joined in, shouting her version of the words 'pretty' and 'lady', between nuzzling her face into the inviting, sheeny material, leaving some fetching dribble stains on the hem, Jane decided she might as well keep it on. Finding a clean faded apron of Edie's to protect her outfit from further onslaughts, she pulled slouch socks over her stockinged feet and padded downstairs with the children so she could continue with preparations for the meal.

The kitchen, like the rest of the house, heaved with decorations – part of a cottage industry that had been led by Karen back in November, comprising paper-chains, angel and snowman mobiles, as well as galaxies of tin-foil stars across the windows. Just moving from room to room made Jane happy, as did having to step over Harriet, playing with an empty saucepan and several wooden spoons in preference to her Christmas toys, and Tom, eating the carrots he was supposed to be helping to peel.

Julia and Olaf arrived when she was still in her baggy socks and frilly apron.

'There's brandy butter on your cheek, or something equally delicious,' said Julia, licking her lips after planting a kiss of welcome. 'Try the other side, Olaf, you might find something even tastier there. I love the dress, by the way – what I can see of it. When and where did you buy it?'

'Guildford, ages ago,' said Jane quickly, the encounter with Anthony's wife and daughter being something she had, and always would, keep to herself. Olaf helped move the moment on by confusing her with a handshake then kissing both cheeks as well. They had met only once before, when Julia brought him down for a flying visit and a mid-morning coffee, and were still learning how to be; although Olaf's evident affection for her dearest friend had made Jane like him instantly. 'And I hope you approve of my chic footwear,' she joked, waggling her toes in the thick socks. 'I might stay in them all day.'

'Chic is the word,' laughed Julia, pulling a bottle of champagne and a bottle of red wine out of one bag and taking another, bulging with gifts, into the sitting room.

'Yes, they are beautiful socks,' agreed Olaf, in his endearing dead-pan way. He had found the old, stained apron Jane had meant to put in the washing machine and tied it round his smart dark blue suit. 'And now, Jane, please give me instructions to assist.'

It was several hours later, once the meal was almost over and Harriet had caused general consternation by choking on – and almost swallowing – a little silver horseshoe from her mini portion of Christmas pudding, that Mattie burst into the room.

'Surprise!' she shrieked, tipping presents between the uncleared dirty dishes and prancing round the table to bestow kisses on the bemused faces of the children, on Julia, and even on Olaf, whose mouth happened still to be filled with a sizeable amount of stilton cheese.

She got to Jane last, hesitating before putting her arms round her, so that her elder sister had time to register the translucent glow radiating out from every inch of her – the soft, but unmistakable light of happiness. 'I've so much to tell,' she whispered, as they hugged. 'You do look well, Janie – all this country living, I suppose. Have you left us any food? We just couldn't resist the idea of a surprise – we would have got here hours earlier only the flight was delayed – typical, or what? They gave us turkey on the plane though, which was rather sweet – and free drinks, which was sweeter still.'

Jane was still puzzling what Mattie meant by 'we', when she glanced up and saw Christopher framed in the doorway, waving at them all as best he could, with several bags over his shoulders and clasped in his hands. He too, looked radiant. Mattie and Christopher. They had made something of each other after all. It should have made her glad. She *was* glad, Jane scolded herself, fighting shame at her meanness of heart as she helped to move chairs to make room for them, finding more glasses, food and cutlery, as well as two extra crackers.

After what turned into a very prolonged lunch, followed by more presents, Christopher lay invitingly on the rug behind the sofa to play roly-poly with the children, who showed as much respect for his body as they might a trampoline. Nearby, Olaf and Julia sat side by side, not holding hands but clearly wanting to, as self-conscious as teenagers. Jane meanwhile, still discombobulated, but doing her best not to appear so, asked Mattie vibrant questions about Boston and teaching art, without listening properly to any of the answers. It was a struggle not to seek out the dark eyes of her brother-in-law; the keen urge to study his face superseded only by the fear of being caught doing so.

After a respectable while, she sought refuge in the kitchen.

'Thank you for your letter.' Christopher picked up a drying-up cloth and began to help with clearing the draining board.

'Thank you for yours.'

'How have you been?'

'Fine.'

'Of course. How silly of me.' He threw down the cloth. 'You're always fine. Everything's always fine.' He thrust his hands into his pockets and strode from the room, almost bumping into Olaf on the way.

Jane stared at the yellow washing up gloves immersed in the bowl of frothy water in front of her, as if powerless to extract them. Her negative mood had annoyed him. He knew her too well. She could fool her best friend, her sister even, but not him. Beside her, stacks of plates, caked with congealed mixtures of bread sauce, gravy and cranberry jelly, awaited attention. Olaf tapped her lightly on the shoulder.

'I would consider it a privilege if you would let me do this washing. I have eaten so well. You are a fine cook, Jane.' He gripped an imaginary tyre of spare flesh through his crisp white shirt and grinned, his blue eyes disappearing in clusters of wrinkles. 'I shall have to go on my diet now, or your Julia will turn me away.'

'I'm sure she won't do any such thing.'

Jane reached for a dirty plate to wash, but he took a firm hold of her wrists and shook his head gravely.

'Go and sit. Talk to your sister and her friend. Julia and I will do this.'

'You heard the man, get out,' commanded Julia, appearing with a full glass of port in one hand and an unlit cigarette in the other. 'I shall direct proceedings. It will give me enormous pleasure. Find out why the hell Mattie's looking so well – I can't get her to tell me a thing.'

Jane slipped away obediently, amazed at the obtuse cheerfulness of people in love.

* * *

With everyone having accepted an invitation to stay over, there was a flurry later on about beds. There were four bedrooms in total, three large and one small. Since both sleeping children were already settled in one of the big ones, and the other two had double beds, Jane pronounced herself more than happy to move into the single, promptly flying upstairs to make up the beds up accordingly. She came back down to be greeted by Julia, putting her head round the kitchen door to say that Olaf hadn't drunk that much, and just as soon as they had finished a last bit of clearing up – with which Jane was forbidden to help – they had decided to gather up their things and head back to London after all. The door was closed before Jane could protest. She took the opportunity to slip on a pair of boots and grab the nearest coat off a peg to go for a breather outside, first checking on the sitting room where Mattie was snoring gently in the deepest of Ernest's chairs and Christopher was too engrossed in a book to look up.

The cold night air felt marvellous. Jane inhaled and exhaled deeply several times as she walked, dispelling the throb in her head wrought by the roaring heat of the open fire and too much wine. Her footsteps in the wellies made slight squeaks on the wet grass. Her dress swished round the top of them, its bright green now only the merest shimmer under the shadowy moon. Jane proceeded at a fast pace, down past the climbing frame towards the gate in the fence that separated the garden from the copse. She leant her arms on top of it, resting her chin on her knuckles, shivering a little from something that felt like more than being cold. Overhead, the sky had grown too cloudy for stars, taking the last hint of the moon with it.

A rustling sound made her jerk round. 'Christopher – I thought you were a ghost.' Jane put her hand to her chest, panting slightly from shock.

'Do you believe in ghosts?'

'Sort of – not really.' Though her breathing was back to normal, her voice still sounded high-pitched and strange. 'I believe in the power of the past, though I suppose that's not quite the same thing. Sometimes it's a nice feeling – like sensing Ernest out here and in the house – but other times it seems no more than a horrid way of getting bogged down, of not being able to go forward...' Jane stopped, feeling she had talked too much, wishing she could make out his expression more clearly in the dark.

'Jane...' He took a step nearer.

In the same instant, Julia's voice rang out from the front of the house. 'Coooeee down there. We're going – I'll be in touch.'

'Hang on,' Jane shouted, 'I'm coming.' She began to run across the garden, her stockinged feet – the slouch socks having been swapped for smart shoes and tights after all – sliding awkwardly inside the wellingtons. Christopher, after jogging behind her for a couple of yards, suddenly began to run properly himself, grabbing her hand as he did so, pulling her on to match his pace. They flew across the dark, wet lawn, slowing only to negotiate the pathway round to the drive. Olaf's grey Mercedes glistened in the dim glow cast their way by the porch light.

Julia, still full of port and festive spirit, dominated the farewells. 'What a lovely day – thank you so much. We'll be in touch again soon. Tell the children I don't need thank-you letters, and if Harriet secretly hates her jumper – though yellow is *so* her colour – then don't be afraid to tell me – I can take it. I'll get something else – I don't want it sitting in the bottom of a drawer. And do give Mattie our best – we didn't want to wake her – see you sooooon...' She had wound down her window and was still blowing kisses through it as the car moved away.

In the silence that followed, with her heart not having settled from the running, and wondering what to make of how he had held her hand, Jane felt at a sudden loss. 'Do you need help with getting anything from the car?' she ventured, purely for something to say. 'I mean, do you and Mattie have anything else that needs taking upstairs?'

'To Mattie's and my quarters, you mean?'

'Yup. Exactly.' Jane started walking towards the blue Ford Fiesta that had apparently been hired at the airport.

'You know, for an intelligent woman, you can be astonishingly dim,' Christopher remarked, making no move to follow.

'Well, thanks very much. I'll take that to mean that you don't need any help.' Jane changed course, giving him a wave to indicate her intention to head back round the side of the house to the garden. She would stay outside a little longer, let Mattie and Christopher sort themselves out.

'Jane.' Christopher walked towards her, looking purposeful and alarmingly severe. 'Do you realise that you are the only person still labouring under the illusion that Mattie and I wish to share a bed?'

'Oh, well... but... of course that is fine too...'

He made a funny moaning sound that could have been laughter, and could have been irritation, dropping his chin to shake his head and then raising his face to look at her. 'Jane, your sister and I are no closer than good friends – ones who now laugh about our imprudent encounter earlier in the year when the earth moved only by virtue of the alcohol levels in our blood streams.'

Jane opened her mouth to say something, but then couldn't think what it was. She dropped her gaze to her wellingtons, aware of a sudden bad drip on the end of her nose, and rootling in the pockets of the coat for something with which to wipe it away. On one side, the lining was ripped so badly that her entire hand poked through the hole. On the other, there was just grittiness and something that felt like a stone, or possibly an old conker. She sniffed loudly instead. 'Right then, well, thanks for putting me right...'

'By the way, that's my coat you're wearing.'

'Is it? Sorry. I just took the first one on the peg. You haven't got a hanky, have you?'

'Yes, but at your own risk.' He pulled a crumpled grey handkerchief from his trouser pocket and handed it over. 'Was there anything else you wanted to say?'

'Only, please do go back inside – I mean, you must be cold...'

'I meant about Mattie. And me.'

'Oh, I see... not really... except that you never mentioned her in your letter, whereas I know you also wrote to Michael and told him you'd spent loads of time in Boston and loved it up there, which is what made me think...' Jane ran out of steam, embarrassed at her gabbling, and needing to breathe.

'It made you think all sorts of foolish things, is what it did,' Christopher said quietly. He was still standing a few feet from her, but held out his hand – an offering, it looked like, to bridge the gap. 'Come here, Jane. You're the one who looks cold and there is something I want to say, while we are alone.'

She shoved the hanky in the pocket with the conker and shuffled nearer, letting him enfold one of her hands between both his. They were warm, and very smooth; the heat of them like balm.

'I did go to Boston a few times,' he said quietly. 'Mattie had some problems – which she was trying to blank out in inadvisable ways. Luckily, she let me help. I found her someone to see, footing the bill until she can pay me back. She swore me to secrecy and I didn't want to worry you anyway.'

'Oh, Christopher... my goodness. I don't know what to say. Except thank you. Thank you. I sort of suspected as much – at one point last year – I should have *done* something...'

'Enough, Jane. Enough.' He held her fingers a little more firmly, pulling her nearer. 'Mattie is no longer your responsibility. That she ever was, must have been such a burden for you to carry, along with everything else, all these years. And for the record, she's going back to the States in a few days, straight into the incomparably safe and adoring arms of a vegetarian baseball player who does press-ups before breakfast. They met through counselling. He's an exhausting companion, but very well-intentioned. Mattie's in love with his triceps and he thinks he's landed an eccentric English princess. I'm not sure anything so old-fashioned as marriage is on the cards, but they talk frequently about producing offspring. When she tells you, pretend you haven't heard it from me. Okay?'

'Okay.' Jane laughed. Her head was spinning, making it hard to speak. 'Thank you again, Christopher. That is *such* good news...' She broke off because the hand-squeezing had somehow segued into having both his arms round her. 'When do you go back?' she managed in a small voice, aiming the question at his shoulder, which was level with her eyes, in a bid to fill a silence that he seemed little inclined to break.

'Never.'

'Never?' She could feel his breath on the top of her head as he talked.

'By mutual agreement, the English faculty of Georgetown and I have severed our contract for good, citing irreconcilable differences as the cause. They found me rather odd – far odder than the generally accepted level of lunacy expected from an Englishman.'

Jane giggled, relaxing into the pleasurable warmth of being held. 'Heavens, what did you do?'

'I forced my students to write poetry. I banned the reading of literary critics. I tore up essays that were too long – as fat as books some of them. Dreadful crimes, I know, but I'm unrepentant.' He released her enough for them to be able to look at each other properly, adding softly, 'So you see, there's nothing to stop us now.'

Jane swallowed. She felt as if she had entered some sort of dream, a parallel universe. A light rain had started to fall, landing on his face and long dark eyelashes. 'Nothing to stop us what?' she managed hoarsely.

'Nothing to stop us kissing.'

'It's raining,' she murmured.

'Yes, isn't it wonderful.' He released his hold in order to cup her face and bring it closer to his. 'I want to kiss you. In spite of the rain. Do you mind?'

Jane shook her head, very fast, following instincts that had nothing to do with coherent thought.

'Thank you, and thank goodness.' He brushed each of her eyebrows with his lips. 'I thought I might feel guilty, if this moment ever came, but I don't remotely, because – and there is no need to respond to this, Jane, now or ever – I have always loved you. Always. From the moment I laid eyes on you. Michael found such treasure and then didn't look after it.'

They started to kiss then, without hurry and with great ease, like two old friends who had found each other, which was what they were.

When they paused for breath at last, Jane brushed a straggle of wet hair back off his forehead. 'I never expected this,' she stammered. 'I didn't realise... I didn't dare... I didn't know... but is it going to be all right? Will *we* be all right?'

'Who knows?' Christopher widened his eyes at her. 'Maybe I'll get drunk on Friday nights and beat you with a saucepan. Or maybe you'll get fed up and start a torrid affair with a librarian.'

'So, we're doomed.'

'Almost certainly.'

They both laughed and then started kissing again. The rain had stopped suddenly, leaving the darkness dripping around them.

'Where the hell have you two been?' cried Mattie, sitting bolt upright in her chair the moment they stepped through the French windows into the sitting room some ten minutes later, carrying their wet footwear. 'I thought I'd been abandoned in a spooky house with two orphaned children. Christ, you're both soaking? What's the joke anyway? Where are Julia and Olaf? I succumb to a spot of jet-lag and wake up to find that the whole world has changed. I wish you'd stop laughing and tell me what's been going on.'

'We'll do our best – but it's a bit complicated,' said Jane, escaping in search of warm towels, while Christopher made tea for them all, carrying the mugs through on a tray into the sitting room. It wasn't until he set about rubbing Jane's hair dry, both of them tucked together in one end of the sofa, that Mattie's mouth dropped open – a spontaneous reaction which was followed by an eye-roll and the grinning announcement that she would leave them to it and take her tea upstairs, if Jane could direct her to the right room.

'Use the big spare, next to the children,' Jane said at once, staying snuggled next to Christopher but not looking at him, 'Olaf and Julia were going to use it, but changed their minds and went back to London.'

On the mantelpiece above the hearth, the beady grey eyes of

Ernest seemed to glint in the firelight. 'Here's to Dad,' said Christopher, raising his mug just as Jane was thinking about the dear old man too. 'He knew,' he chuckled, 'the clever, scheming codger. He always knew.'

They chinked their mugs and nestled closer among the cushions and towels. In the fireplace, the flames curled greedily around a big disintegrating log, releasing celebratory gun-shot crackles up the blackened chimney. Outside, the rain started again, along with a wild wind that raged against the windows and garden doors like an uninvited guest.

ACKNOWLEDGMENTS

I would like to express heartfelt thanks to the whole team at Boldwood Books for their continuing commitment to republish and promote my backlist. It is an undertaking that requires new jackets, as well as careful editing of revised material, not to mention the marketing effort to entice new readers.

Special gratitude goes to my wonderful editor, Sarah Ritherdon, for her invaluable support and expertise, and to Sue Lamprell for her meticulous reading of the manuscript during its final stages.

MORE FROM AMANDA BROOKFIELD

We hope you enjoyed reading *The Wrong Man*. If you did, please leave a review.

If you'd like to gift a copy, this book is also available as an ebook, large print, hardback, digital audio download and audiobook CD.

Sign up to Amanda Brookfield's mailing list for news, competitions and updates on future books.

http://bit.ly/AmandaBrookfieldNewsletter

ABOUT THE AUTHOR

Amanda Brookfield worked in advertising and as a freelance journalist in Argentina, before writing her first novel in 1986. She has two grown-up sons and lives in London.

Visit Amanda's website: https://www.amandabrookfield.co.uk/

Follow Amanda on social media:

- facebook.com/amandabrookfield100
- twitter.com/ABrookfield1
- instagram.com/amanda_and_mabel_brookfield
- bookbub.com/authors/amanda-brookfield

ALSO BY AMANDA BROOKFIELD

Good Girls

Relative Love

A Family Man

The Lover

The Other Woman

The Split

Alice Alone

The Godmother

Boldw**oo**d

Boldwood Books is an award-winning fiction publishing company seeking out the best stories from around the world.

Find out more at www.boldwoodbooks.com

Join our reader community for brilliant books, competitions and offers!

Follow us
@BoldwoodBooks
@BookandTonic

Sign up to our weekly deals newsletter

https://bit.ly/BoldwoodBNewsletter

Printed in Great Britain
by Amazon

30823487R00196